WILDWOOD ROAD

ALSO BY CHRISTOPHER GOLDEN

The Boys Are Back in Town
The Ferryman
Straight on 'Til Morning
Strangewood

The Shadow Saga:
Of Saints and Shadows
Angel Souls and Devil Hearts
Of Masques and Martyrs
The Gathering Dark

WILDWOOD ROAD

CHRISTOPHER GOLDEN

BANTAM BOOKS

WILDWOOD ROAD
A Bantam Spectra Book

Published by
Bantam Dell
A Division of Random House, Inc.
New York, New York

This is a work of fiction. Names, characters, places, and incidents either are the product of the author's imagination or are used fictitiously. Any resemblance to actual persons, living or dead, events, or locales is entirely coincidental.

Bantam Books, the rooster colophon, Spectra, and the portrayal of a boxed "s" are trademarks of Random House, Inc.

ISBN 0-7394-5201-0

Printed in the United States of America

For Charles L. Grant
A quiet one.

ACKNOWLEDGMENTS

Many thanks to my editor, Anne Groell, for shepherding this strange dream. My loving gratitude, as always, to Connie and the kids, Nicholas, Daniel, and Lily Grace. Thanks are also due to Tom Sniegoski, José Nieto, Amber Benson, Rick Hautala, Bob Tomko, Allie Costa, Wendy Schapiro, Maria Carlini, and Amy Young.

WILDWOOD ROAD

CHAPTER ONE

The night of the masquerade was a kind of mad, risqué waltz, the voices louder and the laughter giddier than anyone would have expected. That was the nature of masks.

Michael Dansky leaned against the wall with a Guinness in his hand and studied the ebb and flow of the bright costumes and the body language beneath them. There was something about a masquerade that changed people. Inhibitions slipped away, and not only because of the alcohol present. The question, Michael thought, was whether putting on a mask allowed the wearer to lose themselves in the pretense that they were someone else, or if hiding their faces let them show more of who they really were, down inside.

The Wayside Inn was a charming spot where one could imagine the nineteenth century had never ended. From across the ballroom, Michael watched his wife Jillian move through the masquerade in her Elizabethan gown, smiling beneath an elegant half-mask. Michael had never thought of her as anything less than sexy, but tonight she was more than that. There was a sultriness to the way she moved across the floor, a sensuality in her eyes behind that mask, that took his breath away. As she passed through the room another woman caught her arm and the two struck up a conversation of smiles and moving lips, words lost amidst the churning voices of the masquerade. Jillian's hair was a rich chestnut brown, and her hazel eyes seemed alight with mischief. The woman she spoke to was a thin blonde dressed as a genie.

Michael pushed away from the wall and started across the ballroom toward them. He was vaguely aware that the bottle of Guinness in his hand undermined the effectiveness of his own costume: the cape, boots, hat, and blade of the dashing D'Artagnan of *Three Musketeers* fame. Yet there was a swagger in his walk that might have sprung from either the ale or the costume, or more likely both.

The ballroom was accented by a pair of grand staircases that curled up either side of the room to a second-story balcony that looked down on the main floor. There were chandeliers, but nothing so garish as what he had seen at weddings held in hotel ballrooms. The masquerade was an annual event held in support of the Merrimack Valley Children's Hospital, and in the three years since their marriage he and Jillian had never missed it. It was Saturday night, three days before Halloween, and though the holiday had become overrun with more modern costumes, the organizers of the event insisted that no one wear a disguise inspired by something post-1900. The music in the room was under the same restriction. Some people Michael had spoken to were bothered by the lack of familiar dance music, but others made the best of it, attempting minuets and waltzes, and even a quadrille, which Miri Gallaway and Victoria Peristere taught the attendees every year.

Michael loved it all. The music and the period costumes harkened back to a simpler time, an era in which people believed in mystery. He worked as an art director for Krakow & Bester, an advertising firm out of Andover, and though his work allowed him to explore the history of styles and images, it also exposed him to far too many people whose minds were an arid desert of imagination.

This was sheer joy.

As he crossed the room toward his wife, he bowed in courtly fashion to a beautiful lady pirate and one of Dracula's brides. In the midst of her conversation with the blond genie, Jillian caught sight of him and a playful smile touched the corners of her mouth. She gave him a tiny wave.

Abruptly, his view of Jillian was blocked by several couples dancing to a jaunty tune. He tried to find another path toward her and nearly ran into a portly Henry VIII and a blood-smeared Anne Boleyn. Michael laughed hard enough that he nearly spilled his Guinness.

"What's so bloody funny, peasant?" demanded King Henry.

"That beard, for starters," Michael replied.

The king sniffed at this insult, but touched at his glued-on beard with concern. His real name was Teddy Polito, and his lovely corpse bride was his wife Colleen. Teddy was a copywriter at Krakow & Bester, a semineurotic whose face seemed etched in a perpetual grimace that was deceiving. Despite his various ticks and peeves, the burly forty-something had a kind heart.

"It took me an hour to get this damn thing on right," Teddy muttered.

Michael tried to conceal his smile, but failed. "That's . . . that's pretty astonishing."

Colleen arched an eyebrow and shot an appraising glance at her husband. "I'd say. You'd expect it to be much more time-consuming to really get that perfect Elmer's glue look."

Teddy put a hand across his heart. "You wound me."

His wife bumped him with a curvy hip. "Big baby." She was a brunette with auburn highlights in her hair, a woman with a face that would have been ordinary if not for her large, green eyes.

"Very true, Colleen. I don't know why we put up with him."

"I'm an enigma," Teddy said happily.

"It's part of your charm," Michael said. He glanced around. "Now where has my beautiful wife got off to?"

Jillian was still with her blond genie friend, halfway up the right-side staircase with a drink in her hand. Even as Michael caught sight of her, Jillian began to laugh. Her face flushed and she raised the back of her hand to cover her mouth—a habit left over from the braces of her youth—and took a step away from the genie.

His heart stopped as her foot missed the stair. From the ballroom floor, in the midst of those dancers and with the sound of lute and fiddle and pennywhistle in his ears, he held his breath and watched her begin to fall.

Jillian let go of her drink and her glass tumbled out over the edge of the banister, falling to shatter on the floor below. She caught herself with that empty hand, the other still covering her mouth, her eyes wide with fear. And then an awful sort of embarrassed amusement lit her face and she turned her back to those below her, attempting to pretend the incident had never happened. She kept her hand to her mouth, and Michael knew she was hiding a smile. The genie was laughing in relief and disbelief. She took Jillian by the arm and led her further up the stairs.

Only then did Michael exhale.

"Somebody might be having too good a time," Colleen said, but there was no accusation in it. Jillian wasn't much of a drinker, and became tipsy if she had more than one glass of wine. The Politos knew that.

"I'm going to see if she's all right," Michael told them.

"You do that," Teddy said. "In fact, we'll come say hello."

"Not to worry," Michael replied, eyes still tracking Jillian, whom he could see talking to Ned Bergh, a local realtor, and his wife, Sue. Jillian was talking rapidly with her hands, her whole face animated as she told a story—possibly about dropping her glass only moments earlier. "We're not ready to turn into pumpkins yet."

Michael turned with a flourish of his cape and the three of them set off toward the stairs. He threw himself into the character of D'Artagnan, one hand on the pommel of his sword, channeling the arrogance of a musketeer.

D'Artagnan led King Henry and the resurrected Anne Boleyn up the stairs. Several people called to Teddy and he waved. Once he paused to lean over and mutter something into the ear of a man Michael vaguely recognized as a local politician. The man responded with a knowing laugh, full of insinuation. Teddy had a flair for dirty jokes. Colleen hadn't heard whatever her husband had said, but she gave him a jab to the shoulder on basic principle.

Michael also saw people he knew, though with the costumes and masks it was difficult, sometimes, to tell who they were at first. Gary Bester, son of one of his firm's founders, waved to him from the opposite staircase, and Michael was pleased to be so far away. Gary was dressed as the Big Bad Wolf and his girlfriend, Brittany, as Red Riding Hood. The girl was nineteen, the agency's receptionist, and the sort that even the most decent-hearted man had trouble keeping his eyes off of. Gary was annoying as hell, a talker without any stories to tell, and insanely jealous of any guy Brittany gave the time of day. It was best to just steer clear of both of them.

From the top of the stairs, the view of the masquerade was extraordinary. The colors in motion, the sounds of fiddle and mandolin, accordion and harpsichord, and the antique décor of the ballroom, all combined to take his breath away. Teddy and Colleen were pulled away by a fiftyish woman Michael did not recognize, and so he paused a moment at the balustrade to soak it all in.

His reverie was broken by the sound of his wife's laughter, and he turned to see her still talking to the Berghs. They had been joined now by several others, including a heavy, olive-skinned man with a bulbous nose and curly graying hair, and a thin Irishman with wispy white hair. Michael did not know the first man, who wore the sombrero and clothing of a Mexican peasant, but the older fellow was Bob Ryan, a city councillor.

Ryan was clad in faded denim, weathered boots, a long jacket, and a hat that shaded his startlingly blue eyes. At his waist, Michael could see leather gun belts that crisscrossed one another. If there was anyone at the masquerade who looked more authentic in his costume, Michael hadn't seen him.

"Lawyers are just the mouthpieces," Jillian announced as Michael joined the circle that had gathered around her. They laughed with her and she favored them with a sardonic grin. "It's just like modern medicine. Nurses do all the work. Doctors get the glory. In a law firm, paralegals do everything, and lawyers just show up for the face time and to sign the paperwork."

The Mexican peasant narrowed his gaze. A lawyer. That much was obvious. "I don't see many paralegals arguing cases in front of a judge."

Jillian waved him away. "Please, Benny. That's the showbiz. I'm talking about the work. Sure, we're not doing the song and dance, but we choreographed it, honey. We wrote the music and the lyrics. Anyway, that's not my area. I do corporate law. There are just as many criminals, but they're behind desks instead of bars."

Even as she said this last, she noticed Michael and her eyes lit up. "Well, hello, my handsome musketeer."

With a flourish, Michael bowed. "Mademoiselle."

"Ah, D'Artagnan," Bob Ryan said, tipping his hat, "Señor Bartolini and I were just trying to convince your lovely wife what a wonderful candidate she'd make for city council next fall."

Michael raised an eyebrow and glanced at Jillian. There was a sparkle in her eye that he knew instantly. She had once set her sights on law school, but after becoming a paralegal and witnessing firsthand the long hours and the stress required of first-year attorneys trying to make it on staff, she had realized she simply wasn't masochistic enough to be a lawyer. Still, she enjoyed learning about the process and she embraced her work at the firm. Paralegal work was a compromise, but it was one she could live with.

Jillian had climbed, in a very short period, to the top of the Boston legal scene. She commuted into the city every day, came home late almost every night. She was the paralegal manager at Dawes, Gray & Winter, the largest and most powerful firm in Boston. And though she did not discuss it often, Michael knew she coveted the top spot, the position of paralegal director.

That sparkle in her eye was her quiet ambition.

"So you're a politician now, huh?"

"Nope," she said. "But I am a woman of the people."

She reached for his hand and Michael offered it to her. As she came toward him, disrupting the circle of people who had been involved in that conversation, there was a sway in her walk that he knew sprang from alcohol, rather than any sultry intention. If she had been a drinker by nature, it would have alarmed him. But instead there was something sweet, even innocent, about her inebriation. Jillian wrapped her arms around him and kissed his temple softly, then languidly unfurled herself from him and stood at his side, facing the others.

"Well, sweetheart," Michael said, gazing at his wife. "You've got my vote."

AT MIDNIGHT THE MASQUERADE WAS still in full swing. Michael and Jillian had danced for hours, spinning around the ballroom together. The Politos had joined them, but the Danskys were younger and in better shape, and soon enough Teddy and Colleen had taken a breather and spent much of the balance of the night with other friends.

The dancing took its toll. Michael's feet hurt in his D'Artagnan boots, and sweat dappled his forehead, his chest, and the back of his neck. Yet with his wife in his arms it seemed to him that they were both like marionettes, that whatever magic had transported them back in time filled them with a childlike glee that made it impossible not to dance.

They did manage to rest from time to time, at least long enough to socialize, and to whisper silly things in each other's ears. They were both burning off some alcohol with their dancing, so Michael didn't worry much about the additional drinks that friends bought them. It would have been rude to decline.

But, eventually, the alcohol caught up to Jillian.

"Time to go home," Michael whispered in her ear.

Her face scrunched up. "Honey. It's still early. Nobody's leaving yet."

She'd had to stop dancing to say this, and when she did she swayed against him. A frown creased her forehead and she glanced down at her feet as though they'd betrayed her. Then she laughed softly and raised her eyes once more.

"On the other hand . . ."

Jillian slipped her arm through Michael's and they began to work their way toward the door, bidding good night and happy Halloween to friends and acquaintances. Her eyes were glazed and, now that she had stopped dancing, Michael could almost see the alcohol affecting her. When she said "see you" to Ned Bergh, Jillian slurred the words. It was a first since he had known her, and Michael resolved never to mention it to her. He knew she would be mortified.

At the base of one of the staircases he saw gunslinger Bob Ryan again, but he averted his gaze and steered Jillian more quickly toward the door. Ryan might not urge Jillian to run for city council if he thought she was a drinker.

She leaned on him more with each step; by the time they made their way through the inn and pulled open the front door, he was quite literally holding her up. A rush of cold air buffeted them as they stepped out into the pool of wan light thrown by the spot above the door. It did not extend very far into the parking lot, but the moon was bright, gleaming off of chrome and glass.

Michael paused and blinked several times. The crisp air made him straighten up. His cheeks stung. It was the end of October, but tonight it felt like December. His breath fogged.

"Michael," Jillian began.

The smile was gone from her face, replaced by embarrassment.

"Hush," he whispered. "Let's just get you home and into bed."

She arched an eyebrow. "That's your answer to everything."

He had to laugh. "What's wrong with that?"

"Not a thing."

Her eyes drifted as she said this last, and her lids fluttered. He thought she might pass out at any moment.

Michael glanced around, reorienting himself. Their forest green Volvo was parked at the far left side of the lot. He took a moment to prop Jillian up better, slinging her arm around his neck, and then he helped her stagger across the lot. If they had been somewhere else he might have simply picked her up and carried her, the way he had lifted her over the threshold of the bridal suite on their wedding night. But they knew so many people here; she would not want anyone to witness such a spectacle.

At the car he was forced to lean Jillian against the door while he fished inside his costume for the keys. She lolled against the cold metal and the marionette image that had come to him earlier returned, but now it was of a puppet whose strings had been cut. A low hum came from her lips, but he could make no sense of it.

"Honey, you are a wreck," he said, smiling softly.

One hand holding her in place, he thumbed the button on his key ring and the locks popped up. It took effort, but he managed to get her into the backseat, laying her down. Her eyelids fluttered once and she reached a slow-motion hand up toward him.

"Love you so much," she mumbled.

"Love you, too," Michael told her, and he watched her eyes close. She looked so innocent there, he could only imagine what she had been like as a little girl. *Not that you were a drunken little girl,* he thought, chuckling to himself.

In the morning, he planned to tease her mercilessly.

He shut the back door and then climbed into the driver's seat.

The moment he was off of his feet he felt a tingling in his face, a little beer buzz working its way through his system. He started up the Volvo, its engine purring softly. He felt it humming beneath him as he opened his window and let the cold night air hit him. For several seconds he took stock of his condition. The truth was, other than that little buzz, he felt more tired than drunk.

Both hands on the wheel, he took a breath and let the cold air wash over his face again. "You'll be fine," he said aloud, his voice strange to him in the car's interior, his hands lit by the glow from the dash. "You'll be fine."

The window stayed open as Michael pulled out of the lot. He glanced back over the seat, one hand on the wheel, to check on Jillian. Wine and exhaustion had conspired to put her into a sound sleep, and she even snored a little. She murmured something and he smiled and returned his attention to the road.

Part of the charm of the Wayside Inn was that it was on Old Route 12, which wound through half a dozen or more towns in the Merrimack Valley but never had much by way of traffic. In the many decades since Old Route 12 had been laid down, other major highways had stretched their fingers up into the region. Three separate interstates crisscrossed the northern part of Massachusetts, and anyone who was in a hurry was wise to use one of them. That left only local traffic for Old Route 12. This time of night it was absolutely deserted.

The streetlights were far apart here, but they passed by overhead with a rhythm of their own, splashing light upon the windshield, illuminating the interior of the car. Black cable was strung from telephone poles, in some places crossing the road high above him. Much of Old Route 12 was lined with trees, and though there was the occasional strip mall or gas station or restaurant, it was mostly homes along that road. Some were recent—sprawling things built in the boom times at the tail end of the previous century or the opening days of the current one—but the majority were older. Michael had often admired the Federals, the Colonials, and the few Victorians along the road.

The windows were all dark, but some of the homes had lights on in front. There were jack-o'-lanterns on the steps and scarecrows tied to lampposts. Down one side street, in a recent development of half-million-dollar homes, he saw a house whose entire lawn was a Halloween scene, with orange lights, giant pumpkins, and a Grim Reaper. It was as though the owners had confused Halloween with Christmas.

The tires thrummed on the road and, in spite of the October wind in his face, Michael began to feel drowsy. The flicker of the streetlights began to lull him. He blinked several times, and when his head bobbed to his chest for the first time, he sat up straighter.

"Shit," he whispered.

He slapped himself in the face several times, just hard enough to sting his frozen cheeks, and he opened his eyes as wide as he could. *Time for music. Something with a pulse.*

There was a long curve ahead, so he waited until he had rounded it before he took a quick glance into the backseat again. Jillian was out cold. He doubted the radio would wake her. But even if it did, better that than to have her wake up in a ditch . . . or worse. Michael turned on the radio and scanned quickly over to Kiss 108. He hated the entire hip-hop/rap scene, but he knew that it would keep him awake. The thumping bass he had heard so often rattling other cars as they passed him or while waiting for a green light erupted from the speakers and he turned it up even louder, grimacing as he did so.

At the back of his skull, a dull ache had begun to grow. He was not certain if it was the Guinness or the music or the cold air. *Probably the combination,* he thought. He became aware of a bitter taste in his mouth and ran his tongue across his teeth. He loved Guinness, but like any other beer, it left a film in his mouth. Michael wanted something else to drink. He tried to remember if there was a Dunkin' Donuts on Old Route 12. If it was still open he could get a coffee. Replace one bitter aftertaste with another.

The road hummed. The engine growled. His eyelids grew heavy again despite the music. His cheeks felt numb, and though he wanted to think it was the chilly October night, he knew better. Mainly because his feet were sort of numb, too, and it wasn't that cold down on the floormats. No, it was the Guinness, settling in.

Maybe he'd had more than he had realized.

The music thudded in his ears and the ache at the back of his skull began to throb. A streetlight strobed past the windshield and he blinked the glare away. The tires on the road were white noise. His mind drifted back to when he was eight years old, taking a bus trip to Florida with his family, riding through Lafayette in the middle of the night.

His head tilted forward, and the motion jerked him awake. Michael snapped his head up, panic trip-hammering through his heart. The road was curving to the right . . . but he was going straight, crossing into the oncoming lane, the nose of the Volvo headed for a pair of telephone poles, a new one lashed to an older one to keep it from falling.

His mouth tasted like aluminum foil. Bile burned up the back of his throat. His face was flush with heat now, no longer numb.

Arms rigid, he pressed himself back into his seat and ratcheted the steering wheel to the right.

The streetlight above him winked out in that moment, casting the corner into darkness.

There was no one else on the road.

His tires shrieked on the blacktop.

A burst of elation like nothing he had ever felt surged up within him as he realized that he was going to do it, that he had righted the car. Then he came around the last of the curve, too far onto the shoulder, and saw the little girl on the side of the road.

She was blond. A tiny thing, caught in the glare of his head-lights, golden hair fringed with that brightness as though she were an angel. Blue jeans. A ruffled peasant blouse. Yet the one thing that stood out most was her eyes. She stared at Michael through the windshield, gazing into the headlights with no sign of fear at all. She looked for all the world as though she had just woken from a nap.

"Jesus Christ!" Michael screamed.

His hands nudged the wheel to the left.

The Volvo passed by her so close that, looking out the passenger window, Michael could see her shake with the change in air pressure. He cursed in the dashboard glow, over and over as he slammed on the brakes. The tires skidded slightly on the pavement, but then the antilock kicked in and the car rolled just a bit before it stopped.

"Oh, my God," he whispered, trying desperately to get his heart to slow, to get his breathing back to normal. He pursed his lips and blew out a breath.

Missed her, he thought. *I missed her.*

The night air rushed in, caressing his face, and that helped him catch his breath. His heart still thundered in his chest, but it was slowing. The radio ground out another rap song and suddenly it was too much for him. He punched the power button and all was silent inside the car, save for his own breathing and the purr of the engine.

His gaze fell upon the clock display, a green-white glow that read 12:21.

What the hell was a little girl doing wandering Old Route 12 at half past twelve on a frigid night, without even a jacket on? As he stared at the clock, there was a moment—only a moment—when Michael was sure he was going to look up to find that the girl was gone. Or, perhaps, that she had never been there at all.

Foot still on the brake, he turned to look out the rear window, and there she was, only a few feet behind the car, bathed in the rich red glow of his brake lights. Exhaust fumes swirled up from his tailpipe and she seemed lost in a crimson fog. Her expression had not changed.

Michael's breath caught in his throat and once more he shivered, but this time it was neither the alcohol nor the cold night air that caused it. It was the vacant, lost look in her eyes.

CHAPTER TWO

Shock, Michael thought. *She's in shock.*

The logic of this filtered through him and he let out a calming breath. He was still turned around in his seat, neck craned as far back as possible without forcing him to take his foot off the brake. The effect of the brake lights that illuminated the girl was eerie, and the exhaust fumes that swirled around her only added to that. But now that he studied her face more closely, Michael was certain she must be in shock.

Why shouldn't she be? I almost ran her over.

The blond girl was perhaps seven, but certainly no more than eight. Her face was expressionless, eyes wide, but more in total blankness than in surprise.

Poor thing.

Michael glanced down at Jillian. She had been lying on her side on the backseat, but the abruptness of the stop had tossed her slightly forward, so that her left arm dipped down toward the floor mat and her legs were tilted away from the seat. She mumbled, but did not wake.

His gaze rose once more. The girl stood there, unmoving, forlorn. Michael turned from her and put the car in park. He killed the engine, tugged out his keys, and popped open his door.

"You all right, honey?" he asked, as gently as he could.

The girl did not move as he approached her. Without the brake lights, she was no longer cast in that crimson hue. Only the moonlight provided illumination now—the nearest working street lamp was too far away—and in that lunar glow the girl's features were washed-out and pale. Michael went to her slowly, concerned that he might frighten her again.

"Hello. What's your name?"

She seemed frozen still, her gaze unfocused. Michael dropped to his knees on the pavement in front of her. He reached slowly to touch her arm and pulled his fingers back instinctively. Her skin was cold. So cold. What else had he expected on a night as frigid as this, with the girl walking around in jeans and a thin cotton blouse? He could not help but wonder what might have happened to drive her from her home. Were her parents terrified for her, or were they the sort of cruel people he read about from time to time, or saw on the news?

"Sweetie? My name's Michael. Can you tell me your name?"

No response.

"Are you lost?"

She blinked. A tiny gasp came from her lips, and at last her eyes focused on him. Her face was angelic, but it became heartbreaking when she nibbled on her lower lip. And then her mouth pursed, just for a moment, into a pout.

"The lights were bright," she said, her small voice filled with the import that often accompanied children's proclamations.

"Yeah. I know. My car. I nearly hit you, honey, but you're all right. Okay? You're all right. So . . . you're lost? Is that right?" He was thinking now that perhaps she had followed a squirrel or a bird or the path of some gulley and gotten turned around. It would be easy to do around here, in the woods.

Halloween. The thought struck him from nowhere. The holiday was still days away, but around here most towns had the kids trick-or-treat the Saturday night before to make it easier on parents who commuted. She must have been out for Halloween, trick-or-treating, and somehow . . .

Michael found himself staring at the stiff cuffs of his D' Artagnan shirt. The hat was on the passenger's seat in the car—or probably on the floor now, he hadn't noticed—but the shirt was enough to jar the realization. The girl had not been out trick-or-treating, not without a costume.

"I'm so cold," she said, her voice stronger now.

"Are you lost?" he asked again. "Do you know where you belong?"

The question seemed to surprise her and she blinked several times, focusing on his face once more. Slowly, she shook her head.

"Do you know your phone number?"

Again, the shake of her head.

A hundred thoughts went through his mind. He couldn't call her parents and get their address. The logical next step was to put her in the car and take her to the police station. But Michael could still feel the flush of alcohol in his cheeks, the way in which he was not quite steady, even kneeling on the pavement. How the hell could he walk into the police station and tell the cops he had just driven the lost girl to them when they were sure to notice he had been drinking?

I could just call the police. Tell them she's here. Where to find her.

But as soon as this option occurred to him, Michael dismissed it. There was no specific code he lived by—he didn't take himself that seriously—but he knew without doubt that he was not the kind of man who would leave a shivering little girl on the side of the road to save his own ass. There was no way to know what might happen. She could wander off again.

He hung his head a moment and when he looked back up at her, there was something imploring in her eyes, as though she wanted to ask him something but could not speak the words. She hugged herself and shivered from the cold. Though she did not seem quite as shaken as she originally had, she was still a bit dreamy, disoriented, and he knew she needed to be looked at by a doctor.

Since the early days of their relationship, he had consulted Jillian on every important decision he had ever made. But Jillian was out cold in the backseat of the car. There would be no smile from her now, no brightly sparkling eyes, no wisdom.

Michael put an arm around the girl as he stood up. "You're going to be all right," he promised. "I'm going to get you home. Back where you belong."

He would take her to the police. It occurred to him that showing up with a missing girl in his car could be disastrously misconstrued, but Michael wasn't concerned. He had been at the party until a short time ago. No one could suggest he had done anything but try to help the girl. He hoped the cops would take that into consideration if they smelled Guinness on his breath.

Stop thinking about it. Just do what's right.

"Here. Hop in and let me get the heat cranking. It'll warm you right up."

Michael got the girl into the passenger's seat. His D'Artagnan hat was indeed on the floor, and just before he could retrieve it, she shifted in the seat, using one foot for leverage, and crushed it. He said nothing, but for the first time since he had fallen asleep at the wheel, a smile flickered across his face. As he shut the door, he glanced at Jillian again in the back and wished she were awake.

Shaking his head in disbelief at the strange turns the night had taken, he opened the back door and rearranged Jillian more comfortably. She was probably too drunk to be disturbed, even if she had flown right off the seat and onto the floor, but he didn't like to see her that way, twisted around like a rag doll.

His keys jangled as he got into the car again and started up the Volvo. The lights came on instantly, casting a jaundiced light into the woods just ahead. The little girl had not put on her seat belt. He had asked her several times, but she had drifted into silence again. He pressed his lips tightly together, worried for her, then he bent over and buckled her seat belt snugly. The diagonal chest belt was too high and came across her throat, so he tucked it behind her, not wanting to imagine what would happen if he was in an accident and the belt went taut.

Michael pulled away from the shoulder of the road at 12:29.

He drove carefully, not too fast, but not too slowly, either. For the moment, the adrenaline surging through him had eliminated any trace of drowsiness, but the recollection was fresh in his mind and he feared its return.

Old Route 12 had been made to follow a natural path through the valley and wound back and forth, several times seeming to turn in upon itself. As he drove he stole glances at the girl. The streetlights flashed overhead, spaced even farther apart now. Twice, cars passed going the other direction, but otherwise the road was deserted. The radio was off, and the silence of the car was broken only by the hum of its engine and a light snore coming from Jillian in the backseat. The girl seemed frozen, her face as slack and her eyes as unfocused as they had been when he had first seen her. She did not look at him, did not even seem to wonder who was sleeping in the backseat, or why.

His brain was still fuzzy. No denying that. Michael still had a metallic taste in his mouth and the numbness had not left him. Now that the adrenaline rush was over, in fact, he felt even less steady than he had before. He had to keep his arms rigid upon the steering wheel to keep the car from drifting, and even then he had to adjust from time to time. The alcohol was starting to settle in. This wasn't just a pleasant buzz.

"Scooter," she said softly.

Michael started.

"What?" he asked, glancing at her.

Her expression hadn't changed. If anything, she looked dreamy. Drugged. He frowned at the thought, wondering if that was possible. And of course it was. Anything was possible.

"Scooter," she said. "You asked my name. It's Scooter. That's what Mommy calls me."

Scooter, he thought. *What kind of name is that?*

His eyes were on her and so he saw her sit up slightly, saw her eyes narrow with interest, and then flicker with sadness. One of her tiny hands floated up and she pointed out through the wind-shield.

"Right there," she said. "Turn right there."

Michael glanced at the road, saw a tiny side street coming up, partially hidden in the trees until he was almost on top of it. He slowed.

"You recognize this street?"

She nodded.

Relief spread through him so quickly his skin tingled with it. The girl wasn't lost anymore. He could take her home. He wouldn't have to take her to the police station, which meant no trouble for him with the cops.

"Fantastic," he said, and as the street came up quickly on his right, he took the turn, a little too fast. They both swayed left, but then they were rolling along past even thicker woods, the occasional house hidden back in the trees.

"Just keep an eye out. Let me know where to turn," he told her.

The girl sat with her hands in her lap as though she was at church. She clutched the hem of her peasant blouse in her fingers and studied the road ahead. And yet there was something about her sudden alertness that caused Michael to glance sidelong at her time and again.

Her breath did not come quickly, but it had a little hitch to it, and as her chest rose and fell he thought he could hear her heart fluttering like a frightened bird's. Though her gaze searched the splash of the headlights on the road ahead, her eyes shifted every few moments to the dark woods around them, as though she feared some predator stalked her through the trees.

"There. Turn there," she said, with another nervous glance into the darkness between a pair of split-levels.

Caught up with her anxiety, Michael found himself searching the trees on the right side of the car as well. It took him a moment to register what she had said. When he did, he glanced up to see a green street sign gleaming in his headlights. A left turn. In the glare he could not read the street name, but he turned, distracted by the girl's agitation. As he made the turn she glanced over her shoulder, looking out through the rear window. Michael checked the rearview mirror.

"What are you looking for?" he asked, a bit surprised by the sound of his voice, by the tremor in it.

"I don't like the dark."

He didn't bother to point out that he had found her walking along by herself at night on a stretch of road that had been pitch black except for the moon.

They drove like that for a while, mostly in silence, and from time to time the girl told him to turn. One street was very suburban, lined with lampposts, cars in driveways, Halloween decorations on nearly every stoop. Another was almost entirely woods. Several times, Michael looked in on Jillian in the backseat, but she snored on peacefully. Though his thoughts were muffled by the Guinness, he found his mind wandering, or at least drunkenly stumbling. The girl was afraid of something. First she was lost. Then she wasn't. She recognized a street, but now they had followed an odd zigzag through the valley so that he was no longer certain they were even in the same town.

Several times he began to drift and had to jerk the wheel to keep the tires from hitting the rutted shoulder of the road. They were now on a broad, winding way that led up a hill. Ranch houses hid in the trees, and he spotted an A-frame, which he'd always thought one of the oddest choices for a home. His face felt pleasantly warm, his hands as oddly numb as his feet. He was tired, and combined with the alcohol in his system and the warm air pumping out of the heating vents in the car, the tiredness was catching up to him.

Michael opened his window about halfway. The October air rushed in and he breathed it in, enjoying the feeling of it in his lungs. Fresh, crisp autumn air, with more than a hint of winter. He blinked, sat up a bit straighter, and glanced over at the girl.

She made no response, only continued to search the road ahead. Whatever had spooked her about the trees before no longer seemed to bother her.

"If you're cold, I can close it."

As if she had not heard, she raised a hand and pointed through the windshield. "That one. That's where I belong."

About time, Michael thought. But when he looked out through the windshield, he frowned, and without even being aware of it, moved his foot from accelerator to brake, slowing the Volvo's ascent up the hill.

The house was in a dead-end circle at the top of the road. The hill continued upward, however, and though set back and surrounded by trees, the house loomed over the road as if it stood watch. It was an enormous, sprawling thing with darkened windows, the property untended. Once it would have been called a mansion, but Michael felt that size alone shouldn't earn a place that word. Its condition had to count for something. Michael knew only a little about architecture, but even so he felt that the house was an odd combination of styles. In front there was a single turret splitting a gabled roof, and a porch that seemed entirely out of place, wrapping around one side of the house's face but not the other. In the moonlight he could see that several shutters were hanging, shingles were missing from the roof, and at least one window was broken. The place was simply falling apart.

Yet someone was home. A light burned in a second-floor window, and another up in the turret.

This is where I belong, the girl had said.

Michael shook his head, brows knitted. In the backseat he heard Jillian mumble softly in her sleep. She whimpered, as though she were having a bad dream.

"Listen, are you sure—" he began, turning to the girl.

But even as he spoke, she popped open her door.

"Wait. Wait a second," he said quickly.

She held the door open and turned to him. Her face had gone slack again, the same distant eyes, the same vacant expression she had worn when he had first gotten a close look at her illuminated by his brake lights.

"Come find me," she whispered, her voice smaller than ever. She sounded even younger, then. A tiny child, afraid to go to sleep alone at night. Afraid of monsters in the closet.

"Find me if you can. Will you?"

Michael blinked, trying to make sense of it. He nodded. "Sure. Sure, I will. But listen, sweetie, I don't think you should—"

She turned away, running up the hill toward that dark shambles of a house. Her blond hair flew behind her as she ran, catching the moonlight, though the rest of her seemed to be enveloped by the night.

There was a dinging noise inside the Volvo. She had left the door open. Michael swore and glanced into the backseat. Jillian's expression was troubled, reinforcing his thought that she might be having a nightmare. He got out of the car, engine still running, and walked around to shut the passenger door. The interior of the Volvo went dark, save for the glow from the dash.

He turned to watch the girl as she reached the front porch of the house. She went up the steps and in moments she had disappeared inside as if the place had swallowed her. No one had come to the door to greet her. No other lights had come on. Save for those two illuminated windows, in fact, the place looked deserted. Uninhabited.

Michael took a step toward the house.

Wait. What the fuck are you doing? He stopped, staring up at the house, conflicted. He swayed, his balance off, and bent his knees a little to keep from falling. *Just go. Get in the car and go. You heard her say it. This is where she belongs.*

The temptation to drive away was powerful. Her parents had to be there. They were probably sleeping. Was she young enough to realize that she could just sneak in and they wouldn't know she was gone? Was it possible they could have been sleeping the whole time? But that made no sense. He had picked her up miles from here. On foot, it would have taken a long time for a little girl to travel that distance.

So what, Michael? What's your plan? If the place is empty, you'd have to go to the police. And if it's not, if the parents are freaks and that's why she was nervous, well, you'll still have to go to the police. It's like quantum science, that German physicist and his cat. As long as you don't go up there, you'll never know, so neither option is true.

He started around the front of the car, unwilling to even look up the hill again. But when he reached his door, when he opened it, he knew he was fooling himself. He had to know that the girl was safe.

Besides, he thought, glancing around at the road and the woods, *you don't have a goddamn clue how to get out of here. Without some directions from her parents or whoever, you won't get home till morning.*

With a sigh, he glanced into the backseat to check on Jillian. She was still completely out, but he felt a moment of trepidation leaving her alone in the car. Another look around, however, and he realized that the chances of another car going by, never mind anyone on foot, were next to nil at this time of night. Michael reached into the Volvo and turned the engine off. He pulled his keys out, shut the door, and clicked the button that locked the doors. The locks slid into place with a reassuringly solid thump.

Michael gazed up at the house again. Though his extremities were still sort of numb, he felt the bite of the chilly wind on his cheeks as he started up the hill. The moment he began to climb toward the house, however, he felt his equilibrium failing again.

How many bottles of Guinness did I have? he wondered, and for the first time, realized that with his friends buying him drinks, he had lost track. Now here he was in the middle of nowhere, getting himself involved in something that was clearly none of his business.

He managed to stumble up the hill, though the longer he stayed on his feet, the more his stomach began to feel queasy. Michael was determined now, though. He was practically at their doorstep. There was no way he was going home without finding out exactly what was going on here. What kind of people were they?

Only when he reached the porch did he pause to really look at the house again. He gazed up at it, craning his head so far back that he nearly tumbled down the hill. It was even more dilapidated than he had thought. Several windows were cracked. On the porch there was a swing; it rocked gently, set in motion by the wind, emitting a steady creak that sent icy fingers of dread dancing up his spine.

The front door was not entirely closed. Even from the base of the stairs he could see that it hung open several inches, only darkness inside.

He wanted to turn around. To go straight to the car, to his blissfully unconscious wife, and get out of there. To forget about the little girl, and this entire night.

"Scooter?" he called, and immediately felt an utter fool. The name was so silly that saying it out loud was like nails on a blackboard.

"Hello?" he ventured. The only response was the creaking of the porch swing and the silence from the dark interior of the house.

Michael hesitated, glancing back down at the car. The face of that little lost girl was etched deeply in his mind.

Find me if you can. Will you?

What the hell had that meant?

He started up the steps, agonizingly aware of the moldering house. The paint was peeling, flaking. And as he climbed the stairs he caught a scent on the breeze, the smell of old newspaper and of decay.

"Hello?" he tried again.

Someone's got to be here. The girl went right in the front door. The place might feel empty, but it isn't. It can't be.

There was no doorbell.

Fuck it. Someone *is* here.

Michael knocked on the door three times in quick succession.

The sound echoed down the hill and inside the house. The force of his knocking swung the door inward, until it hung half open.

"Hello," he said again. Or perhaps this time he only thought it.

With one final glance down at the car, he took a breath, nodded determinedly, and went inside.

CHAPTER THREE

The house creaked with age and the wind. Michael had expected dust to fill his nose, had expected the place to be empty, save for dirt and broken furniture and cobwebs. But the house was not at all what he expected. What he found instead was worse, in a way.

Moonlight streamed in through the windows, casting a yellow gleam of illumination, though the corners were lost in shadow. It seemed odd, that luminescence. The moon had not seemed quite so bright when he was outside—not nearly bright enough to provide him so much light.

The house was clean. That was the thing that really surprised him. Not a single dust mote floated in the splashes of moonlight that dappled the foyer. Something struck him as odd about the wallpaper, and the paintings on the walls. As he ventured deeper into the house and peered into the moon-washed parlor to the right, Michael realized what it was.

The house was a relic out of time, as if it had been decorated in the 1940s and had remained untouched since then. It reminded him of his childhood, and of old Mrs. Standish, who had been born in the house across the street and had lived there until she died. Whenever Michael had to sell chocolate bars or raffle tickets as school fund-raisers, Mrs. Standish was always generous with her time and her money. By then she had lived in the house nearly eighty years, and even the knickknacks on her shelves had yellowed.

This place was like that. Blanched. Yellowed, and not just by the moonlight. The sofa and the carpet and the divan in the parlor were all faded. Michael stood in the foyer, looking in, and then his gaze drifted toward the grand staircase ahead of him, and the corridor that ran alongside it into the heart of the house.

It was like stepping into an old sepia-toned photograph.

Despite the cracked windows and the disrepair of the exterior, someone obviously lived here or it wouldn't have been kept clean at all. Michael shuddered as he thought of that little girl having to live in this dreary old place.

The girl.

He realized that he had not heard a single sound since he had entered. Now he took a deep breath and moved deeper into the house. He ought to call her name. He knew that. Yet he was reluctant to disturb the silence, as though doing so might awaken something better left sleeping.

He licked his lips to moisten them, the rich, earthy taste of stout still on his tongue and palate.

"Hello?" he ventured. His voice was a dry rasp, and the house seemed to swallow the sound.

Listing slightly to one side, as though trying to keep his balance on shipboard, he started down the corridor that ran beside the stairs. The air inside the house was crisp and unsettlingly odorless, so that when he caught just the whiff of a scent, it made him pause and blink his eyes several times, trying to determine what it was.

Cocoa. Hot cocoa.

Michael shook his head, knitting his brows. That made no sense. And anyway, the scent was gone almost the instant he had recognized it. He started forward again, only to stop himself at the realization that the arched entrance to the dining room was on his right. His head felt muddled again, worse than it had before. He peered into the grand old room, with its wide windows, its crystal chandelier, and the high-backed chairs around its long, elegant, claw-foot table.

Perfectly clean, yet the wallpaper here was just like elsewhere in the house, and the upholstery on the seats was faded.

How? his mind ventured. Michael glanced back the way he had come and realized he had no memory of having walked the last dozen feet or so of that corridor. He glanced about him. The corridor continued straight ahead. To his left, beneath the stairs, was a heavy door that he felt sure led to the cellar. *Not there,* he told himself, shivering. *No way did that little girl go down there.*

Ignoring the door under the stairs, he continued along the corridor. It was ridiculous, the way he swayed, as though he had continued drinking long after he knew he had stopped.

For the first time, Michael began to wonder if someone had doped him, or dropped something into his drink. Ecstasy, maybe. He had no experience with the drug, so he could not compare this light-headedness to its effects.

"Shit," he said, pausing to bring a hand up to squeeze the bridge of his nose. He sighed and dropped his hand away.

And discovered he was standing in the middle of the kitchen.

"Jesus," Michael whispered. He flinched back from what his eyes saw, D'Artagnan boots heavy on the kitchen floor. Abruptly he felt absurd, standing there in the kitchen of strangers in his masquerade costume.

He should leave, he knew that. He was intruding. A drunken man—*and yes, you are drunk. No use denying it.* An idiot in a costume, wandering around a house that didn't belong to him. What would the girl's parents think if they found him there, now? Would anything he could say to them come out right? Thoughts of the police continued to plague him.

But the house . . . there's something not right about this place.

"Fuck it," he whispered. He had seen her come in. Despite its outer appearance, the place was clean enough. Someone lived here. That meant there was someone here who was responsible for her.

Michael felt himself fading again. The alcohol. *Or maybe it's not. Maybe it's just this place. Maybe I'm fading just like the wallpaper. Just like the furniture.*

A frisson of alarm went through him. What the hell had he been thinking, coming in here? An image of Jillian passed out on the backseat of the car swam up into his mind. His responsibility was to her.

Heels rapping on the kitchen floor, he turned in a circle as he got his bearings. One door probably led to a pantry. There was another tall, wide door that he assumed would take him back to the main corridor. And then there was a narrow door that hung open to reveal a set of steps leading upward. Back stairs, not at all uncommon in houses of this age and size. But with the luminous moonlight not extending itself up into that stairwell, there were only shadows up there.

Fire.

Michael frowned, nostrils flaring. He sniffed the air, and caught the scent again. Logs burning in a fireplace.

He took a step toward the exit.

Peppermint.

Another, and he froze.

Popcorn. Fresh popcorn, with plenty of butter.

A breeze came from somewhere else in the house, one of the cracked windows, he assumed. It caressed his face, and brought with it the smell of new-fallen snow. Yet with the next draft he was sure it was not that clean winter scent, but the smell of spring rain and flowers.

Michael listed so badly to one side that he nearly fell over.

It occurred to him that if someone had put something in his drink, he could be hallucinating. A finger of dread traced along his spine, and yet he also found the thought oddly comforting. It was, at least, an explanation.

He took a deep breath, careful to inhale through his mouth to avoid any more strange aromas. Then he started for the door again, intent on getting out of there. Whoever lived in this fucked-up house, he was happy to leave them to it. A tiny voice in the back of his head reminded him that he had no way of knowing how to get out of the neighborhood, but he ignored it. He just wanted to be gone from here.

His hand was on the knob. His eyelids fluttered and he thought he might black out again, or whatever it was that had been happening to him before. His fingers curled more tightly on the brass door handle, and he refused to let go. The feeling passed. He tugged the door open and was relieved to see the hall-way beyond. A bit further down was the entrance into the dining room. On the far end he would emerge into the foyer, and the front door was waiting for him.

Come find me.

He blinked. The little girl—*Scooter, she said her name was Scooter*—had said those words. But now he'd heard them spoken again. Somewhere nearby. In the house.

Come find me.

Michael dragged the back of his hand across his mouth and glanced over at the narrow doorway, and the steps that rose up into darkness beyond.

"Olly-olly-all-come-free!"

The voice was distant, drifting down those stairs to him, but it made him stagger back a step, just the same. It was not in his head. It had not sprung from a bottle, like the cottony taste in his mouth and the way he had lost seconds here and there since entering the house.

The voice had broken the silence, and now it was followed by a rapid scatter of footsteps upstairs. Children. Not just the one girl, but several of them. He could hear their laughter, a distant trilling like morning songbirds, like water over stones in the brook behind his childhood home.

His hand came off the doorknob.

He blinked, took one swaying step, and opened his eyes to find himself on the third step up that narrow, shadowed stair-well.

Michael hesitated. His foot hovered, ready to descend, to re-treat. But the laughter came again, from upstairs. In his mind he heard those words again. *Come find me.* Hadn't she seemed frightened then, when she spoke those words? Or, if not frightened, then at least very sad?

She had. He knew she had.

But now there was this sound, the giddy laughter of little girls.

The house was a mystery. One that made his skin crawl with doubt and reluctance. Michael just wanted to be gone, but that did not keep his foot from moving up instead of down. One step. Then another. Passing up through the inky blackness of the back stairs until he emerged in a long second-story corridor, lined with rooms. Every door hung open. The moonlight spilled like mist from those open doors, illuminating the hall.

It's a dream, he thought with a smile of disbelief. *I've passed out somewhere. That's the only answer. I'm asleep.*

But the texture of the costume was rough on his skin. The boots were too tight on his feet. And he could still taste the stout in his mouth.

Cinnamon. There was no breeze this time, but his nostrils were suddenly filled with the scent. Not just cinnamon, but sugar and baking apples. Apple pie, maybe. But layered with cinnamon.

A floorboard creaked behind him, down in the kitchen. Michael glanced down; in the narrow outline of the door at the bottom of the steps, something shifted. He was looking at it dead on, but it moved like the sort of phantom that usually appeared only in peripheral vision. So quickly that it was little more than an afterimage.

It left him only with the impression of silver, the color of moonlight on the surface of a lake at night. A ripple of silver. And a whisper. There had been a whisper, too. Not words. And not the wind. The whisper of something moving, pushing the air around it. Rustling down there in the kitchen, with not even a light sheen of dust to disturb as it passed.

Michael stared for several seconds down those stairs, trying to get another glimpse of whatever he had seen.

Another chorus of girlish laughter came to him from the back of the house. He looked down the hall.

Something flashed in the moonlight, ducking into one of the rooms back there. A little rush of air escaped his lips, and he stared again, narrowing his gaze, trying to make sense of what his eyes were showing him. A ripple of silver. An afterimage that stayed on his eyelids when he closed them, as though he had looked at the sun too long.

"That's enough," he whispered, the words painfully simple.

He turned his back on the giggles and the shifting moonlight and started toward the front of the house. Far along the hall, he could see the balustrade at the top of the grand staircase. Michael began to move more quickly, his pulse racing. His own breathing was too loud in his ears. All he wanted was to get the hell out of there before he blacked out again, before his feet could take him in a direction no sober man would go.

Smells assaulted him now. Too many for him to separate them. It was as though he stumbled now through fairgrounds or a carnival, so overwhelming were the odors that filled the air. His stomach churned and bile burned up the back of his throat. His legs felt weak. A shudder went up his spine, and he knew if he turned and glanced back the way he had come he would see those silver ripples slipping from room to room, or gliding up the stairs in pursuit.

A soft chant began up ahead, coming from one of those side doors.

One, two, buckle your shoe.
Three, four, shut the door.
Five, six, pick up sticks.
Seven, eight, don't be late.
Nine, ten, do it again . . .

He stood frozen in the hall, listening, his heart pounding so hard in its bone cage that his chest hurt.

A little bit faster or your turn will end.

The laughter of small children seemed to fill the hall, streaming from every room. It was joined by a rhythmic shuffle, the backbeat of a jump rope. The sound of footsteps echoed off the walls. Michael shifted his gaze from left to right, certain he would see a little girl run into the hall, or do a ballerina pirouette.

The singsong chant faded. Once more he began to move, thinking only of leaving, of getting to the front stairs and the hell out of there. He reached an open door on the left. From within he heard a soft, lisping, baby-girl voice singing "I'm a Little Teapot." Trembling, he paused an instant, then stepped over the threshold.

A child's bedroom. Pale and bleached of life, washed in moonlight. No sign of any occupant at all, and now the voice he had heard was hushed, distant, as though it came from a closet, or from outside the window.

". . . *Here is my handle, here is my spout* . . ."

Spiders of dread crept all over his body. He flinched, staring at that empty room. As he turned to withdraw, he noticed the scrawl. Graffiti snaked all over one wall of that bedroom, but these were no filthy limericks or spray-painted gang tags. *Miss Friel Cuts the Cheese,* announced one. *Nikki and Danielle were here. Ruthie Loves Adam. Lizzie & Jason, TLA.*

TLA. Michael hadn't seen those three letters put together since grade school, but their meaning was fresh in his mind. *True Love, Always.* The sort of notion kids believed in, before they began to understand just how many obstacles there were to get in the way. *TLA* seemed so damned simple then. But *True Love, Always* could be hard work. Even when you got lucky, like he had, finding Jillian. Even then, it was work.

Jillian. He could imagine her face in front of him, her grin, the way she always seemed to have one lock of hair hanging in front of her eyes. *Oh, Jesus, honey, I just want out of here.*

A door slammed. Michael spun, heart pounding, and let out a long, shuddering sigh when he saw that it was not the door to this room. He staggered into the hallway.

A trickle of sweat ran down the back of his neck.

Michael broke into a run for the end of the hall, for the top of that grand staircase. There were higher floors, more stairs that went up and up, to the very top . . . to that one window at the peak of the house where he had seen a light on. He didn't care about those stairs. He only wanted the ones that went down.

His boots thumped the floor as he ran, stumbling toward the stairs, building momentum.

Giggles erupted from the rooms he passed, but now he did not want to look inside them. Still, he could not avoid the images his peripheral vision sent to him.

A swing set, chains creaking as they swayed in some unseen breeze.

More graffiti . . . in every room. Names in chalk and crayon and marker, and maybe in other substances he did not want to think about. *Heather. Sarajane.* Michael picked up speed. The hallway seemed impossibly long. *Barbie. Alisa.* His arms were pumping, legs flying under him. The stairs were getting closer, at last. *Tracy. Erica. Scooter.*

Scooter.

He tried to stop short, twisting himself around to get a better look inside a room on his right, a little study with a desk and bookshelves and children's names finger-painted in watercolor on the side of the desk. But he was running too fast. Michael tripped over his own legs and for a moment he was airborne. Then he hit the wood floor and slid. The fabric of his costume jacket tore.

He lay panting, eyes closed tightly, wishing it would all go away. Someone had given him something bad, and here he was running around some stranger's house like a lunatic. Scooter's house.

His eyes opened. The temptation to go back to that small

study, to look at her name painted on the side of the desk, was strong. But he was through with succumbing to curiosity. It could wait until morning, until he was sober. Or straight. Until he got his head on right.

Michael pushed himself to his knees and glanced along the hall toward the top of the stairs. The whole corridor was dappled with splashes of moonlight and shadows, but there were other things there as well. Things that were neither light nor darkness. Silver things that shimmered like heat off the summer pavement, that only really seemed solid if his eyes were half closed.

They were between Michael and the stairs.

Without ever seeming to move, they came nearer. It was as though they blinked out of one spot and appeared in another, flickering from one gloomy place to another, becoming visible not in the patches of shadow or the shafts of moonlight, but only ever in those slashes of nighttime twilight where shadow and light met.

Michael froze, staring. His stomach lurched again and he gasped for breath. He shook his head and started to back away, moving down the hall. But images flickered in his mind, silver ripples he had seen down in the kitchen, and back along that hallway. He did not have to turn around to know that they were behind him as well.

Out of the corner of his eye he could see the open door of that little study, *Scooter* scrawled in lime green finger paint on the desk. Erica had used yellow, Tracy a metallic gold. Another picture flashed through Michael's mind . . . of his own finger, dipped in bright blue paint, tracing a capital M onto the wood. . . . His every muscle fought the urge to go in there.

But the ripples flickered nearer still.

The sounds had all but died in the house, but now they returned. The laughter was a madhouse cacophony, a schoolyard full of songs and giggles and jeers. And the scents, that carnival of smells . . . popcorn and cinnamon and baking pie, rosemary and roasting turkey, spring rain and flowers, smoke from a wood stove. Somewhere in the house he could hear calliope music . . . maybe from a carousel, but he thought he recognized the tinny buzz of this particular tune. It was the ice-cream man. The one from his street. His high-school English teacher, Mr. Murphy, owned the truck and spent his summers making the rounds. There had been a faded caricature of a clown on the side of the truck, its hair the same bright rainbow of colors as Michael's favorite sno-cone. The clown had scared him, despite the fact that the paint that gave it life was dim and chipped, as though time had taken steel wool to the image.

That was it. The calliope music of Mr. Murphy's ice-cream truck. He could almost taste that sno-cone. Almost see that clown, with its squat, ugly body and bulbous nose, and that leering grin that said, *Come on, kiddies, I'm your friend. Just mind the teeth, and you'll be all right . . .*

He bolted, surging up from the floor. Feet still numb, he stumbled into the doorframe, slamming his shoulder hard enough to send spikes of pain through him. The room was empty. At least, for a moment it was. Then, once more, figures shifted in his peripheral vision. But these were not silver ripples, moonlight wraiths . . . these were glimpses of phantom children. There were pale girls skipping rope. A sullen dark-skinned girl in a corner. Another pair playing rock-paper-scissors.

No way out.

One final glimpse showed him an ocean of silver gathering outside in the hall.

He scrambled up onto the desk and hurled his body at the window, pulling his limbs close in hopes that he could shield himself from the glass as it shattered. Then he was falling, limbs flailing, glass shards glittering in the moonlight as they cascaded down around him.

The ragged grass seemed to rush up toward him.

The impact knocked the air out of him.

Darkness closed in, the shadows swallowing the moonlight.

His mouth was still filled with the rich, earthy flavor of stout.

CHAPTER FOUR

Tap, tap!

The first bit of awareness that slipped into Jillian Dansky's mind on that Sunday morning was the prickle of gooseflesh along her arms. She shivered from the cold, and drew her legs up beneath her, pulling into a fetal ball, yet there was no warmth to be had. Her nipples were painfully erect from the chill. She had neither sheet nor blanket to huddle beneath.

Tap, tap, tap!

As she slowly emerged from sleep, she became cognizant of the light beyond her eyelids. Simultaneously, she woke to the bone-deep aches that wracked her body. Her neck was stiff, and a line of dull pain ran up the back of her skull and panned out across the top of her head, settling into her forehead and temples. A tickle in her stomach was almost nausea, but not quite. More a whispered hello, putting her on notice that if she tried anything more ambitious than opening her eyes it might turn into full-on puking.

Jillian shivered again and let a tiny moan escape her lips. It was a sound born not of pain, but of regret. All she wanted, body and soul, was to stay precisely where she was. But she knew that the cold would never be abated if she did not move.

Tap, tap!

Eyes still closed, she frowned. What was that noise? She had heard it before, but had not registered it. It sounded like glass, like something rapping against—

"Rise and shine!" called an impatient voice. A man's voice. And it was not Michael's.

The pieces of this strange puzzle were all there, but her brain was slow in putting them together. Then, in an instant, the connection was made. The stiffness. The feel of the seat beneath her, and at her back. The cold. And that tapping . . . tapping on the window of the car.

Jillian opened her eyes. Late October sunshine made her squint, but she could see the blue uniform clearly enough. She was lying on the backseat of the car, peering up at a gruffly handsome young police officer who stared in through the glass at her with a disdain in his eyes that she had never felt directed at her before, and hoped never to feel again. An autumn leaf struck the window, blew across the glass in front of his face, then disappeared. Their eyes had made a connection, and that leaf had severed it.

"Oh, Christ. Michael!" she cried, sitting up too quickly, heedless of her hangover headache.

With a hiss she pressed the heel of her right hand against her temple and squinted against the pain. All of this was foreign to her. Jillian had been drunk enough to have a hangover perhaps three times in her life, and never one as bad as this. Certainly never one with which she had awoken in the backseat of a car. Her own or anyone else's.

The cop was tapping on the window again, motioning for her to get out of the car. Didn't the guy know she had the mother of all headaches? Her Elizabethan gown was stiff and unyielding, wrinkled and pleated in places where no pleats ought to be. She squinted her eyes even more tightly and then forced herself to open them again, to swing her legs beneath her and sit up all the way in the backseat so that she could lean forward and look into the front, where Michael lay huddled much the way she had been only moments before. Even the rapping of the policeman's nightstick on the window had not roused him.

"Ma'am?" the cop called, his voice muffled by the glass. "Please step out of the car. Now."

This last was said calmly, but with such an air of command that it could not be debated. There was a second police officer, she noticed at last. He was on the other side of the car, the passenger's side, and he was trying to get a look at Michael in his torn, wrinkled D'Artagnan costume, a grave expression on his face. For the first time, Jillian wondered why her husband wasn't waking up.

"Oh, no," she said, in a tiny little voice that did not sound like her, even to her own ears. She reached into the front seat and grabbed his shoulder, shaking him with all the strength her hangover would allow. "Michael! Michael, wake up!"

"Ma'am!" the cop shouted.

Jillian had been numbed by sleep and her hangover, but with this snap from the policeman, her heart leaped into a sprint. Her face felt flushed and she raised both hands to signify that she was surrendering to his demand. As she moved toward the door, Michael began to stir in the front seat. She felt a mixture of relief and fury. He was alive, that was good. But what the hell were they doing there on the side of the road in the first place?

Michael, what the fuck have you done? she thought as she unlocked her door and eased it open.

The wind rushed in, whipping a cascade of chestnut hair across her face. She ran her fingers through it, pushing it away from her eyes, and hated how it felt, unwashed. Michael had begun to sit up in the front seat. There was a dark bruise on his face, covering most of his left cheek. She had no idea where he'd come by it, or the tear in his costume. But now wasn't the time to ask.

She had heard the hum of engines as she was waking up, but only now that she was out of the car could she see other vehicles passing by. Even now a gold minivan that looked vaguely familiar passed, and she prayed no one would go by who might recognize her, standing there in her costume. What would she say, then? Just thinking about it made her headache worsen.

"Ma'am?" the policeman said, and his voice was stern. "I don't suppose you've got some ID in that outfit?"

Jillian's cheeks blossomed with the heat of embarrassment. She looked down again at the wreck of her beautiful costume. A stray thought danced through her mind; she wondered what had become of the traditional half-mask she'd worn in front of her face for most of the night. At some point, she recalled having handed it to Michael, but somehow she doubted she would find it again.

"No, I . . ." She met the policeman's gaze, and stiffened. Her first impression had been correct. He was handsome, a broad-shouldered mid-twenties guy with a square jaw darkened by permanent five o'clock shadow, and the kind of eyes that could melt a girl's heart. But what had brought her up short was the look in those eyes.

He was pitying her.

It made her feel small. The tickle in her stomach wasn't quite so ticklish anymore. She felt sick, but not so much that she would actually *be* sick.

"I'm sorry. I don't. My purse is in the car"—*I think*—"I can get it." She ducked back into the car before he could argue with her. Her headache sang a funeral dirge, and her stomach churned as she bent over.

Michael was wide awake now. Or, at least, he seemed to be. There was something unspoken in his eyes. He looked almost stoned, but Michael had smoked pot exactly once in his life, so that was out of the question.

"Jillian? Jilly, what—"

The cop on the other side of the car wasn't as polite or as patient as the one Jillian had come to think of as *her* policeman. Michael's policeman slapped his open palm down on the roof of the car, making them both jump, then bent to glare in the window.

"Sir, step out of the car now, please. Right now."

"Yeah," Michael said. "Yes. Yeah, of course." He slid over to the front passenger door and unlocked it.

The policeman stood back, one hand resting on his holstered gun. Jillian didn't think Michael noticed that little detail, but it gave her an icier chill than the October wind. No, Michael wasn't noticing much. His expression was mystified. His eyes were wide, as though he had woken up to find himself lost in Oz. His hangover must have been even worse than hers, though how that could be she did not know. She wanted to scream at him, to hurl blame at him for putting her in this situation. Instead she just asked him to hand her purse back to her, and he did so.

"I'll need your license and your registration, please," Michael's policeman said curtly.

Jillian stepped out of the car again, even as her husband got out on the other side. She pulled her wallet from her purse, then opened it and retrieved her license, handing it over. Her policeman glanced from the picture on the license to Jillian and then back again several times.

"All right, Mrs. Dansky. Stay right there a minute, please."

He held on to her license as he made a circuit around the car. Jillian watched as he approached Michael and the other officer, and she realized that the two had separated them purposely. Probably just their usual procedure, but it made her feel even more isolated than she already had. Her policeman took Michael's license as well as the Volvo's registration, said something to his partner, and then started back to the police car. He slid behind the wheel; through the windshield, Jillian could see a gray silhouette as he picked up the handset for his radio. She had been stopped for speeding twice in her life, so she understood that he was checking to make sure the car belonged to them and that there were, God forbid, no warrants for her or Michael's arrest.

An eternity seemed to pass.

Her mouth felt full of cotton and there was a tight little knot in her belly. Though her hearing seemed dull, she caught some of the exchange between Michael and his policeman.

". . . very late," Michael was saying, "and I was falling asleep behind the wheel. My wife had had a little too much to drink—"

"What about you, Mr. Dansky?" the policeman asked, cut-the-bullshit in his tone. "You were nodding off at the wheel."

Michael nodded. "I'd had a couple of beers, yeah. I don't think I was drunk, but throw in how late it was and the kind of day I'd had . . . I thought it would be better to just pull over and sleep an hour or so than end up in a ditch or wrapped around a tree. I never thought I'd end up sleeping until morning."

"It's not the kind of thing we recommend."

"Do you recommend driving when you can't keep your eyes open?" Michael asked.

At this, Jillian spun and stared at him. His tone up until that point had been conciliatory, but now Michael was staring at the cop, standing up to him, turning the whole damn thing around. His mother had always said he would have made a wonderful lawyer, and Jillian had often agreed. Michael Dansky knew how to win a debate. What was the cop supposed to say now? No, sir, you should have driven on home, no matter how tired you were or how much you'd had to drink? Never going to happen.

The cop glared at him. Jillian turned away before Michael's policeman could see the tiny smile that flickered at the corners of her mouth. But her amusement only lasted a moment. There was nothing funny about any of this.

She shivered. The wind was cold, but the sun was bright and warm. It was a beautiful Sunday morning in October. People were on their way to church, or to a farm to buy pumpkins or pick apples with their children. If there were any apples left on the trees. And here was Jillian Dansky, her humiliation on display. How would this go over with Bob Ryan and Benny Bartolini, last night's gunslinger and Mexican amigo, who wanted her to run for West Newbury City Council?

Not too well, she thought. And a little piece of her heart broke off, leaving a jagged edge. Jillian had worked very hard to achieve what she had in her career. She loved the community she and Michael had embraced as their own. They wanted roots here. Wanted to have children who would grow up here. But something like this . . . God, if word got around it would haunt her forever.

For the first time, she glanced around at the police car parked behind the Volvo. North Andover. A tremor went through her as she saw the name of the town stenciled on the side of the car, and she spent a moment thanking God, in whom she did not always believe. They hadn't gotten all the way home to West Newbury. It was bad, but not as bad as she had feared.

Her policeman returned from the patrol car. He held the registration and Michael's license in his left hand, but he handed Jillian's ID back to her. His eyes, gentle and kind, searched hers. If she hadn't felt so ridiculous, she might have hugged him, for his eyes told her all she needed to know about what was going to happen next. The registration had not raised any red flags, and neither had their names. Any annoyance she'd felt at being pitied a few minutes earlier disappeared.

"You're free to go, Mrs. Dansky. Your husband broke a city ordinance about overnight parking, and there's a vagrancy issue that comes into play, but nobody wants to cause trouble for you here. I really hope this was a one-time thing, one bad night. I really do."

There was a sermon waiting in his gaze, but he left it unspoken.

So do I, she thought. But what she said was, "Oh, it is. Honestly. We're really very boring. We're not drinkers at all, but last night there was this masquerade, and—"

"Sort of figured that one out," the policeman said. He smiled and gestured toward her costume.

"Of course. I just—"

"You have a good day, Mrs. Dansky." He nodded to her, then started around the car.

Jillian glanced over at Michael, who looked on expectantly,

brows knitted. She gave him an encouraging nod as the police officer approached him and they exchanged a few quiet words. The other cop was giving Michael a hard look, but Jillian's policeman handed her husband's license and registration back, and a moment later both officers were walking back to their car.

Jillian stood where she was and watched as they got into the patrol car and drove off. Her policeman waved at her as they passed. A moment later, Michael came to stand beside her on the roadside, car keys jangling at the end of one finger.

"Do you want to drive?" he asked.

"No," she said, surprised by the venom in her voice. She and Michael rarely fought, and on those rare occasions it was more healthy debate than bitter argument. At the moment, however, she wasn't in the mood for a healthy debate.

"You drive," she told him, walking around toward the passenger's side. "And on the way, you can explain what the hell just happened."

IN THE MONTHS BETWEEN HIS junior and senior years at Emerson College, Michael worked a summer job at the secretary of state's office, right up on Beacon Hill in Boston. He had grown up in Sudbury, thirty minutes west of the city, and the commute was a bitch. But he had spent enough time delivering pizzas and working in video stores, and wanted to have a real job on his résumé. As always when it came to city politics, strings had been pulled to score him the job. More than a decade earlier, his father had been a state representative out of Sudbury. The old man had been taken by cancer when Michael was in high school, but he'd been well liked and the connections remained. Teresa Dansky had made a few phone calls on her son's behalf, and quick as you please he had a job.

Other than its location—Michael loved Boston Common and the State House—the job was wholly unremarkable. He answered phones and filled out paperwork; the department had half a dozen people doing the work of two. He sketched a lot, working on covers to imaginary CD's and books, and sometimes he even read, there at his desk.

But the job was not a total loss. If he hadn't made that trek into Boston all summer, if his mother hadn't made those calls, if his father hadn't been in state politics, he never would have met Jillian.

One July morning, he sat at his desk typing up a form and trying to ignore the uncomfortable closeness of the air. The air-conditioning wheezed from vents in the ceiling as though on its last gasp. His desk was nearest the window, and the glare of the sun on his back combined with the failing air conditioner to make his work space almost stifling. They were supposed to get around to fixing the a/c soon, but Michael had no faith in what "they" said. It was a government building, after all. It took two to do half the work of one, and that was on the off chance they weren't on break. He figured they'd get around to fixing the a/c just in time for the cold weather to come blustering in.

The office was filled with conversation, a steady hum of voices. Michael typed the date at the bottom of the document he was completing, then tapped the key to print it. He stood to stretch, and glanced around. Kara, the woman who headed up his department, was on the phone. Sheila was bent over her computer, doing a background search on a corporation. He had no idea where the others were. Their area was separated from a much larger room of files and computer stations where paralegals could come and do UCC searches for their firms' clients, but his missing coworkers were nowhere in sight.

"Michael?"

He turned to Sheila, who had pulled her focus away from her computer long enough to get his attention. She smiled and gestured toward the long open counter-window at the front of the office.

"You have a customer."

The girl on the other side of the counter stood patiently, a file clutched against her chest. Michael felt a warmth kindled in his gut that had nothing to do with the faltering air-conditioning. He knew her name, of course. She came up to the Corporations division at least twice a day to do UCC searches or to get certificates of good standing for her firm's clients. There were other things he knew as well. She was Italian. From Medford. She had only just graduated from Suffolk University, and in addition to her B.A. had earned a certificate that allowed her to work as a paralegal.

As Michael strode toward the counter, Jillian Lopresti glanced up at him and her eyes lit up. He drew a sharp breath through his nostrils and held it, trying not to smile like an idiot. Jillian reached up and pushed a stray lock of chestnut hair away from her face and laid her folder down on the counter.

"I was beginning to think you had the day off," Michael told her.

Jillian rolled her eyes. "I wish. I could use a day off. I'd rather be at the beach."

Michael tried not to imagine her at the beach—in a bikini—for fear that his eyes would trail downward and she would catch him looking, catch him imagining.

"What've we got today?" he asked.

She opened her file and withdrew several documents. "The usual. Three separate corporations, all owned by the same client. I need to know if they're in good standing. If not, how far back do we have to file to get a certificate?"

He nodded, taking the pages from her. There were a dozen little bullshit things he could have said, just to shoot the breeze, but he was not in the mood for small talk. Michael had other things in mind.

Jillian looked at him expectantly, clearly wondering why he wasn't off to look up the corporations in question. She raised her eyebrows.

"So, what do you usually do for lunch?" he asked.

One corner of her mouth lifted in an adorable smirk. Perhaps she was only a year older than he was, but there was so much confidence in her. Michael admired that. He also found it incredibly alluring. Even more so than the images his mind had conjured of her in a bikini.

What do you usually do for lunch? he had asked.

Jillian studied him. "Eat."

Michael laughed politely, but he was not deterred. "When's your lunch hour?"

Her smile turned sly. "When I'm hungry."

"Well, when you're hungry today, I'd love to take you to lunch."

She let out a little breath and shook her head. "Sorry. I have plans."

All the air seemed to go out of him. Those hazel eyes sparkled, and her smile remained, but apparently Jillian hadn't been nearly as interested in him as he had been in her. Michael had been taken by her the very first time he had seen her. She carried herself with the air of someone much older, and she always had a pleasant word for the others in his department. That first day she had worn a burgundy blouse and a black skirt with a slit up one leg. He could still hear the echo of her heels the way they clicked on the linoleum on the other side of the counter.

There had been no overt flirtation between them, just an exchange of pleasantries. Not very different from the way she spoke to anyone else in that office. But, still, he had hoped.

Michael forced a smile that he hoped didn't reveal how foolish he felt. He waved the documents at her as if she needed to be reminded what he was doing, and started back toward the computer at his desk.

"Isn't tomorrow your birthday?" she said to his retreating back.

He frowned as he turned to face her. How did Jillian know it was his birthday? "Yeah?"

She shifted her stance, putting all her weight on one foot, her hip outthrust beneath her skirt. It was a defiant pose, and heartbreakingly sexy. "Do you already have plans?"

"No."

"Well, then, why don't I buy *you* lunch tomorrow? To celebrate?"

Michael stared at her a moment. Then he nodded. "I'd like that."

She played me, he thought. *The girl played me. She was busting my balls the whole time.*

I think I'm in love.

MICHAEL FELT LIKE SHIT.

It had been only a few hours since their rude roadside awakening. They had come home and showered, and immediately he had retreated to the basement to avoid Jillian.

The house was only three years old. They had bought into a new development and watched excitedly over the months as the house went up. West Newbury was expensive, but not in Andover's league. With their joint salaries, they had still been overreaching, but had hoped that in a short time their income would catch up with their expenses.

With Jillian's promotion last year to paralegal manager, they at last had a little breathing room. Now it was time to do some of the things to the house on Persimmon Road that they had been holding off on. One of those was finishing the basement. Michael had begun framing for walls in July. It was the sort of thing he had to do in spurts, when he had the time and inclination.

No day like today, he thought.

He was nearly done. A couple of hours of work remained, and then he would be able to go out and buy the insulation and the sheetrock. That would be a big job, however, and it wasn't something he was going to worry about today. Not with the thudding headache that had settled like storm clouds across his skull. Not when every quick move shot him full of so many aches that he felt a hundred years old.

The Patriots were playing Dallas today. Kickoff was at one o'clock. Once the game started, he could hide in front of the television. Jillian didn't mind football, but it held no interest for her. With the game on, she would find other things to do in the house, perhaps even go out to do errands, as she so often did on Sundays. By the time the game was over, it would be dinnertime.

By then, Michael hoped that her anger would have cooled some. Then, maybe, they would be able to talk about what had happened the previous night. Their conversation in the car had been clipped and tense. Never in his life had he been so confused, and yet the person to whom he would naturally have turned for help was in no mood to lend him comfort.

It had taken Michael several minutes just driving around before he was able to get his bearings enough to find his way home. Jillian had wanted to know what had happened, how they had ended up spending the night on the side of the road. To his shame, Michael hadn't been able to tell her. He knew he must have had some flash of insight and realized he had to pull over before he passed out behind the wheel, but he couldn't remember any of it. Images of the previous night were jumbled in his mind, many of them disturbing and some, he felt, possibly only dreams or drug-induced hallucinations.

He remembered the masquerade perfectly, including their departure. He could recall Jilly passed out in the backseat. But the drive home from the Wayside Inn was all a blur. The hum of his tires on the road, of the car engine. He had been sleepy. Drunker than he had thought. *God, how could you have driven like that?* But that was the key, wasn't it? He had not felt drunk when he had gotten behind the wheel. Then again, wasn't that what they all said?

A ripple of silver. Come find me.

Michael winced at the picture that flitted across his mind, like the lingering colors on the inside of his eyelids after a camera flash had gone off. And a voice. A little girl's voice . . .

"Jesus," he whispered to himself. He shook his head. None of it made sense. He had had only a few bottles of Guinness. Certainly not enough to induce this kind of blackout. He knew it was possible, of course. Had experienced it before, waking up in the morning to discover himself guilty of some fairly

embarrassing behavior. But it had been years since he had been
that intoxicated. Since college, in fact.

But to drive that way, to park on the side of the road and
sleep it off and not remember how he got them there?

Michael was almost as angry with Jillian as she was with him,
but most of his hostility came from guilt, and from the terror
that filled him when he thought about what might have happened to them. As humiliating as it had been to be woken by the
police rapping on the car windows, it was nothing compared to
the worst-case scenario that had played out in his mind again
and again since they had reached home that morning.

Not his own death. No, the worst thing would have been if he
had gotten Jillian killed, and survived to know it.

He squeezed his eyes tightly together and took a long, shuddering breath. Then he steadied himself and drove another nail.

There were images in his mind that confused him. The last
thing he remembered—really remembered—was nodding off at
the wheel. But there were other things

Come find me.

Other pictures in his head. A little blond girl, a halo of light
around her head. An old, rambling house on a hill, dark and
abandoned. A nightmare. It had to have been. For how else to explain the feeling of unease that crept up his spine when he
thought of such things? He could picture himself even now, in
the midst of that nightmare, standing in an unfamiliar kitchen.
He had a vague memory of a chorus of little-girl voices singing
jump-rope songs.

One, two, buckle my shoe.

And something . . . some weird trick of the light that in his
dream had frightened him.

Some trip. Some fucking trip. The sleeve of his D'Artagnan jacket
was torn, and there were several small cuts on his face. Little pin-
prick things that Jillian hadn't noticed. *Of course she hasn't noticed
them. She won't look you in the face.*

Some fucking trip, he thought again. Michael was certain that's
what it had been. Someone had dropped something in his beer.

What other explanation could there be? Maybe there had been a house and a girl and he'd tried to keep driving afterward and couldn't make it home. Maybe. If so, they were both fortunate he had had the sense to pull over and park for the night. But he wasn't ready to talk to Jillian about it. Not when things were like this between them. It made his belly hurt to remember what it had been like driving home with her this morning. She had sat in the passenger's seat with her arms crossed, expressionless, gazing out at half-stripped trees as they drove.

Now, in the basement, Michael propped a two-by-four in place, plucked a nail from his lips, then hammered it into the wood with four solid strikes. He added a fifth unnecessarily, and it marred the wood in a strange crescent.

In his mind was an echo of the last words Jillian had said to him this morning, just as they had pulled into the driveway.

"I can't believe you let this happen."

Michael had dropped the car into park and responded without looking at her. "You weren't exactly the picture of sobriety. I had to carry you to the car."

He heard her swear under her breath, and knew what was going through her mind. That sort of public display was something she would have found disgusting in anyone else. The idea that she had done such a thing, that others might have witnessed it, appalled her.

Of course, he had exaggerated. He had certainly had to support her to get her to the car, but he had not carried her. Just then, however, Michael was stinging from her anger and disappointment, so he was in no rush to alleviate her concerns.

A flash of guilt went through him now as he recalled that sin of omission, but he was not prepared to correct it. Not yet.

Michael and Jillian were lucky. In one another they had found love and patience and good humor. When they fought—as all couples did—their arguments usually sprang from anxiety over money, or from disagreements over their respective families. Michael had only his mother and his older brother, both of whom lived on Cape Cod. Jillian had a large Italian family spread across half a dozen North Shore cities and towns. They did things differently, of course. Had different approaches and expectations about holidays and family events, a hundred little social differences. Such things took time for a couple to adjust to. But even these things were small. In the eight years since they had first met, they'd had only a handful of arguments that had lingered.

This one was simmering.

Michael stepped away from the wall and regarded his handiwork, hammer dangling in his grip. All that remained was to frame the little pantry he had decided to add. Jillian was always wishing for more storage space in the kitchen and, if they were going to finish the basement, it only made sense to take advantage of the added room.

His stomach gave a sudden lurch and Michael burped softly, then scowled at the bitter taste in his mouth.

"Shit," he whispered. His legs felt weak and he slid to the cold floor, the hammer taking a chink out of the concrete.

Come find me.

"What the hell?" he asked aloud.

As if in answer, the door at the top of the stairs opened. He could not see Jillian from where he sat, but he could feel her there.

"Michael?"

"Yeah?" He was careful to keep his tone flat and emotionless, just like hers. Like walking across a field of land mines, hoping to get to the peace that lay on the other side.

"I have to go to the cleaners and to the bookstore to pick up the book the club's reading next month. I thought I'd bring the costumes back. I've got them all together, but I can't find your hat."

"Is it in the car?"

"I don't know," came her frosty reply. "Is it?"

The muscles tensed across his back. It took great restraint, but he said nothing. The only thing he could do was hope that he could remember more of what had happened the night before, and wait for the lingering bitterness and awkwardness between them to blow over.

With a sigh, Michael climbed to his feet and trotted up the stairs. As soon as she saw that he was coming, Jillian retreated into the kitchen and busied herself unloading the dishwasher. He paused a moment to stare longingly at her back. If he just reached out now to touch her shoulder, to give her a moment of tenderness, he could probably put an end to the issue right there. But he couldn't, not yet. His own anger was still too fresh. It didn't matter if he was angry with Jillian or with himself. It needed time to fade. Soon enough, one of them would defuse the whole thing.

I'm sorry, he thought, wishing he could communicate with Jillian mind to mind, so she could feel what he felt, and maybe make better sense of it than he could.

He went out through the kitchen door and into the garage. As soon as he found the hat he would go in and put his arms around Jillian at the sink. He would kiss the back of her neck. She would stiffen up at first, resisting him. Michael could almost see it playing out in his mind. But then he would whisper to her how sorry he was, how much he loved her. He would tell her the truth, that he had helped her to the car, but not carried her, and that would settle her nerves. And then, at last, he could share with her his fear that someone had drugged him, and the images that were plaguing him every time he closed his eyes, even for a moment.

The dream he'd had. The nightmare.

They never locked the car when it was in the garage. It just wasn't that kind of neighborhood. Wasn't that kind of town. Up here in the Merrimack Valley, there were probably people who still didn't lock their front doors. The Danskys weren't willing to go quite that far, but the garage seemed safe enough.

Michael tugged open the passenger door and the hat was there, on the floor of the front seat. He reached in to retrieve it and saw that it was misshapen.

For an instant he thought Jillian had stepped on it that morning, getting into the front seat.

Then that aluminum taste returned to his mouth and he sagged against the open car door. He squeezed his eyes shut and he could *see* her, there in the car. He could see her foot coming down on top of the hat. The little blond girl on the side of the road, silhouetted in the glare of his headlights, about to be run down. Then in his car. Lost. Alone.

No, not lost.

"Right there. Turn right there."

"You recognize this street?"

Clutching that black felt hat in his hands, Michael began to remember.

CHAPTER FIVE

All day Michael had moved silently through the house, the air heavy with the tension between him and Jillian. Each time he felt the urge to reach out, to smooth things over, his body and mind felt sluggish, as if frozen by the chill. It was ridiculous. He could speak to Jillian about anything. She was his closest friend.

But not that day.

He had given her his costume, including the hat. Though it was obvious that they would have to pay for the damage, Jillian said nothing more about it.

His mind was filled with images of the night before, of shattered fragments of memory, of sights and sounds and even smells. Michael could not remember everything. The details were muddled, as though the previous evening had been a fresh deck of cards and someone had shuffled them, removing a random few. He had trouble putting them in order, and he could not tell what was missing. But he had enough to construct a basic mental sketch of those bizarre events.

The little girl in the road. That house. What the hell had possessed him to go inside in the first place? Yes, he'd been concerned for the girl. He remembered that much. But to go wandering around inside . . . it would have taken a lot more than a few Guinnesses to get him that inebriated.

Late on Sunday afternoon he was raking leaves as the last of the sunlight slipped away, the indigo sky bleeding into black. He wore a battered leather jacket and thin gloves, but when the wind blew the chill cut into him. It was too early in the autumn for the nights to be this cold. Or, at least, that was what he told himself. Obviously he was wrong. The proof was in the air, and the way his cheeks stung. His eyes watered. There were bags of leaves all over the lawn. The wind had forced him to collect them as he went, or he'd have been raking until the snow fell.

The second story was dark, but a warm golden glow radiated from the windows of the living room and the kitchen. Jillian had muttered something to him, noncommittally and without meeting his gaze, about making some sort of pasta dish tonight. His stomach rumbled as he paused, leaning on the rake, leaves rustling. Several blew away from the pile in front of him, drawing his attention.

Michael caught the scent of a wood-burning stove. A smile touched the edges of his mouth . . . the first one in hours. The Greenways, two doors down, had one of those stoves and used it all fall and winter. It was a wonderful smell, one that reminded him of autumns back home in Sudbury. Several people in the neighborhood had had such stoves. For just a moment, there in the gathering darkness, he closed his eyes and remembered.

And flinched.

That had been one of the smells in the girl's house. If it even *was* the girl's house. Several times during that day he had tried to open up to Jillian about it. But what would he say? How would he explain what he thought had really happened?

The one thing that was growing clearer in his mind was the progression of his drunkenness. His memory was murky now, but it seemed to him that he had felt only a little buzzed when he and Jilly had left the party. But that wasn't right, was it? Once he had gotten behind the wheel he had realized that he was drunker than he had thought. He might have had four bottles of Guinness instead of three. Maybe—and this was an enormous maybe—but maybe even five.

Still, though, that did not explain what happened afterward. It did not explain the blacked-out portions of his memory, or the way in which his judgment and perception had been impaired. The images of the house were practically hallucinatory. When he thought about it, he felt dread seize him. He was—

Terrified . . . you were terrified . . .

His eyes snapped open. Michael stood in his backyard, an eddy of chill wind spinning autumn leaves away from the pile he had made. It gusted, and he swayed, staring at the leaves as more and more slipped away. This was useless. He blinked away the encroaching darkness and then glanced upward. The night was deepening and the moon had emerged, frosted with a white corona, a kind of ghostly doppelgänger.

He *had* been terrified.

The small cuts and the bruise on his face were obvious, but he had done his best to hide the gash on his right forearm from Jillian. It bordered on needing stitches, and there was no way he was letting her talk him into going to the hospital. They would want to know how he had been injured. What would he say? Michael had only the vaguest memory of the fear that had sent him crashing through a window.

"Jesus," he whispered, the word stolen away by the breeze. He shook his head, holding the rake as though it were some walking stick to keep him from falling. *Did I really do that?*

The cuts told the story. As did the pain in his ribs when he inhaled deeply; probably some massive bruising there. His back ached and his right cheek was swollen.

Michael had done some incredibly stupid things in college under the influence of alcohol. He had shattered a car's headlights. One night he had done a back flip into a fountain in front of a hotel in Cambridge. He had thrown a beer mug at the head of one of his best friends, barely grazing the guy's skull, but left with the knowledge that he could have done serious damage. Freshman year he had said terrible things to a girl at a party, and remembered not a word later. Perhaps worst of all, he had walked a fourth-floor balcony railing as though it had been a circus high wire.

Those memories troubled him, but not nearly so much as the idea that he had somehow gotten so obliterated that he could have fallen back into that sort of behavior.

He glanced at the house again. The golden glow from within was irresistible. *What the hell are you still doing out here?* he thought. *You're freezing your ass off . . . and your wife is inside.*

With that, the last of the chill that he had felt separating him from Jillian seemed to burn off, the ice melting. Whatever resentment he'd held on to was gone, and now, as ever in such situations, he felt like a complete ass for having nurtured those feelings at all.

"Screw it." Michael let the rake fall to the lawn, abandoning it and the last pile of leaves he had gathered. He walked around to the front of the house and into the garage. Now that night had arrived the garage was quite dark, but he kept it neat and there was no chance of his tripping over anything. He could just make out the two crude wooden steps he had never gotten around to replacing.

The door from the garage into the kitchen was unlocked. He opened it and stepped inside, greeted by the almost overpowering smell of onions, peppers, and garlic frying. Jillian stood in front of the stove, her hair tied back as she stirred the contents of the pan to keep them from burning. Michael's eyes watered from the smell, and his stomach growled. She had the sleeves of her green cotton blouse pushed up to the elbows, and one lock of hair fell across her face. He smiled at the sight of her.

"Hey," Jillian said without turning.

"The wind was too much. I'll have to finish it another day."

"The snow will cover it all soon enough," she replied, a tentative lightness in her voice. "Don't worry about it."

Softly, Michael let out a long breath. He crossed the kitchen and moved up behind her. His hands seemed to act of their own accord, sliding around her waist. He kissed the back of her neck. Jillian stiffened a moment before releasing a tiny sigh. Michael held her tightly from behind, and Jillian turned her face just enough so that he could kiss her. Their lips brushed together and then the kiss became something deeper.

She set aside the wooden cooking spoon she had been using and turned toward him. For the first time that day, she really looked into his eyes, and then she slid her arms up to clasp her hands behind his head and drew him down to kiss her once more.

"I'm sorry," she whispered, laying her head against his chest. "I was just . . ."

"Freaked, I know. I don't blame you." Michael held her to him, relishing the feeling of Jillian in his arms. The kitchen was redolent with the smells of their home, their married life, and he felt like a fool for fighting with her. "I'm sorry, too. I don't know what happened. I swear I wasn't that drunk. I only had a few—"

"Oh, wait!" she said softly, eyes going wide as she spun to stir the vegetables that were frying in the pan.

The onions had started to burn. Michael could tell from the smell, but as he peered over her shoulder he saw that they had not yet blackened.

"Looks like you've rescued dinner."

Jillian shut off the burner and turned to look at him. "I've been more annoyed with myself than I was with you. I just keep wondering what people would think if they saw us on the side of the road. Or even if they saw you helping me into the car."

"You worry too much about what people think."

"That's—" she started, angrily, and then took a breath and shook her head. Jillian laid a hand on his chest. "Maybe you're right. Anyway, look, I was thinking about what you were saying. About how much you had to drink. It doesn't make any sense. Do you think somebody could have—"

"Put something in my drink?" Michael finished for her, his brow furrowing. "Yeah. I'm definitely thinking that. Nothing else fits."

"God. Who would do something like that?"

He shrugged and turned from her, going to the refrigerator and retrieving a root beer. "I don't know. It could have been totally random. Probably was. Just some asshole playing a prank."

As he spoke, Jillian had gone to the sink and picked up a strainer full of bow-tie pasta. She had a pot of tomato sauce simmering on the stove with chunks of sausage in it. Dinner was looking promising.

"Some prank," she said, dumping the pasta into the sauce pot. "We could have been killed."

Michael watched her as she added the onions, peppers, and garlic into the pot as well, and then began to stir.

"Jilly."

She raised an eyebrow and turned to look at him.

"It's still fuzzy . . . but I remember some of what happened last night."

THE LAW OFFICES OF DAWES, Gray & Winter were located in the heart of Boston, at One International Place. It was a rounded tower whose upper floors provided one of the best views in the city. There was always chaos on Monday mornings, as the firm's engines got up and running again. Business did not cease for the weekend, but those who were fortunate enough to be able to abandon it on Friday afternoons had to play catch-up come Monday.

Jillian relished the Monday morning rush. Paralegals who had been working on closings in the corporate department over the weekend were always burnt out by then, and she did whatever she could to arrange for them to leave early on Monday. Sometimes that was impossible. Documents had to be changed and re-filed, new signatures had to be obtained. That could be difficult. By far the least entertaining part of Monday—of the entire job, in fact—was refereeing conflicts between attorneys and parale-gals.

She had just walked through the marble lobby with its splash-ing fountains, a place with the size and elegance of a cathedral, and was getting on the elevator when Brad Klein caught up with her. He called her name and trotted up just as the doors were sliding closed, thrusting out one hand to stop them. He was a junior associate, a fortyish man who might have been decent looking if he'd had the common sense to shave his head down to stubble instead of trying to pretend he wasn't going bald. The way he combed his hair was not yet the rat's nest such things could become, but it was on the way.

"Good morning, Brad. How was your weekend?"

The doors slid closed and they managed to jockey for posi-tion next to each other, despite the other half dozen people on the elevator.

"It could have been better."

Jillian glanced at him. It was obvious from his tone that he was talking about work. He'd been working on a buyout—Downtown Corporation was acquiring Lyons Publishing—and they had been supposed to close on Friday. When Jillian had left the office, they had still been working on it, but she'd assigned Barb Hagen and Vanessa Castille to the closing, and she trusted both of them.

Obviously, Brad wasn't happy with her judgment.

"What happened?"

The attorney moved his briefcase from one hand to the other. His gaze shifted toward her, and then he went back to watching the numbers light up above the door. Neither one of them said another word as the elevator made its stops and the other passen-gers made their exodus at various floors. Only when they were alone, three floors away from their own destination on thirty-nine, did he address her again.

"Lyons and Sons Publishing Partners, Incorporated. That's the legal name of the company," Brad said.

A sick feeling churned in Jillian's stomach. She glanced at him. "They got it wrong?"

"We had to start from scratch. Every document just said Lyons Publishing. Vanessa has been with the firm two years. This is not the kind of mistake an experienced paralegal should make."

Shit! Jillian thought. But she nodded gravely and did not speak that particular sentiment out loud. "I'll talk to her first thing."

The elevator stopped on thirty-nine and the doors slid open. They stepped off together and Brad turned to look at her. He was an intelligent man, and had always been pleasant enough to deal with. Today none of his kindness was in his eyes.

"This is the second time in as many months that something like this has happened with her. At the beginning of September we had the Havilcek thing? That had the wrong address. When it's our mistake, Jillian, we don't charge the client. Vanessa has cost the firm a lot of money in the last couple of months. And she cost me a Saturday watching my son play football. I'm not happy about that. She's got two strikes."

They stood in the foyer, just outside the frosted glass doors of the firm's reception area. For the moment they were alone, and Jillian was glad. She did not want to have this conversation where anyone might hear.

"Do we understand each other?"

Jillian nodded. "Three strikes and she's out."

"We can't afford her if she doesn't clean up her act."

"I'll handle it," Jillian assured him.

His expression softened and at last he seemed himself. "I know you will. That's why you're the manager, and not someone like Vanessa Castille."

Brad swiped his key in front of the scan pad and there was a soft beeping noise. He tugged the door open and Jillian followed him inside. Without another word they went their separate ways. She hurried down to her office, her purse heavy over her shoulder. A grim weight had settled onto her, and she felt a perverse pleasure in it.

This was good, really. This was exactly what she needed today. If she had office politics to address, mistakes to be corrected, and subordinates to warn of imminent job loss, she wouldn't have to think about how she had spent her own weekend. Wouldn't have to think about the disjointed story Michael had told her the night before, over dinner.

"This girl . . . there was this girl . . ."

Jesus, he almost killed a little girl. And then he had just left her off at a house in the middle of nowhere. A house he did not even remember how to find. It was obvious from his story that he had been hallucinating, flying on something. No question now, as far as she was concerned, that someone had mickeyed his beer. When she thought about what could have happened, not just behind the wheel, but what might have gone down if the owners of that house—the girl's parents or not—had caught him wandering around inside.

Drunk driving. Breaking and entering. Never mind any thought she might be giving to running for city council.

She did not blame Michael at all. None of it was his fault. But it still terrified her. And she worried about that little girl. Even if it was her house, no one could have been home. If they had been, certainly they would have discovered Michael staggering around the kitchen. They must have been out looking for their daughter. That was the only explanation that made any sense.

God, she thought.

Then, *no. You're not going to do this today. There's work to do. Focus, or you'll make mistakes. And guys like Brad Klein don't look too kindly on mistakes, no matter what your distractions are.*

As she reached her office, the phone was ringing. The view out her window drew her eyes as she dropped her purse on the desk, slipped on her headset, and tapped the blinking button to answer the call.

"Jillian Dansky."

"Hey, Jilly! Happy Halloween!"

In spite of her stress, she smiled. "Hello, Hannah. You're one day early."

"You're no fun. Those of us with a weakness for chocolate celebrate Halloween as long as the world will let us. I think I've got mine up to a week this year."

The familiar warmth of her sister's voice, and her laugh, allowed Jillian to relax, at least a little. But she had work to do, bad news to deliver, and the truth of the matter was that she knew if she stayed on the phone with Hannah she would end up talking about what had happened Saturday night, about her embarrassment Sunday morning and her fight with Michael. This was neither the time nor the place for such a conversation.

And, in her heart, she really did not want to tell Hannah—or anyone else, for that matter—about fighting with her husband. It wasn't anyone else's business. Michael was the one to whom she bared her heart and soul. Hannah usually only got the silly stuff.

"So, what's going on with you, sis? I haven't talked to you in, like, weeks," Hannah said.

"I'm sorry, Nah-ni. I just got in and I've already got some fires to put out. Can I call you later? Or tomorrow morning even?"

"Sure," her sister replied, but not without some obvious disappointment. "But don't call me Nah-ni, or I will run you down in my new, incredibly un-PC, gas-guzzling SUV."

"Whatever you say, *Nah-ni.* I'll scold you sometime this afternoon."

They said their good-byes and hung up. The message light was blinking and Jillian stared at it a moment. She knew she ought to pick up her voice mail and e-mail before doing anything else, just in case there was anything truly urgent. But she wanted to speak to Vanessa as soon as possible. She thought of herself as a good manager, but Jillian felt that the first step in managing other people was managing herself. The longer she waited to have an awkward conversation with someone, the more she built it up in her mind into something awful. It was best for her to get it out of the way, to save herself the trepidation.

The blinking voice-mail light beckoned, however, and so she made a compromise with herself. Voice mail now, e-mail as soon as she got back to her desk. Voice mail was likely to be more urgent anyway. She picked up the phone and keyed in her security code.

"You have . . . thirteen . . . new messages."

Jillian sighed, but it turned out not to be as bad as she anticipated. Two of the messages were from friends in the city—paralegals with whom she had worked at her first job at Savage & Young—trying to set up a lunch for the three of them. Three were from attorneys who had new closings that needed paralegals assigned. One was from Human Resources, hoping to schedule some interviews for an open position in her department. An even half dozen were from Brad Klein or from Vanessa, all of them over the weekend when the shit was hitting the fan. She was about to deal with all of that.

Message thirteen had come in only minutes before she had arrived. *While I was on the elevator,* she thought. It was from Councillor Ryan.

"Hello, Jillian, Bob Ryan calling. Just thought I'd give you a ring and let you know how much we all enjoyed speaking with you on Saturday night. If you're really interested in running for city council, let me know. I can tell you that you'd have some significant backing from incumbents."

He rattled off his phone number and Jillian was left just staring at the phone. She had to replay the message in order to write the number down, and as she did a tiny shudder of relief went through her. *Apparently, nobody saw you make an ass of yourself.* And, apparently, nobody had recognized her and Michael on the side of the road Sunday morning.

It occurred to her that what Bob Ryan had liked—the person he wanted to run for city council—was a slightly intoxicated Jillian Dansky. But the main difference between Jillian sober and Jillian shit-faced was the propensity to speak her mind a bit more readily. If she was going to run for city council, that would not be an issue. Jilly had no problem giving her opinion, but she hesitated to do so without an invitation. Running for office was an invitation all its own.

The last of her anxiety over her weekend antics was gone. As she rose from her desk and left her office, heading toward Vanessa's cubicle, she had to fight the smile off of her face. The last thing she wanted was for Vanessa to think she was amused by the conversation they were about to have.

ON HIS DESK, MICHAEL HAD a Macintosh with the biggest damn personal computer screen he had been able to find. For someone in his line of work, it was a thing of beauty. Graphic design was the perfect job for an artist whose greatest skill was in visualization, and in combining research and invention to create just the right image for whatever project he was working on. Of course, he wasn't just a graphic designer now. He handled client accounts, so the title was art director. He'd worked hard for that. Michael loved all aspects of the job. His office was wall-to-wall with books whose pages were filled with art and stock photos. And not merely the traditional sort. There were histories of pop culture, comic books and graphic novels, advertising portfolios, and old, dusty books with the most stunning illustrations he had ever seen. His favorite was Dante's *Divine Comedy*, with the Gustave Doré plates.

Whatever he couldn't find reference for in his books was easily available on the Internet. Half the time he found it first online, and then searched through his office for a hard copy. When trying out images it was simple to snatch up bits and pieces of things off the Net. When he was assigned a new advertising campaign, Michael worked it both ways. Sometimes he sketched first, doing up as many as a dozen separate designs before choosing a path to follow, then searching for reference for the elements he wanted to include. Other times, when he had no immediate ideas, he would surf on-line in a sort of weird free association. A tour company specializing in Ireland might prompt him to look at everything from Celtic myth to castles to biographies of famous Irish Americans.

Today he was just sketching. His drawing table was set up on the opposite side of the office from his desk. Krakow & Bester had just picked up Newburyport Premium Ice Cream. It was a small company, but they had put together a cadre of investors with enough capital so that they could roll out a national campaign. If Michael and Teddy Polito did their jobs effectively and the thing was a success, the client would reap enormous benefits, and the agency would have a new major client on their hands.

Up until now, Newburyport Premium had taken what Michael thought of as the *Saturday Evening Post* approach, using Americana images of grandfathers and kids. That was a solid choice for advertising ice cream in New England. But going national meant appealing to every possible consumer . . . which was impossible. Michael would have preferred to spend the time dreaming up something fantastically clever, but even he had to admit that clever was a risk. It could alienate the audience by being too smart or too quirky—what he and Teddy called the Dennis Miller effect. Both the agency and the client had decided the way to appeal to the broadest spectrum of customers and alienate the fewest was to go with the lowest common denominator.

Sex.

While Michael would've preferred risking the Dennis Miller effect and doing something clever, he had no fundamental disagreement with doing something sexy. It was sort of a game, trying to figure out exactly how suggestive they could be and still get away with it in a national advertising campaign.

He smiled as he bent over the drawing table. He and Teddy had brainstormed the basics on Friday and now they were getting down to business. Teddy was working on a variety of slogan suggestions, and copy for this ad. Now Michael's pencil flew as he began the basic sketch. The image was almost fully formed in his mind. A sexy blonde standing on the beach, one hip cocked insouciantly, come-hither look in her eyes. She holds an ice-cream cone in one hand—vanilla, of course, to complete the innuendo—and it is dripping down over her fingers, maybe a few drops on her chest or belly. The tag line would be something like "It's a Sticky Situation" or "Come and Get It Before It Melts."

But that part was Teddy's job.

There would be other options. He was already formulating an idea of a similarly sexy woman in sexy lingerie, sprawled in a big plush chair in front of the television eating a pint of chocolate ice cream. That one Michael already had a tag line for, and he was going to insist. Teddy could write the rest of the copy, but the tag could only be one thing: "All Dressed Up and No Place to Go."

Sometimes the lowest common denominator could be fun.

The pencil scritch-scratched on the heavy paper, images forming. When the phone rang, Michael did not even stop sketching. He reached out with his left hand and picked it up, propping it between his ear and shoulder.

"Michael Dansky."

"Hey, sweetie."

He smiled. "Jilly. Don't tell me you're having a quiet Monday morning."

"Not even close. I just had to tell you that Bob Ryan called."

Michael stopped paying attention to what he was drawing. The pencil still flew over the page, the scritch-scratch continued, but he was on autopilot. It was common for him, once he had the image in his mind, to talk on the phone while he worked. He could easily focus on the conversation and still have a small portion of his brain left over to make sure the drawing came out the way he wanted it.

"And are you the local scandal queen now?" he asked.

"Nope. He just wanted to let me know how serious he is about wanting me to run."

He let out a small breath he'd been holding. "Excellent. So, are you going to go for it?"

"I think I might."

Michael laughed. "Okay, Ms. Noncommittal. You should run for president with answers that concrete."

They chatted briefly about what kind of time commitment was involved in campaigning for city council. Michael offered his services to come up with a poster. He suggested "Vote Jillian Dansky, Sex Kitten" as a slogan, then pretended to be mystified when she chided him about it.

"I'm *your* sex kitten. Not Bob Ryan's."

He could almost hear the smile on her face. Jillian knew how much he respected her for her intelligence and her wisdom. But she also sort of liked it when he let her know how sexy he thought she was.

"Aren't you going to get in trouble, talking like that at work?" he asked.

"No. Everyone here knows I'm a sex kitten," Jillian said, lowering her voice to a sultry rasp. Then she laughed. "Besides, I have my door closed."

"Really? Well, maybe you should be my phone sex kitten."

"I have to *go* now," she replied, adding just the right amount of disdain to her voice.

Michael laughed and reminded her how much he loved her before he hung up the phone. By any standard, the weekend had started nicely and spiraled into a shit-storm. For the most part, that was all over now. There was the lingering question of who had decided to drop Ecstasy or whatever into his beer. And if he was going to be honest to himself he was still somewhat concerned about that little girl, hoping that she had stayed in until her parents had come home.

But he was doing his damnedest not to think about such things. *The important thing is Jilly's happy. Forget the rest. Life goes on.*

There was a rap at the door and Teddy Polito poked his head in. "How's it going, *artiste?*"

"It's going, scribbler. I think I have a handle on the second one that you're going to love."

Michael started to explain his idea about the lingerie-clad woman pigging out on Newburyport Premium in front of the TV. Teddy came into the office and glanced over his shoulder at what he had been working on, and Michael saw a look of confusion pass over his face.

"Umm, Mikey, don't you think she's a little young-looking for this campaign?"

He injected the question with the right amount of jest, but his expression was troubled. Michael frowned and looked down at his drawing table.

The sketch was all wrong. Where there should have been a sexy woman in a bikini, there was a young girl in blue jeans and a ruffled peasant blouse. Blond. With wide and innocent eyes. And not just any girl, either.

That girl. The little lost girl on the side of the road. Michael had zoned out while talking to Jillian and somehow the pencil had taken over. His subconscious had changed the sketch, had filtered into his hand. He had drawn her without even realizing what he was doing.

A shiver went through him. The likeness of her face was enough to push a picture into his mind, an image of that little girl outlined in the glare of his headlights, those big eyes sad and more than a little afraid. For all that he had been trying not to think about her, it was obvious that he couldn't let it go. Couldn't let her go. *Scooter.* Her name still made him want to laugh. What the hell kind of name was that? A sudden rush of guilt went through him as he wondered what had become of her.

"Michael?" Teddy prodded.

"Huh?" He glanced up at his partner again.

Teddy's brow was furrowed with concern. "Are you all right?"

"Yeah, fine." Michael waved the inquiry away, heart fluttering with embarrassment. "This is . . . this isn't what we talked about, I know. But I was thinking maybe . . . maybe we should give the client a more familiar option. Kind of merge their *Saturday Evening Post* track record with a hipper, today's-kid kind of thing. Go for the younger demographic."

For a long moment Teddy only stared at the drawing. Then he shrugged. "We could bring it up, but not yet, I don't think. Do you? If the campaign starts to work, we can start segmenting demographics. For now I really think we should focus on what they've asked for. Play it safe, at the beginning, at least."

Michael nodded. He was bullshitting, and from the look on Teddy's face, he thought his partner probably knew it. But the last thing he wanted to do was try to explain. And how would it look, anyway, him obsessing over the girl so much that he was drawing her into his work?

Teddy studied him. "You going to tell me what happened to your face?"

Michael forced a wan smile. So far, most people had been too polite to ask. Those who had, however, had all received the same bullshit story.

"Tried to get the neighbor kid's cat out of a tree," he said. "It didn't feel like coming down."

For a long moment Toddy regarded him dubiously. Then he smiled.

"All right. I'll let you get back to it," Teddy said. He rubbed his hands on his prodigious stomach. "Don't forget we have lunch at one."

At the door, he paused and glanced back into the office. "Oh, and seriously, artiste. Leave the slogans to me. I don't know what you're going for with that, but it's kind of creepy. If we were doing a riff on old milk cartons or the Amber Alert or something, all right. But it's ice cream. No Dennis Miller effect, all right?"

Michael didn't know what he was talking about. When Teddy had departed, he glanced down at the drawing table again. His attention had been focused on the sketch itself, but now he saw that there were other things on the page. Words, drawn in pencil. Big and bold, and small scribbles as well. Block, logo size letters, and elegant script. And all of them said the same thing.

Come find me.

For an instant, Michael had the disconcerting idea that this was not some obsession erupting from his subconscious, but a kind of message, a reminder. The idea was foolish and he dismissed it, but he found that despite the heat ticking in the vents in the ceiling, he was cold all over.

What the hell is wrong with me? he thought. He sat back in the chair and took several long breaths, trying to clear his head. His nostrils flared. Then he froze, inhaling sharply, his eyes wide.

Popcorn. Fresh popcorn, with too much butter and plenty of salt.

There was just a hint of that smell in the air. It was a homemade popcorn smell, not that chemical movie-theater stuff. People didn't often make popcorn that way anymore.

But you've caught that same smell somewhere else recently, haven't you?

In that house.

Troubled, he rose from the chair, needing air, needing to be away from his office for a minute or two. He went out into the hall and glanced around at the cubicles, at the doors to the other offices. There was a break room down the far end of the hall.

"Does someone have popcorn?" he asked, feeling foolish even as the words left his lips. Phones were ringing, people were rushing about, doing their jobs. Somewhere there was a radio on. Conversations taking place. It was too early for lunch. And as Michael inhaled again, he discovered that the smell was gone.

He took a long breath and turned back toward his office.

Once more he froze, head cocked, trying to listen hard, searching for a sound he had heard a moment before. Just the tiniest snippet of music. Calliope music, the sort of tinny, buzzing music that piped out of the speakers on top of an ice-cream truck in the summertime.

CHAPTER SIX

Downtown Andover was a colorful strip of quirky little shops, upscale consignment stores, and restaurants. There were few chains—a pharmacy, a doughnut shop, an ice-cream place—and the street was impeccably cared for. The cars parked along the curb were Benzes and BMW's and the occasional Volvo. Students from nearby Merrimack College strolled the brick sidewalks alongside mothers pushing their babies in canvas-and-steel jogger-strollers. The moms weren't jogging, of course, but those all-terrain baby carriages were the rage.

Michael stood in front of Sacred Ground, the finest coffee shop in town. Somehow the owners managed to convey a Bohemian atmosphere and love of exotic coffee beans while remaining as snootily upscale as most every other business on the strip. Bohemian and snooty was not an ordinary combination, but their product was so good they could afford to be unorthodox.

After an hour bent over his drawing table, he had gotten nothing done. The sketch with the lost girl on it—and those words—had gone into a drawer, and all he had succeeded in doing since then was to pencil in the rough outline of a female form that looked more like a balloon animal twisted up by some party clown than an advertising campaign.

Finally, he had surrendered. It was lunchtime, and though he was not at all hungry, he needed fresh air desperately.

He told himself it was just to clear his head. That the October chill would shake him out of the strange fugue state he had been in most of the morning. And it was nice to be outside, no question. Michael leaned against the back of a bench—unwilling to sit at the moment—and sipped at a double cappuccino. His breath came in slow, purposeful inhalations, and the day was brisk enough that it steamed a bit when he exhaled.

The scent of the cappuccino was strong, wafting up from the hole he'd torn in the plastic cover of his cup. The bank just across the street attempted to put forth the ambience of an earlier age, a Frank Capra age, and so from early autumn to early spring they had a wood-burning stove inside. The smell of its smoke was a pleasure. Even the exhaust fumes from passing cars and buses were welcome.

"Michael?"

It took him a moment to register that someone was speaking to him. Then he blinked and glanced over his shoulder to find Brittany Hurley staring at him curiously. The girl looked even younger than her nineteen years, and was not as dim as most people assumed. She was sleeping with the boss's son, after all.

"Are you all right?"

He gave her a smile and tapped one finger against his temple. "Just cogitating. Working on the new campaign."

Brittany flashed him a cheerleader's smile. "Oh, cool! No wonder you looked so far away. But aren't you cold?"

"That's what double cappuccino is for." He toasted her with his cup and took a sip, pleasant enough to be courteous, but just wanting her to go away.

Miraculously, she did, cooing that she would see him back in the office. It occurred to him that Brittany was the perfect combination of sweetheart and slut for the Newburyport Premium campaign. As he returned his attention to the cars rumbling through downtown Andover, he knew he would use her as a mental model for the sketches he was supposed to be working on. That was good. Having a picture of her in his mind would help keep the other image out.

The image of the lost girl. Scooter.

Come find me.

The words came back to him, and for the first time he realized that they were really what had driven him out into the chilly air. The coffee, the walking, the crisp breeze, they were all helping to clear his head after all. Subconsciously or not, he had been obsessing about her. Michael was an intelligent man. He understood why. In the condition he had been in on Saturday night, and with what little he remembered of the house, and the circumstances of his leaving her off there, he felt responsible for anything that might have happened to her.

There was only one solution for that.

He was going to have to find her.

A sudden gust of wind whipped up, blasting amongst the shops and restaurants, and his cheeks stung with the cold. Michael tipped back his coffee and took a long gulp, the heat of it warming him from within. His upper lip curled and he glanced down at the cup. It tasted bitter to him, suddenly. He tossed it unfinished into a nearby trashcan and turned back toward his office.

There was work to be done, but he knew he wasn't going to be able to focus on it until he got this other thing out of his head.

A trio of women had gathered on the sidewalk in front of him, physically different but all glowing with health and affluence. Friends, he thought, who had been out and about on various errands and run into one another by happenstance. They laughed about something or other, and there was a brightness to their eyes and a warmth in their features that made him smile, helping to further dispel the shadow of the weekend.

Upstairs, Michael ignored the bustle at Krakow & Bester and went into his office, turning to the computer. Stray puzzle pieces drifted around in his mind and he tried to put them together. All he knew of the girl was her description and a nickname. But he had seen her home, had driven her there himself. No matter how inebriated he had been, he felt certain that he could put together the bits and pieces of memory from Saturday night and figure out where she lived.

The place to begin was where that surreal evening had begun. The masquerade had been held at the Wayside Inn in North Andover. Michael did a quick Net search for the place and found it had its own Web site. There was no map, but it did give him the exact address. With that, it was a simple matter to call up a map of the area with the inn as its center point. It was too broad, so he magnified the image.

Old Route 12 was there, a thin red line running through the Merrimack Valley. The road had long since been supplanted by more modern streets, but Old Route 12 had been relied upon by locals since the nation was young. Much like Boston Post Road, however, it was used by very few outsiders, because they had no idea just how far they could travel on that one street.

Should've taken 125. Or gotten on 495. The recriminations came unbidden into his mind. Either of those options would have been the long way around, far less direct, and yet might actually have been faster. The Danskys preferred Old Route 12 because it was peaceful and beautiful, particularly in the autumn. In addition, Michael would always prefer the most direct route, and traveling to West Newbury from the Wayside Inn made Old Route 12 by far the most direct course to take.

He dragged the cursor over the map, using it as a guide. For a moment he retreated into his mind, trying to picture that night. His memory was gray and hazy, yet somehow the hum of his tires on the pavement was fresh in his head. He focused on that sound and was able to recall driving down Old Route 12, Jillian snoring softly in the backseat. He had nearly wrecked the car, and righted it just in time to come within scant feet of running down that lost girl.

Where the hell had he been when that happened?

Michael clicked on the tab that magnified the map even further. A couple of miles down Old Route 12. No more than that, surely. The entire road at that point was a scribble on the map, where it twisted and turned as it wound through the Merrimack Valley.

Maybe if I drove out there, he thought, peering at the screen.

He ran a fingertip along the curves of that red line, and he paused, tapping the screen. It was a bit further along than he thought, but the most harrowing of the turns seemed the most likely place for him to have nearly run off the road. Once more he magnified the map onscreen.

Could be.

He drew the cursor over to the northeast corner of the map and clicked there, shifting the image in that direction, revealing the next segment of Old Route 12. Somewhere along that way was a tiny little side road, buried in the trees, that seemed an unlikely conduit to several other neighborhoods. His initial turn had been a right; he recalled that clearly.

"Turn right here."

Then, a little ways further on, he had taken a left. There had been a lot of streets, plenty of houses, roads that gently rose up a long hill, at the top of which was the dilapidated mansion the little girl lived in.

Come find me.

"Exactly," he said aloud. Self-conscious, he turned to make sure no one was standing in the open door to his office.

When he looked back at the screen, he noticed for the first time how inadequate the map was. It was a tiny little square. To search for anything by shifting that square around was ridiculous. He needed a better map.

He closed the screen and went out of his office, pausing a

moment to glance around the various cubicles and at the doors, closed and open. Karlene Dietrich's cubicle had fresh flowers in a vase. Barry Waid had posters and magazine cutouts of thirties Art Deco images all over the interior walls. Those were the only two that Michael could see from just outside his door, but he ran through most of the employees in his mind, trying to figure out who could help him. On the door to Vic Birnbaum's office were crayon masterpieces done by his children.

A thought struck him and he went back out toward the foyer. Brittany's desk was the only thing in the foyer of Krakow & Bester's offices, aside from a pair of sofas and a coffee table for people waiting to be admitted for an appointment. There were the double doors of a coat closet, and some modern art on the wall that looked more like junkyard trash. Frosted glass separated the advertising firm from the building's main corridor.

When he came out into the foyer, she gave him a frankly appraising look.

"Brittany," he began.

"What's up?"

"You live in Boxford, don't you?"

She shrugged. "Well, my parents do. I moved out earlier this year. Can't afford to live in Boxford myself. But I grew up there."

"I'm not sure it's in Boxford," he forged ahead, "but I drove through this neighborhood off of Old Route Twelve this weekend, without paying attention to how I was going. Got a little turned around, you know? Anyway, it was an interesting place. I'd like to get some pictures or sketches out there. It was on top of a hill, sort of a few different neighborhoods all dovetailing off one another, the way a lot of them do around here. Y'know, one built in the twenties, then the next in the forties, then the sixties, then some new development. But at the top of the hill there were just a few houses, all pretty big. Must have been wealthy people living there once upon a time, but the neighborhood's kind of rundown now."

Brittany listened carefully and he could see from her expression that she was trying to figure out what the hell he was talking about. He could also see that nothing rang a bell.

"This one house was fairly ugly, but it might have been beautiful once. It has a turret, sort of Victorian, but is a weird mix of architectural styles that—"

Her eyes lit up. "Know what? I think I have seen that house, now that you mention it. Not for years. In junior high, I had this friend, Sarah, who would invite me to her birthday parties and stuff. I think we used to pass it going to her house. It's not in Boxford, though. Could be Jameson. I mean, chances are it's probably not the same house you're thinking of, but it might be in the same neighborhood."

"Could you give me directions, do you think? Or find it on a map?"

Brittany's eyes went wide and she shook her head. "Oh, I don't know. Sorry." Her lips pulled into a pout. "No way on the directions. But if I had a map I might be able to figure out the general area."

Shit! Michael gnawed his lower lip a moment and then nodded. "Could you? That would be helpful."

"Sure!" She stood up from behind her desk and crossed to the closet. Pulling open the doors, she reached up to a shelf above the coat rack. There were half a dozen phone books up there, an old coffee machine, and random winter mittens, hats, and scarves that people had left behind over the years.

From amongst the phone books Brittany pulled down a thinner volume and brought it to him. Michael glanced at the cover. It was a complete street map of eastern Massachusetts, dated the previous year. At her desk, she opened up to the pages for Boxford and began skimming through. He stood in front of the desk and, even upside down, had no trouble spotting the place where Old Route 12 passed through the northwest corner of the town. There were several sharp curves on the map. Brittany traced her finger along it, frowning.

"Not Boxford, I don't think," she said without looking up.

"Try Jameson," Michael said, unable to disguise the urgency in his voice.

She glanced up at him and smiled. "You must really want to find this place. Sure you don't have some old girlfriend you're trying to find?"

A shiver went through him. He shook his head but did not smile. "I don't really have any old girlfriends. Not serious ones. Jillian and I have been together since I was in college."

"Lucky girl," she said, smiling as she returned to perusing the map. She flipped to the double-page spread of the town of Jameson. Old Route 12 passed right through its center, winding up from southwest to northeast, then into Georgetown.

"Hanover Street," Brittany said, tapping the map.

"Is that it?" Michael said, snapping off the words more abruptly than he'd meant to.

She frowned. "No." Her fingernail traced the short road that ran north from Old Route 12 in Jameson, just south of the Georgetown border. "There used to be the most amazing ice-cream stand right there. Hanover Street Cone Corner. On the way home, my mother would take me there, but it was a little further away than Sarah's house. So . . ."

Brittany drew an invisible line with her finger around a section of the town to the south of Old Route 12.

"It's got to be in this square somewhere." She gave him an apologetic glance. "Sorry I can't be more helpful."

"No, no, that's a start," Michael told her. He lifted up the map book. "Can I borrow this?"

She shrugged again. "As long as you bring it back eventually."

"Thanks, Brit."

She told him he was welcome, but by then he was already pushing through the door that led into the interior offices of Krakow & Bester. The map book felt oddly cold in his hand as he carried it back to his office. Teddy Polito's office was on the way but Michael did not feel like talking to him about the Newburyport Premium campaign at the moment, so he took a detour amongst some cubicles.

The map in his hands made him feel as though he had accomplished something. It was a beginning. This weekend he would drive into Jameson and do some poking around, see if he could find anything that looked familiar. His guilt at having been so negligent with this girl would go away if he could find her house and know that she was safe. All he wanted was to get her out of his head.

In his office, he set the map book down and went to his drawing table. There was a broad sheet of sketch paper there, with only the basic female figure penciled in. In his mind's eye he could still see the wide-eyed face Brittany had made earlier, and he started working on the features of the woman in the sketch. That would be the expression on her face as she glanced down at the melting ice cream dripping on her bikini-clad breasts and bare belly.

His pencil flew across the paper, scratching quietly.

A kind of peaceful contentment filled him. Yes, he would find the girl. But for the moment, this was what he needed. Get a little work done. Get lost in his art.

His nostrils flared.

Cinnamon. He smelled cinnamon, and something more. His stomach rumbled hungrily as he recognized that smell. Cinammon-apple pie, baking in the oven. But there was no oven here, and the door to his office was closed.

The tip of his pencil broke off and Michael froze. A wave of cold air seemed to rush over him, as though the heater had just clicked over to a/c. He glanced up, and something moved in the corner of his eye.

The sunlight streaming through the window washed her out, so that she was like a transparency superimposed over the world. Blue jeans. A ruffled peasant blouse. The sunshine passed right through her, silhouetting her like the headlights of his car. For just a sliver of a moment, he thought perhaps he had killed her after all, and now she was haunting him.

He gasped and blinked.

And she was gone.

"Oh, hell. You have got to be kidding me," Michael whispered to himself. His hands were shaking. And when he looked down at the sketch he had been working on he found that just above the bikinied Brittany with her drippy ice cream cone, just where his pencil tip had broken, stabbing a dark mark onto the page, he had written the words again.

Come find me.

His eyes darted to the map book.

"I'm trying," he whispered. His hands came up and he ran them over his face and hair, then leaned back in his chair, glancing around the office, which had become only ordinary again. "I'm trying."

ON WEDNESDAY NIGHT, WITH THE wind outside the only sound, Jillian lay beside her husband in bed, feeling more alone than she had ever felt before. Three nights in a row she had lain awake like this, feeling lost. Never in her life, if she had been asked, would she have thought she could have felt lonely in her own bed, with Michael at her side. It wasn't the fight they'd had. She was pretty certain they had cleared that all up days ago.

So, what, then?

Her face felt warm, flushed with emotion. The clock read 1:07 but her pulse was racing too fast. There was no way she was going to go to sleep. Not yet. All she could do was lie there with her arms crossed, corpselike, across her chest. Beside her on the nightstand was a reading lamp. Her book was on the floor. But it was too late to start reading, too late to turn on the television.

She had a history of insomnia—maddening, crippling stuff. The first time had been the night before her brother's wedding. As maid of honor, she had been expected to make a speech, and though she was normally outgoing, the prospect filled her with such anxiety that sleep eluded her. From that point on, any time she went to sleep late, she would remember what it had felt like and dread its return. It had been a terrible period in her life but she had gotten past it. Mostly.

Now, here it was again. Monday night had been difficult, but she had been asleep a little after midnight. Tuesday had been slightly worse. Now, with the fear that the torment of persistent insomnia was returning and the hollow feeling in her chest that sprang from the distance she felt between herself and Michael, she felt as though she might never sleep again.

1:11. She stared at the painting on the wall, proper Victorian ladies walking through a park. Its hues were darker in the night, deeply shadowed. Almost as though they were strolling long after midnight.

1:26. Michael lay so still beside her, no sound of snoring nor really any sound of breathing, that she wondered a moment if he was dead. Or worse, if he were lying there awake, listening to her rustling the sheets and not wanting to speak, unwilling to comfort her. She considered very seriously the question of which option would be worse.

1:33. Listening to the gears of the clock.

1:39. Wistful thoughts began to fill her mind. She dredged up images of the past. Though she had felt frozen before, she found herself able to turn now, and placed her right hand on Michael's hip, wishing he would turn toward her. Wishing he would open up his eyes and kiss her. Or, even better, that he would let her hold him and kiss away whatever was weighing so heavily upon him. This Michael—the one who had come home on Monday night with such faraway eyes—he was so different from the Michael she had first fallen in love with. The Michael she had first made love with.

1:41. Jillian at last closed her eyes, but still she did not sleep. In her exhaustion she fell into a kind of half-wakeful limbo, and with a grateful heart she let herself follow the path her thoughts had laid for her. Her mind drifted back to that night . . . that first night with Michael.

• • •

LATER ON, JILLIAN WOULD MAKE the distinction that it was not their first date. They had, after all, been to lunch half a dozen times previous to that evening. But the truth was that in her heart and mind she considered it the first real date they had been on. Michael had suggested they leave campus and go into Boston for dinner, even suggested a restaurant and bar in Quincy Marketplace called Seaside.

Jillian loved Quincy Market. The aquarium was only a stone's throw away, and Boston Common not much farther. The abominable bit of concrete architecture known as City Hall was just up the street. But Quincy Marketplace, with the historic Faneuil Hall as its centerpiece, was one of her favorite spots in Boston. It was vibrant with color and with the music of street performers who roamed the cobblestones, and the scents of the various food carts and flower sellers battled it out on each breeze.

On that night they walked, hand in hand, past a juggler on a unicycle; she marveled at the face-painted performer for a moment. When she glanced at Michael, she found that his attention was not on the juggler, but on her. While she had been smiling and laughing at the man's antics, Michael had been watching her, and his smile was not so much different from her own. She had loved him a little bit, right then. Though it would be a long time before she said it.

The truth was that Jillian believed—and told all of her friends—that Michael was just going to be a summer fling. But her heartbeat quickened when she saw him looking at her that way, and her step felt lighter as they continued along the cobblestones. He bought her a flower, a single red rose, and he did it so nonchalantly, with so little fanfare, that it seemed not like some grand romantic gesture but as a matter of due course, as though the very idea that he might not have bought her one was ridiculous.

The long summer day was coming to its close, the sun having lasted well into evening, when they abandoned the tourist-trodden thoroughfares of Quincy Market and stepped into Seaside. They had reservations, but they were still told they had a twenty-minute wait ahead of them, and so they took a seat at the bar.

They both had wine, sitting close together to be heard over the din. He held just the ends of her fingers in his hand and there was a light in his eyes, a confidence and passion for life that excited her. The conversation leaped from one topic to another, but they talked about family, and about life and ambition . . . about the future.

A strange feeling swept through her and she blinked and smiled.

"What?" he asked. "What's wrong?"

"Nothing," she said, face warm. Jillian took a sip of wine and urged him to go on.

That strange feeling, so odd in the midst of the crowded, noisy bar, was her own arousal. How could she feel that way with all of those people around, with this guy that she had only just begun to get to know?

"Listen, Michael," she said, shyly dropping her gaze.

"Yes?"

She raised her head. Acting coy would not get her message across. She locked eyes with him. "I like you. I really like you. But I just want to get it out of the way now, so we can enjoy the rest of the night. This is our first real date, and I need to know somebody a lot better than I know you before I'm comfortable enough to . . ."

Jillian offered a small shrug, hoping that would suffice. It did.

Michael nodded sincerely. "Oh, yeah. Of course. I'm . . . well, it's certainly not as if I was expecting the night to end that way."

There was a moment when they gazed at each other as she interpreted the underlying message of that statement. It wasn't what he expected, but it wasn't as though he had written it off as impossible.

"Just so there are no misunderstandings," she said.

Totally earnest, he nodded again. "Of course."

Four hours later they were on the roof of the university library with the most breathtakingly romantic view of Boston she had ever seen as a backdrop. Jillian had told him what she wasn't *going* to do, but that left a great many questions about just what she might be *willing* to do. Kissing him was certainly within the realm of possibility.

His face was limned with moonlight and he slid his hands behind her head, dipping his chin to kiss her. Jillian felt as though the ground was giving way beneath her. Her arms went around his back and she found herself kissing him in return, her body molding to his. Michael's hands caressed her back, gliding down over the curve of her ass. When one of his hands slid up beneath her skirt she had a moment of utter conflict. Everything in her mind was telling her to close her legs, to push his hand away . . . but her legs would not obey. Instead, they shuddered and threatened to give out beneath her, and she had to lean back against the railing.

Without hesitation, Michael pushed her panties aside. He kissed her sweetly, gently, as he touched her there, fingers tracing her, teasing her.

A fire blazed up inside her, burning away all of the reservations and hesitations she had so carefully constructed. She whimpered as she pulled his face down for another kiss and then she reached for his belt. The leather slapped her wrist as she unbuckled him, then unzipped his pants. They were out in the darkness, in the shadows atop the library roof, but people came up here all the time. They might be interrupted at any moment.

Jillian didn't care.

When Michael lay down on the stone roof and pulled her to him she slid her panties down over her ankles and then climbed onto him, kissing his face, letting her hair hang down, cascading into his face. Her skirt covered both of them, but she did not need to see. She could feel him there, inside her, and she stared into his eyes with amazement at the heat, at the passion that had come over them. Her breath came in quick gasps, timed with the rhythm of her hips as she rose up and down upon him. He looked into her eyes as though she was the only girl he had ever seen.

She could barely breathe.

Just a summer fling.

NOW IT HAD COME TO this. The two of them in bed together, and her heart aching, feeling as though he was a million miles away.

Jillian had hoped that whatever had been troubling him on Monday night would fade, but if anything he had seemed more distant than ever tonight. She had felt it the moment she had walked in the door. Michael had made dinner, a chicken stir-fry, and he had done and said all of the right things. But it was in his eyes.

"Are you all right?" she had asked as they sat down to dinner. "You've been on autopilot all week."

"I'm okay. I guess I haven't been feeling that well." He had glanced away.

For a long time she had studied him, forking stir-fry up to her mouth without ever really tasting it. He did look pale. There were dark circles under his eyes. She had wondered if it was just the lingering effect of their horrible weekend, and if it was, what about it was staying with him. Someone had slipped something into his beer, but that should be long out of his system by now. Maybe he was fighting the flu, or something.

Or maybe it wasn't anything physical. Jillian had not wanted to think about it, but she had to consider that it might be nerves. That it might be remnants of their fighting over the weekend. Or worse. Maybe it was her. The way he wouldn't meet her gaze, the way he gave that little laugh when she asked him about it.

Something was haunting Michael, and he didn't want to talk to her about it. Jillian had felt herself closing off from him at dinner. Even her own body language had changed, her arms in tight to her body, her legs turned away from him under the table. Normally he was so perceptive with that kind of thing, but he failed to notice at all. He was too wrapped up in whatever was going on in his head.

Now she lay beside him, remembering that first night they had made love by the light of the moon, with the Boston skyline as their backdrop. A flicker of the thrill of that night still lingered in her heart. This was Michael. She loved him. And one of the things he had always said he loved about her was that she never suffered other people's bullshit.

Enough, she thought.

Jillian kissed the back of his neck and reached around to trace her fingers down his chest. Then she moved her hand lower, pushed beneath the waistband of his cotton briefs, and gripped his cock in her hand.

On the third stroke, he woke up.

He seemed to wake all at once, and a small gasp escaped his lips. "Jilly? What are you doing?"

"Sssh. What does it feel like I'm doing? I can't sleep. If I have to be up," she said, stroking him erect, "then so do you."

Michael laughed, and her heart shattered with relief at that sound.

When he rolled over, though, the two of them there beneath their down comforter, in the private warmth of the bed they had shared for years, there was still a distance in his eyes, a sadness that she did not understand. If she had not known better, she would have thought what she saw in him was fear. But what did Michael Dansky have to be frightened of? She had never known him to be afraid of anything.

He pushed his fingers through her hair, caressed her face, and bent to kiss her on the nose and then on her eyelids. His hand began to run over the curves of her body and he snuggled up even closer to her.

"Come back to me," she whispered.

His brows arched, eyes filled with alarm at first, and then with sorrow. "Sorry. I . . . it's been the strangest week."

"Why didn't you talk to me about it?" she asked, not accusing him, but trying to lead his straying mind back. "When you're troubled, baby, this is where you always come. Home to me." Jillian took his hand and placed it over her heart. "You bring it here so that you're never alone." She lowered her voice but her gaze did not waver. "When you don't, I'm scared for you, and for us, and then we're both alone."

Michael drew in a long, shuddering breath. He continued to caress her and Jillian's own fingers danced up and down his chest, then back down to stroke him again. But there was no seduction there. It was all a part of who they were. Sex and passion and friendship and love, an adoration that combined them all.

"I know," he whispered. "I'm sorry."

"Can you talk to me about it now?"

She felt him begin to soften in her hand.

He drew her to him and kissed her hair, kissed her tenderly on her mouth, then softly on the neck, where it sent a ripple of pleasurable shudders all through her.

"Tomorrow. Let me sleep on it tonight, and I promise I'll tell you about it tomorrow. In the daylight."

For some reason, she shivered at this, and not at all with pleasure. Jillian pushed him back so that she could stare into his eyes again. "I'll never be able to sleep if I don't at least know what it's about. Only the worst things come to mind, especially in the middle of the night. We can talk about it tomorrow, but at least let me know what it is that's troubling you. What it's about."

Michael hesitated a moment, but then he swallowed and nodded. When he spoke, he drew in a quick breath first as though he was afraid he might not have the air to get the words out.

"I think I saw a ghost."

For a long time they only stared at one another, Jillian searching for some explanation, something further in her husband's eyes. She wanted to know more, but she knew the conversation was over for tonight. Then, softly at first but with growing urgency, Michael kissed her once more. His hands moved over her skin and she found herself responding with a ferocity that shocked her. She needed him. It was as though they were escaping into one another, fleeing from this thing that haunted them.

CHAPTER SEVEN

On Thursday morning Michael told her everything. They sat together at the rustic table in their kitchen, the November sun halfhearted as it spilled through the windows and across the floor, and Jillian pulled her feet up beneath her on her chair and cupped her hands around her coffee mug, watching him with equal parts compassion and astonishment. She wore flannel pajama pants and thick white cotton socks. Normally the sight of her like that would have taken his breath away. With the mischief of the previous night glinting in her eyes and stray locks of dark hair falling wild across her face, the earnest innocence in her stumble-out-of-bed wardrobe was incredibly, unintentionally, sexy.

But Michael was immune to his wife's charms at the moment. The dreadful chill that shivered up the back of his neck was far too much of a distraction. He traced one finger over the handle of his coffee mug, furrowing his brow a moment as he noticed the way that the sunshine coming through the windows stretched just far enough to envelop Jillian in its brightness, leaving him in shadow, a slashing line dividing the table in half.

"So," he ventured. "I'm wigging out, right?"

Jillian laughed, but there was an unsettledness to it, something shrouded beneath her gaze when she looked at him.

Michael had told her everything he could remember from Saturday night, all of the thoughts he had been having, the way he had been obsessing about the lost girl and his responsibility to her. He had told her about the way he had subconsciously worked her into his sketches, and about the weird sensory events, the things he kept smelling. Most important, of course, he told her about *seeing* the girl.

"And you haven't seen her since Monday?"

He shook his head. "No. But I keep feeling like I'm going to, like I'll turn around and she'll just be there, as if she's here, but not here. I know how it sounds, trust me."

"Scooter?" Jillian looked at him. "You're sure that was what she said?"

Michael nodded. "It must be a nickname or something."

She smiled. "I hope so."

He realized that Jillian was stalling for time, hedging as she tried to process everything he had said. But he couldn't blame her for needing a couple of minutes to take it all in. He tried to imagine how he would have reacted if their situations were reversed, and could not.

Wasn't it strange, how most of the time the hum of the refrigerator and the ticking of the floral clock on the wall were inaudible, and yet at other times they seemed impossibly loud? Now, for instance.

"Well?" he said, at last.

It seemed to pain her to respond. She pursed her lips together and gave a barely perceptible shake of her head. "You never believed in ghosts," she said softly.

"No, I didn't. I'm still not sure I do." The heat of embarrassment warmed his face. "I mean, what's more likely, really? That I'm being haunted . . . or that my head's shaken up from what happened Saturday night? All of it, I mean."

Jillian's usual confidence slipped back into her expression and she smiled as she reached across the table, shattering that line between daylight and shadow. She twined her fingers with his and tilted her head, drawing his gaze and holding it.

"I think you know the answer to that."

With a nod, Michael sighed. "Yeah. I do. And to be honest with you, sweetie, I think I'd almost rather be haunted."

"Hey," she said softly, squeezing his fingers. Her brows knitted in consternation. "Don't do that. You're talking to insomnia girl, remember?" And he did remember. Jillian had suffered from terrible insomnia the year Michael had graduated college. "I couldn't shut my mind off for months. I thought things at three in the morning that wouldn't make sense to anyone. Your mind can play tricks on you. And very few of them are funny.

"Look, we've already established that you weren't drunk enough by half for what happened to you Saturday night. So someone slipped you something. How are we to know the effects of whatever it was? We don't even know *what* it was. So what have you got so far? A bit of obsession, which is understandable if you're feeling guilty for having left the girl at that house when you're not sure she was safe. You were messed up, Michael. You're not responsible. But I can't tell you not to feel that way, 'cause I'd probably be stressing about it, too.

"What else do we have? Paranoia, for sure. Weird sensory experiences. That sounds like the effects of drugs. All right, you've had one massive hallucination—seeing this girl—but even that could be due to whatever was in your drink, or the mental stress, or a combination of the two. I think you should see a doctor—"

Michael nodded, sighing. "A shrink."

"Well, yeah," Jillian agreed, nodding in punctuation. "But that's not what I meant. I think you should see a *doctor* doctor to make sure that whatever you were doped with this weekend isn't going to have lasting side effects. Who knows what's in your blood right now? And then I think you should talk to a therapist, just to get rid of the stress you're under. You're so tense, you've latched on to this girl. Maybe you need to talk to someone whose job it is to combat that stuff."

The smell of coffee was strong in his nostrils. Michael noticed that the morning sun was rising further into the sky and the line of shadow had moved back some, so that now the place where he and Jillian held hands was washed in sunshine. The warmth of it felt better than he would have cared to admit.

"You're okay. You're just a little out of focus at the moment," she said.

"Like when the TV starts fritzing out," Michael agreed, smiling with some small effort. "Maybe if you just whack me in the side of the head?"

"Don't tempt me."

They stayed like that for several long moments and then Michael nodded. "Thanks, Jilly. I'm sure you're right. I think I knew all that, but I needed to hear it from you, too."

What he didn't tell her was that the hallucination of the lost girl in his office had seemed so real that he had needed to talk about it to Jillian to soften it in his mind, to make it seem less real. Talking about it out loud helped him push it away, reassure himself that the rules of the world he knew still held fast. And it had worked. Now that they had spoken of it and Jillian had echoed his own internal attempts to make sense of it, Michael could embrace the idea that there was something wrong with him. Something that could be fixed with a couple of doctor's visits, maybe a prescription or two.

Now she watched him again with those gentle eyes, her smile playful as she leaned over the table to kiss him. Her lips brushed against his.

"You'll be all right, Michael. If you need to try to find that house, just do it. That might make you feel better. But first, call the doctor. And set up an appointment with a therapist. You'll be right as rain."

He had to grin at that. It was an antique expression, one her mother had always used, and Jillian put it into conversation almost without realizing it.

"You know," he said, "you really are something. Level head. Always got an answer for everything. Maybe you should run for office one of these days."

She laughed. "Maybe I will."

Michael had been teasing her about her interest in running for city council, but he was glad she seemed to be taking it seriously. It would be good for her, and good for the city.

"Actually," she said, "we're going to have dinner with Bob Ryan tomorrow night."

"Really?" He was pleased, and a bit surprised she hadn't brought it up sooner. Michael had the feeling Jillian wasn't sure if her husband was really in favor of her getting into politics. "Somewhere nice, I hope."

"Dorothy's."

Michael sat back in his chair. "Great. I could use a night out. Guess I have to be on my best behavior, huh?"

"Yes," Jillian said, wagging a finger at him. "No ghosts."

Traffic was heavier than usual on the way to the office. Halfway there, Michael wished he had gone all the way out to Route 495. It would be the long way around, but with the traffic on the back roads it might well have gotten him there sooner.

Driving south on Route 125 he listened to the morning talk on Kiss 108, even though he couldn't stand the music they played the rest of the day. Their A.M. drive show was the best in the city. Even so, he was only half listening. There was a pleasant ache in his hips from his lovemaking with Jillian last night, and he could still feel her touch on his hand from their conversation at the kitchen table this morning.

The rest of his life might still be out of sorts, but as long as things between him and Jillian were on solid footing, he was sure everything else would work out. Hell, as long as he had Jillian, not much else really mattered. He loved his work, but it wasn't nearly as important to him as his marriage.

As he drove south, he barely paid attention. This was a route he had traveled hundreds of times. He could have driven it with his knees. Hell, he could have driven it with his eyes closed, nearly. The window was open several inches to let in the cold, crisp November air. The visor was down to protect his eyes from the sun, but he still had to squint as he rounded a corner just past Butcher Boy.

Out of the corner of his eye he saw a lone figure standing on the sidewalk in front of the ice-cream stand on the left. A ripple of some trace memory went through him and for a moment he was sure it was her again, the lost girl. Scooter.

But when he glanced over, careful to keep the car on his side of the center stripe, he saw that the figure was too tall. Instead, it was someone in a long, shapeless coat. Perhaps a homeless man, though this would be an unlikely place to see a vagrant walking. With the sun cutting down at a harsh angle, the man's face was bleached and pale. In that glimpse it seemed his face was misshapen, as though he wore a mask. Michael shifted his focus back to the road, adjusted the steering wheel slightly, and then glanced back to try to get a better look, but he had driven too far past the man now and all he could see was the strangely shambling shape on the sidewalk.

The radio had been rambling through a series of inane advertisements for this week's television lineup. November was a network ratings sweeps month, after all, so there were all sorts of stunts on the various sitcoms and dramas. Jillian and Michael didn't watch a lot of television.

Now the ads segued into a hip-hop beat, a woman sang the same sweet words over and over in the background, and a deep-voiced man launched into a rap in dangerous tones. Michael rolled his eyes. It was all the station played these days, and it all sounded the same. He reached out and punched buttons on the radio, gaze ticking upward to make sure the traffic light ahead was still green.

Two of his preset stations were oldies, and he smiled now as the blistering guitar riff from Eric Clapton's "White Room" squealed from his speakers.

Content, he sat back.

The light was yellow and he was just about to coast under it. The intersection was a large one, and half a dozen vehicles were waiting to come in from the right, where the China Blossom restaurant sat on a small rise overlooking the road. A breeze whispered through the window. Clapton's guitar wailed. It was too late to stop for the light, which would turn red any second, and so he accelerated. A pickup truck loaded with paint supplies, ladders hanging off the sides, had already edged partway out into the intersection in anticipation of the light change.

The paint truck's driver laid on the horn as Michael sailed through the intersection. Michael ignored him, though the urge to make an obscene gesture was pretty strong.

Then he was passing by China Blossom, a big orange-and-white barn of a place, with very little overt Asian influence, despite the offerings on its menu. His stomach growled. He had eaten breakfast, but still felt hungry.

"Is it lunchtime yet?" he muttered to himself, chuckling.

And then he frowned and sniffed the air. Perhaps it was hunger, or just the thought of food, that had summoned up the scent, but if so it was an odd one. He inhaled it, a smile tugging at the corners of his mouth. He glanced at the control panel for the heat and a/c, wondering if somehow it was coming from the engine or drifting in from outside, but the fan wasn't even on.

Michael smelled chocolate. *No, not chocolate. Hot cocoa.*

He breathed it in again, but this time there was only a trace of the smell. And then it was gone entirely and he was left wondering if it had been his hungry stomach and his vivid imagination after all.

He put down his window and the chilly air rushed in. The traffic stopped abruptly ahead of him and he hit the brakes. The car shuddered to a stop. Another frown creased lines in his forehead as a disturbing thought struck him. This wasn't the first time he had noticed a smell that seemed out of place to him, and he wondered if it could really be some aftereffect of whatever he might have been drugged with.

Jillian was right. The sooner he saw a doctor and found out what was happening to him, the better. If he was going to sit in traffic—up ahead there was some construction going on, a new high school, he thought—then he could make use of the time. Keeping his foot on the brake, he popped open the glove compartment and pulled out his cellular phone.

As he sat up again and began to dial, he glanced to his right.

The sun had disappeared behind gray prewinter clouds and the daylight was dreary now.

On the side of the road were two figures, nearly identical to one another. Nearly identical, also, to the homeless man he had seen a short way back on the other side of the road. Long, shapeless coats. A sort of stoop to their shoulders.

They stood as though waiting for a bus, but they were looking directly at Michael. At his car. Through his car. Watching him.

And now that the sun was hidden in gray sky, he saw that it was not the glare of the morning light that had made the face of the first one look bleached. These two were equally pale and had the strangest features, as though their faces had been stretched and distorted. Yet Michael could see their eyes—wide eyes with irises so dark they seemed black as tar—and they stared at him.

Not masks, he thought.

Sympathy touched him, pity for them, and curiosity about what sort of affliction caused something like that. But sympathy had not been his first reaction. In the moment when he had realized that they shared their deformity with the other man he had seen—the moment when he'd realized they were looking at him—the first emotion to reach his heart had been fear. It passed and was quickly forgotten, but a trace of it lingered beneath other feelings.

He tried to make sense of their features, of what he was seeing, and somehow he could not. It seemed difficult to focus on their faces. His attention seemed to want to shift, to pull back and take in their entire forms, those shapeless coats and hunched shoulders.

His vision blurred and he reached up to rub at his eyes, the engine purring and the radio moving on to something with a thumping backbeat. He smelled exhaust fumes. Traffic was frozen.

When he looked again, they were gone. Just like Scooter. Just like that lost girl.

The traffic started to move again.

Car horns blared.

Michael forced himself to drive, breathing slowly, wondering about what had been done to him Saturday night, when the effects would wear off.

If they would wear off.

TEDDY POLITO COULD NEVER GET comfortable in the chair in front of his desk. Maybe it was ergonomics and maybe it was just that he had a hard time focusing on his work. He fidgeted a lot, sitting up straight, then slumping back down. It was one of those typical office chairs, metal arms painted black, black fabric covering the seat and back. Most everything else in the office was a comfort to him, from the photograph of his wife in the silver frame on his desk to the spider plant in the corner to the old-fashioned green glass banker's lamp he had had with him since college. But that fucking chair did him in every goddamned day.

You're fat, Teddy, he thought. *You can't get comfortable because you're fat.* And there was that, true enough. But he did not think it was just his weight that made him so uncomfortable, put him in constant motion. It certainly didn't help, though, especially with the pain in his back.

The new Liz Phair played quietly in his computer's CD drive. He didn't dare have it any louder. His door was closed, but if anyone came in he did not want to have to listen to complaints about some of the more ribald lyrics Liz came up with.

He sat back in the chair, stretching, popping the muscles in his neck with a twist, and then just stared at the computer screen. As his mind worked, he tapped a pen against the edge of the desk in a rapid one-two rhythm.

Most days, he didn't have a clue why he couldn't get comfortable in his chair, why he had such a hard time focusing on his work. Today, though, he knew exactly what was unsettling him. Michael had come in late for work, and more than a little. He had muttered an apology to anyone who asked him about it, but hadn't even offered an excuse for why he was late. The guy had looked pale, even a bit shaky.

At his desk, now, Teddy closed his eyes and massaged the bridge of his nose. He had grown up with a father who drank far too much; when he had looked at Dansky this morning, images had flashed through Teddy's mind. Ugly images. Shattered bottles and empty cans and bruises on his mother's face. The truth was, Michael Dansky looked a hell of a lot like a man who either had a vicious hangover, or someone who badly needed a drink. Either option spelled trouble.

With a sigh, he stood up and stretched his back. One of these days he was really going to get serious about losing weight. Getting into shape. What he needed was a nice little heart attack to motivate him. Nothing serious, just something troubling. Something to scare the hell out of him.

These morbid thoughts were his way of distracting him from what was really bothering him at the moment. He glanced out through the clear glass that bordered the door to his office. The beehive was at work. Garth was making the rounds with the mail cart. Paul Krakow, the big boss, was standing in the midst of the bullpen of cubicles that made up the lion's share of the production, sales, and accounting departments. There were some junior copywriters and designers out there as well. At the moment, the distinguished older gentleman who had started the agency was engaged in an animated conversation with Heather Vostroff, a recent hire. Heather was a talented girl, a designer with her eye on Dansky's office, and his job.

No wonder she was sucking up to the boss.

Not that Paul Krakow minded. She was feeding him charm and sex appeal like candy, and he was gobbling it up.

"Michael, you idiot," he whispered to his otherwise empty office. "Don't fuck this up."

He wasn't just talking about Dansky's career, but the Newburyport

Premium account. Heather Vostroff wanted Dansky's job, but there were half a dozen young writers at Krakow & Bester who would love to pick up the assignments that Teddy Polito got, and if Michael screwed up the ice-cream campaign, it might have a serious effect on Teddy's position at the agency as well.

"All right. All right," he muttered to himself. He shook his head and opened the door.

Without pausing to speak to anyone, he moved swiftly across the main floor toward Michael's office. Krakow noticed him on the move and raised a hand to acknowledge him. Teddy smiled and waved back, nodding politely. The last thing he wanted to do was to get into a conversation with the old man today about Newburyport Premium. Bester the younger, the talentless sycophantic hack who'd gotten the job because his father was the junior partner at the place, was already breathing down the back of his neck for the first round of test ads so that the management team could discuss them.

Heartburn seared Teddy's guts and he wished he had picked up the bottle of Tums back in his office. He might not get that jaunty little cardiac event he'd been hoping for, but he damned sure was on his way to a mighty evil ulcer.

Michael's office door had been closed since he had arrived this morning. It was after eleven o'clock now and nothing had stirred from within since then. The guy was either hard at work, or asleep at his drawing table. Dansky was his friend, but Teddy reluctantly admitted to himself that he wasn't sure which of those was true.

He rapped his knuckles lightly on the door, not wanting to draw attention to himself, or to Michael's office. There was no reply from within, not even any sound that might indicate the guy was getting up to open it. Teddy felt a burning sensation at the back of his neck and reached up to scratch at it. It wasn't an itch, though. It was just his certainty that someone was watching him, that there were eyes following his trek down to Michael's office and awaiting the outcome. Maybe old man Krakow was watching him, maybe he wasn't. Teddy didn't want to go barging in on Michael, but he thought that might be better than the appearance that anything was wrong.

Or maybe you're just being paranoid.

Still, he didn't want to draw attention, so he opened the door and stepped inside. Michael was seated at his drawing table, talking on his portable headset. He was slightly hunched over, as though he was in pain, and though he was not looking at the paper on the table, his pencil scratched across it even as he spoke into the headset.

"No, today. I just . . . I'd really like to get in to see him today. It's sort of hard to explain. I'll take whatever time I . . . quarter after one is fine. Just . . . it's fine."

Michael held up one finger to let Teddy know he'd only be another few moments. He was still pale, and there were dark circles beneath his eyes that Teddy hadn't noticed before. His gaze darted around as though he were searching the corners of the room for something he'd lost. Michael seemed almost skittish, and if Teddy hadn't been almost certain it was ridiculous, he would have thought the guy looked frightened.

"Thank you. Yes, I'll be there," Michael said. He thumbed a small button on the headset to disconnect the phone and then slung it off of his head and onto the drawing table. His pencil went down beside it and he looked up expectantly.

"Hey, Teddy. What's up?"

For a moment, Teddy had no idea how to respond. It was such a goddamned stupid question. Didn't Dansky have a clue? Wasn't Teddy's concern obvious from the expression on his face?

"Look, Michael," he began, closing the door behind him. "I don't want to get into your business, but . . . I mean, we're friends, right? Aside from work?"

Michael frowned, but even with that he seemed distracted. Twitchy. "Yeah. Of course we are."

Teddy let out a long breath. "Buddy, you've got me worried. You look like shit. You come in late. It's been days and I don't have even initial sketches from you on the ice-cream campaign. Gary's already been bugging me about it. The clock's ticking, and you're making me nervous."

He blinked, realizing how all of that sounded. "But it isn't just work. I'm worried about you. I don't know what's up with you, but whatever it is——"

"Okay." Michael held up a hand to stop him.

Knitting his brows, Teddy only stared at him.

"I . . . That was my doctor's office."

Michael let the words hang there between them for a long moment. He'd spoken them with such gravity that Teddy began to wonder—and to worry—that whatever was going on was even more serious than he'd thought.

"I look like shit because I feel like shit." There was a moment of hesitation, as though Michael had been about to go on, to tell him something else . . . something worse, maybe. But then he sat back in his seat and just shrugged.

"All I can say is I'm sorry. I wish my head wasn't so fucked up right now. I'm leaving early. I've got an appointment to see the doctor. And I'm going to stay home tomorrow, work from there. I swear to you, give me the weekend and I will finish not just sketches but full designs for the ideas we've talked about. I will, Teddy."

Michael stood up and began to gather his things. His hands were shaking. "But right now . . . right now I've got to get out of here. I've got to see the doctor."

Teddy nodded. He was sure he said something comforting, something reassuring, told Michael not to worry. Mainly, though, he was focused on staying out of the way as his friend collected the things he needed to work from home. Whatever was wrong with Michael Dansky, Teddy didn't want to catch it.

Not with Heather Vostroff brewing trouble for both of them.

An art director could work from home and show up with something brilliant, and nobody ever wondered how long it had taken him to create. It was taken for granted that art was a time-consuming process. But as a writer, he never worked from home, even though Krakow & Bester certainly would have allowed it from time to time. It was all about perception.

He stood in Michael's office and watched his friend go through the warren of cubicles, portfolio case in one hand and his jacket in the other. Only after Michael had departed did he glance down at his friend's drawing table and notice the charcoal image he had been doodling while on the phone. Shades of gray that formed the face of a little girl, the same girl Michael had drawn into his sketches on Monday.

What the hell's going on with you, Dansky? Teddy wondered to himself. But he wasn't at all sure he wanted an answer.

THAT NIGHT MICHAEL COULD NOT sleep. Long after midnight he lay in his bed, staring at the ceiling, his hands at rest upon his chest as though he were a corpse, set out for viewing. The room was dark save for a dim, diffuse glow from the streetlight just across the road from the Danskys' house. His chest rose and fell, his breathing even, but his mind would not turn off.

He could not stop the echo of the things Dr. Ufland had said to him during his appointment. Michael had returned home from the doctor's office before three o'clock, and he had been hearing those words over and over since, seeing the doctor's face in his mind.

"Anything like this ever happened before, Michael? And with these enhanced olfactory episodes, the heightened smells you were talking about . . . any of your other senses behaving the same way? Have you noticed an increase in the intensity of other stimuli? Do things sound louder? Do things seem more colorful? Flowers more fragrant?"

No. No. And no. Nothing like that.

"It certainly sounds like you might have been dosed with something that caused you to have blackouts and altered your perception. Kids are brewing up all sorts of unique drugs these days. I'll run some tests, but I have to confess

that their inventiveness has us behind the curve. I might not find it even if it's there. And that was Saturday night. It's unlikely it would still be affecting you now.

"As far as you seeing the girl . . . absent any of the other symptoms we've talked about, I'm fairly skeptical that there is a medical explanation for this. I will do an MRI, just to rule out a tumor, but this is so specific and individualized that I can't imagine dementia manifesting like this. We'll test as we can, but Michael, you should know that I suspect we're looking at more of a psychological issue than a physiological problem. You're obviously troubled by the episode over the weekend. Burdened with guilt about this girl you mentioned. Worrying that something might have happened to her. That may be what's causing all of this. I'm going to make an appointment for you with Helen Lee. She's an old friend, and a damn fine doctor."

Doctor. Helen Lee wasn't just a doctor. She was a psychiatrist. And the truth was, nothing Dr. Ufland had said had surprised Michael. Intuitively, he had understood that the things that were wrong with him were too focused to be the result of some malady. The twisted part of that was, he would have expected himself to be happier at the thought that he probably didn't have a brain tumor.

But there might be worse things than a brain tumor.

Michael lay in bed next to the only woman he had ever loved, his eyes burning with exhaustion and with the sting of unshed tears. He gnawed on his lower lip. Beside him, Jillian breathed deeply, lost in slumber. He wanted to look at her, to watch her sleep. It calmed him to do that, on nights when he had trouble falling asleep. Not that it happened often. She was the one who had suffered from insomnia. Now, though, he was beginning to understand what she had gone through.

Not that this was the same. Far from it.

He wanted desperately to turn and watch his wife's sleeping form, to watch her chest rise and fall, her features silhouetted in the barest golden glow from the illumination coming in through the window from the streetlight. Michael wished he could reach over and caress her face, even perhaps lean down and kiss her forehead, or the spot just behind her jaw where she had a tiny mole.

But he did not dare to turn toward her, did not dare to even look at her. For they were not alone in the room.

In the far, shadowy corner, untouched by the dim golden glow and yet somehow containing her own faint illumination, was the lost girl. She had been standing there for more than two hours, silently watching him. Michael refused to look at her now, but earlier he had not been able to stop himself. Maybe the doctor was right and it wasn't drugs or a brain tumor; maybe he was just losing his mind. He wanted to watch her, to see her. And so he stared at the little blond girl standing there in the darkness. She only watched him, and she wept silently, fear etched upon her features. But fear for herself or for him he couldn't tell.

Time had passed since he had last looked over at her. From his position he could see the digital readout on the cable box on top of the television. It was going on two in the morning. Perhaps by now she had gone.

But he shivered under his covers, and gnawed his lip harder. For he knew she was still there. He could *feel* her.

Come find me. She had not spoken the words. Even her tears were shed in silence. But still, Michael heard them in his head, an echo of the first time she had spoken.

Now he lay in his bed and he waited. Waited for the dawn. It was a long way off, but he knew he would not sleep. He had a powerful hope that when the sun rose, its light would somehow disperse the image of the girl in the shadowed corner of the room. Until then, he would not look. And he would not . . . absolutely not . . . wake Jillian.

What frightened him most was not that he might have a brain tumor, or even the prospect that he was losing his mind, though that was certainly terrible. What froze him there in his bed was the fear that whispered through his head and shivered up his spine, the fear that neither of those things was true. That if he woke Jillian up and told her to look into the corner, she would not tell him he was imagining things. His greatest fear was that he would wake Jillian and she would see the girl.

And that would make it all real.

So Michael lay there, very still, listening to Jillian breathe, and praying that she would sleep until morning.

And that the morning would make a difference.

CHAPTER EIGHT

Jillian was long gone by the time Michael dragged himself out of bed the next morning. The sky was chalk white, the daylight pale and wan where it washed through the windows. Nothing fell from the sky. Not a raindrop, nor a hint of hail or sleet. On the street outside the Dansky home, the world looked too quiet, too empty, as though some silent apocalypse had taken place during the night.

True to the vow he had made to himself, the darkness outside his window had lightened to an impossible indigo and then the night had begun to bleed into morning before he had finally fallen asleep. Jillian had shaken him awake less than an hour later, and Michael recalled muttering something to her about needing to sleep, about working at home today. Now he glanced at the clock and saw the digital numbers burning an accusatory red atop the television: 10:47 A.M.

Just a few hours' sleep. Not nearly enough.

But the day was wasting, and there was something he needed to do. Something of vital importance. The appointment that his doctor had set up for him with the shrink wasn't until next Wednesday. Which might as well have been a hundred years away, to his mind. An eternity separated now from then.

Michael stretched, muscles in his back and neck popping. He

pulled off the white T-shirt that he had worn to bed and tossed it into the laundry basket beside the long dresser beneath the mirror he and Jillian shared. His reflection revealed gray circles under his eyes and a shadow of stubble on his chin. His face was puffy and he reached up to touch the places beneath his eyes, where the elasticity of his skin seemed to have given way. Staring into his own eyes, he could see an emptiness there, a kind of void where some of the emotion he ought to have been feeling had spilled out. He felt numb, as though an echo was rebounding inside his head. His eyes were dim.

Haunted.

On his nightstand was a full glass of water. Michael and Jillian both took water to bed with them at night, and normally both glasses were nearly empty by morning. But during the night Michael had not taken a sip. He had not dared to reach for the glass.

A splinter of pain punctured his chest, perhaps a little tear in the fabric of whatever he had used to blanket his fear and dread. For a long moment he stared at Jillian's side of the bed. Her glass was empty. The book she was reading—a family drama from Joyce Carol Oates—lay there on top of a copy of the latest *Bon Appétit*. The drawer of her nightstand was open and a pair of cotton French-cut panties had been left sticking out, like the top tissue in a Kleenex box. She had been in a hurry this morning. Had she been running late, or just in a rush to get to work?

At last he remembered why she was in a hurry. Jillian wanted to leave the office early tonight to get home in time for dinner with Bob Ryan and whichever of his political cronies were joining them. An image flashed through Michael's mind of Ryan at the masquerade that night. The gunslinger. The Man With No Name. And the guy had the cold, flinty eyes for the role. Perhaps he looked more like Clint Eastwood's costar in those old movies, Lee Van Cleef, than like Eastwood himself. But that was better, in a way. For in Michael's mind, Bob Ryan would always be remembered in that outfit, would always be the cruel-eyed, hawk-nosed Lee Van Cleef.

Michael realized that Bob Ryan frightened him a little. Not for real. Not in any way that meant something. But the man was intimidating.

"Okay," he whispered. "Okay, Jilly." For Jillian, he would be back here and dressed and ready to go to dinner by six o'clock. But the time between now and then belonged to Michael.

Or, really, to Michael's obsession. If he ever hoped to overcome it, he was going to have to find that girl. To find that house.

Even with the pallid daylight that filled the bedroom, Michael had managed to avoid looking into *that* corner thus far. The corner where the ghost of the lost girl had stood throughout the night, watching him. Crying. Pleading with him in silence. Now, though, he did look.

The corner was empty.

The house was empty, except for him.

Michael let out a long breath and nodded to himself. He stepped out of his underwear and tossed it into the laundry basket as well, then went to the TV and turned on CNN. A woman in Louisiana had driven her car off a bridge and into a river, with her seven-year-old son, and her five-month-old baby strapped into a car seat in the back. The seven-year-old boy had saved the baby and swum to safety. The mother had drowned. According to police, the boy reported the mother declaring that there was too much evil in the world and that the three of them would be better off in God's hands.

A still photograph of the boy came up onscreen. His eyes were wide and his sandy blond hair was tousled. He wore a grin, as though he had just been surprised. Michael wondered how long it might be before he smiled like that again.

When the next story came on, about the current standings in the NFL, he felt relief, as though he had been set free of the sadness of the story before it. With the television on the house was not so quiet and he did not feel as lonesome. But that was the irony of television. Too many people considered it a friend, but it was a friend that lacked the courtesy not to tell you what you didn't want to hear.

His body smelled stale. He turned the volume up on the TV, then went into the bathroom and turned the water in the shower to its hottest setting. Steam began to fog the room moments later, clouding the mirror over the sink. The drone of CNN voices combated the noise of the shower. He was glad for the voices, and for the steam. When he stepped in and closed the glass door of the shower stall, he kept his gaze fixed on the interior wall and did not look out into the bathroom.

Michael Dansky had never been claustrophobic, but of late he had grown hesitant to enter enclosed spaces. His shower was brief, and he hurried out of the bathroom, dripping onto the carpet as he dried off in front of the television set, letting the news story about some political imbroglio distract him.

After the long, sleepless night, he wanted very much to be out of his house. But he was not foolish enough to believe that things would return to normal once he was out the door. The world had been twisted up, and it would take more than a new day to fix it.

He did not bother to shave. Once he was out of the shower, it felt as though he was being propelled, as though he was on fast-forward. Michael put on blue jeans and shoes, a fresh T-shirt, and a hooded New England Patriots sweatshirt that would probably not be warm enough.

As he went out of the house through the door that led from the kitchen to the garage, he noticed a note from Jillian on the kitchen table. There was a big heart drawn on it. Michael did not even slow down to figure out what the note said. Something about dinner with Lee Van Cleef, he was sure. But he would be back in time for that. It would be getting dark at that point, though, and he hoped that Jillian came home before nightfall.

He didn't really want to be in the house by himself when it got dark. The first time he had seen the girl it had been in his office, with the sunlight shining outside. But at night it was more difficult for him to believe that it was all in his head, all his imagination.

IT WAS A WORK DAY for most people, so the traffic was light, but the roads weren't completely deserted. So much for his personal apocalypse. He drove out Old Route 12 but went directly to his destination without stopping. It would be better to start from the beginning, back where it had all begun.

The Wayside Inn was not open for lunch on weekdays. Michael parked at an odd angle in the center of the lot and climbed out of the car. There were no other vehicles there but he went up to the front door anyway. Some invisible tether inside his chest seemed to guide him, as though there was an anchor here, as though he might grab hold of one end of his lifeline and follow it out to the point where his whole world had fallen apart. Michael was an optimist by nature. And still a young man. But not so young and not so optimistic that he believed anything could be that simple. Life did not work that way. If you broke something, you had to fix it. There was no going back and undoing it.

Especially if it was a human thing. A life. A friendship. A trust.

A mind.

So there was no magic to be found here. But perhaps if he could follow that tether back out to the place where it had all gone wrong, if he could retrace the steps he had made that night, he could set his mind and heart at ease. And if he could, then maybe the lost girl, regardless of whether she was a ghost or an obsession, would stop haunting him.

The pavement scuffed under his shoes as he left the Wayside Inn and crossed the lot back to his car. A cold wind eddied down low, and an empty beer can rolled and then tumbled end over end across the tar. Michael paused to watch. The wind hesitated and then gusted several times, teasing the beer can, almost letting it go and then seizing it again, carrying it away.

He glanced once more at the Wayside Inn. In his mind's eye

he could see quite clearly the festivities from that night. Jillian, so beautiful in her gown. The glass she had dropped over the banister. Teddy Polito in his Henry VIII costume. And Michael as D'Artagnan. Bowing with a flourish. The feather in that stupid hat.

Escorting Jillian to the car, hoping she wouldn't fall down.

The face of the Wayside Inn was closed, the windows secure, the doors locked, the lights off. The place wasn't dead, though. It was only sleeping.

Back in the car, he turned the key in the ignition and sat a moment while the engine purred. He imagined watching himself load Jillian into the backseat, watching himself back out of the space and then start out of the parking lot. Michael put the car in gear and gave it some gas, picturing his Saturday night self driving off ahead of him. He pulled out of the parking lot of the Wayside Inn, in pursuit of a memory that he hoped would heal him.

In his mind he tried to re-create that night. He could remember Jillian snoring lightly, unconscious on the backseat. Following the same route he had used on Saturday evening, he made his way to Old Route 12 again and started back toward home. More than ever, he could recall with perfect clarity that he had not been drunk when he left the Wayside Inn. At the masquerade, he had had several bottles of Guinness, but Jillian had been the drunk one. He had to look out for her. And he would never have gotten himself drunk when he knew that he had to drive his wife home. No way would he have risked Jillian for another bottle of Guinness.

The tires hummed along the road, now, and Michael's sleepless night was catching up with him. His eyes felt heavy. The chalk white sky had burned away a bit and there was some blue up above. Sunlight gleamed off the hood. He continued to follow his memory.

Here, he thought.

He blinked and glanced out the windows at both sides of the

road. There was an antique-looking gas station coming up on the left, one of the first in the state; the owners cultivated its appearance to make it part service station and part tourist attraction. It was a bit of the local color of living in the Merrimack Valley.

Right about here he had become very drowsy, and the feeling of drunkenness had deepened. His head had felt as though it was stuffed with cotton; even now, days later, with the sun shining and the sky turning blue, he could taste the aluminum flavor in the back of his throat. The memory merged with his lack of sleep and Michael reached out to turn up the radio, tuning it to a hard rock station. Something that would thump along in time with the ache that was beginning to pulse in the back of his skull. He opened the window, letting the cold air in, and continued to pursue the echo of his Saturday night.

Old Route 12 wound lazily through the valley on a path that was fascinatingly circuitous. Nobody would approve such a road in modern times. It would be considered ridiculously inefficient. But with the hills rising up on both sides and the thick woods that banked the sides of the road in many places, it was a peaceful route to travel. Even the small strip malls were bordered by forest. There were houses set back in the trees along the road, and numerous streets branched off of Old Route 12 at varying angles, leading into neighborhoods and developments that could have been used to trace the history of housing in Massachusetts for the past half-century.

His eyelids fluttered. "Shit," Michael whispered, and he sat up straighter. He drove past a convenience store on the left and instantly regretted it. A coffee or even a bottle of Coke would have been welcome at the moment. Anything with caffeine. He let out a long breath and pushed the fingers of his left hand through his hair.

He forced his mind back to Saturday night again, watching the road ahead. There was a signpost: ENTERING JAMESON. The road gently curved to the left, then cut dramatically back in the other direction. It straightened out for a couple of hundred yards. The tires hummed and the engine purred and he nodded to himself as his eyes focused on the turn up ahead. The road turned right again. Straight ahead there were only trees, including a massive oak whose trunk split about ten feet up into a towering wishbone.

Right here. You could have died here, he thought. *Could have killed Jilly, too.*

The effects of the Guinness and whatever else was in his system had gotten the better of him right here. He had closed his eyes and, for just a few moments, had fallen asleep behind the wheel of the car. Now, six days later, with the sun shining on a cold November afternoon, he slowed and took the turn with both caution and attention.

In his mind's eye, he saw what happened immediately afterward. He had regained control of the car, stopped the tires from skidding, gotten the steering wheel straightened out, and then looked up just in time to see the girl on the side of the road. He was too far over, on the soft shoulder. She was silhouetted in his headlights, big eyes and a halo of blond hair, blue jeans and that peasant blouse.

Too cold. She wasn't dressed for the cold, he thought. *Where was her jacket?*

But the lost girl had not seemed as though she was cold. When he had gotten her into the car, Jillian still snoozing in the back, Scooter had not seemed cold at all. Just lost. A bit numb. Distant. As the car now rolled on past the place where he had nearly killed the girl, where he had picked her up, he went over his memory of her again. Her house—or at least the place she had guided him to—was quite a walk from Old Route 12. Or it seemed that way. Michael wondered if, as the crow flies, it might have been shorter. She could have stumbled into some woods behind the house and become lost, wandered for a time. Other kids would have been out trick-or-treating, but not Scooter the lost girl. No jacket. And no sense of direction. Even if she was on the younger end of possibility—he figured her for eight, but she

might have been as young as six—she still ought to know uphill
from downhill.

And the house was uphill. Even as he drove, Michael glanced
up the side of the valley on his right, where the trees soaked up
the autumn sunlight. Uphill. His memory was vague, but that
was one thing he was sure of. The place was at the top of a long,
winding road, overlooking the valley.

"Shit." Michael hit the brakes, glancing over his shoulder. A
soccer mom in a minivan blasted her horn at him as she swerved
to avoid a collision. There were no other cars behind him, and he
waited while several cars passed going southwest, then pulled a
U-turn.

The grinding music on the radio had given way to an ad
for windshield glass replacement. Michael punched the button and the radio clicked off, plunging the car into silence
save for the engine and the rapid beat of his own heart in
his ears. He backtracked a short way, letting the car roll along
the shoulder until he reached the spot that had drawn his attention.

A narrow side street with trees grown up on both sides. There
was a pole, but no sign on top of it. It was deceiving. Anyone
who did not know better would assume that it was some dead
end, or some minor street that looped around to nowhere. But
Michael knew better.

"Turn right here." Scooter had recognized the street, and to
his astonishment, he had remembered it, too. Hidden away.

A FedEx truck rumbled past him, shaking the car. When the
street was clear, he took a left and went up that road. The sense
of familiarity that swept over him was both encouraging and unsettling at the same time. There were houses set back in the
woods, but he wasn't paying much attention to them. The next
turn was a left. That much he recalled. Perhaps a quarter of a
mile up the street, and there it was.

Michael had to stop, engine idling with his foot on the brake,
and stare at that left turn. It seemed somehow impossible. His
experience on Saturday night had such a dreamlike quality that

to find this place while he was awake, while the sun was shining, seemed unreal.

He turned left, the road immediately curving right, turning uphill.

His memory of the rest of the journey was unclear. There was nothing for him to do but explore, and so he began. For more than an hour he drove around the back roads that branched away from that street south of Old Route 12, rising up the side of that hill. There were new developments and others that had been built as far back as the fifties. Down one street, he spotted a house still bedecked with a showcase of Halloween decorations. It sparked his memory. He had passed this way.

Similar clues let him fill in his path. Michael had the copy he had made of the map of the area, and he marked the streets with a green highlighter that had snuck out of the office in his pocket.

An A-frame house. Perhaps not the same one, but he would take that risk. How many of them could there be up here? The style was rare enough that it was worth betting the odds.

His stomach rumbled. Michael realized he was hungry. He let the car roll to a stop in front of the A-frame, and a smile played across his features. Hungry was such a normal thing. He passed several people bicycling, two women power-walking, and an overweight, bearded man smoking a cigarette while he walked his dog. But that was it. No sign of *her.*

The ghostly girl who had spent the night haunting the corner of his bedroom seemed less real, less tangible, after hours in the car.

Because this feels real. This makes it real. The hidden road was there. The suburban neighborhood with the garish Halloween decorations. The A-frame.

If he searched long enough, he was certain to find that long, curving street that would take him up to the circle at the top of the hill, to that dilapidated, sprawling old house with its shattered lantern and hanging shutters, with its dark-eye windows.

The home of the lost girl. *Where I belong,* she had called it. And what an odd way to say she was home.

But it was not long before his optimism began to bleed and weaken. Michael tried every side street that appeared to lead uphill. Several wound around and did, eventually, make it near what appeared to be the apex of this particular ridge. But none of them led to that house. To *her* house. As he began the third hour of his search, Michael used the word "fuck" more than he had in a month. With his map out, he marked all of the streets he had traveled, and in time, he found himself at the top of Briarwood Terrace, in a circle that deadended much like the one where Scooter lived, and he was at a loss.

With a sigh he climbed out of the car, killing the engine and pocketing the keys. He pulled the map out and laid it on the hood, bending over to examine it more closely. The wind ruffled the edges of the map. He traced his highlighter over Briarwood Terrace and stared at the names of streets, at the green lines that showed his search.

East, he thought. *It's got to be further east.* Michael ran one finger over the paper toward the eastern edge of the map. Then he stepped back and glanced around, looking at the trees on the horizon in a full circle. Yes, to the east, the ridge seemed to rise even higher. It was hard to gauge the distance, though, because the blue sky was darkening, the shadows on the treetops growing deeper.

A shiver went through him. Michael glanced around, frowning as he peered into the trees behind the century-old Victorian behind him. Nothing moved in the woods. Most of the leaves had already fallen. Yet he felt the cold, familiar feeling of someone watching.

Nervously he gathered up the map and looked around again. The only way out was to drive back down the way he'd come, so he was nowhere near the street he was looking for. *But maybe I'm getting closer,* he thought.

As he climbed into the car and started it up, he noticed once again that the sky was a deeper blue than it had been. Nightfall was still a ways off, but much closer than he would have liked. Jillian was expecting him home so they could go out for dinner with Bob Ryan. Michael brought up his right hand and ran his palm over his stubbled chin. He would have to shave before he dressed for dinner.

Time to go home.

It was frustrating to abandon his search, but he did not feel the hours had been wasted. The map showed him where he had searched and where he had not. And he had let his stomach growl emptily for long enough. These were compelling reasons to go home, to come back another day. But in his gut, the real reason was obvious. The woods were casting long shadows on the road now; sometimes the night could be clever, stealing across the valley on cat feet, darkness swallowing day before anyone was prepared. It was that time of year. The night coming earlier with every passing day.

Yes, it was time to go home.

But only for now.

With an entire day gone by without any strange incidents, and with the landmarks he recognized as solid evidence that the previous weekend's events had actually taken place, he was more convinced than ever that he was suffering some obsession. A psychiatrist might be able to help, but finding the house and the girl would go a long way toward erasing that obsession, and setting him free of it.

He would find her. And that house.

Now that he had begun, Michael was not the type to give up. Once or twice as he searched a strange thought had occurred to him, that perhaps the house did not want to be found. Ridiculous, but that was what a couple of hours of sleep could do to him.

No, Michael would find that house. He would find answers.

JILLIAN WATCHED THE WORLD GO by outside the windows of the train. She loved the autumn, even after dark. The houses she could see had warm lights on inside, and she saw many with smoke rising from their chimneys. She could practically smell that wonderful scent of burning wood that made a chilly night so much more pleasant. Sometimes she and Michael liked to make hot cocoa and sit on the front steps of the house on a night like this, smelling the chimney smoke and watching the stars.

A sigh escaped her lips and she pressed them tightly together. She was worried about her Michael. Regardless of the tests the doctor had ordered for him, she was fairly certain there was more to his anxiety and hallucinations than someone slipping him a mickey in his beer. If anyone even actually called it that. A mickey? What was the origin of that phrase?

Her mind was wandering because she let it. Better that than to think about her certainty that Michael needed a shrink. No shame in it, absolutely. But a hallucination was serious business. She was hoping it was a combination of factors. Stress, over-work, and some asshole drugging him might all have combined to do it. Jillian had a dozen little speeches that she ran through her mind, telling herself it was really nothing. That it would be taken care of by the doctors. Michael would be all right, mind and body, in no time.

But that was a bullshit placebo for the little burning ember of terror that sparked in her heart at the idea of something truly awful happening to him. She couldn't bear even the thought of it. In all her life no one had ever really understood her, ever seemed to even *want* to know all of her, never mind being capa-ble of it, except for Michael.

He's going to be fine. A couple of days of sleeping late and work-ing at home were exactly what he needed. Dr. Ufland and Dr. Lee would take care of him, and Jillian would do her best to dis-tract him from thinking about such things.

The truth was, as excited as she was about dinner tonight and about the prospect of running for the council, she had been tempted to cancel. It felt wrong, somehow, to be thinking of herself. But that would only feed Michael's anxiety. And a night out like this might be exactly what he needed.

The train began to slow. Jillian let her gaze focus beyond the windows again, and she could see over the backyard fence that ran behind a row of houses. It always fascinated her, seeing people's lives from that angle. There was laundry out hanging on a line, despite the temperature. One house had piles of raked leaves that had not been picked up and had started to blow around again. Another had an old car up on blocks—a rusty Thunderbird, if she recognized it correctly—and a stretch of earth that had been a garden only a couple of months earlier.

From the train she could see people's backyards, the things that they were hiding from the world behind the faces put on by the fronts of their homes. She tried to picture her own backyard and could not even remember what was back there.

With a hiss and a loud clanking, they slowly crawled into the station. It had been recently renovated; the lampposts on the train platform were elegant, reminiscent of another age. Already there were Christmas decorations hanging from the posts. Wreaths with bows, and holiday lights. The sight gave her a bit of hope in her heart, a reprieve from her worried thoughts.

He'll be all right, she told herself again.

Jillian was running late. She had phoned Michael from the office to let him know, but there had been no answer at home. On the machine she left a message that he should just meet her at Dorothy's Restaurant, that they were supposed to be there by seven o'clock. Much as she would have liked to go home and change, there was nothing to be done for it. She looked all right to go out for dinner, in a chocolate-brown tailored suit with a hunter green turtleneck under the jacket. But after being in the same outfit all day, it would have been nice to freshen up.

Life was simply like that, sometimes. You had to roll with it.

From the train station, she drove directly to Dorothy's. It was almost a quarter after seven by the time she pulled into the lot. The restaurant was on the expensive side, despite its strangely quaint location. It was actually the first floor of the home of the family that owned and ran it, and the entire place was decorated in homage to *The Wizard of Oz*. The food was wonderful, though, and the place was small, so reservations were difficult to come by. She had felt a bit of trepidation at not having been able to reach Michael, and the underlying concern for him that had been with her all day, but as she stepped out of the car and started toward the front door of the restaurant, other concerns took precedence.

Can I really do this? she wondered. Jillian was a woman with opinions, and the will to do something about it. But her image of politicians in general was so poor that the idea of becoming one of them was laden with doubts. Then again, what was that saying? Something about the only thing necessary for the bad guys to win was for the good guys to do nothing.

Well, I'm not a guy, and I'm not riding a white horse or anything, but . . . She did not finish the thought in any concrete way. There was no need. Her feelings on the subject ran deep enough that it wasn't necessary to formulate them into full-blown sentences. Jillian Dansky certainly did not picture herself as some kind of hero, or martyr, but she did believe that she could help. That she could do some good.

When she walked into the restaurant, the buzz of conversation struck her and set her at ease. There was a large fireplace on either end of the long dining room, and both were blazing. Behind a podium by the door was Dorothy herself, a fiftyish woman who refused to dye her graying hair, but wore it in a stylish cut.

"Good evening, and welcome to Dorothy's," she said. "Meeting someone?"

"A group, actually," Jillian confirmed. "It might be under Ryan. They should be here——"

"Oh, you're with Bob's party," Dorothy said pleasantly, a twinkle of mischief in her youthful eyes. "Poor girl. Right this way."

The woman led her to the far corner, where a loud group were chatting and drinking around a large table by the fire. Bob Ryan was there, of course, with his wife, Yvonne. She saw Ben and Carole Bartolini. It took her a moment to recognize Mary Elizabeth Tilden, who was also an incumbent on the council, and she assumed the man with her was her husband. With these three on her side—if they were on her side—she would have an excellent chance of being elected. But she was well aware that if they were on her side, that also meant that she was on theirs. Town politics were bitter and hard fought, with grudges going back generations. If she allied herself with these people, she'd be gaining the support of their friends, but she would also be earning the spite of their enemies.

Something to think about.

At the moment, however, all such thoughts were banished to the back of her mind.

For at the back of the table, his back to the corner, Michael Dansky sat, smiling and laughing and entertaining the people she hoped to make her cronies. He wore a white collarless, button-down shirt beneath a brown suede jacket that she knew he kept on more because it looked nice than because he was cold. His eyes sparkled as he whispered something funny to Yvonne Ryan and they laughed together. He was freshly shaven and his cheeks shone in the glow of the fire.

Her husband looked like himself again. This was *her* Michael. Happy and relaxed. He had a glass of wine in front of him, and as he spotted her approaching he raised it in a silent toast to her, one corner of his mouth rising in a lopsided smile.

It was that smile that had seduced her. That smile that had won her. He wasn't arrogant, but he was a passionate man, and he wanted to share that enthusiasm with others.

Seeing him like that, Jillian could not stop the small laugh that bubbled out of her. She took a deep breath, and it was as though the fear and anxiety floated away with it. With Michael there, and at ease, she would feel comfortable with Ryan and his friends. With him backing her up, she was capable of anything.

Michael stood as she approached the table. The other men did as well, and she said her hellos all around, shaking hands and kissing Ryan's cheek. When she at last made her way over to the empty seat next to her husband, he pulled it out for her, but before she could sit down he took her by the hand. Jillian studied his face. There were dark circles under his eyes. Obviously he had not gotten enough sleep the night before. But the change in him was clear.

"Hey," he said. "How was your day?" He kissed her, just a soft brush on her lips.

"Hectic. How was yours? You seem . . . better."

Michael smiled. "Not completely. But I think I'm getting a handle on things." He lowered his voice and whispered to her. "It's possible I've only lost a few of my marbles, instead of the whole bag."

With a soft chuckle, she glanced at him, one eyebrow raised.

"Sit down, Jillian. Order a drink," Bob Ryan called pleasantly. She gave him a polite smile and then looked back at Michael.

"I'll explain later," he continued, still whispering in her ear with the intimacy of husband and wife. "For now, let's enjoy dinner. You've got votes to win."

As THE HOUR BEFORE MIDNIGHT wore on, Michael lay on the dark red floral print sofa in his living room and watched Humphrey Bogart bicker with Katharine Hepburn. His eyes burned and his body ached with exhaustion, but he had passed the point of ordinary sleepiness earlier. What he needed, after the surreal haunting of the previous night and the all-too-solid and ordinary effort he had put into searching for Scooter's house that day, was some time to wind down. *The African Queen* had been just starting when he and Jillian had come in from dinner. It was one of Michael's favorite films, and he could think of no better way to let the tension slip out of him than spending a couple of hours with Bogey and Kate.

Jilly had joined him at first, kicking off her shoes and snuggling up with him on the sofa. In what seemed like minutes, he had heard her breath deepen and settle into a steady rhythm. Only when he jostled her did she open her eyes.

"Maybe I should go wash my face," she said. "I want to get my makeup off. Get out of my work clothes."

Michael had smiled at her. "Need any help with that?"

"I think I can handle it, Mr. Dansky."

"Well, if you change your mind, you know where to find me," he had told her.

But he knew she wouldn't come back down. It was late, and her history of insomnia made her reluctant to stay up past midnight or so, as though that might be inviting a sleepless night. Usually, Michael would have gone up with her and just watched the movie in bed while she burrowed under the covers beside him. But tonight he was comfortable right where he was, and the truth was he was in no hurry to go back to their bedroom, no hurry to discover if that shadowy corner by the bed was occupied again.

Dinner with the council members had gone very well. If anyone had ever told him he would have enjoyed himself at a table with a bunch of politicians, he would have told them they were full of shit. But to his great surprise, he had found it easy to relax around them. It was nice to be around a group of people who had such strong opinions and were just itching for intelligent conversation and debate. The truth was, he thought he might have had an even better time than Jillian.

But there was an even deeper truth, and that was that maybe Michael had been working at it. Maybe he had been trying very hard to have a good time. Not only for the sake of Jillian's political aspirations, but because he needed it. Needed to unwind. To let go.

Whatever it was, it had worked. He felt more at ease than he had all week. A tremor would go through him anytime he would think of the strange things he had seen—or thought he had seen—but he reminded himself that that was why psychiatrists existed. If people didn't get a little fucked up now and then, the shrinks would all be out of a job. The best news of all, though, the part that comforted him the most, was the fact that he had not seen anything at all out of the ordinary since waking up that morning. Seen, or smelled, for that matter. No popcorn. No cinnamon apple pies. Nothing like that.

He was going to be all right. It might take a little time, but if he could just take a deep breath now and then, and keep his head on straight, he would be okay. Jillian was a big part of that. Just seeing her at dinner tonight, the way she glowed, the way her eyes sparkled when she laughed, was enough to start to fill up all the empty places in him. And this, lying here for a while with *The African Queen*, eyelids drooping and a warm, soothing feeling of tiredness washing over him . . . *this* was taking a deep breath.

In the midst of such thoughts, with the unshaven Bogart looking down upon him from the television screen, he drifted off to sleep.

IN HIS DREAM, HE IS driving along Old Route 12. His headlights burn the darkness ahead. The road curves left, and right, and left again. Around each turn his sleeping mind expects to see her, the little lost girl, the blond angel in the peasant blouse, caught in the glare of the lights. He feels a dreadful certainty as each turn approaches, an utter sureness that this time he will not be able to swerve in time to miss her. That the car will strike her, shattering her bones, driving her down under the tires, bumping over her and leaving only a bloodied, misshapen mess behind.

It is a terrible dream, but in its repetition, in its unforgiving redundancy, it builds to a crushing nightmare. He feels himself weeping. He wishes for the road to end, for the morning to come, for the headlights to wink out so that he will not have to see her there, pinned against the darkness as though she is some sacrifice set out for him.

He can hear the hum of the tires on the road. Oddly, he smells cotton candy.

D'Artagnan, a tiny voice whispers beside him.

His fear is for nothing. She is there in the car, on the seat beside him. He continues to guide the car around each dark corner, headlights parsing the gathering night shadows, but he can breathe easier. Beside him, her wide eyes are heavy with sorrow.

Come find me, *she whispers.*

What kind of a name is Scooter? he asks, apropos of nothing. He doesn't care. He is just glad he hasn't killed her. That he will not turn the next corner and feel the impact of the car's front grill on her flesh and bone.

Scooter, *she tells him, giving him a little-girl shrug.* Scoosan. Hilly could never say Susan.

He blinks. The smell of Thanksgiving dinner—of turkey and gravy and sweet potatoes and sausage stuffing—fills the car. The lost girl—Susan—is gone.

His gaze shifts back to the road ahead just in time to tug the wheel to the right, to avoid the massive split-trunked tree that loomed up ahead. The tires shriek as the car tears around the corner. And there she is. Captured by the head-lights. Going tharn. That was what the rabbits in Watership Down *called it, that paralysis that comes on when the headlights capture you. Going tharn. The girl is going tharn.*

The grill crushes her chest. Her body crumples and her head slams down on the hood with a wet crack. Michael lets go of the steering wheel, screaming, and he understands in that moment that he wants to die.

". . . OH," HE SAID, JUST THE tiniest little oomph of air, as he jerked awake on the sofa, heart hammering in his chest.

For a long moment he stared at the television screen. He recognized a young George C. Scott but the film was black and white, something he did not think he had ever seen before. Where was *The African Queen?* Even as he wondered, fractured images of the dream came rushing into his mind and he fought to catch his breath. His chest hurt with the grief that lingered after the dream, and yet already it was diminishing. Already the pieces of the dream were dissolving, being lost down the drain of the subconscious where all of the other dreams of his sleeping life had gone. Michael had always considered it a terrible loss, the way that the rich imaginings of his unconscious mind were cast aside upon waking.

But he had rarely been so happy to let go of a dream as he was at that moment—although something about it had been of value. He was sure of that. In his mind he could almost hear the girl's whispered voice, but he could not hold on to her words.

He shook his head and then swung his legs over to sit on the edge of the sofa. With a deep breath, still a bit disoriented, he stood. A quick glance at the clock on the cable box told him he had slept for less than an hour. Long enough for the movie to have ended and another one to have begun. He stretched and went into the kitchen for a glass of water. The light above the sink was on so he hit the switch, plunging the room into relative darkness. He drank the water and left the glass in the drainer. Out in the living room, he took a few moments to watch George C. Scott curiously, wondering what the film was. He could have used the remote control to access information about it, but his curiosity was not as powerful at the moment as his desire for the comfort of his bed and the warmth of Jillian beside him.

Michael shut the TV off and double-checked that the front door was locked. Memories of the previous night remained, but they shared space now with those of the day, and of the content-ment of his evening out. It was obvious to him from the episode on the sofa that he wasn't going to have trouble falling asleep tonight, and he took heart from that.

At the top of the stairs he went left, toward the master bed-room.

Something heavy and damp shifted in the darkness of the hall behind him. It sounded like the flap of a flag, or the rustle of a wet raincoat as it was removed.

The urge to turn, to investigate, struck him even as he reached the open bedroom door. But he never did turn. He was frozen, instead, by the sight that greeted him.

The bedroom was thick with shadows, alleviated only by the faint glow of the streetlight across the street, its illumination casting a hint of twilight across the Danskys' cherry sleigh bed.

There were five of them in a circle around the bed. Bald, stooped figures in their long, shapeless coats. Yet for the first time he noticed the wisps of silver hair, the shape of their mouths, and he realized they were not male at all, but female. Their pale skin gleamed in the darkness, gleeful expressions gruesomely phosphorescent. Jillian lay on the bed, her eyes wide and her mouth open in a silent scream as one of them bent to kiss her, mouth open so wide it seemed almost as though it might try to swallow her. The others had their hands on her, but they were not holding her down. Their fingers massaged her flesh, and in the single moment when the tableau was etched upon Michael Dansky's soul, he saw that their fingers seemed to have burrowed into the flesh of her arms and her bare legs. There was no blood, and yet they worked their fingers into her skin as though she were made of potter's clay.

Michael screamed.

Icy fingers clutched his own arms from behind. A hand clamped over his mouth, sliding down to his throat. Sharp fingers punctured his neck.

Stay away. The words felt like icy mercury injected into his vocal cords. They were spoken by his own lips, with his own mouth, but it was not his voice. They were not his words.

You can not help her. She is ours. If you continue to search, you will not like what you find.

The chilling grip on his arms sapped the strength from him, so that when he was set free, he collapsed instantly to his knees on the carpet. Like the withdrawal of a quartet of needles, the fingers retreating from his throat tugged at the flesh there. He coughed. The penetration had bruised the muscles there, but as he clapped a hand to his neck, he felt no wound. No blood.

Wheezing, gritting his teeth against the sensation that something was still lodged in his throat, he grabbed the door jamb and struggled to stand. He glanced around, but there was no sign of them. Not a single trace of that phosphorescence, the unnatural moonlight of those terrible, expressionless faces.

"Jilly," he rasped.

In the instant before he managed to focus upon their bed, he was suddenly sure she would be gone. The sight of her lying in the center of the bed with the spread drawn down, her chest rising and falling evenly, was enough to make his legs weaken beneath him. A rush of gratitude unlike anything he had ever felt filled him. He took several steps into the room and just stood over her, staring down at her, studying her to make sure there was no sign of any wound.

Jillian was pale, but otherwise she seemed unharmed. Michael shook his head. He was grateful, but he knew they had done something to her. A tremor went through his gut and he took a step nearer. She seemed to be sleeping, and he wondered how much of what just happened she would remember, and if she would think it had been a dream. He would shake her, just to be sure she was all right.

He listened to the darkness, glanced around the room for sign of any further intrusion. Already he was doubting himself. He had felt the fingers in his throat. Still felt the aftereffects of it. He had felt the words forced through his vocal cords, had been made to speak them. But he had read enough to know that it was possible that it was all still in his head. If so, well, then he was completely out of his mind.

A shrill little laugh bubbled up from inside him.

Jillian was the proof. If she had seen it. If she had felt it. If she remembered.

Yet as he reached for her shoulder to wake her, he hesitated. If she *had* seen them, what then?

As this final thought struck him, her eyes snapped open. Her gaze locked on him and her brow furrowed angrily.

"What are you looking at?" she demanded, her voice biting and cruel. In all the time he had known her, Jillian had never spoken to Michael that way. She had never even looked at him with such disdain. Now she only rolled over, turning her back to him.

"Go to bed, Michael."

For long minutes he could only stand there in the dark, watching her and trembling with exhaustion and fear, and the weight of dread crushing him. She was entirely unaware of what had happened . . . and yet they had touched her. Violated her.

Whether she recalled it or not, how could she experience that and not be wounded by it?

Michael feared that the answer was simple enough: She could not.

CHAPTER NINE

On the day Michael proposed to Jillian, nothing went as planned. As far as she knew, he was out of town on a business trip to New York to present a new campaign to a client. His position at Krakow & Bester in those days could best have been described as coffee boy. Technically he was a designer, but little to nothing of what he had sketched or conceived since being hired had actually been used. His work on the Lifeboat account was about to change that. Despite the odd name, the company sold men's and women's clothing—mostly comfortable, earth-toned apparel. Every other campaign had been some funny twist on boating, or on an actual lifeboat. People sitting in a small watercraft staring at one another. The company wanted to get away from that.

In a meeting in which he was the junior member of the team, Michael bluntly told them he thought that was a mistake. He had put his job on the line with those words. Rolled the dice.

"What do you mean?" the marketing director of Lifeboat, Chet Griggs, had asked.

The weight of the attention on him was almost more than he could bear.

Michael had shrugged and attempted to appear relaxed. "It's just . . . well, for instance, what about this? Instead of people on a lifeboat, let's riff off of *Titanic* a little. A bunch of people are already in a lifeboat that's starting to be lowered down to the water. A few people are jumping into it. Except our guy, the guy dressed head to toe in *your* clothes, he's got this heavy steamer trunk and we can see a shirtsleeve sticking out, like it was packed in a hurry. And your logo is all over the trunk, right? And there's a member of the ship's crew, a purser or whatever, stopping him. 'Sorry, pal, you have to leave your trunk behind. No room for your belongings.'

"Our guy, though, he seems pretty calm. 'You go on ahead, then. I'll take my chances.' He won't get off the ship without his clothes. We do it as a series of ads, three or four, telling the story in sequence, and the last one is the best one. In the middle of the ocean, the guy's sitting on top of his trunk, sort of bobbing on the waves. Logo prominently displayed on the trunk. Lifeboat. And he's cool as a cucumber, just sitting there, or even lying back and enjoying the sun, abandoned in the middle of the ocean. But damn, he's got that trunk of Lifeboat clothes, so he's happy. And the tag line . . . I don't know, I'm not a writer, but something like 'Lifeboat. Apparel for every occasion.' Maybe 'every adventure.' Something like that."

When he had finished, they were all still staring at him, but now their expressions revealed their surprise. Carl Berger, who'd been the senior art director at Krakow & Bester then, had frowned, sensing the change in the tone of the meeting. The clients were paying attention to Michael now, and not to him. Maybe he would have said something then, something to swing it back into his control. But he hesitated a moment too long.

The marketing chief, Griggs, smiled at him. "That's not what we were looking for, kid."

Michael had blinked, face flushing with heat. "I know. It's just, I—"

"It's better," Griggs went on. "Much better than any of the limp-dicked shit that we came up with." He pointed at Carl,

Michael's immediate superior back then, and his grin widened. "And it's much better than any of the crap you've suggested, Carl. Truth is, I wasn't thinking your agency was going to be able to give us what we need. But the kid may have just scored you the gig."

"That's . . . well, yeah," Carl Berger had muttered. "Michael's got a great eye. Great instinct."

That was what he had said. But Michael already knew enough about the business to know what Carl was thinking: *You little prick, you upstage me like that one more time and I'll have you gone from Krakow & Bester so fast they'll put your goddamned picture on a milk carton.*

Lifeboat wasn't going to give them an answer that day, so Michael had driven back up to Massachusetts with Carl, a dreadful silence filling the car most of the time. Carl hadn't even wanted the radio on. Michael had known the guy was pissed, but hadn't understood why Carl could not just be pleased that it seemed they had a shot at the account. He could not have known that the man's job was already in jeopardy.

Krakow & Bester scored the account. The marketing director, Griggs, made no secret of the fact that it had been Michael's ideas that won them over. Paul Krakow gave the account to Michael, along with a promotion to art director. Carl quit the next day.

A week later, it was easy to convince Jillian that he had to go down to New York to make the presentation of the concept sketches to Lifeboat. Jillian was thrilled for him, and Michael was more than a little excited himself. But not about Lifeboat. Not on that day.

He had arranged everything so carefully, which made it almost funny when it all fell apart. Jillian's little sister Hannah had arranged for the two of them to meet for lunch at the Publick House on Beacon Hill in Boston. It was the place Jillian had taken Michael for his birthday on that first day they'd had lunch. It was a dark little pub, with dim lights and candles, even during the day. But it was quaint, and the food was good, and they'd enjoyed themselves quite a bit and gone back several times. Once, they had brought Hannah, so it wasn't a total giveaway that Hannah would ask Jillian to meet her there.

Lunch. Then maybe a quick shopping trip in Downtown Crossing. Jillian was always nervous about taking long lunches, but she could get away with it from time to time. It all made sense. It was foolproof.

But it was a Tuesday. And the Publick House was closed on Tuesdays.

Michael had taken the day off and slept a little late. When the phone rang, he had just stepped out of the shower and started to lather up his face to shave. He cursed, ran for the phone, and picked it up just in time to cut off his own voice on the answering machine.

"Hello?"

"It's Hannah."

He knew immediately, just from her tone.

"What's wrong?"

As she told him, Michael began to cuss and he stomped his foot. Flecks of shaving cream sprayed off of his face. He ought to have known, he told himself. It all seemed too perfect.

"I'm sorry, Michael. I guess I should have called and checked first, but, I mean, who's closed on a Tuesday? Monday I could understand, but Tuesday?"

He consoled Hannah, telling her not to worry. After all, he was the one who should have checked the whole thing out, but it had never occurred to him, either.

"I could call her, tell her we'll go somewhere else. But she said she was going to be in a meeting all morning."

"Don't worry about it," Michael told her. "Just call and cancel. I'll take it from here."

"What are you going to do? I mean, she knows it's coming, right? She just doesn't know when. So how are you going to surprise her?"

He laughed softly to himself, holding the phone slightly

away from his face to keep shaving cream from getting on it. "I don't know. I'm Indiana Jones, today. I'm making it up as I go along."

An hour and a half later he was in Boston. He had put on a brand new, crisp pair of blue jeans and a dark green sweater. His shoes were a bit scuffed, but not so badly that anyone would notice. The sky was a milky blue, as though it wasn't entirely sure whether it felt like being cloudy or not. It wasn't quite lunchtime yet, but already there were people swarming the streets, walking rapidly along with briefcases in their hands, or clutching cell phones to their ears. Women wore suits, many of them skirts, with sneakers for comfort. It was a strange sight, unique to big cities, and he never got used to it. But it always made him smile.

There was a chilly breeze sweeping through the streets of Boston, coming in from the harbor and making flags and awnings flap. Even so, it was a nice day in Boston. A day for walking through the Common with someone special, or window-shopping on Newbury Street. But Michael had more important things to do.

His first stop was at Milk Street Florist, where he picked up a dozen long-stemmed roses in a vase. He was improvising, so the vase was a necessary expense. The same thing applied when he stopped at a liquor store to buy a bottle of champagne. Perrier-Jouët was expensive enough without the pair of fluted champagne glasses he bought to go with it. He never hesitated, however. These were the things he needed for this moment. Jillian was worth it a thousand times over.

All through this morning marathon, his pulse was racing. His face felt flushed and his hands shook. He was nervous and excited all at the same time, on the verge of giddy laughter every moment.

From the lobby he called Jillian's number. Her group shared a secretary and he said a tiny prayer that she would answer the phone.

"Jillian Lopresti's line."

"Kyra, it's Michael Dansky. If Jillian's there with you, don't let her know I'm on the phone," he said quickly.

"Michael?" the secretary whispered back. "No, she's in a meeting. She'll be out any minute, though."

He thought his heart would burst if it didn't slow down. "No, look. I'm downstairs and—"

"I thought you were in New York."

The girl meant well, but he wanted to throttle her. "Kyra, please, listen. I'm coming up. I need you to meet me at the main desk and sneak me back to her office. I want to surprise her."

"Oh, seriously?" Kyra asked, a little-girl thrill in her voice. "Is today the day?"

"Yes. Please don't blow it for me."

"No way!" Kyra replied. "Hurry and get up here, though. She's seriously going to be out of that meeting, like, any minute."

"I'm coming."

It was the longest elevator ride of his life. Michael was disoriented when he stepped out onto Jillian's floor, but then the door on the far right opened and Kyra beckoned to him. Her giddy smile made him laugh. Co-conspirators, they hurried through a row of cubicles to avoid using the main corridor, and in moments she had safely ensconced him in Jillian's office.

"I'll call her number and let it ring once when she's on the way."

Michael nodded and then Kyra closed the door, shutting him in. His arms were full and he was careful not to drop anything. He unwrapped the roses and put them in the vase, ignoring the price sticker on the crystal and not bothering to put any water in it. There was time for that later. He pulled the champagne out of its paper bag and set the two fluted glasses beside it on her desk. Then, from his front right pocket, he withdrew the small, black velvet case.

When he opened it, the diamond engagement ring glittered in the harsh office light.

He took one last, very deep breath, and arranged the open box on the desk so that she could see it when she walked in. Then he sat in her chair and waited for the phone to ring.

It never did.

Jillian walked in less than two minutes after he had sat down. Michael felt like he couldn't breathe. His heart skipped every other beat. His throat was dry. But when he saw the expression on Jillian's face, everything changed. Her gaze swept the office, staring at him a moment; then she blinked and focused on the desk. On the roses, and the champagne.

On the ring.

"Hi, sweetie," Michael said.

Jillian raised a hand up to cover her mouth, but she could not hide her utter surprise and joy. A little, wondrous laugh came out of her and she shook her head, not in denial but in amazement. The best thing about her reaction was that she had known he was going to propose. Known that he was going to buy the ring, even. But the moment had snuck up on her so entirely that it had taken her by surprise in spite of that knowledge.

"Oh, my God," she said, as Michael stood up from her chair.

He went to her, picking the ring up off the desk and holding it up for her to see. "Jillian Lopresti, will you marry me?"

Tears filled her eyes and rolled down her face. Her smile was radiant. "You're supposed to be in New York," she said, slapping him on the arm.

Michael laughed. "That's not an answer."

Jillian nodded. "Yes. Yes, of course."

And she slid into his arms, shaking, and he held her tight, supporting her, for in that moment it felt as though all the strength had gone out of her and his embrace was the only thing keeping her on her feet.

But that was all right.

Michael would have been happy to hold her like that forever.

•   •   •

By Monday morning, Jillian was dying to get out of the house. Michael wasn't sick. He was depressed or having a breakdown or something, but he wasn't sick. On Friday night he had seemed his old self again, but all day Saturday and Sunday he had been stumbling around the house, as pale and just about as eloquent as a zombie. He was "working from home" again today. She had tried to be as understanding as she could, but there was a point at which reality had to kick in.

Get over it, she thought. *Deal.*

When she reached One International Place she stopped in the lobby to get the biggest, blackest, most caffeinated coffee she could find. For some reason she felt exhausted this morning, and no amount of concealer had been enough to hide the dark circles beneath her eyes. Jillian felt like crap, and she knew she looked like crap. It was shaping up to be a wonderful day.

There were too many people on the elevator and she felt claustrophobic and fought the urge to hit someone. No one from the firm was on the elevator with her except a Dominican mailroom boy with bad skin. Jillian avoided looking at him.

She waved her key card at the pad beside the frosted glass doors, then pushed her way inside. The receptionist brightened immediately upon seeing her.

"Morning, Jillian. How was your commute?"

Jillian barely slowed down as she passed the desk. "I managed to get here without killing anyone. I guess that passes for good."

The receptionist's eyes widened and she made a little o with her mouth. Only when Jillian was already a dozen feet down the corridor did she hear the girl behind the desk mutter "Je-sus."

Jillian froze, then turned on her heel and marched back to the desk. The girl blanched when she appeared once more, glaring down.

"Did you say something, Gabrielle?"

"Um, no."

"Well, *um*, it sure sounded like you did. Do you have a problem this morning?"

Gabrielle's eyes narrowed. She bit her lower lip, and it was clear that whatever she wanted to say, she was holding it back. "You were in such a hurry I didn't have a chance to tell you that Ron wants to see you. He asked me to tell you when you came in."

For a long moment Jillian only stared at her, trying to decide how far she wanted to go with it. She had always gotten along with Gabrielle, but this morning the girl's tone had really pissed her off.

She nodded. "Fine."

Phones were ringing as she strode through the office of Dawes, Gray & Winter. People hurried past her, arms loaded with contracts and briefs, documents to copy, or trays of coffee, bagels, and muffins headed for one meeting or another. Voices clashed in the air like some mercenary room in the Tower of Babel, talking about stocks and money and litigation. Her own office was off to the western side of the building, but she kept on straight through the beehive center of activity and then into a corridor that was painted in gentle colors, its walls adorned with tasteful art. There were potted plants here, and each office door had an engraved nameplate.

Ron Balfour was a partner in the firm, a silver-haired snake-oil salesman whose nose was red from drink and whose face matched that color anytime he became the slightest bit annoyed. He had a reputation as an excellent attorney, particularly in the courtroom. When he grew impassioned speaking to a judge or jury, spittle flew from his mouth. But he won. Jillian had no idea how many times Ron had successfully defended airlines against the claims of the families of crash victims, or chemical companies from class-action suits in communities with high cancer rates.

He was a good lawyer.

The glass wall of Ron's office was opaque, but the door was

partially open. Jillian rapped once and then ducked her head in. Ron was just hanging up the phone and gestured for her to join him.

"Jillian. Good morning. Come on in."

She stood just inside the door, arms crossed over her chest, managing to clutch her massive cup of coffee even in that position. If she let the guy stare at her tits he'd never get a sentence out that she could understand.

"What can I do for you, Ron?"

He hesitated, glancing at the door as though he wanted to ask her to close it. Jillian looked down at him impatiently, and he nodded as though she had prodded him.

"I've had a complaint from a client about one of your paralegals."

One of *your* paralegals. She didn't fail to notice the emphasis. They were his employees, but when there was some shit to sling, suddenly they belonged to her.

"Which client? Which paralegal?"

"Spence Rosen from RoyalTech called. Apparently this girl was very rude to him in a meeting the other day. I get the impression that he questioned the accuracy of certain documents and she snapped at him."

Jillian rolled her eyes and sighed. "And which *girl* would that be, Ron?"

The attorney's face darkened, flushing a deep red to match his nose. He sat back in his chair and studied her. "I don't think I like your tone, Jillian."

"And I'd say that in the hands of the right attorney, the pejorative use of 'girl,' as if your female employees are teenage chambermaids, would constitute the creation of an uncomfortable work environment related to gender issues, Ron," she said.

He opened his mouth to form some retort, then shut it again. His face flushed so deeply red it looked as though it were covered with fresh blood. With that color against his silver hair, he looked ridiculous, like some first-time Florida tourist with a lobster sunburn.

"It was a poor word choice," he said slowly, dangerously. "But I hope you aren't suggesting that I—"

Jillian shifted her weight from one foot to the other, arms still crossed, and tilted her head to glare at him. "Ron. Please. It's Monday and I've got a lot to do today. If I'm being enough of a bitch that you can't stand it, fire me. If I'm doing my job well, chalk it up to PMS and just tell me who to ream."

He blinked in shock, suddenly the picture of propriety. "Jesus, Jillian."

"Ron," she said tiredly.

"Her name is Vanessa something."

"Castille," Jillian said with a sigh. "Vanessa Castille. Third strike. She's out."

"That's a little harsh, don't you—"

"Brad Klein made it clear to me that if Vanessa screwed up again he wanted her fired. Are you telling me not to fire her?"

He contemplated that a moment and then shook his head. "No. Go on ahead. Just make sure we have a paper trail on her performance."

"Fine. Write me a memo about the complaint you got on her."

Without waiting for any further reply she turned and left his office. The day was looking brighter by the moment. As she strode through the bustle again she sipped at her coffee. It scalded her lips, but she didn't mind. Her mood could not have been any fouler.

When she reached her own little corner of the Dawes, Gray & Winter fortress, she slid into the chair behind her desk and scowled at the red light blinking on her phone. Reluctantly she put her coffee down, punched in the code for her voice mail, and listened to the messages. Her sister had called, but Jillian was in no mood for Hannah right now. There were half a dozen work-related messages that she scribbled down onto a pad to deal with after she had finished her coffee. There was a message from Michael that she deleted without even listening to. Bob Ryan had left her two messages, and there was one from a reporter at the *Eagle Tribune*, one of the larger local papers, who wanted to discuss the following year's election with her. She had not even made her candidacy official, and Ryan or one of his cronies had already leaked it. What was she supposed to say to a reporter? Hell, what was she supposed to say to Ryan, today?

Jillian let her head drop, her forehead banging the desk. *Shit. What the fuck is wrong with me?* She didn't feel like herself. The way she was behaving this morning wasn't giving her any pleasure . . . or maybe a very little bit. But if she couldn't play nice with Ron Balfour she was going to be headed out the door right after Vanessa Castille.

You stupid ass, she thought. *If you call Bob Ryan like this, your future in politics is over before it starts.* She stared at the message she had scribbled on her pad. No. Tomorrow she would call him, apologize and say she had been too busy to talk to him. Tomorrow, things would be better. Maybe Michael would even have gotten his act together and gone back to work.

Shaking her head, Jillian picked up the phone and punched in Vanessa Castille's extension. The paralegal's voice mail picked up.

"Vanessa, it's Jillian. I need to see you in my office. Now."

Her eyes hurt and itched. Her head ached. Jillian set the phone down and leaned back in her chair, massaging the bridge of her nose. She felt like she had acid on her tongue, or some kind of snake's venom, and she just wanted to spit it at people. It was the strangest feeling. There was a kind of echo in the back of her mind telling her that she ought to feel guilty, but instead she was exhilarated.

She reached for her coffee. The phone rang and she spilled some of it onto the notepad, blurring the words.

"Mother*fucker!*" she snarled.

Cursing again, she snatched up the phone. "Hello?"

"Jilly? What's wrong?"

Hannah. Jillian sighed. Of all the people she wanted to talk to this morning, her sister would have been pretty close to last on the list.

"Jilly?"

"Hannah, didn't you leave me a message?"

Her sister hesitated. "I . . . yeah, I did. I just wanted to tell—"

"Did I call you back?"

"No. Jillian, what's wrong with you? Did something happen? You sound like someone just killed your dog. If you had a dog."

For a moment Jillian could only clench her teeth and squeeze her eyes closed. Then she laughed softly.

"Hannah, if I haven't called you back that means I don't have time for you right now. That's what voice mail is for. When I do have time, I'll call you back. Until then, just let me breathe, okay? I'm your sister, not your fucking boyfriend."

All she heard on the phone was a little gasp. But she knew Hannah. Any second now her sister would start in with the hurt feelings and all of that.

Jillian hung up on her.

It wasn't half a minute before there came a knock on her door and she looked up to see Vanessa Castille standing in the doorway. The woman's expression showed plainly just how worried she was. Jillian had no patience for trying to be her friend today. She was the boss. It was time she started acting like it.

"You wanted to see me?" Vanessa began.

"Any idea why?" Jillian asked.

Vanessa shook her head, trying to mask the obvious, like someone getting pulled over for doing seventy in a thirty-five-mile-per-hour zone and acting all mystified about why the cop would bother her.

"The other day when I talked to you about the Lyons Publishing thing, I thought I made it clear to you that you needed to avoid making any other mistakes."

Vanessa stared at her. "I didn't. I mean, I don't think I did."

There was a hurt-little-girl thing going on with her, both in her face and her voice, and it made Jillian want to slap her.

Maybe Ron Balfour had used the right word for Vanessa after all.

"One of the senior partners had a complaint from a client about your behavior. You were rude, apparently."

Vanessa tried for solemn indignation. She stood a bit straighter. "I think I deserve at least to know what I've been accused of and who's doing the accusing."

Jillian nodded. "You're probably right. But I don't have the stamina for dealing with bullshit like this right now, so you're going to have to get the details from Human Resources during your exit interview."

"My . . ." Vanessa began to hyperventilate a little and she took a step back, shaking her head. "Jillian, come on. Don't . . . my exit interview? We're friends. What are you doing?"

It was funny. Jillian couldn't help it. She laughed.

"Friends? We get along, Vanessa, but it's not like we're chatting on the phone every night about the size of our husbands' dicks. You're an employee of this firm. I'm your boss. Now, seriously, I don't have the time for this and my head hurts like a bitch. Pack up your crap and get out of here by lunchtime. Call H.R. to make an appointment for the interview. We'll mail your last check."

THE AFTERNOON SUNLIGHT REACHED LONG fingers across the floor of the Danskys' living room. Dust motes danced in those shafts of autumn light and Michael watched them, entranced. He lay upon his side on the sofa, legs tucked up under him in near-fetal repose. The television had not been on today. He had not read a single page from a book. The morning newspaper still lay at the end of the driveway. The postman had come, but the mail remained in its box.

In the silence of the house he could hear the hum of the refrigerator and the tick of the clock from the kitchen. He could hear trucks passing by on the main road, not far away. All weekend he had moved through the house as though he himself had become the ghost, haunting it. He had spent today on the sofa, not moving except to piss and to eat a bowl of Cheerios when his stomach growled. He barely tasted them. The house seemed to breathe around him. From time to time he had the distinct impression that he was not alone. The pressure in the room changed and he felt certain that if he looked behind him, he would see the girl there.

Scooter.

Or, worse, the ugly women in their shapeless coats. Misshapen women whose long fingers had been like daggers as they slipped into Jillian's skin, sinking into her flesh without leaving a wound. . . .

"Oh, Jesus," Michael whispered, breaking the silence.

But there was no one in the house to hear him. The clock ticked. The refrigerator hummed. The dust motes danced. And there he lay, frozen. Outside the living room window he saw figures moving along the street and he held his breath, held down a scream that pushed against the backs of his lips.

Voices reached him, muffled by the windows. Laughter.

It was just kids, fresh off the school bus, walking home. Even now he could hear the rumble of the bus as it trundled along to its next stop. A girl passed by, perhaps twelve years old. She had black hair and a bright red jacket, and she swung her backpack as she went past the window. Two boys followed her, bumping each other and laughing. All on their way home.

Michael felt trapped in his own living room. He wished he could call to them, ask them to come in and watch television in his house, just for company. Just for life and laughter. But he could never have done such a thing. What would their parents think?

And what might happen to them here? he wondered. Would the ugly women appear again, to touch them with fingers that passed through flesh like water?

He swallowed and his throat burned. A shiver went through him, and abruptly he felt tears burn at the corners of his eyes as he recalled the fingers that had been thrust into his throat, the words that had been forced out of his mouth in a voice that was not his own. His stomach churned at the utter alienness of that touch. It had tainted him.

But that was nothing. Not in comparison to whatever they had done to Jilly.

Jilly. Sweetie, what did *they do?*

He was afraid to go outside. The house was no safer, yet he felt safer here. In the living room. Downstairs. Michael had not dared go upstairs all weekend, and had slept on the sofa in front of the television every night. Nothing could have made him go into his bedroom. Scooter might come back. Or the ugly women.

The two were connected. He knew that. They had warned him. *You can not help her. She is ours. If you continue to search, you will not like what you find.*

Michael bit his lower lip and squeezed his eyes closed, swallowing the grief he felt. Whatever they had done to Jilly had been a warning. It was all about the girl, somehow. And none of it was in his head. None of it. Fucking psychiatrists couldn't help him. Not an army of them.

With his eyes pinched shut, the images from Friday night were too sharp, too clearly etched in his mind. He opened them.

The phone rang, and he let out a shout as though someone had crept up behind him and tapped him on the shoulder. The ring was tinny and shrill. Part of him was drawn by instinct to answer the phone, but the rest of him was unwilling to rise off of the sofa.

On the third ring he sprang up and raced into the kitchen. He snatched the portable phone from its cradle and pressed Talk.

"Hello?"

"Michael, it's Hannah."

Hannah. He felt a wave of hope go through him. If he told Hannah about her sister, she might be able to help. Just telling someone, sharing what he was feeling, sharing the burden, would be a relief.

"Michael?"

"Yeah, hi, Hannah," he said. "Listen, I'm . . . I'm glad you called."

"I'll bet. What did you do to her?"

He blinked several times, frowning deeply. "What? What are you talking about?"

"I talked to her this morning. She was a total bitch, Mike. Not at all like her. In all my life, I've never heard her like this. So what's the story? Are you messing around on her or something? 'Cause Jillian's not going to just go off like that without a reason, and I racked my brain to figure out what it could be, and all my questions lead back to you."

Michael shivered. He took a deep breath and tried to calm himself so that he would not scream.

"It's nothing like that, Hannah. I don't know what it is. Something's happened to her."

There was a long silence, as though his wife's sister was trying to decide if she believed him or not.

"I'll talk to her," Hannah said. "Try to figure out what it is. You really don't have a clue?" She sounded a bit lost as she said the latter, as though the idea of Michael being unfaithful was infinitely preferable to having her sister's behavior a mystery.

"I don't. And I think . . . I'm not sure there's anything you can do to help."

"She's my sister, Michael."

"Right. Of course." He sighed. "I'll . . . talk to you soon."

He hung up the phone and stared at it for a moment. Instead of making him feel less alone, Hannah's call had made him feel more isolated than ever. What could he have said to her that wouldn't have sounded insane?

It's on you, Mikey. You've got to do something.

Like what?

Both hands on the kitchen counter, he leaned there for several seconds, just breathing. Listening to the clock and the fridge and his heart.

Stay away, those nightmare women had said. But if what they had done to Jillian was connected to the lost girl, then staying away was not the answer. The answer was going to be in finding her. It might lead him to nothing. It might make them come back and do to him what they had done to Jillian, but it was a far better option than living on his sofa and letting his mind break down while he waited for the bitch his wife had become to come home from work.

Come find me, Scooter had said. And now Michael believed that he had to, that *everything* relied upon him doing exactly that.

He started back into the living room and the phone rang again behind him, startling him once more. When he went to pick it up, he saw on the caller ID that the call was from Krakow & Bester. He let the answering machine pick it up.

"Michael?" came Teddy Polito's voice. Angry. Cold. "Michael, pick up the goddamn phone if you're home. Look, I've been worried about you, but I'm getting past it pretty quick and moving onto being pissed off. You said you'd have the designs to me today, but you didn't show up, and I haven't heard from you all day. If you don't get those designs in by the end of the week, you're going to blow the whole account. Even if Gary assigns someone else, it's still going to reflect badly on me. He might even go with a completely different team. Which would suck for a lot of reasons, not the least of which is that we've got a good campaign for them. Look, if you want to piss away your own career, that's your business. But don't fuck up my livelihood in the process."

There was a pause, as though Teddy spent a moment wondering if his tirade would convince Michael to answer the phone. Then he hung up. The answering machine recorded the day and time, and then it was quiet in the house again.

Michael stared at the phone.

"I'm sorry, Teddy," he whispered aloud. "But it just isn't important."

My wife is losing her mind. Something took away everything sweet in her, everything kind. Every damn thing that makes her Jillian.

Nothing else matters.

Nothing.

CHAPTER TEN

Johnny Carson is on the TV. Which is weird, isn't it? Johnny hasn't been on TV since Michael was a teenager. And the man looks good, that's the strangest thing about it. Looks like he hasn't aged a day. Michael laughs as he watches Carson on TV, sitting behind that old desk. He's tapping a pencil and making a point about something, but it's hard to hear with the audience laughing like that. He arches his eyebrows and glances at the camera, to let the folks watching at home in on the gag.

That Johnny. He's the best.

The camera cuts away to Ed McMahon for a reaction shot. The big man's guffawing, shaking in his chair. When the angle shifts back to Carson, he's wearing that crazy feathered turban, the Carnac the Magnificent turban. Michael laughs just looking at him. Carson holds up several envelopes, inside which are the questions, for which Carnac / Carson now has to supply the answers.

Michael leans back on the sofa. It's the red sofa, the itchy, uncomfortable pullout that used to be in the basement of his parents' house, the one he fell asleep on so many nights while he was growing up, watching Johnny Carson. The King of Late Night. The hell with all of the other guys who came in later. Nobody can hold a candle to Johnny. Nobody can replace him.

Weird. Replace him? Why replace him? He's right there on the TV. Michael sprawls across that itchy red sofa in plaid flannel pajama pants. He hasn't worn pajamas since the age of twelve, but damn, aren't they comfortable? A ripple of laughter comes from the TV. Johnny has broken character as Carnac and is snickering about something, his face flushed red. Michael has no idea what the joke was but laughs anyway. Carson is just funny. He's Carson. He's like everyone's naughty uncle Johnny.

In the shadows of the corner behind the television, Scooter stands and watches him. She's in that same peasant blouse. Those same jeans.

Michael doesn't want to look at her. He keeps his eyes right on the TV. On Carson. Uncle Johnny.

"Next, oh Great Carnac?" prompts Ed McMahon.

"Mm-hmm," Carson replies, mugging for the camera as he pretends to concentrate on the small envelope he holds against his forehead. "I love you, the check's in the mail, and I promise I won't come in your mouth."

The television flickers. On the Tonight Show *set—the classic one, not the slick setup that the replacement will use later—the lights darken. Ed McMahon is laughing again, that deep, bust-a-gut-cough-up-a-lung laugh that seems simultaneously the fakest and most genuine thing Michael has ever heard. His eyes are damp and he's brushing at them as though at any moment he'll weep with merriment.*

Carnac tears open the envelope. " 'Name the three biggest lies men tell women,' " he reads from the card.

Michael frowns. This isn't Carson. Uncle Johnny could be a wiseguy with the double entendres and the naughty, knowing looks, but . . . not this. Not crude.

His stomach burns, suddenly, and twists with the need to vomit. There's something in his throat, some phlegm he can't hack up or swallow, like there are . . . what? Like there are fingers in there.

On screen, the Tonight Show *set darkens even further, but now the camera pulls back and Michael can see that the set is not complete. It's just the desk and the chair and a bit of background, and beyond that it's a house. A massive, rambling old house with cracked windows, a place where time has moved on and no one has updated anything—curtains, wallpaper, carpet—in half a century.*

What the hell is this?

Carson's still wearing the turban, but he's in his suit now. The rest of the costume is gone. He holds the next envelope up to his forehead. "And what is your next stunning revelation, oh great sage of the East?" McMahon asks in that bellowing voice.

"Susan," Carnac / Carson / Uncle Johnny says.

His eyes shift and he's staring out at the TV audience again. But not at everyone. Just at Michael. Twelve-year-old Michael in his pajamas. Grown-up Michael, impossibly sprawled on the itchy red pullout sofa from his parents' basement.

"Her name is Susan, you jackass. She told you, don't you remember? She whispered it to you. Her little sister, Lily? Millie? No, Hilly—I knew it was something like Jilly. You did, too, didn't you? Hilly couldn't say Susan, she always said Scoosan, and that's where Scooter came from. Jesus. Wake up, moron. You promised you'd find her. Take my advice and do it. Quick. Damn skippy."

Carson isn't smiling. He isn't mugging for the camera. He isn't smirking. Good old Uncle Johnny, Carnac the Magnificent, the King of Late Night . . . Johnny Carson is pissed off.

"Wake up, Michael. Go find her."

Ed McMahon just laughs and laughs.

The screen goes dark.

Michael flinches. He lifts his gaze and sees Scooter—Susan—standing behind the television with the cord in her hand, plug dangling from her grasp. The TV is dead. The image is gone.

Susan.

"Susan what, though?" Michael asks. "Susan what?"

Scooter mouths a word. A name. Maybe her last name. But no sound comes from her lips and Michael can't read lips. One word, though. One syllable, even. That name.

The lost girl glances around and now it is her eyes that go wide. Scooter's eyes. Susan's eyes. Michael sees terror there on the face of that girl, the pretty little angel who is limned with golden light that is the only illumination in the darkness of that room. His living room.

But it isn't, is it? His parents' old pullout sofa was in the basement of their house. Basement. Living room. He looks around and sees that this is neither one.

The itchy red sofa and the unplugged TV are next to Johnny Carson's desk on a stolen swatch of Tonight Show set in the middle of a crumbling, creaking old house. Things shift in the dark.

Michael smells popcorn.

•   •   •

HE OPENED HIS EYES AND sucked in a lungful of air with a rasp, as though someone had been holding a pillow over his face while he was sleeping. Michael's heart was hammering and his body was shaking. A chill went down his back in spite of the trickle of sweat that raced it from skull to tailbone.

"Oh, Jesus," he whispered, rocking himself over and over on the sofa in his living room. His living room. His and Jilly's. Not the itchy sofa at all, but a soft, plush, blue thing they had gotten at Jordan's Furniture in Nashua. On the TV, a pair of cute, scrappy British women instructed a third how to dress, and it all came back to him. It was Wednesday night. Five days since those gray, misshappen things had fallen upon Jillian in the dark, had touched Michael. Three days since the two of them had even spoken to one another. Michael was afraid to try, afraid to look into her eyes and see nothing of the kindness that had always resided there.

His appointment with the psychiatrist, Dr. Lee, had been scheduled for today, but he'd blown it off. After what had happened five nights ago, he was certain no doctor—for mind *or* body—was going to be able to help him.

No. It was up to Michael to figure out what to do next. If he could just get up off the sofa.

This afternoon he had switched on BBC America and promptly fallen asleep.

It was dark in the living room, save for the strange blue light from the television. How odd, he'd always thought, that the color of the light didn't seem to change with the colors on the screen. Outside the windows there was only the night and the darkness.

Michael frowned as he glanced at the digital readout on the cable box. It was nearly a quarter to ten. Late. Not one light had been turned on in the house. He groaned as he pushed himself to his feet, stretching, bones popping. Questions swirled in his mind as he crossed the room and hit the switch, throwing the light from half a dozen recessed bulbs into the living room. The night had been visible outside the windows before, but with the glare within they were just black now. It might have been a coal mine outside, or the inside of an oil well, or the end of the world.

He felt better with the lights on. Instantly he was more awake. Scattered fragments of his dream went cascading down into the well of his consciousness; in his mind he snatched at them, not wanting to let them go. Most of it went away despite his efforts. There had been something about Johnny Carson.

And there had been the girl in the shadowy corner behind the television. Now the shadows were gone, the room drenched in light, but he was reluctant to look over there in any case. She might still be there, a wisp, a shimmer of color. A ghost.

Scooter.

"No," Michael corrected himself, his voice a tired rasp. "Susan."

Even with the British women chattering on BBC America, the sound of his own voice was startling. It echoed strangely in the house and though he had no proof of it, he felt inside a strange confirmation of what he had suspected from the moment he awoke.

Jillian had not come home.

There was no alarm in him. Until the events of Friday night he would have panicked, thinking that some terrible fate had befallen her. Was she dead in a ditch on the side of the road? Had she been in a car accident? But now . . . now he only felt a bone-deep dread that resonated inside of him.

"Jilly?" he called into the empty house, receiving only an echo in reply. It was a lonesome certainty, the knowing she was not there. And yet he felt that he had to go through the motions, had to confirm it, because you simply could not go through life functioning on instinct.

He went up the stairs and checked their bedroom, turning on lights as he went. The spare room was also empty. The home office. But there was no one there. No one home but Michael and the shadows. Michael started back down the stairs, but stopped halfway and sat heavily, hanging his head.

Find the girl. Like you promised you would, he thought.

It all came down to that. It was all connected.

Michael was a pragmatic man, or had been until recently. It was one thing to attribute that Saturday night's events to hallucinogenics, but the situation had gone way beyond that. Ghost or not, the little girl was haunting him. She needed his help. Whoever these gray, twisted women were, they did not want him to get involved.

They want to frighten you away, to drive you off. You've got them worried. Which means that you can help, Michael. Or they wouldn't have bothered with you.

He had tried to find her and come up empty. That had likely been what prompted them to come after him and Jilly. But they didn't understand people. Didn't understand love and marriage for sure. If they had, they would have understood that by doing whatever they had done to Jillian, they had taken away the one thing in his life that he would sacrifice anything for.

Michael Dansky had nothing left to lose.

There had been enough lying around on the sofa. He had been shell-shocked by what happened. But his dream was lingering. He did not know if it was something unnatural, some way in which the ghost of the girl had touched his sleeping mind, or if it was simply his unconscious telling him, but he knew it was all tied together. His wife had not been mugged or raped. There were no police for whatever had happened to her, no detectives, no one out to get justice for that violation.

It's up to me, he thought.

Michael rose from the stairs and continued down. He would wait for Jillian, all night if he had to. But while he waited, he would set out the map he had been using when searching for the old house where he had brought Scooter—Susan—and see if there were any small side streets he might have missed. There had to be something. It was there. He had been inside. The house was real. He wasn't sure how he could have missed the street, but—

They don't want you to find it.

No, of course they don't.

Now he nodded. Those ugly women in their shapeless coats weren't normal. He had no idea what they were capable of. It was possible they had misled him while he was searching, thrown him off the trail. He would be more thorough tomorrow. Very thorough. No matter what the cost. He was frightened of them. The feeling of fingers inside his throat, of his voice being used by someone else, of this thing just taking him over, still left him feeling unclean. But what other choice did he have?

His stomach rumbled. He hadn't eaten anything all day.

Again he glanced at the clock. *Where are you, Jilly?*

The smell of popcorn lingered in his nostrils—or, rather, in his mind, leftover from his dream. Michael went into the kitchen and began opening and closing cabinets and the refrigerator. He wasn't up to making himself a meal, but he was hungry. When he came across the box of microwave popcorn a wave of nostalgia swept through him. That wasn't what he had been smelling. His bizarre olfactory "hallucinations" were very specific. It was old-fashioned, homemade popcorn he had been smelling. *But what the hell,* he thought. *Why not?*

Michael put a bag of popcorn into the microwave and hit the timer. It hummed to life, the numbers on the timer ticking silently down toward zero. For a few moments the microwave seemed to be doing nothing, but then there came a single pop, followed by a burst of several at once, and then a steady, staccato sound, like tiny fireworks in a drum.

Ding!

Even after the bell, several last kernels popped. Michael's stomach growled loudly. He opened the microwave door and reached for the puffy, overstuffed bag.

His hand froze inches away from it. The heat from the popcorn steamed against his fingers.

There were greasy stains soaking into the bag from the inside. But these were not random streaks. They formed a pattern.

Letters. A name.

Barnes.

Even as he stared, the greasy streaks ran and the name was obscured. But it had been there. Michael was certain of that.

A tremor in his hand, he reached out and slammed the microwave closed. In the glass door he saw his reflection . . . and the reflection of the little lost girl, the blond angel who stood behind him in the kitchen.

Michael cried out and spun around, stomach lurching, heart pounding against the inside of his chest as though it might tear free. But the girl was not there. He was still alone in the house.

Slowly he faced the microwave again. He opened the door. The bag of popcorn was just that, now. The oily streaks were barely noticeable. But the name was seared into his head. The lost girl had been doing everything she could to try to communicate with him, but something didn't want her to. She was bound, somehow, and couldn't really reach him. In some way he knew that. But she managed, still. She managed.

Barnes.

Susan Barnes.

JILLIAN PULLED INTO THE DRIVEWAY a little before one A.M. and did not bother to try to get the car into the garage. She was not so drunk that she didn't realize she would likely scrape one side or the other going in. There was a kind of delicious feeling burning low in her abdomen. Her lips seemed very dry and she licked them over and over. At some point she had taken off her shoes to make it more comfortable to drive, and they were on the seat next to her. Jilly left them there as she got out of the car and slammed the door.

Her suede jacket was not warm enough for the chill of a November witching hour, and even with the alcohol in her she shivered as she hurried to the door. The cold pavement of the walkway stung her bare feet and swirled around her legs, flapping her skirt. Jillian purred softly to herself with the thrill of that cold wind caressing her.

It took her a moment to realize that her keys were clutched in her hand and she snarled at them as though they had conspired against her. Teeth chattering, she scraped the key against the door several times before finally sliding it home and twisting it.

When she closed the door, her keys were still hanging from the lock. She noticed for a moment, and then just as quickly forgot. The warm buzz in the most primal part of her brain had not blocked out the most vital bit of information. She had to work in the morning. Time for bed.

She went up the stairs with her jacket still on, holding the rail to steady herself. Her palm made a shushing noise on the wood that she liked.

A dull drone of voices came from the bedroom. Jillian paused at the top of the stairs and frowned deeply. Her nostrils flared. *Fuck,* she thought. *Fucking Michael.* The light from the television flickered from that open door. After a second or two she rolled her eyes and continued on.

When she stepped through the door she found Michael still awake. He sat propped against his pillows, watching something black and white. A tall man was arguing with a short, stumpy guy and a blond-haired woman with a masculine voice and the body of a prison matron. Michael had a plastic tub of popcorn on his stomach. There were bits of it spilled onto the bed. On the sheets. Some on the floor. Two empty microwave bags were on the nightstand beside him.

Michael's gaze shifted to her, then back to the television.

"What the hell are you up to?" Jillian asked, swaying a bit as she walked into the room.

"What does it look like?" Michael replied.

She flinched. Unbelievable. He was lazing around having himself a grand old popcorn fiesta and she was working to pay the goddamn mortgage. Beautiful.

"Did you finish your sketches for that client?" she asked.

Michael resolutely refused to look at her. This was the last thing in the world Jillian was going to put up with. Who the hell did he think he was? She shifted position, blocking his view of the TV. For several seconds he continued to stare straight ahead, as though he could see through her. Then, with hateful slowness, he at last met her gaze.

"Go to bed," he told her.

"Fuck you. You don't talk to me like that," she snapped, hand on one hip. "What the hell have you been doing around here all day and all night?"

His breathing quickened and his eyes grew moist. He bit his lip. "Me? What have I been doing? It's one in the morning, Jilly. What have you been doing? Besides drinking. I can smell that much from here."

She saw his gaze dart to her legs, and he winced as though the sight of her bare flesh hurt him. Her husband was a good-looking man. Darkly handsome with plenty of what she called Grrrrr. He hadn't shaved in days, but that usually only added to his appeal.

Not tonight.

Jillian smiled and withdrew her pantyhose from the right-hand pocket of her suede coat. Michael seemed to crumble a little, right before her eyes.

"I got a run in them," she explained.

A glint of hope lit his gaze.

Then she pulled her lavender lace thong from her left-hand pocket. "This, though . . . this I took off just for fun."

Michael stared at her. In the flickering television light she could see his Adam's apple bob as he swallowed several times in quick succession. He gritted his teeth and nodded slowly, as though making his mind up about something. And the truth was, something had changed in his eyes then. Jillian saw it. She just had no idea what it was.

"What did they do to you, Jilly? Can you tell me that? Do you even know?"

A slow grin crept across her face. She felt it, uncontrollable. "How much detail do you want?"

Confusion was etched in his features, and then dawning surprise and revulsion. Michael seemed speechless. Jillian liked that. She gestured at the TV, where the black-and-white sitcom played on. "What is this shit, anyway? Why the hell are you watching this?"

Michael froze. His face went slack and his eyes widened. He looked at her as though he had never seen her before in his life. Jillian did not like that look. Something about it got under her skin, and not in a way that pissed her off—like everything seemed to—but in a way that made her a little afraid.

"What are you talking about?"

He got out of bed, spilling the bowl of popcorn all over the floor, and barely seemed to notice it as he took a step toward her. It crunched under his foot. His eyes were wild. In his underwear and a Donald Duck T-shirt, he looked like a lunatic.

"This . . . this show," she said, uncertain now, taken off guard by his reaction. The revelation of the thong wadded up in her pocket ought to have gotten a very different response.

He drew in a long, shuddering breath and stood up straighter. "It's *The Dick Van Dyke Show*, Jilly. How can you not know that? I know you haven't seen it since you were a kid, but you've told me a dozen times you used to watch it with your father when you were little."

A ripple of something unpleasant went through her. "I've never seen it before. And it's black and white, Michael. Do you think I'm stupid? This show is too old for me to have watched it as a kid."

"Reruns, Jillian," he said, narrowing his eyes, his head twisting slightly to one side as he studied her. "How can you not remember that?"

Twitching, she stuffed her thong and hose back into her pockets and doffed her jacket, throwing it over the edge of the bed. The question bothered her and she did not want to talk about it, did not want to deal with Michael anymore at all.

"Hold on," he whispered.

She spun on him. "What? Hold on to what? Stop *looking* at me like that!"

All traces of the pitiful Michael were gone. Grim and determined, he reached for her face. Jillian flinched as he caressed her cheek and though she wanted to slap him, to claw at his eyes, she held back.

"Have you forgotten other things?"

"I don't know what you're talking about."

Michael dropped his hand. "What was the name of the guy who took you to your prom?"

She scowled. "Andy Hollings. He forced me to give him a blow job and I threw up in his lap."

Her husband's face twisted in distaste, but then the contemplative look returned. "Talk to me, Jillian. For better or worse, remember? Have you forgotten other things? You forgot *The Dick Van Dyke Show.* What else? I've been trying to figure out why you've been acting so . . . why you haven't been yourself. I know you feel it. Well, what if it's something really wrong with you? Some chemical imbalance or . . . or worse?"

"Me? How's *your* head, Michael? You're the one who was seeing ghosts."

"Jilly—"

She gave him the finger and turned her back on him, unzipping her skirt and letting it fall to the floor, showing him her bare ass. He swore under his breath, but it wasn't from admiration. She grinned to herself, relishing the flavor of the wine in her mouth and the warm tingling ache between her legs.

She tried to unbutton her shirt but the operation proved problematic for her fumbling, drunken fingers. She tugged the shirt off over her head and grabbed a clean T-shirt from her closet. When she pulled it on and turned toward the bed, Michael blocked her path.

"Get out of my way," she snarled.

But Michael had been thinking. That was plain on his face.

"You don't want to answer, or you can't answer?"

"Get out of my way, Michael."

"Who was your first-grade teacher?"

"Michael," she muttered, warning him.

"What about fifth grade? Seventh? Who was your eighth-grade teacher, Jillian? What about high school? Who was the principal in your high school?"

Trembling, and furious at herself for it, she tried to push past him. Michael grabbed her by the shoulders.

"Rita Welch! My high-school principal was Rita Welch!" she cried, hating how shrill her voice sounded.

Michael closed his eyes and let out a long breath. He nodded and opened them again. "All right. Now we're getting some-where. Do you remember what your mother bought Hannah for her eighth birthday? You were so jealous."

"Of course I do."

"What was it?"

She scowled and rolled her eyes again, stumbling a bit. Michael caught her. Jillian met his gaze fiercely, wishing now that she wasn't a little drunk. Wishing she was sober enough to outsmart him.

"You don't remember. Do you remember anything?" His voice rose to a panicked pitch. "Hannah? The beach house your family always rented on Cape Cod? The first boy you kissed?

Chasing the ice-cream man? Do you remember the trip your family took to Florida when you were ten?"

"Of course I do," she said, not liking the quaver in her voice.

Michael took a step away from her. "You've never been to Florida in your life. Not ever." He ran his hands over his face. "Jesus, Jilly, what did they do?"

It was the same question as before, but this time she did not misconstrue it. The question had nothing to do with her absent thong or the pleasant throb up inside her. It was about something else. But Jillian was entirely mystified as to what that something else might be.

And it frightened her. What if there really *was* something wrong with her mind? A brain tumor or something?

"Jilly, please, just tell me. What's the earliest memory you have?"

She was still trembling, but now she began to shake her head back and forth violently. "Stop it," she said. "Just stop it, Michael. Leave me alone! Stop with this psychoanalysis bullshit. I can't . . . I don't want to know!"

The words were out of her mouth before she knew they were coming. Once they had escaped her lips she gave a little hiss of surprise. Then she felt a change sweeping through her. Her head shook harder, her teeth grinding down, and her hands clenched into fists with such ferocity that her fingernails slit little crescent wounds into her palms.

"Jilly—"

"Don'tyoufuckingcallmethatyousonofabitch!" Jillian began to beat him then, raining her fists down on him. She caught his jaw with a hard right that felt like it might have broken a knuckle or two, but it was worth it. It felt so good she nearly came all over again.

Michael was off balance and Jillian followed through. She stepped after him, slapping and punching. Her left hand flashed out and she scratched his cheek, but he rolled with it and she did not gash him as deeply as she wanted to.

"Fuck you, get out of my house! Get out of here!"

She kicked him, aiming for his balls, but he moved enough so that she caught him in the shin instead. Michael hissed in pain, staggering back again. In a second she'd back him up against the bed and he'd fall down and then she'd have him. *Fucking asshole. Son of a bitch.* Who the fuck did he think he was?

"Who the fuck? Who the fuck?" she asked, turning it into a chant, saying it over and over.

"It's my house, too. I live here," he said.

Jillian spit in his face.

Michael's mouth dropped open in abject horror.

They both froze.

"Get the fuck out of my house. And keep away from me."

He shook his head with an expression of utter despair. A single tear slipped down his cheek. When Jillian saw it she scoffed, her upper lip curling.

"Pussy. Get out."

She crossed her arms and watched him as he pulled on his blue jeans and a sweatshirt, threw some things in an overnight bag, and left. His footsteps went down the stairs and she heard the door slam. The rumble of his car starting floated up from the garage; she went to the window and watched as he jockeyed around her car, which was parked at an angle across the driveway.

Then he was gone.

Jillian picked up the remote control and raised it to change the channel, but then she froze, staring at *The Dick Van Dyke Show*. She was mesmerized, watching the actors. They were wretchedly happy and kind. The jokes weren't funny. The laugh track couldn't have convinced her otherwise. Where was the charm in this?

She lay down on the bed, still tender all over—the two guys at the bar had used her mercilessly and she had urged them on— and she watched that old black-and-white relic on the television. Within her was a vague awareness that something was missing, and that its absence should have hurt her. But she was only bored.

Bored, and cold.

Moments later she fell asleep, and slumbered on undisturbed by conscience, or by dreams.

CHAPTER ELEVEN

Michael Dansky's world had been twisted so completely in the past few days that he could no longer look at anything the same way. The very fabric of things had been undone. Or perhaps it was only that the curtains of reality had been drawn aside and the real performance was only just beginning. The apparition of a little girl appeared and disappeared at will. Strange, malformed women spied upon him from the side of the road and appeared in the darkness of his bedroom to violate his flesh, to attack his wife. To taint her.

All that he had known for certain about the world now had to be unlearned.

And yet . . .

He drove from home to the office of Krakow & Bester with the window down, the November chill promising an early winter as it whipped at his face. WBZ news radio said nothing about the alteration of reality. There had been a double murder in Newton, a woman and her daughter killed by an unknown assailant. The weather was supposed to warm up in the morning, with the possibility of some rain. The Patriots were primed for another banner year. Ordinary life continued.

But the real and mundane had now become surreal to him. How the reversal had taken place, Michael did not know. But as he drove the winding road into downtown Andover his gaze shifted frequently to street corners and to the shadows between buildings, and he found himself surprised not to see ugly, emotionless faces staring back, watching him. There was no sign of the girl, either. Of Susan Barnes.

After a while, it began to worry him. If she was no longer appearing to him, and those misshapen women were no longer watching, did that mean something further had happened? Had they *caught* her? It was a strange thought, but Michael felt certain the girl was thwarting them somehow by appearing to him.

Even as he turned left at the light in Andover center, a turn that would take him right past Krakow & Bester, he chuckled softly to himself at the perverse irony. He was anxious because the specters that had been haunting him were now leaving him alone. Despite Jillian's aberrant behavior, everything else seemed normal. He thought of a story he had seen on television about a teenage surfer girl who had lost her arm in a shark attack. The shark had come and done its damage, and then moved on, leaving the girl forever changed. Yet everyone behaved as if things could continue as if nothing had ever happened. Life would return to normal, somehow.

The sharks had come and they had mutilated Jillian, sure enough, though her wounds were invisible. And now things were returning to normal. But like that surfer girl, the damage was done.

And in this case, the sharks were still out there.

There was no traffic on the road. Streetlights went from green to yellow to red and back to green again in a silent display. Fluorescent lights flickered in shuttered storefronts. Others were dark behind metal gratings. It was after two o'clock in the morning and the world was asleep. An ordinary night. Yet no matter how ordinary the world seemed, for Michael life could not go on as usual. Things would never return to normal.

Not unless he *made* them.

Jillian had changed completely, and now he knew that those changes were more than behavioral. She had no recollection of her childhood. Michael felt certain that those twisted women had somehow destroyed part of her mind, that they had damaged her. He did not know if there was any way to help her, but if one existed, he first had to find out what they were, those shapeless figures. And the key to that knowledge was the lost girl.

Michael parked in front of the office. Before getting out of the car he took a careful look around. The street was deserted. Only one other car was parked on that entire block, several spaces back, and it had a couple of parking tickets under the windshield wiper. Whoever owned it wasn't coming back anytime soon. Idly, he wondered what had happened to the owner. It reminded him that other people were living their lives and had their own problems. Somewhere out there, he reasoned, there must be others who had touched the truth the way he had—or had it touch them. It made him feel less alone.

He left his overnight bag locked in the car. As he let himself into the building with his front door key and went up the stairs, he realized he had never come here in casual dress. With Jillian shrieking at him, he had dressed in blue jeans, sneakers, and a Patriots sweatshirt. Now he felt like a thief, breaking into the place. There weren't any lights on but when he unlocked the office doors and slipped inside, he found that the lights from the street outside provided more than enough illumination to keep him from crashing into filing cabinets or the copy machine.

More than ever, in that strange combination of gloom from neon and moon, he expected to see Scooter. Everything seemed washed in a dull golden glimmer. If ghosts were to appear they ought to come now.

But he was alone in the office with the hum of equipment that had been left to run all night. A refrigerator. The copy machine. Computers. Unfortunately the heat was not among them, and he shuddered with the cold that had settled into the office overnight. He did not want to turn a lot of lights on. It was unlikely anyone would notice from the street at this hour of the morning, but it still felt like a bad idea. The heat, on the other hand, no one was going to notice.

Once he had found the thermostat and dialed up a more comfortable temperature, Michael went to his own office. Inside were the remnants of the days he had been absent from Krakow & Bester. Mail was piled on his chair. The red light on his phone blinked rapidly, demanding he pay attention to the accumulated voice mail that must await him. Half a dozen yellow sticky notes adhered to his computer screen. He stripped them off, ignored the blinking light on the phone, and dumped the mail from his chair onto the floor, immediately forgetting all of it.

His eyes burned with exhaustion but he felt as though his mind had gotten a second wind. From his car he had made a call to the Hawthorne Inn, just a few miles away, and he knew a comfortable bed awaited him there. But he had things to do before he could rest.

"Miles to go before I sleep." That was the Robert Frost poem, wasn't it? *Yes. ". . . Promises to keep, and miles to go before I sleep."*

Both so true.

In the darkened office he turned on the computer and typed in his password. Once it gave him access, he opened his Internet browser and began to search for Susan Barnes.

It was a massive exercise in frustration. There were dozens of search engines that promised results. Many of them required him to sign in, some with a credit card, and among those, some guaranteed an answer if he would just pay the one-year membership fee. It was a reckless pursuit. Susan was a girl; no child that age would have her own telephone or address listing. But an e-mail address—or photographs on a family Web site—those things were not impossible. He typed "Susan Barnes" into the most reliable search engine on the Net.

There were 45,700 results.

He bit his lip and nearly wept. For well over an hour he keyed in additional words and combinations. "Massachusetts." "Missing." "Abducted." Even "death." If she was a ghost, surely that word would be a part of any article about her. An obituary, even. But in all that time, his frustration only grew. The Internet was supposed to be the answer to every question a person might have. You could buy or locate anything that way. But though he found reference to hundreds of women named Susan Barnes, even girls, there was nothing that even hinted that any of the entries might be the girl he was searching for. Some had pictures and looked nothing like her. Most were far too old, or lived too far away, even in other countries.

The closest he came was an Amesbury real estate agent. She lived only fifteen minutes away, but her picture on the real estate company's Web site revealed her to be in her fifties. Her hair was dyed a strawberry blond, but as Michael studied the picture something made him take a closer look. If he was looking for a relative of the lost girl, of *his* Susan, there was enough of a resemblance to this woman that she would certainly be on his list. She was too old to be the girl's mother, but a grandmother or an aunt, perhaps.

He nodded to himself. That wasn't a terrible idea. If he could find a relative with the same name, that might be the lead he needed.

He hit the address and phone number search engines and developed lists of women named Susan Barnes, not only in Massachusetts but throughout New England. Rubbing his eyes, he checked the clock as he printed them up. Half past three. Reams of paper accumulated on top of his printer. If he had to call every single one of them, he would.

Exhausted, he sat back in the chair and scanned the pages. There was only so much he could do in one night.

Michael glanced at the clock to find that it was ticking toward four in the morning. The last thing he wanted was to still be here when the first person showed up in the morning.

Reluctantly he shut down his computer and stacked up the pages he had printed. Tomorrow he was going to search for the house again, while it was still light out. And then, tomorrow night, he would begin making phone calls. For now, though, there were things he didn't want to leave the office without accomplishing.

By the time Michael left Krakow & Bester, locking up behind

him, it was just after seven A.M. on Thursday morning, the ninth of November, and the sun was on the rise. Already there was life on the street, people walking their dogs or jogging by, light traffic on the road, a short line inside Starbucks.

He had never been so happy to see the morning. It energized him, made him want to go out and search for the house right then, take full advantage of the daylight. But he had not slept in far too long, and just the thought of a soft mattress at the Hawthorne Inn was enough to coerce him.

Sleep. At least a few hours.

He hoped that he would not dream, or that if he did, he would not remember.

TEDDY POLITO HAD HIT THE snooze button on his alarm clock one too many times this morning. Running a bit late, he had foregone breakfast and regretted it the instant he pulled out of his driveway. One stop at the Dunkin' Donuts drive-through later, he had remedied that situation. His stomach rumbled gratefully in response, but he left the cinnamon bagel in the bag while he drove the rest of the way into work.

With the Dunkin' Donuts bag in one hand and the biggest damn cup of coffee they dared to sell in the other, he marched up the stairs with the determined dignity of a condemned man. Work had sucked miserably the past week. Michael had fucked up the Newburyport ice-cream gig and Teddy was certain that when the campaign was reassigned, there wouldn't just be a new artist chosen, but a new copywriter too.

The worst part of it was that he couldn't really even be that pissed off. His star at Krakow & Bester had risen thanks to its being tacked onto Michael Dansky's, like the tail nailed to Eeyore's ass in the old Winnie the Pooh cartoons. Only Michael was anything but a donkey. Which made it all the more upsetting to Teddy the way he'd been behaving. He was no saint; his primary concern was for his own livelihood. But he was concerned about Michael as well.

He tugged the door open and walked into the agency's reception area. Brittany was behind the desk. Her eyes lit up as he entered, and he perked up a little. Brittany was the kind of girl Teddy Polito had never had a chance in hell of bedding, not even back in college, and to see the sparkle in her eyes as she greeted him, to know that she was fond of him, always gave him a lift in his step.

"Morning, Teddy," she said.

"Good morning, Red," he said.

Brittany rolled her eyes with a good-natured grin. She had been Red Riding Hood at the masquerade party and Teddy always enjoyed reminding her.

"Any sign of Dansky?" he asked, lowering his voice a bit.

Her smile disappeared. "No. He hasn't called, and I haven't seen him yet."

Teddy sighed and thanked her. As he was walking past her desk, though, Brittany called him back.

"Listen," she said, her voice hushed. "Michael's a good guy. If he's having a rough time . . . I guess what I'm saying is that if Gary tries to stir up trouble for him, you'll let me know, right?"

Brows knitted in surprise, Teddy felt like he was seeing Brittany for the first time. She was sweet, and stunning, but not very bright. All those things he had known. But he realized now what kind of person she was. The girl was screwing the boss's son, but she knew right from wrong. She knew the stand-up guys from the scumbags, even if her heart sometimes got in the way of that perception. She was willing to use her relationship with Gary Bester to help Michael out, because Michael was a good guy.

"You're all right, you know that?" Teddy said. It could have come off as insulting, in a way, but the sentiment was genuine and heartfelt, and Brittany must have realized that, because she blushed and thanked him.

"Just let me know," she said.

Teddy nodded. "Absolutely."

The sun had been shining when he had dragged his carcass out of bed, but now, as he strode through the bullpen full of cubicles that was the heart of Krakow & Bester, the day had turned gray outside the windows. His mind rewound the morning news bites from the radio and he recalled something about the threat of rain.

As he did every morning, he thanked the gods of commerce that he didn't have to work in a cubicle anymore. Teddy managed the doorknob without crushing his bagel and shoved the door open with his knee. He flicked the light on and went in, dropping the Dunkin' Donuts bag onto the little table against the wall and setting his coffee down to shrug off his jacket. He picked up the cup and took a sip, enjoying the heat of the coffee.

Only when he at last went to sit at his desk did he see the enormous black portfolio folder propped on his chair.

His brow furrowed and Teddy reached for the portfolio, setting the coffee on his desk. He propped the bottom of the portfolio against his voluminous belly and lifted the cover.

The sketch was extraordinarily detailed and perfectly shaded. An ice-cream truck with *Newburyport Premium Ice Cream* stenciled on the side. At the sliding window through which ice cream was served, instead of the classic ice-cream man, there was a breathtakingly sexy brunette in a barely-there, teeny tank top, her breasts practically spilling out the top as she leaned over to hand a cone to one of several gawking boys gathered around the truck. Chocolate ice cream dripped over her fingers. Her breasts were quite clearly the focus of the illustration.

There was even a tag line already. *Perfect Scoops. Every time.* Nice double entendre. Short and sweet. Teddy's work was done for him.

It was fully half a minute before he even turned the page. This one was the idea Michael had been working on before he started to freak out. A sexy blonde on the beach, one hip cocked arrogantly, all attitude and sass. Her vanilla ice-cream cone was dripping down over her fingers. Once more, the tag line was in place: *It's a Sticky Situation.* With the company logo at the bottom.

"Damn," Teddy whispered. They were the finest work Michael had ever done.

The third page was a redhead in lingerie, sprawled across a loveseat in front of her television, eating a pint of strawberry ice cream. Only then did he get that Michael intended for the company not to pick one of these, but to use them all. The brunette for chocolate, the blonde for vanilla, the redhead for strawberry. And yet again, Michael already had a tag line in place: *All Dressed Up and No Place to Go.*

Teddy had come up with dozens of possible slogans. One or two of them might work as a consistent line to go beneath the corporate logo, but otherwise Michael's ads worked perfectly exactly as they were.

"Son of a bitch," he whispered. Then he laughed. "You son of a bitch."

He spent another five minutes just studying them, over and over, relishing the knowledge that despite how much of a fuckup he'd been the last few days, Michael had saved both of their asses. Teddy could make the pitch to the client without him. He had done it before.

I'd like to see Gary try to make trouble for Mikey now, Teddy thought.

Suddenly he felt very guilty for the way he had spoken to his partner. Not that he hadn't had reason, but with all the work they had done together over the years, he ought to have had more faith that Michael would come through.

He looked again at the first illustration, the one with the ice-cream truck. It was brilliant. The clients were going to love it.

Yeah, Teddy would cover for Michael for as long as he could. It was the least he could do.

MICHAEL WOKE ABRUPTLY, REACHING FOR his throat to tear away the hands that were choking him, cutting off his air.

There were no hands.

Gagging, he sat up, heart thundering in his chest. He wheezed as he drew in long drafts of air, calming himself, becoming oriented to his surroundings. His gaze darted about the room. Framed prints on the walls. Lamp, alarm clock, TV on top of the bureau. The little cardboard sign that sat on the TV advertising HBO in the room caught his eye. For some reason, staring at it helped him to relax.

The drapes were open partway. The sky was overcast, clouds ominously gray and pregnant with the threat of rain. A light drizzle misted the window. He glanced at the alarm clock again, noticing the time: 12:47. He had slept less than five hours. But that would have to be enough. Every moment that passed with Jillian like this, he felt himself drifting farther away from her. And there was no telling what she would do. Nausea churned in his stomach as he remembered the things she had said to him. An image swam up into his mind of her pulling her thong from her pocket and he bit his lower lip, refusing to allow himself to dwell on that.

She'd been wounded. Violated. Her mind had been damaged. Michael knew it was possible she couldn't be helped, but he had to try.

He dragged himself out of bed and rubbed at his eyes as he gazed out at the gray day. Sleep still had a grip on him, but he knew that a shower would help. Clean clothes. Caffeine. Idly, barely aware that he was doing it, he ran a hand over his throat where one of those things, one of those malformed women, had touched him. When he realized what he was doing he pulled his hand away.

Whatever dream or nightmare had driven him so violently up from sleep, he could not remember it. Michael considered that a small mercy.

With the television on for company, he took a shower and dressed quickly. His jacket was rainproof canvas with a thick lining, but even so he hurried to his car. The drizzle of rain was icy cold, and the chill seeped into his bones. He felt weak and shivery, and it was not until he was a mile away from the Hawthorne Inn that his preoccupied mind settled down enough for him to realize why. In the previous twenty-four hours he had eaten nothing but popcorn.

The light rain misted the windshield. Low music droned on the radio. The swish of the windshield wipers combined with the whisper of his tires through the puddles on the road to become nearly hypnotic. But his day was only beginning, and he would not succumb to his exhaustion. With the window halfway down, the cold and wet sweeping in, he spotted a strip mall ahead. Athena Pizza seemed an afterthought, a tiny place squished between a CVS pharmacy and a bicycle shop.

It was while he was waiting for the Greek girl behind the counter to make his gyro sandwich that he had an idea. Frustrated that he hadn't thought of it earlier, he borrowed a pencil off the counter and slid into a booth. Turning over the paper placemat, he began sketching on the blank sheet. The image in his memory was fuzzy, but as he focused it began to take on clearer edges, more distinct features. The pencil flew over the paper and he gave himself over completely to the work.

Michael did not look up until the olive-skinned girl tapped him on the shoulder. He jumped in his seat, startled, and looked up into her dark eyes.

"I'm sorry," she said. "I called to you, but I guess you kinda went to Bermuda for a minute."

Her smile was playful, but not flirtatious. She handed him his sandwich, wrapped in white paper and stuffed into a brown paper bag. Her gaze went past him, then, and she looked at the drawing he had just finished. It was a sketch of Susan Barnes's house. Or, rather, the house where he had brought Susan Barnes on the strange night when all of this had begun.

"Wow. You're really good," the counter girl said.

"Thanks. You don't happen to recognize the place? Ever seen this house before?"

She stared at it for several long seconds, frowning as though she wasn't quite sure. Then she seemed to drift, a strange, faraway look in her eyes. After a moment she knitted her brows, troubled by something.

"Are you all right?" Michael asked.

The girl looked at him as though he had just woken her. Then she blinked several times and shrugged, adding a small laugh. "It does look sort of familiar, but I don't think I know where it is. Sorry." She turned to go back around behind the counter.

"Wait."

The girl paused, turning to him, shifting uncomfortably.

"You recognize it." It wasn't a question.

"It's weird," she said. "I must've seen it at some point. Couldn't tell you where it is, but I must've seen it. It just feels like . . ."

"Feels like what?"

"It feels like something I dreamed about once."

Her words echoed in Michael's head long after he'd left Athena Pizza behind. If the counter girl had dreamed about the house, he wondered how many others had as well. Of course it could have been a coincidence, just her own strange reaction to the drawing.

He drove out to Old Route 12 with the drawing on the passenger seat and the gyro sandwich nested in its wrapping paper on his lap. Michael was a cautious driver, never understanding why people found the need to make phone calls or put on their makeup, or eat or consult a map while driving. But none of the rules of his old life seemed to apply anymore.

Even without the atlas—which lay on the floor in the backseat—he had no difficulty finding the place he had originally turned off the road. He had been back here once already. He had hoped to show people the drawing and ask if they'd seen the house, but the day was still shrouded in gloom and light rain continued to fall. Cars sailed past him in the opposite direction from time to time, but no one was out for a walk or working in their yard.

As he ate his sandwich, he managed to navigate several turns that he was certain had been his route that night. The area alternated between thick woods and forest rising up toward the peaks of the hills and neighborhoods tucked in amongst the trees. Now he found himself on a long road that sloped slightly upward. He drove slowly for half a mile, looking at every street and driveway. Even so, he nearly went right by a narrow road he had not seen the last time he had searched the area.

"Damn," he muttered, hitting the brakes. The remains of his gyro slid off of his lap and tumbled to the floor. Grumbling, he kept his foot firmly on the brake and fished around on the sandy floormat before retrieving the sandwich. He wrapped it in its paper, wiping dressing on the bag, and set it all on the floor in front of the passenger seat.

The windshield wipers squeaked dry on the windshield. The rain had ceased. Michael switched the wipers off and at last looked up again at the road on his left. There was no sign, and the trees on either side of the road had grown so large that their branches intertwined above the pavement, creating a kind of dark tunnel.

Michael felt his pulse speed up. There was a constriction in his throat and his chest hurt. This could be what he had been searching for. As that knowledge swept over him, a torrent of emotion was unleashed. His face contorted with grief and pain as the words and images of the previous night came back with terrible force. The hatred in Jillian's eyes. The hiss of nylon as she drew her pantyhose out of her pocket. Then the thong.

He had smelled it on her. Not just the alcohol, but the sex, too.

Michael glanced over his shoulder to make sure the coast was clear, then turned into that tunnel of branches. In spring and summer, he imagined the entrance into the road would seem even more like a tunnel. Now, though, it was only the dead, skeletal branches that twined above him. Somehow, that seemed worse.

The road led straight up the hill a hundred yards or so and then curved to the right. The first house to come into view was a massive Federal Colonial that looked as though additional wings had been added to it over time. It was painted rose pink. Though the color was dull, he was not certain if it was aging or if the gloom of the day was to blame.

Michael drove past the rose house slowly. At first glance he had been disheartened. How could he have missed such an enormous house painted such a conspicuous color? Yet it had been dark, that night. And he had not been sober . . . or in his right mind.

The road continued upward; the other houses were of a similar age to the first, all of them from the late nineteenth or very early twentieth centuries. Some were at skewed angles to the road, and too close, a result of their having been built long before the street had been paved. Several had barns. All of them had well over an acre of land. Despite the state of disrepair one or two of them were in, there was money here. Old families, or new arrivals with high salaries and an appreciation for old homes.

Then, abruptly, the road ended in a cul-de-sac. A beautifully restored Victorian thrust up from the hillside on the far side of the circle, as though the owner was the lord of the land, looking out across his fiefdom.

Michael pounded the steering wheel, letting the car idle in the circle as he stared at the house. He knew right away he wasn't high enough. The decrepit house in his illustration was at a higher elevation. For several minutes he sat there, trying to figure out what to do next.

The door to the restored Victorian opened and a heavyset woman emerged onto the porch. She locked the door behind her and Michael watched as she walked down the path to the BMW parked in the drive. He gauged her age at perhaps fifty, though her hair was dyed dark.

"Screw it," he muttered.

He drove into her driveway, pulling up right behind the BMW. It always amazed Michael that despite all the horrors that happened every day in the world, people were still basically trusting. If he had meant her harm, she would never have been able to reach safety. As he climbed out of his car he was glad to see there was at least a hint of caution in her gaze. She pressed a button that caused her BMW to unlock with a chirp, and she opened the door, prepared to climb in at any sign of trouble. In a strange way, it made him feel better.

"Can I help you with something?" she asked, her tone as polite as could be without masking her wariness.

"I hope so." He had snatched the placemat illustration in one hand as he got out. Now he approached her slowly, holding the drawing up so that she could get a look at it. "I'm pretty lost. I'm trying to find this house. A . . . an artist friend of mine was driving around up here and drew me a picture. He said it was for sale. I thought I might take a look, but his directions make no sense and I keep getting turned around."

She seemed to take a moment to decide if she believed him or not, but as her eyes focused on the picture, she became convinced. "Your friend is very talented."

"Yeah," Michael laughed, trying to put her at ease. "He thinks so, too."

The woman smiled and studied the drawing. "Well, I do feel like I've seen it." Her smile wavered.

Like the waitress, he thought. And, now that he thought of it, like Brittany, who had not seen an illustration but reacted just to his description of the place. He wondered if they could all really have seen the house before, what the chances were of that, or if there was something else going on here. He wondered how many women in the area would react the same way, and if it would be just women.

"Gosh, I have no idea where, though," she went on. "It must be nearby. I'm fairly new to the neighborhood." Her eyes lit up. "You know what, though? Go on down to Bill Ginsler's. That pink house right at the bottom of the street? You must have noticed it. He's lived here his whole life. If anyone knows the streets around here, it's Bill. He roamed all over the woods around here growing up."

A rush of excitement went through Michael. He nodded. "The pink house. Yeah, that'd be hard to miss. But . . . it's the middle of the afternoon. Would Mr. Ginsler be home now?"

The woman laughed. "He's a Web designer, so he's home almost all the time. Tell him Marjorie sent you down."

"Thank you so much for your help." He waved the placemat at her and climbed back into the car.

Michael turned around and headed down the hill, with Marjorie following not too far behind him in her powder blue BMW. When he turned into the driveway of that rose pink house, she tooted her horn and drove on by. He waved out the half-open window, not knowing if she could see him or not.

With the placemat still in his hand he strode quickly up to the front door and rang the bell. Ginsler must have heard him pull in, for he was there almost instantly. The door opened to reveal him, a man about Michael's age in a white T-shirt and blue sweatpants. His short hair was a mess, sticking up at odd angles, and he needed a shave. It was clear he hadn't bothered to take a shower yet that day.

Must be nice to work at home, Michael thought.

"You're not selling anything, are you?" Bill Ginsler asked.

Michael smiled, feeling a little giddy, like he'd just been sucking helium out of balloons. He almost laughed, but instead he shook his head. "No, Mr. Ginsler. No, I'm not. I just spoke to . . . Marjorie? Your neighbor up the street. She thought you might be able to help me."

He gave the same basic bullshit to Ginsler about his friend the artist, and like Marjorie, the man didn't question the idea that someone would sit and do a fully rendered sketch of a house for a friend who was in the market to buy one.

"All right. Let me have a look."

Michael handed him the placemat, which Ginsler turned over for a moment, smiling at the logo and menu for Athena Pizza. Then he returned to studying the illustration. After a moment he nodded.

"Yeah. I know the place. Didn't realize it was so run down, though."

The breath stilled in Michael's lungs. His heart took a

hesitant pause. This wasn't the vague recollection that Marjorie and the waitress had. Ginsler was sure. Last night's scene with Jillian played over in Michael's mind, along with pictures of Susan Barnes, of that first night he had picked her up and she had told him her name was Scooter.

"You don't . . . you don't know the name of the family that owns it, do you?"

Ginsler shook his head. "Can't help you there. But the house is on Wildwood Road."

Michael frowned. He didn't remember any Wildwood Road on the map he had in the car. Ginsler apparently noticed his confusion, for the man began to nod.

"Yeah, yeah, I know. I'm sure there's no sign. Just like there isn't one on this street. This is Ledgewood. The whole area used to be called Juniper Hill, at least when I was a kid, but nobody really calls it that anymore. Not since all the new developments started going in during the nineties, down by Route Twelve.

"Anyway, if you take a left coming out of Ledgewood and keep on for a couple hundred yards, the road starts to curve. It'll be on your left. It comes away from the road at an angle, so it's easy to miss. But it's there." He handed the illustration back to Michael. "This place is all the way at the top of the hill, in the circle."

Barely able to form words, Michael managed to thank him and hurried back to his car. He pulled out of the driveway. By the time he glanced back as he was making the left back onto the winding road, Bill Ginsler was gone.

Michael followed his instructions. He did not so much drive as he did steer those two hundred yards, letting the transmission roll the car along. When the street began to curve he stared into the trees off to his left. There were no houses here. But there were also no breaks in the tree line. No Wildwood Road. Not even a dirt path.

Assuming Ginsler had misjudged, he drove on a bit further and at the next curve he did the same thing, examining the woods as he passed. But still there was no road. Michael drove another quarter of a mile before he came to a well-marked intersection, where Nixon Road led into a neighborhood of well-kept ranches and split-levels from the sixties and seventies.

He turned around.

As he completed the turn, he saw movement in his peripheral vision. A figure in a raincoat.

Michael hit the brakes. He swung around to get a better look and only when he saw the German shepherd the man was leading on a leash did he relax. He felt like he had never been closer to finding the house. If those pale, twisted women wanted him to stay away, now was the time that he would see them.

His hand went to his throat and he swallowed. It felt as though something was lodged there. He wondered if it would always feel that way.

"This is crazy," he said, his voice too loud in the car. Then he drove back the way he'd come, watching the woods on his right for any hint of a road or path there. When he reached the curve where Ginsler had said he would find Wildwood Road, there was still no sign of it so he pulled the car as far onto the shoulder as he could manage, killed the engine and got out.

Michael stood on the side of the road, staring into the woods. He craned his neck back, trying to get an idea of how near the top of Juniper Hill he was.

He recalled the hatred in Jilly's eyes. The venom. And the huddle of figures who had surrounded his wife, tearing at her like pigs at a trough. As though they were feeding off of her.

"Fuck this," he whispered.

Michael pressed the button on his keychain that locked the car. It beeped quietly, but he did not even turn to look at it. He went right into the woods, moving in amongst the trees, and began climbing.

The ground in the forest was blanketed with fallen leaves; they were wet and slippery from the rain. There were many bare trees in there—maple and oak and birch—but plenty of evergreens as well. Yet even with the fallen leaves, it was still dark in the woods. Only a few feet from the road it seemed as though dusk had arrived, with only the weakest, palest light reaching him.

The hill grew steeper very quickly. Michael gritted his teeth. This was where Wildwood Road was supposed to be. If it wasn't here, it was near here. He would climb to the top of Juniper Hill and he would find that road. That house.

His feet slipped constantly and he had to grab bare branches to keep himself from falling. All along he kept his focus upward, searching for a break in the woods, for a clearing that might mean the road was ahead. His hands were scratched. The trees grew closer together and he had to duck under branches to pass.

In the dusky gloom, his own hands looked gray. Once, as a boy, he had been swimming at a lake in Upton with his cousins. Some guy had gotten drunk and tried to swim across the lake. Tried and failed. When they dragged him in, Michael and his cousins had gotten a glimpse as they tried to hustle him out of the water and to the waiting ambulance. His skin had been gray like this.

The ambulance had not been in any hurry when it drove away. No lights. No siren. No rush.

The memory was vivid, now. The very air around him seemed leeched of light and color.

He slipped on wet leaves. His fingers tried to grasp a branch but he could not hold on, and it scrapped his flesh raw. Michael went down on one knee, and the moisture from the day's rain soaked through his jeans.

After taking a moment to compose himself, he grabbed hold of the trunk of the nearest tree and began to get back up. Once more he turned his gaze upward, searching for a clearing.

There was movement in the trees.

For a moment his eyes struggled to adjust. In the gloom of the forest, that absence of color, they were almost invisible. But they were moving, and as they did he found he could make them out more clearly. Shifting behind trees and moving nearer and nearer, they were uncannily nimble.

Expressionless, and yet their features were terrible. Elongated. Inhuman. Every one of them with her mouth open impossibly wide as though in a silent howl.

CHAPTER TWELVE

The women seemed almost to dance through the trees as they came down the hill toward Michael. With their strangely stooped forms and long coats, there was something grotesque about this swift and elegant motion. The treacherously steep grading of the hill gave them no trouble with their footing, nor did the thickness of the forest. Somehow, in spite of the darkness of those woods, their black eyes gleamed like polished ebony, or perhaps more like hot tar, for one glimpse of those eyes and it seemed to Michael that they might draw him in like quicksand.

His instinct was to run, but for several heartbeats he felt trapped by those eyes. Their faces were so unreal, like hideously contorted masks, that all the world suddenly seemed like some bit of perverse Greek tragedy.

There were nine of them by his count. They seemed to slow as they moved nearer, tilting their heads to study him like curious birds. There was something terrible about that look. One of them flowed in amongst the others, drawing his attention with a kind of twirling dance. It seemed almost float down the hill, slipping behind trees and appearing once more as though it were putting on a show just for him.

They were still perhaps twenty feet from him when he took a

step back and his foot slipped on the rain-soaked leaves. The sound of his own tread, of his weight upon the ground, hammered home an observation that he had made unconsciously and not been able to recognize in his conscious mind.

They were silent.

Their footfalls made no sound upon the wet leaves or the ground. No earth was disturbed by their passing. Yet he was certain that they had mass and solidity. These were not ghosts. But they were nothing natural, either.

They floated down toward him.

Get out of here! he thought, panic awakening his previous inaction. Somehow they were in his head, muddling up his thoughts and his reason. His mind felt fuzzy and he flashed back to that night, coming home from the masquerade, and the way he had felt then.

Nobody had drugged him at the masquerade, he realized. He had been buzzed and sleepy, but after he had picked up Scooter, when he had begun to get disoriented and off balance, and later when he had blacked out . . . it had been them, somehow.

Now that he knew, he fought it. He shook his head, gritted his teeth and forced himself to move. Even as he took two more steps backward, trying to gauge the distance between himself and the road, his left foot slipped on wet leaves and he began to fall. He reached out and grabbed the nearest branch, looking back. The twisted women had paused, there on the hill, with their stretched, plastic faces and their crude oil eyes. The nearest was barely half a dozen feet away. Michael's heart pounded the inside of his chest so hard that it hurt. Whatever had remained of the mesmerism they had worked upon him, it was shattered now.

"Oh . . . oh shit," he whispered, barely aware his lips had moved.

Silently, gracefully, they closed in on him.

No. He tried to stand but could not get his footing. The trees were thinner here, and the leaves were even wetter. He slipped again and his knee struck a rock. Michael cursed as the pain shot through him, clearing his mind even further. There was nothing surreal about them now. They were more real than anything he had ever experienced.

Then they were on him. Fingers as thin as the tips of branches clamped on his arms and shoulders and forced him down again. Michael started to scream and a frigid hand clamped over his mouth. One of the women came around in front of him while two others kept him on his knees. She . . . but he could not really think of this creature as *she*. No, *it* stared into his eyes with those black orbs and there was nothing for him to see in its expression; no emotion there, no question, no comment.

It reached out a finger, touched the center of his forehead, and then *pushed* the finger through skin and bone without breaking either. The creature's own flesh moved through his as though it was a ghost, but he knew it wasn't. It was as though it filled the spaces between his atoms, like water soaking into a sponge.

Michael shuddered, his legs and arms spasming. He felt the other hands upon him begin to push into his body as well, through his clothes and his skin. Terror raced through him and he opened his mouth in a silent scream, tears forming in his eyes.

Once more, he felt words forced to his lips. *"You were warned,"* the creature said with his voice, his mouth. *"You have brought misery to Jillian. Her joy might have drawn us to her one day, but instead it was your foolishness that led us to her. Yet still you will not stay away. What more must we do to you? We hunger, meddlesome man, and you will not be allowed to interfere."*

Michael struggled. His muscles were rigid, frozen fast by the thing's violation of his body. He tried to clamp his jaws closed, but it used him as a puppet, spoke through him. His upper lip curled into a sneer and his eyes narrowed to slits. It was the smallest of rebellions, but the creature was, at least, not entirely in control of him.

A thousand images of Jillian flickered past in his mind. Vital moments—making love on the library roof, watching her walk the aisle toward him, the anxiety before he dared to ask her to lunch that first day—and hundreds of tiny ones. Jilly asleep in bed beside him, weeping in a darkened theater, laughing at some idiocy he had uttered. Scattered in amongst the others were less pleasant pictures. Jillian pulling her thong from her purse. Swearing and spitting at him, screaming for him to leave the house.

Even as the creature threatened him, Michael felt bitter anguish clutch his heart. He was utterly forlorn. With the thing's finger still pushed into his skull he forced his muscles to obey his will, just enough for him to shake his head slowly, sneering as he glared into its eyes.

"What did you do to my wife?" he snarled.

The other creatures flinched and backed away a step. A breeze swayed branches overhead. The malformed woman who had touched Michael so deeply now snapped rigid, just as he was, its body twitching. They were connected by that touch, by a circuit it created between them. Michael began to jitter as though an electrical current passed through him. His muscles were still not his to command, but he managed to force more words through his clenched jaw.

"Jillian! What did you do?"

"Jillian," he said again, but this time he had not spoken the word. It issued from his lips, but it was the twisted thing that had spoken.

Its tar pit eyes widened.

Then Michael saw nothing. His mind—all of his senses— were flooded with not merely image, but experience. Memory. Slices of childhood, moments of innocence and bliss.

But they were not moments from his own childhood.

They belonged to Jillian.

His mind was torn in half. One part of him wallowed in the horror of what the creature was doing to him, of the truth of their existence. But that part of his consciousness was nearly obscured by the other . . . the part that was, momentarily, Jillian.

Jillian at her first Communion, in her pretty white gown so much like a wedding dress, her daddy telling her how beautiful she looks. She keeps her hands pressed together and her back straight as she walks down the aisle of the church. A hundred times she has been inside this place and yet today it feels so huge, so full of peace. Suddenly she realizes she is out of step with the others and she giggles softly to herself and quickens her pace to fall into rhythm.

Laughing, she hurls snowballs at Hannah. Her little sister's face is flushed red with cold and laughter; they know that their mother will have cocoa for them when they go inside.

Seventh grade, and her heart flutters at the dance. The song is something old. Something her parents would like. But she is barely paying attention, because Billy Marcus—the cutest boy in her class, the same boy who has been her nemesis since kindergarten—is asking her to dance. And he seems embarrassed and hesitant, and though she can't put it into words, there's something wonderful about that. Something that touches her.

Building sand castles in Ogunquit with Dad and Hannah.

Homemade brownies on the back porch, watching the August sun burn down over the horizon.

The endless bus trip to Chicago that year, all the strange sights as they pass through city after city, the sunlight fading and the bus rumbling on all night, her head bouncing off the window as she tries to sleep. Loud people and funny people and the odd nighttime life in the bus stations. It is the farthest she's ever been from home, and it makes her feel as though she wants to keep traveling, keep riding that bus until she has been through every city in the world.

Mom, baking cookies and letting her stir, letting her lick the spoon.

Daddy, singing silly songs to her to get her up for school in the morning.

Michael blinked. His vision cleared for just a moment, blurry, but not so much that he could not see the elongated, ghastly face of the woman. Its hand was still up, fingers pushed through his forehead, but something was wrong with her. With it. That hideous face was twisted worse than before, contorted in pain, and withered to a haggard thinness. There were hollows around the eyes and even its body seemed to have deflated into a hunched, cadaverous figure.

Its mouth was open and a kind of hiss issued from it, like air leaking from a punctured tire, and he had the irrefutable impression that the ugly woman was hollow inside, that whatever it and the others had taken from Jillian, they took to fill that void within.

Jilly. Her memories had flowed from the thing and into Michael, yet that had obviously not been its intention. Somehow—

Then it was happening again. His vision swam and darkened, all of his senses surrendered to memory. But these were not Jillian's recollections. They were faded and ancient. A gray world coalesced around Michael's consciousness, and he could sense the age of it; the scent of the very air was different.

The sun gleams upon the blue water of the Gulf of Tunis. All of the priests of Kart-hadasht gather this morning at the Byrsa. They march with her now, though she leads. They give her that dignity, this virgin girl. She is to be honored, this day.

Tears burn her cheeks and she does not understand them. All of the land will reap the rewards of her sacrifice. An honor.

Her lips tremble with words unspoken and her heart breaks with love unspent.

"Hush," one of the priests snaps, his voice rough. "Do not shame yourself. You must go smiling to the Hall of Moloch, so that you are acceptable to him. If you are unsuitable, all of Kart-hadasht will suffer."

The scene shifts. Stone columns tower all around an earthen plaza. The scent of the sea caresses the air. Birds cry warning to one another and veer away from this place, instinctively avoiding it, sensing the dark power that emanates from the stones and the earth. If not for the stone structure before her and the heavy wooden door, she could still have seen the blue water. The view is denied her.

She will never feel the warmth of the Gulf waters again.

Never feel that joy.

She will never laugh again. But she knows that there is still time for her to weep. And so she does, and the priest's warning be damned.

The susurrus of excited conversation surrounds her. The priests are there, but beyond them are thousands of others, come to see her off, come to worship Moloch with her blood, and to thank the god-king that she is not their sister or daughter, or themselves.

The doors are drawn open. The darkness yawns within. It is a tiny structure, really, for inside there are only shadows, and a set of stone stairs leading down into the earth, underneath the city. Moloch lives in the heart of Kart-hadasht. The god-king is the city's very essence.

She takes a single step, stumbles and falls to her knees. All the strength is gone from her. Her tears flow freely now and she has bitten through her lower lip. Warm blood streaks her chin, but it is the only warmth she can feel.

"Foolish girl. You shame not only yourself but your family. You face your duty now. Moloch has chosen you."

None of it means anything to her, save the words about her family. Her destiny has arrived. There is no thought of escape. But if the priests are required to force her through those doors, to hurl her down the stone steps, it will be more humiliation than her father can bear.

She stands, the priests helping her to her feet.

The door is really not so far away at all. The gown in which she has been cloaked rustles against her bronze skin. Her bare feet whisper upon the stones set into the ground. Tasting the salt of her own tears, the tang of her blood, she steps over the threshold and starts down the stairs with no further hesitation. Once she has entered the Hall of Moloch, there is no hope for her. She shall never emerge.

Only when the doors are closed behind her—a muffled cheer audible from the crowd outside—does she notice the glimmer of light far below. She descends forever, one step after another until her legs are so weak she fears she will fall, tumbling the rest of the way.

Then she has reached the bottom at last. The Hall of Moloch. Torches flicker upon stone walls. The chamber is vast, the heart of the city, but there are several tunnels leading away into utter darkness. She cannot breathe as she studies each of them in turn, searching for the god-king, wondering from which he will emerge.

Only then does she hear the thump of his footfall behind her, feel the moist heat of his breath on her neck.

She turns and is frozen in the gaze of Moloch, the god-king Baal-Melkart. He is stooped, yet massive, muscles rippling beneath a coat of dark hair that gleams in the torchlight. His massive phallus hangs pendulously beneath him. Hooves strike the earthen floor. The head is too heavy for the body, too large, and though all icons of the god represent him as like a man yet with the head of a bull, she understands now that this is an ideal. The face is twisted and elongated, *snoutlike. The horns are long and curved, deadly sharp. It is easy to see the comparison. But the god is no animal. He is hideous, a monster.*

He is Moloch.

In his eyes, there is no spark of benevolence, nor even of intelligence. There is only savage hunger.

The god-king dips his heavy head and moans with anticipation as he reaches out for her. She has been so frightened she could not move, but now at last she tries to turn to flee. Even the darkness of one of those tunnels beneath the city would be preferable to his touch.

Moloch grasps her. Bones crack in his grip as he turns her to face him. Once more he dips his head and then he thrusts forward, one of his horns impaling her. Yet there is no pain, only discomfort. Only a terrible coldness. She stares down at the place below her left breast where the horn has entered her, pushed through fabric and flesh, and she realizes that it has not gutted her. It is as though Moloch's horn has passed through her without harm. It is inside her. But there is no wound, no real pain, only . . .

She flinches. Begins to shake.

Her tears flow freely now.

The god-king has not opened his mouth, but where they are connected, Moloch has begun to feed on her. Draining strength and hope from her as surely as if the monstrosity were leeching her blood. She wants to cry out for her mother, wishing that she could be coddled, once more, in that good woman's arms, just as she had been as a small child.

Then the urge has passed, for she cannot recall the feeling of such comfort and safety.

There is only sorrow in her now.

Moloch has begun to moan again with the pleasure of his feast. Her vision begins to dim and she ceases any struggle, falling limp in his arms, her head lolling to one side.

And she sees them, emerging from the darkness of those tunnel mouths. Wisp-haired women in shapeless cloaks, faces stretched and distorted, nearly as hideous as Moloch himself.

Hungry.

"Nnnnnnnnnnnnnnnnno!" The sound began with Michael grunting through his teeth, and ended as his fingers sifted through wet leaves and closed around the same rock he had struck his knee on earlier.

They still held him tightly, but the one before him was little more than a wraith now, a hollow, withered shell. Yet its fingers were still anchored inside him. With an incoherent roar he forced himself up, twisting around and swinging his arm to slam the rock into the face of the misshapen woman whose fingers were sunk into his left shoulder.

The rock tore open its face. Its flesh. As the wound gaped open, a silver mist began to spill out, like a tendril of fog made of mercury. It hissed as it slid from the gash and the wind through the trees began to pull at it. The silver mist swirled languidly away, like blood in the ocean.

Blood, he thought. *They can bleed. They can be hurt.*

This realization took a fraction of an instant, and then he drove his elbow back into the chest of the other who had been holding him. The one in front withdrew its finger from his forehead and Michael hurled the rock at it. The stone caved its face in with a puff of dust and a crackling noise, a dried husk breaking.

It fell.

The others hesitated.

He turned and hurled himself down the hill, unmindful of the incline or the wet leaves, hardly feeling the branches whipping around him. He ducked beneath a bough, grabbed hold of it and swung himself past. His heels slipped and he began to slide. He could see the place below where the trees thinned and the incline began to level off, where the light of the overcast day seeped in. His heart leaped with a frantic hope unlike anything he had ever felt before.

His arms wavered and he tried to keep his balance. Tried, and failed. Michael tried to grasp low-hanging branches but he only continued to slide. His ass bumped over rocks and roots and it was all he could do to keep from somersaulting ass-over-teakettle the rest of the way down. An image swam in his mind of his head striking a tree trunk and splitting like overripe fruit. Like something was rotten inside his skull.

And maybe it was. The taint of those images, those memories, was still inside him.

His back and neck crawled with the fear that the twisted women were dancing and floating in pursuit, coming down the hill through the trees after him. But he would not turn, would not even glance over his shoulder. He didn't want to see them. Branches tore at him as though they, too, wished to hold him back, and then Michael reached the bottom of the hill. His knees nearly buckled as he adjusted to the level ground, and then he exploded from the trees and ran to his car.

Stay away, he heard, a whisper on the wind, a suggestion in his ears. Or perhaps in his mind. Or in his veins, where their touch had tainted him. *Stay away.*

He dared not look up while he tore open the door; once he was inside, he locked the car and started the engine, ratcheted it into gear, and hit the accelerator. The car leaped forward, spitting sand from under the tires, and only then did he glance around.

The twisted women—the husks—were gone.

He shook all over, barely able to keep his hands on the wheel, but he did not pull over. It was not until he was back out on Old Route 12 and passing by a strip mall that he brought the car to a stop, threw it into park, and held himself, rocking and staring wide-eyed at nothing, trying to make sense of the impossible.

WHEN MICHAEL AND JILLIAN HAD announced that they planned to go to Austria for their honeymoon, the prevailing wisdom amongst their family and friends was that this was sheer lunacy. The recommendation, spouted from dozens of sets of lips, was that they spend the days subsequent to their wedding in warmer climes. A Caribbean cruise, for instance. Mexico and Bermuda were also popular suggestions.

Aside from the fact that both Jillian and Michael loathed the idea that they should choose a destination solely based on its popularity, there was the additional obstacle of Michael's despising the beach. His mother had been, and still was, an inveterate sun-worshipper. As a child he had been dragged to the shores of Maine, Cape Cod, and Florida so frequently that body-surfing, collecting seashells, and building sand castles no longer held any appeal for him. Like any child forced to engage in any activity so often, even when he had no desire for it, he had developed a certain antagonism toward the whole enterprise. In fact, during the entirety of their relationship thus far Jillian had been able to drag Michael to the beach exactly once, and that had been in Maine the previous New Year's Day. Not the ideal climate for sun and surf.

In response to the dismay with which their friends met their plans, Michael could only remind them that when it was their turn to go on a honeymoon they could choose whatever destination their hearts—or the latest trend—demanded. But he and Jillian had other interests.

The truth was that Jillian would have been more than happy to take a Caribbean cruise. In fact, had she insisted, or seemed even the least bit upset about the options Michael presented, he would have submitted without argument. He loved her, after all. The important thing was for them to have time together, away from their usual lives, to recover from the chaos that accompanied any wedding.

However, for his own part, he wanted more than lying out under the sun, drinking daiquiris and margaritas and things with little umbrellas in them. He wanted history and adventure; he wanted discovery. He wanted to spend time investigating whatever locale they chose. Most of his friends would have been appalled to learn that one of the destinations they had considered was Alaska, until they'd set the wedding for October. Austria would be chilly that time of year, but Alaska . . . that was too much even for Michael. Those same friends would have been astonished if he and Jillian had announced the honeymoon spot they had settled on initially. Michael had always had a fascination with Egypt. So much so that despite the turbulence and violence in that region, that marvelous adventure had been their plan right up until the very moment he discovered that the coolest month to visit Egypt was January, when it was still ninety-five degrees in Cairo and one hundred and ten on the Nile. He would have endured a lot to see the Great Pyramids, visit the Sphinx, and cruise along the same waters that had once carried Cleopatra's royal barge, even ignoring travel warnings from the U.S. government. But there were limits. Someday he hoped to visit Egypt . . . but not in October.

The morning after the wedding was a wonder. As tired as they were, they were filled with a kind of energy that neither of them had ever felt before and both doubted they would ever feel again. It was pure exhilaration. As they drove to the airport together, and later on the plane to Vienna, Michael looked at her dozens of times and repeated the same words.

"You're my wife."

To which Jillian would reply, "Yes, I'm aware of that."

Michael would gaze at her in amazement and shake his head. "No, you don't understand. You're my *wife*."

There was a wonderful period of adjustment to that idea. They had been married less than twenty-four hours and already he found a kind of peace and comfort in her presence that he never could have imagined. Jillian treated it as though she thought he was being silly. Charmingly so, but silly nevertheless. Yet he could see in her eyes that she understood and that she felt that same calm, that sense of rightness.

Upon their arrival in Vienna, they thanked God for taxicabs. Much like many of the other old capitals of Europe, Vienna was a diamond in the rough. The rough consisted of the industry that had grown up to surround the heart of the city during the twentieth century. There were office buildings, factories, and featureless apartments that could have been part of any city in the world. But once they had crossed the Danube Canal, the old city rose around them. There was romance in every stone of the architecture. The artist in Michael rejoiced.

When the cab stopped at a red light beside a tower in which was housed the most intricate glockenspiel he could have imagined, Jillian scrambled for the camera. But Michael did not want a photograph. He pulled out a pad and sketched madly, grateful for the traffic and the red light. Two minutes later as they pulled away, he craned his neck to get a last glimpse and then closed his eyes to sear it into his mind. He spent the rest of the ride sketching furiously. Jillian said nothing, only watching over his shoulder. She reached over to stroke the back of his neck, fingers twirling in his hair. She understood. Hell, that was one of the reasons he married her.

He would carry that pad wherever they went in Vienna, but then, in the madness of nearly missing their stop at Salzburg, he would leave it on the train. Later, he would vow to himself that he would return once more to Vienna, just to draw. But so far, no luck.

Still, the loss of his sketch pad was yet to come—like so many losses and victories, small and large. On that day they wove through narrow back streets. Without the cab driver they never would have found the Hotel Kärntnerhof. It wasn't on a main street, or even precisely off a main street, but in a small alley called Grashofgasse, which seemed hidden away off of a side street. Even after they had found it, the hotel seemed hidden from the rest of the city.

They lugged their bags from the car, checked in, and spent only moments in the room before finding a map and heading out onto the streets of Vienna after dark. The hotel was quaint and seemed impossibly far from everything, yet in moments they found the magic in the city they had been hoping for. At a tiny restaurant in which no one spoke a single word of English save "hello," Michael ate something he couldn't pronounce but guessed was a kind of potato dumpling. Jillian ordered Wiener schnitzel, because after all, it was their first night in Vienna.

A short walk through a narrow arcade just around the corner from the hotel brought them into the midst of Rotenturmstrasse, and minutes later they were standing in a broad open plaza staring up at the extraordinary façade of St. Stephen's Cathedral. It stunned Michael with its combination of architectural styles, from the Romanic foundations of its basic structure to the stunning Gothic traditions of its towers. He knew he had to draw it, but that would have to wait for daylight. Lights burned in the tower and the windows, accenting the mystery of the place.

They continued on from the plaza, strolling along Kärntnerstrasse, a pedestrian street lined with elegant shops, chocolatiers, cafés, hotels with globe lampposts, and one extraordinary structure after another. It was evening in Vienna, and this seemed the city's beating heart. There were Austrians on the street, but Michael heard half a dozen other languages spoken by people passing by. He strolled arm in arm with Jillian, gazing in shop windows and just soaking up the amazing history of the place, the clash of architectural styles that gave it its unique flavor. The city had been a jewel of Europe, fought over for centuries, and it reflected the influences of its various suitors.

Walking around he realized how chilly it was, and they bought scarves for twice what they were worth. Jillian dragged Michael into a bakery café called Linzner's. As Jillian looked at Michael over her Sacher torte and he licked whipped cream off the rim of his cocoa mug, she laughed.

"Well, I'm married now. I guess it doesn't matter anymore if I have three desserts a day and put on forty pounds in a week."

He winked. "We'll get fat together."

While they didn't visit Linzner's three times a day, they were there at least once, usually twice, a day for the duration of their stay in Vienna. In between visits for chocolate, coffee, and tortes, they wandered the city, ducking into tiny antique stores and taking tours of the grand baroque palaces of the Austrian capital. They explored the Vienna Woods, and walked through the Tiergarten at Schönbrunn Palace, the oldest zoo in Europe. They took in the Sigmund Freud museum, and the Imperial Crypt of the Hapsburgs.

On their final afternoon in Vienna, Michael told Jillian he had a surprise for her. He had just finished a sketch of St. Peter's

Church, whose origins as a house of worship dated back into the mystery of the fourth century, though Charlemagne himself had supposedly founded a church on the site four hundred years later.

Now he posed her so that he could take a photograph of her with the church in the background.

"I have a surprise for you," he said from behind the camera.

"Oooh. I like surprises."

From his inside coat pocket he withdrew a pair of tickets and held them out for her. Jillian snatched them from his hand, gazed at them, and her eyes widened.

"Oh, my God, Michael. I can't believe you did this. They were so expensive."

"It's our honeymoon, Jilly. We're allowed to splurge a bit."

The tickets were for *La Traviata* at the Vienna Opera House. Neither one of them had ever been to an opera before.

"Oh, shit. I don't have anything to wear. What am I supposed to do?"

Michael laughed. "Wear blue jeans, sweetie. You're an American. They don't expect much from us."

And that's what they did.

They weren't the only ones at the opera house dressed down, but they were in the minority. Most of the people who attended *La Traviata* at the Staatsoper that night were in elegant gowns and tailored suits. As he and Jillian went up the grand staircase in that bastion of class and style, Michael found a kind of freedom in being there in a sweater and blue jeans. In a way he felt like a man who had just stepped back in time, as if he and Jillian had just transported themselves to an era when the arts were preserved and presented in a setting of opulence and wealth, kept for the nobility and the upper classes as though only they could appreciate it.

They sat in their box and watched the opera. Though he did not understand a word of Italian, the entire evening was a thing of beauty. He relished the French Renaissance style of the architecture. He watched the other people in their boxes and wondered what the dreams and lives had been of the people who had sat in those boxes a hundred years before.

When the opera was over it was quite late. They walked back along Kärntnerstrasse and found it transformed. There were still lights on, but the cobblestoned street was deserted, the shops closed. Only a handful of other people passed them, most of those also returning from the opera. At the end of the street they found themselves in the vast plaza in front of the cathedral, alone.

The moon hung full and storybook bright above the cathedral and bells rang the lateness of the hour. In the center of that courtyard, in the midnight shadow of the cathedral tower, Michael Dansky took the hand of his wife and together they waltzed in the moonlight.

They laughed a moment, but then the laughter died and their smiles faded, and they waltzed in perfect rhythm and with utter sincerity. In that single moment they knew that their suspicions had been correct all along.

They were meant for each other.

HALF A MILE AFTER MICHAEL had collected himself enough to drive away from the strip mall, he was struck by the realization of what he was returning to. Though it had been driven from his mind for a time—the only tiny mercy in a day that had completely unraveled all that remained of his faith in the world—now the memory of Jillian's behavior the night before returned to him. This sweet woman, with whom he had waltzed in the cathedral square in Vienna, had been corrupted.

His mind was fraught with confusion. The memories that he had . . . tasted. What a strange word, and yet it felt correct. He had tasted some of Jillian's memories. That husk of a woman had forced a connection of flesh and mind. It had violated him to use him, to communicate, to warn him again or frighten him away. But his desperate fear for Jillian, and his anger, his hatred of them, had done something. Just as the thing had tapped in to his mind, he had tapped in to hers. He was sure of it.

Michael had felt its mind, and a terrible dark void inside, a black, yawning hunger, and then those memories had come spilling out of her. Memories Jillian had lost. He had experienced them firsthand, flooding into him as though they were his own memories and he was only now recalling them. Still they lingered in his mind. Though they were only a few fragments of what she had lost, it tore him open inside to feel so intimately the joy of Jillian's childhood.

How? That was the word that haunted him now. What was wrong with Jillian wasn't brain damage. Somehow those things had stolen all of the memories of her innocent years. They had attacked her like rabid dogs, and the result was the absolute bitch she had become. Without the core of hope and pure happiness those memories provided, all that was left was bitter cynicism.

A handful of those memories had been in the mind of that soulless husk that had thrust her fingers into his flesh, and maybe it was just Michael's yearning for Jillian to be returned to herself . . . but some of those memories had spilled into him.

And then . . . others. Ancient memories. Dark and terrifying. *Moloch,* he thought. He had to make sense of those images, those memories. If he could understand what these husks really were, he might be able to help Jilly, to restore what had been stolen from her.

If there was any of it left.

He slammed on the brakes and swerved to the side of the road. A truck following too closely behind laid on the horn and his car shook as it thundered by.

What about the girl? Or the things you've been smelling and hearing? He had no answers to those questions. Not yet. But already he was beginning to postulate. He had first caught those scents when he had entered that house the night he brought Scooter home. When Scooter was near, he had smelled some of them again. In the car, when he had first seen those misshapen women on the side of the road, he had smelled them again. The lost girl had been nowhere in sight, but now he wondered if she might have been there after all, with him, yet invisible to him. Trying to get to him, to make him see, to communicate.

She had touched his dreams. Had tried to speak to him when she manifested in his office or his bedroom. The letters in grease on the popcorn bag. He had promised to find her, had tried to help her, and maybe all along she had been trying to get back to him, to help him find her.

He didn't really understand how any of it was possible, or what it meant. All of his guesswork was not answering any questions. Not really. But it would lead him to answers, of that he was confident.

Another question occurred to him and his brow furrowed. *Why not me?* Rage and grief burned inside him. He had been the one searching for Scooter, for Susan Barnes, and yet they had gotten to him not by hollowing out his own childhood, but by stealing Jillian's. It made no sense.

Or perhaps it did. That other memory, that ancient memory, belonged to a girl whose innocence was being sacrificed to her city's god, to a monster. The husks themselves were women. Could it simply be that he was a man? There had to be more to it than that. Yet another memory struck him now . . . one of his own this time. He recalled clearly the vaguely dreamy expressions on the faces of the waitress and the other woman to whom he had shown his drawing of the house on Wildwood Road. As if they remembered it, but only from a dream.

"It's too much," he whispered, barely aware that he spoke aloud.

His head ached, the front of his skull the worst of all. Part of it might have been the touch of that husk—who had withered to almost nothing even as she had forced those memories into his head—but he knew a lot of it was simple confusion. Too many questions. Too much new information to process.

There was a great deal he did not yet understand, a lot that still did not make sense to him. But it would.

Michael put the car in gear and pulled back onto the road. He drove slowly, watching both sides of the road and the rearview mirror for any sign of them.

All right, now what? So you understand, or you think you do. How does that help Jillian?

Once again, the answer came back to that night on the side of Old Route 12 and to the lost little girl who had made him promise to find her. Susan Barnes was the key. Those hollow husk women wanted to keep him from finding that house, wanted him to stop looking for the girl. Michael had thought she was a ghost, but if that was true, why would they interfere?

These were his thoughts as he drove down Old Route 12 past that classic gas station that was a relic of an ancient time, a little out-of-the-way spot that wasn't on any tourist map but would delight anyone seeing it for the first time. A perfectly preserved piece of the past. Nostalgia come to life. A memory.

Two blocks further on he saw a FOR SALE sign in front of an old Cape that butted up to the edge of the road.

Susan Barnes stood beside the sign.

Dusk was coming on and he could see the fading light of day passing through her translucent form. Her face was contorted with sadness and desperation. As he drove past, craning his neck to look at her, she mouthed the words silently.

Come find me.

Michael slowed the car and looked back, but she was gone.

The next FOR SALE sign was three miles down the road, in front of a sub and pizza shop whose windows were soaped over.

She was there, too. Mouthing those words. Chills ran all through him and his heart broke for the little girl all over again. He wished he could ease her pain, wished he could pull over and let her climb in, just as he had done on that first night, the night she had been wandering on the road. What had she been doing, that night, so far from home? That run-down mansion had been her destination, but he had always doubted it was her home.

By the time he reached the Hawthorne Inn he had passed a total of eight FOR SALE signs. The spectral form of Susan Barnes waited for him beside each one, lips moving in silence. And yet it was only after he'd let himself into his room at the inn and lain down on the bed that he understood what it was she was trying to tell him.

CHAPTER THIRTEEN

A cold rain began to fall as Jillian drove home from the train station, a frozen drizzle that spattered her windshield and coated the road with black ice. The urge to stomp on the brake, to test the slick blacktop, was strong. It made no sense, but this was just the sort of idiotic temptation that had been teasing her mind of late. She resisted, keeping her hands firmly clutched upon the steering wheel, but her mouth was curled into a sour twist and she fumed as she drove.

Another bitch of a day. Another day as a bitch. For the second day in a row she had fired one of her paralegals. This time, however, it had been her call and not something demanded of her. Alisa Gordon had gone off to meet some girlfriend for lunch and had reappeared nearly three hours later carrying shopping bags from Neiman Marcus. There weren't any attorneys waiting on documents from her. She had recently completed a major closing and was just beginning the groundwork for a new one. But still . . . three hours? Jillian had never taken a lunch that long in her life. It was just blatant abuse of the relationship Jillian had tried to forge with her paralegals.

So she'd fired the idiot.

A ripple of surprise and indignation had gone through her department. Attorneys had come by to ask her what had happened—none of her paralegals had dared—and she had told them they could read it in her memo. Presumptuous assholes. She was aware of how icy she'd been with the attorneys and vaguely cognizant of the fact that this was a bad idea, but she could not seem to muster up much concern. Something had changed inside her, and she felt as though she had woken up from a long, pleasant sleep to a grim reality.

This was the world. Most people were stupid or incompetent, and the majority of those who managed to rise above the chaff weren't exactly scintillating company. A sick feeling had been spreading through her all day long, an ache in her gut that was part pain and part nausea. She wondered from time to time what had become of Michael, where he had gone when he'd left the house last night. A rancid bitterness boiled up in the back of her throat whenever she imagined his expression the night before. What kind of a man was he? What sort of loser was confronted with what he'd been confronted with and just took it on the chin, just packed a bag and walked?

It pissed her off, actually. He was her husband. If he was going to take off, they ought to at least have it out. All day she'd thought about the fight they should have had, about the screaming that hadn't happened and the way she imagined it would have been to hit him, and have him hit her. Not that she wanted to be hurt. But if he had a problem with what she'd done, he should have been willing to fight about it.

The November chill seeped into the car despite the heat. In the wake of her thoughts about Michael, her mind returned as it had all day to the night before, to sweaty, risky sex with two college boys in the men's room at a bar near Government Center. Images flashed in her mind of the rush she'd gotten, and of the way she had despised them and herself even as it happened. She'd relished every second of it—the filthiest, most wonderful sex she'd ever had. In her whole life, Jillian had never fucked or been fucked like that. She'd thrown one of them against the wall of the bathroom, grabbed the top of the stall, and hung there, riding him.

The car swayed as she turned a corner, tires sliding on black ice. Frozen tears struck the windshield like a shower of diamonds.

A smile crept across her face and a warmth spread up from between her legs as she became wet.

The twist in her gut spoiled it. A feeling lingered in her as though she was hungry, but no food would erase it. There was some hollow part of her she couldn't fill, and it was maddening.

Her smile disappeared and she slammed a fist on the steering wheel. The horn beeped, the wheel spun, and she hit the brake even as the car began to skid. Her heart sped and she gritted her teeth as she gripped the wheel. The car spun lazily in a circle, completely out of her control. The front tires bumped against the curb, and the back end swung around and knocked over a stop sign with a crunch of metal.

Jillian gripped the wheel, waiting for something worse, some impact. But nothing else happened. The rear driver's side would be dented, but when she gently pressed the accelerator, the car rolled forward. She turned herself around and continued toward home, knuckles white on the wheel. In those moments when she was out of control, anything could have happened. She had been lucky.

Lucky. She understood the concept, but she couldn't feel it. Didn't know it.

Still, she was careful the rest of the drive home.

The house was dark when Jillian pulled into the driveway. The windows were like black eyes watching her approach. Ice had started to build up on the grass, making the lawn look like it was composed of sewing needles. It was too early in the year for this. Too early for ice, for winter weather, for nights when the sky forced you home.

Jillian killed the engine and sat in the darkness watching the house. Her head was all fucked up. Anger clawed at the base of her skull; it was an effort to prevent spite from curling her lip. She wasn't stupid. The conversation with Michael about her memories had not been lost on her. And it was true: She could not remember anything before the eighth grade.

But that bothered her less than the things she *did* remember.

Her memories of high school were intact. Of college. Of her job and her love for Michael. Love. She scoffed at the word, but a pang of something echoed in the hollow that was inside her. Jillian remembered laughing because she was happy. She could recall that it felt good when Michael held her in his arms. But these things didn't make sense to her, now. Just the thought of their honeymoon, how romantic they had been, filled her with self-loathing.

It was all bullshit. Pleasure was an ephemeral thing to be had from a moment's triumph or a durable lover. Nothing else mattered.

So why was she so empty inside?

A scowl tore across her face and Jillian let out a little shout of frustration. She banged her head on the steering wheel and pushed her fingers into her hair. Her chest rose and fell rapidly as she slumped, forehead against the wheel.

"Stop your fucking whining," she whispered to herself, the desperation obvious in her voice.

Then she popped open her door, dropped her keys into her purse and slid out. She cursed again as she slammed the door. The urge to hit something was strong and she wished Michael were home. For that, and because it was so dark there, inside the house. And it seemed that though she could no longer understand certain emotions, loneliness was not among them. That one she could summon up just fine.

When she pushed the door open and stepped inside, closing it behind her even as she slid out of her shoes and dropped her bag, the only sounds from within the house were the hum of the refrigerator and the ticking of the heat. Then, as if to greet her, the phone trilled.

Jillian jumped, startled, her pulse quickening. The sound came again and she strode over to answer it, annoyed by the noise

and by the fright it had given her. Shadows shifted in her peripheral vision and she jerked her head around. Something had
moved there in the darkness. Or had it?

The phone rang again.

Scowling, she picked it up.

"Hello?"

"Hi there, is this Jillian Dansky?"

Her brow furrowed. "Who's asking?"

"Mrs. Dansky, this is Harry Crenshaw from the *Eagle Tribune*.
Bob Ryan gave me your phone number. He tells me you're running for city council and that you're going to be the candidate to
beat next year. It sounds like you've got a lot of support. I hoped
I could ask you a few questions, get your take on—"

"Now's not a good time," Jillian interrupted, biting off each
word.

Crenshaw hesitated. He was getting the message loud
and clear. "Right. I'm sorry about that. We can set it up for another time. It's just that, well, Bob thought you'd want to
get some press going right away, get your name out there early,
and—"

"Bob Ryan should mind his goddamned business."

"I'm sorry?" The voice was horrified.

Jillian bit her tongue. Her nostrils flared and she tried to keep
silent. She knew she should say nothing, just hang up, but she
was just so sick to death of people treating her like she was a
character in the movie of their lives. Hannah. Every attorney at
the firm. Bob fucking Ryan the worst of all.

"Look, Mr. Crenshaw, I told you that you caught me at a bad
time. Beyond that, what do you want me to say? That I'm running? Yes, I am. But I need to do things at my own speed, in my
own way. I don't want to be just another crony of the old boys'
network, a chess piece on somebody else's board. When I want
to announce, you'll get a press release. You want to talk then,
fine. But just report the news. Don't do me any favors. Politics
isn't supposed to be about favors and public ass-kissing. It's
about time the city council learned that lesson."

There was a pause. She thought she could hear a pen scratching on paper.

"Can I quote you on that?" Harry Crenshaw asked.

Jillian felt that sick twisting in her gut again. Her head ached. The hollow inside her seemed to grow.

"Fuck off!" she snarled, and slammed down the phone.

But she had not said no.

COME FIND ME.

Michael stood in the darkness in his room at the Hawthorne Inn, staring out the window. Frozen rain whipped against the glass. For some reason the sound it made reminded him of car tires rolling slowly over gravel. His breath fogged the window and idly he raised a finger to draw a smiley face in the condensation.

He blinked, glancing out at the night as though coming awake. For a moment he studied the view from the window, the gauzy veil of storm that had fallen over the night, preventing him from seeing clearly. It seemed to him that Scooter should be out there in the icy rain, on a corner, gazing up at him forlornly. But that made no sense, really. How could she be out there when she was in here with him?

Adrenaline still raced through him, so much of it that he felt as though his body was quivering. And maybe it was. A tiny smile he could not have explained flickered across his features and he turned to look into the darkness of his room at the inn. Even as he did so, he saw her, there in the dark corner between the bureau and the wall. She had her own ethereal glow and yet she was a vague figure, like the afterimage of the sun on the inside of his eyelids.

Then she was gone. His gaze swept the room. She was in the bathroom doorway. She was by the floor lamp in the corner. She was just beside him. The lost girl. In his peripheral vision at all times, as though her image had been permanently burned into his mind, or into his retinas at least. Haunting him. Every few minutes he would catch the scent of popcorn or hot cocoa and he would know she was still there. She was his constant companion now, so close, and yet further away than ever before. The hollow women had seen to that, somehow. They were keeping him from her, or her from him. Frightening her. Frightening Michael, too.

Oh, Jesus, he thought, shuddering as he thought about them again, about their touch.

But no matter what they did, she had touched him, too. And she was with him now for the duration, he sensed. There in his peripheral vision, there on the outskirts of his reality. All along she had haunted him, yet he had no fear of her.

Haunting wasn't about fear. It had taken time for him to realize that, but he knew it now. Haunting was about sorrow.

Come find me.

"I'm trying," he said to the darkness, to the girl who haunted the shadows at the edges of his eyes.

But that wasn't exactly right, was it? No, not at all. For spread across the bed were all of the papers he had printed up at Krakow & Bester the night before, the results of his search for the elusive Scooter, the finding of the lost girl. A girl who, maybe, was never really lost at all.

Michael frowned. How had it gotten so dark in here so quickly? How long had he been standing at the window? Night had been falling, certainly, but now it was here. Dusk had surrendered to the fullness of evening, as always. What was wrong with him?

Yet another question he knew the answer to.

"Shit, do something," he commanded himself.

With a short, frustrated snort of breath, he went over to the nightstand and clicked on the antique blown-glass lamp. This very sort of thing was the reason he preferred an old inn like this to a traditional hotel. The place could have been cleaner, but it had personality. Someone had taken the time to decorate it, instead of creating a thousand such rooms in one pass, like the cubicle in Krakow & Bester he had worked so hard to escape.

Michael sat down on the edge of the bed and surveyed the papers laid across the floral bedspread. Too many names on paper. Names, addresses, photographs. Maps.

And the illustration he had drawn of the house on Wildwood Road. When he'd come back to the inn he had shown it, on a whim, to the woman behind the counter, asked her if she recognized it. At first he had thought she was going to say she hadn't, but then she blinked and wet her lips, her face gone a bit pale. She nodded.

"I think so," she'd said. "I don't remember where. Your friend wants to buy the place?"

Michael had given her that same lie. He nodded. "Yes."

The smile that had touched the corners of her mouth had been almost sickly. "You couldn't pay me to live there," she had said. Then her eyes had gone wide with the realization that she had spoken aloud, that she might have insulted him.

He had thanked her and started across the lobby, more questions in his mind than ever. Nearly at the elevator he had paused. A pair of women sat in the lounge talking to one another animatedly over coffee or tea. There had been accents in their voices and a terrible idea came to him. He was almost afraid to approach them, afraid of the answer. They were visitors, clearly not local women. From their accents, he had guessed they were German or Austrian.

"Excuse me," he had begun.

The women had seemed taken aback. Only then had Michael wondered about his appearance. He'd been stumbling around the woods and it had been days since he had shaved. He had smiled nervously and quickly explained what he wanted.

"Very sorry," said the older one, a thin blonde he had placed in her late forties. "We are not from America."

Michael had held the drawing up, certain that the placemat with its grease stains would make them even more wary of him. "Maybe you've passed it, since you arrived?"

"No, I'm sorry," the blond woman said politely.

But her friend had frowned as she studied the drawing. This second woman was dark-haired and dark-eyed, shorter and stouter than the first. "I do not know this house," she had said, her accent thick. "But it reminds me of something . . . something . . ." She had glanced at the blonde. "A building in Düsseldorf, I think. Do you know the one?"

The blonde had paled, her eyelids fluttering. "Yes. I . . . they don't really look alike, do they? It is simply something about them. Was it in Düsseldorf, though? I can't remember."

Michael had thanked them and walked away quickly, unnerved by their reactions and by their words. What did it mean? There was a house here that every woman he had approached seemed to vaguely recognize, as if from a dream, and seemed to dread. In Germany, there was another. How many others might exist?

Too many questions, and a lot of them distractions. There were many mysteries here, but in the end not all of them were important. His focus was the house on Wildwood Road, and what went on there. What concerned him was Jillian, and the lost girl, Scooter. There were questions he knew he needed to ask, but they would wait. First he had to find that goddamned house.

The paperwork was spread across the bed. His eyes avoided the one printout that he needed, but his fingers knew just where to find it.

Icy needles continued to pelt the window. The lost girl lingered at the edges of his vision. When he glanced toward the night-dark glass, it seemed she was torn away. He almost thought that if he closed his eyes he might see her better. It made no sense, but the thought was there just the same. His fingers slid along the texture of the page, a simple piece of paper he had printed off of his computer at work.

FOR SALE.

It was no coincidence. The girl had haunted him from the

roadside as he'd driven back to the inn. And she had been at not one, but half a dozen For Sale signs.

Michael held the paper closer to the lamp—the shadows seemed to want to crowd in nearer and nearer, encroaching on the light it shed—and he studied the photograph of the Amesbury real estate agent. The picture of a fifty-something woman named Susan Barnes. Her hair was bleached. Her face was that of a woman on the upward climb out of middle age. There were a thousand ways he could have denied that the woman in the picture had once been the lost girl he had picked up on the roadside, the cute blond angel in the peasant blouse that he had nearly run down in his car. But Michael wasn't looking for reasons to deny it. He could not.

It was her. The gossamer specter on the roadside had told him as much. She had been trying to tell him all along. Her real name. *Hilly couldn't say Susan, she always said Scoosan, and that's where Scooter came from.* The words echoed, only now fully remembered from a dream. The popcorn bag. And then, even as they tried to keep her from him, she had been there, on his drive back to the inn.

FOR SALE.

No, believing it was her was not the problem.

Michael shook his head, letting out a long breath, and his gaze drifted across the page. There, beside the picture, was the address—97 Kingsbury Avenue—and a telephone number. He let the page rest on his lap and glanced at the telephone on the nightstand.

What was he supposed to say? *Do you know me? Did you ever live on Wildwood Road? Have you been . . . hurt?*

He ran his hands through his hair, found that his fingers were still shaking. When he glanced at the window again, he thought that perhaps the spectral wisp of a girl lingered an instant longer. He could feel her eyes upon him, watching him expectantly, pleading with him. Her despair was an open wound, and she had put all her hope in him.

Grief cut him, then, and he closed his eyes, wincing. In his mind's eye he did not see the ephemeral figure of the little lost girl, however. He saw Jillian . . . the way she had looked at him on that first night, when they had made love on the roof of the library.

Come find me.

Michael was reaching for the phone even before his eyes were open. He snatched the paper up from his lap, cradled the phone against his ear, and dialed quickly the Amesbury telephone number on the page. It began to ring almost instantly.

"Hello?"

"Yes . . . hello, is Susan Barnes there?"

A male voice had answered. Young. It occurred to him that he had no idea how old the information was that he had found. A wrong number. He would have to start over.

"Who is this?" the voice inquired.

All of the adrenaline he had built up evaporated; he felt himself deflate. Michael ran his tongue over his lips and flexed the fingers that held the phone.

"She . . . she doesn't know me. But I'd like to speak with her about a house."

That was true enough.

"My mother isn't a Realtor anymore. And she can't be reached at this number. You'll have to find someone else."

"No," Michael said, too abruptly. What was he supposed to say now? She was a real estate broker, but it seemed unlikely that this house—if it was home to those hollow women—would be for sale. But she had come into contact with the place somehow. He had to keep Susan's son from hanging up on him.

"I'm . . . it's not my house. I don't even know if she . . ." He hesitated, knowing he wasn't making any sense. "I just thought she might be able to tell me about it. Off of Old Route Twelve, way up on a hill around Wildwood Road."

There was a pause on the other end of the line during which the only thing Michael could hear was the crunch of icy rain on the window of his room. It felt as though it were hitting his back. He shivered with the chill.

"Who the hell are you?" the man asked, bitter and angry.

Shit. Michael did not understand what had set him off, but the man's tone made it clear that he had crossed some line. He had blown it. A moment later and there would be a click and the line would go dead and he'd be no closer to finding her.

"Look, just . . . I'm just trying to find your mother. Maybe if you could give me a number, or just take mine and ask her to—"

"I don't think so."

"Please, you don't . . . it's hard to explain."

"Good-bye. Don't call here again."

"Wait!" Michael snapped. His hands were sweating. He glanced around the room frantically, and everywhere he looked, the shadows danced with the elusive image of the lost girl's ghost. "Please, just . . ."

Susan's son did not hang up.

"Look, just . . . can I ask you one question?"

Still no response, but he was listening.

"When she was a little girl, growing up . . . did she ever get lost?"

"What kind of freak—"

"They called her Scooter. Didn't they? Because Hilly couldn't say Susan, and it always came out—"

Click.

MICHAEL WAS DESPERATE. THE GUY had hung up on him, but that, and the mystery of why she'd given up selling real estate in the first place, were enough to give him hope. This was the path he was meant to be on. And it wasn't going to end with someone else hanging up a phone. Not with the flicker of blond hair and forlorn eyes that existed in his peripheral vision, that ghosted around after him. Not with what had happened to Jillian.

It was an effort not to think about Jilly, not to let hideous images and whispered memories into his mind. *How is it fair?* he thought, time and again. He'd done the right thing, picking up that girl, trying to get her home. And then *Come find me*, she'd said, and she had haunted him. Obsessed him. Needing someone who would save her from whatever hell she was in, whatever the hollow women had in store.

You did the right thing, he thought bitterly, *and all it cost you was Jillian.*

Even that was bullshit. Yes, it had cost him his wife and their relationship, but that was nothing compared to what it had cost Jillian herself. Michael wasn't so selfish that he didn't see that. Just selfish enough to push such rationality away and hold his own pain close as a child with a security blanket.

How is it fair? A grown man, in a cynical industry, with twenty-four-hour news channels galore telling him all the injustices in the world, and he still believed that life was fundamentally fair. How stupid was that?

The radio was off and the car rolled in silence save for the rush of warm air from the heater, the hum of the engine, and the spray of sleet-needles against the windshield. The weather hadn't improved. The roads were slick, deadly, but his mind wasn't muddled tonight as it had been that evening after the masquerade. It was clear. *Crystal.*

He felt as though he might jump out of his skin. Desperation ran through his blood like a heroin spike. His fingers were too tight on the wheel and somehow, despite the heat blasting from the vents, he felt cold. In the rearview mirror he could see traces of the girl in the backseat, a transparent silhouette.

"I think I'm beginning to understand," he said aloud, hoping she would hear him. "I think I'm on the way."

But first, he had a stop to make. Susan Barnes's son had hung up on him, so Michael was going to go there, directly, and confront him. He had to know. Had to speak to the woman the lost girl would grow to become. He had only begun to understand, but he thought he knew what he was going to find. Or had an inkling. But whatever happened, he wasn't going to let the guy brush him off. He would go there and knock on the door and ask questions and pray for answers.

Before that, though, he had to go home.

He had been avoiding even thinking about it, but he could not do that for long. Jillian was his wife. Hell, she was his whole world. Whatever she had done or said, he knew he had to see her. Jillian was not thinking or behaving rationally, and Michael was afraid for her. Afraid of what she might do.

She had already proven that she was capable of anything.

The storm kept people off the road. Sleet rained down in jagged curtains, twisted by the wind. The car rocked with the force of it. The night and the storm enveloped him, carrying the car along toward home. It was nearly seven o'clock when he came in sight of the house he and Jillian had shared, and it brought fresh pain to his heart as a thousand little memories cascaded through him like shattered glass.

Every light in the house was on.

For half a minute he just sat in the driveway with the car running, wipers shushing sleet off of the windshield. He glanced at the street atlas on the passenger seat with the printout of Susan Barnes's picture and address. The lost girl was a glimmer at the edge of his vision.

When he killed the engine and palmed his keys, the gravel-spray noise of the freezing rain on the car seemed to triple in volume. The windows were opaque with accumulation that sweated lines down the glass. But the house burned in the darkness so brightly with all of those lights it was almost like a mirage, teasing him with the promise of an end to the pain in his heart and the madness that haunted him.

Michael popped the door open and stepped out, slamming it behind him as he ran for the front door. He winced and brought his hands up to protect his face from the sleet, his keys still clutched tightly in his palm so he'd have them ready. Then he was on the front stoop, holding open the storm door, working the keys, turning the knob. He pushed the door open and stepped inside.

The house felt empty. That was the strangest thing. It was like being in the office the night before all by himself, or days when he'd come home from work and Jillian wasn't in from Boston yet. There was a void. A quiet. Every single light in the house was on—including one of the recessed lights over the fireplace that had burned out last week and that he hadn't gotten around to changing—but the place felt like a shell. Nothing seemed out of place, but he imagined that the odd sensation that went through him might not be unlike what he would have felt had they been robbed.

And Scooter was gone.

He blinked and shook his head, standing in the bright lights just inside the front door. Sleet dripped down the back of his shirt and ran down his back. Michael slid a hand through his hair, skimming the moisture, and flicked it at the doormat. He closed the door behind him, paused a moment, then started to make his way through the house. Any other night he would have taken off his coat and hung it from the finial at the bottom of the stairs, but not tonight.

He did not call out for Jillian as he moved through the rooms on the first floor. Somehow he did not think she would answer. The house was immaculate. Even the kitchen seemed undisturbed, as though the house had been abandoned. Not a dish in the sink. Not a spot on the counter. Michael made his way back around to the stairs and paused at the bottom, looking up to the second floor.

There was light in the hallway up there, but not like downstairs. Not so much that it could dispel all of the shadows.

The first step creaked as his weight fell upon it. How ridiculous that he should have lived in this house for years, noticed it each time, and then promptly forgotten. As he came up the stairs he could see the open door to the bathroom. The fan hummed inside, but as he crested the landing he could see the mirror. Jillian wasn't there, not even in the reflection of the bathtub. He'd thought she might be. It was often her retreat when she was at her wit's end.

The lights in the guest room were on but Michael ignored it and went instead to the master bedroom. Once upon a time he had carried Jillian all the way up the stairs and into their room, tumbling into bed, flushed with alcohol and desire. That seemed so long ago, now. He wondered if Jilly remembered.

The bedroom was as brightly illuminated as the rest of the house and as precisely neat and tidy, so for a moment he did not even register that the bed was occupied. Jillian lay on her side atop the richly detailed red-and-gold floral spread, curled in a fetal position. Though she was still dressed in her work clothes, her hair was wild and unkempt and her shirt was untucked from her skirt, which rode up well above her thighs, exposing the tops of her pantyhose. There was nothing titillating about this.

Jilly made no sound except that of her own breath coming ragged and too quick. She was moving almost imperceptibly, not even enough to shake the bed, rocking herself the way she had on the night they had spent in a romantic lodge in Vermont, when she had gotten food poisoning.

Michael took a step into the room. The floor creaked there as well.

With a hissing intake of breath, Jillian sat up and spun toward him. Michael recoiled in horror at the sight of her. Her shirt was open and streaked with blood, her bra was undone and hanging loosely beneath her arms. For a moment he feared some assault, but then he saw that there was blood on her hands, on her fingers, and that it had come from long furrows that had been clawed in the flesh of her breasts and the skin between and below them. The wounds were fresh. And she had made them herself.

The time for thinking was past. This was his baby, his love, his wife. "Jilly, oh, my God," he whispered as he started toward her.

She did not wait for him.

Eyes lost in a darkness that came from within, lips curled in a scowl of pure disgust and hate, she lunged from the bed.

Michael held up his hands to urge her back even as she hit him the first time. Her fist connected with his cheek with enough force to jar his teeth and send a jolt of pain through the muscles of his jaw. The next blow struck his chest, and the next, and the one after that. So stunned was Michael that it took him all of that time to react. He tried to grasp her wrists, but Jillian was fueled by rage. Her right hand escaped and she grabbed his throat with her bloody fingers and drove him backward. Michael was in a tumult of emotion and confusion and too slow to save himself from falling. He tumbled to the floor and his wife rode him to the ground.

"Jilly, please, stop it!" he said, tearing her clutching hand away. He could not stop his mind from recalling those images that had soaked into his mind from contact with the hollow women, stolen fragments of Jillian's life.

"Why?" she shrieked, tears springing to her eyes. Drops of fresh blood spilled from the gashes on her scarlet-stained breasts and dripped onto his chest and face. Her tears followed. One tear landed on his lips, and he tasted the tang of salt even as she pounded her fists down onto him again, pummeling him.

"Why what?" he shouted, frantic.

She grabbed his head with both hands, her fingers slipping into his hair, and shrieked again, spittle flying from her mouth. Her eyes were wide with fury and anguish.

"Why do you care?" Her voice was raw and ragged, collapsing in upon itself, even as she began to falter, the strength running out of her with her blood and tears.

Michael grabbed her wrists and tried to connect with his eyes, locking his gaze with hers. "Because I love you, Jilly. How can you ask that? Because I love you."

Her expression was wretched. Her eyes darted back and forth, and he could see she was lost. Misery in her every aspect, she shuddered and shook her head and leaned close to look into his eyes.

"But how do you love, Michael? *How* do you love? I can't re-member."

Then she collapsed upon him and he cradled her there, singing softly to his love, her blood soaking into his shirt. Michael rocked her and stared, wide-eyed, at the ceiling of their bedroom, more afraid now than he had ever been before.

CHAPTER FOURTEEN

In time, Jillian fell asleep in Michael's arms. She had spent the better part of an hour wavering between distraught and furious, and he had endured cruel taunts and barbs right up until the moment her eyes began to flutter and close. Soon her breathing had deepened and he knew that she slept. Only then could he allow himself to feel the sting from her words. For several minutes longer he just held her, gently. She did not know what she had lost . . . only that she had lost it.

But that was a beginning, at least.

Michael slid a pillow under her head and extricated himself, making sure not to disturb her. He pulled back her bloodstained shirt and studied the long scratches she had clawed into her chest. Relief flooded him. They were mostly superficial. Warm water to clean the drying blood and some antibacterial ointment and she'd be all right. But now wasn't the time. Not while she was sleeping.

He shut off the lights and paused at the open door of the bedroom to look back in at her, limned by the moonlight that spilled in through the windows. Jillian was a petite woman; curled there on the bed, she seemed almost like a girl again. Gazing at her there in the dark hush of the bedroom, she seemed so peaceful that he was reminded of the way things had been *before*. Once upon a time. Seeing her like that was a kind of window into the past, a view back to a place he could never return to. Whatever happened next, nothing would ever be the same.

He went downstairs and into the kitchen, leaving all the lights burning. She had found some solace in that, keeping the darkness at bay, and Michael did not want to take that away. The answering machine was blinking with new messages, but he had neither the time nor the inclination to listen to them. Jillian had probably blazed a trail of resentment and anger today, and it would only sadden him to hear the results of her behavior.

Focus.

Jillian's address book sat beside the microwave, stuffed to overflowing with scraps of notepaper and index cards scrawled with cooking recipes. He found Hannah's number easily enough and dialed her right away, leaning against the dishwasher. A stale, dirty smell emanated from it; even as he listened to the phone ring, he opened the cabinet and withdrew a box of dish-washing crystals.

There was a click as Hannah answered the phone.

"I don't want to talk to you," she said in a clipped tone.

"Hannah?"

"Michael? What do you want? What's going on? Did she make you call me, because I'm not going to forgive her this time. She's got a lot of explaining to—"

"Hannah, please," Michael said. "Just listen."

Something in his voice, in the soft tone he took, must have reached her. Hannah had obviously seen on her caller ID that the call was coming from his house and assumed it was Jillian; if his wife had torn a destructive path through her day, Hannah had clearly been one of the casualties.

"What is it?" Hannah asked, unable to hide her concern.

"Look, whatever she did or said to you today, she's not herself."

"Well, no shit. She's my sister, Michael. I still want to know what you did to set her off like that."

He sighed and banged his head on the wall, cradling the phone to his ear. "Jesus, Hannah. I didn't do anything. Could you just for one second stop thinking you have all the answers and listen to me?"

Dead silence on the line. Then: "You've got a lot of fucking nerve. The two of you. I swear to God, if this is how you treat people now, you deserve each other. I'm not your wife, Michael. You can't talk to me—"

"Hannah!" He cursed under his breath and glanced up as though he might be able to see through the ceiling to find out if he'd disturbed Jillian. When he spoke again, his voice was low. Emotion clogged his throat as he tried to put into words why he had called.

"Look, she's not herself, I told you. She's not . . . she's not well. It goes a lot further than her just being kind of bitchy. She's sort of delusional, Hannah. She's having trouble with her memory. There's someone I need to go see. Someone I think can help, but—"

"What do you mean, delusional? Is she on drugs or something? Ecstasy? She always told me you two stayed away from that stuff."

It was all he could do not to shriek at her. Instead he drew a breath and let it out quickly. "We do. It isn't drugs. She's having these . . . episodes. Weird behavior. I think I can help, but I don't want to leave her alone. I'm afraid she might hurt herself."

Or someone else, he thought. But he didn't dare say the words.

"Wait, you want me to come there?"

She sounded so incredulous that Michael had to pause a moment. "Well, yeah. I . . . she's just in a bad way right now, and—"

"I can't. Not that I'm sure I'd be willing to, even if I could. I live two hours away, Michael, never mind that I've got to be at the hospital early in the morning."

Michael frowned. "The hospital? What—"

"My mammogram showed something that isn't supposed to be there. They need to do a biopsy."

"Damn. Hannah, I'm sorry. I didn't know."

"Why would you? I've been trying to tell Jilly for days, but all she does is cuss me out." Hannah sighed. "Is she puking?"

"What?" He shook his head, and began pacing the kitchen.

"Throwing up, Michael. Is she throwing up? Is she physically wounded in some way? Convulsing?"

"No, but—"

"No. And if she was, you'd bring her to the hospital. So, I'm sorry, but whatever it is, I can't handle it right now. Not on top of this, and not when she's been treating me the way she's been treating me. When she feels able to use the phone, she can call me with an apology, and then if she needs to be baby-sat you can bring her here. I don't know what's wrong with you two, but I suggest therapy."

Hannah hung up on him.

Blinking in amazement, Michael held the phone away from him and stared at it. Whatever Jillian had said to Hannah earlier, it must have been pretty nasty.

"Christ," he whispered as he continued to pace. He put his hands behind his neck, stretching to his full height, racking his brain. No way was he going to leave Jillian home alone at this point, but if Hannah couldn't come, his options were severely limited. Several times he started to dial the phone number of one of his wife's other relatives, but that wasn't going to do any good. Jillian wouldn't want any of them to see her like this. And Michael needed quicker results, regardless.

He rested his forehead against the refrigerator, feeling the electric hum vibrating inside his skull. After a moment he pulled away, nodding to himself. The phone was still clutched in his hand and he dialed quickly, his pulse accelerating as he listened to it ring on the other end. He looked out the window above the sink; it was pitch black out there. Perhaps the moon had gone behind some clouds, or was blocked by the trees behind their house. Whatever the cause, it seemed like more than simple night blackness. It was as though the dark had swallowed up the house entirely.

"Hello?" asked a voice on the other end of the phone.

"Teddy."

"Mikey! Hey, bud, you really came through for me. I left you a bunch of messages. Where've you been? You feeling better? Working the cobwebs out of your brain?"

Just the sound of his friend's voice soothed him. Suddenly Teddy was his touchstone of sanity. Michael was being swept along a river of grief and impossibility and terrifying loss, but if he could only get Teddy to throw him a line—

"Listen, Ted. I need your help. It's . . . it's Jilly. I've got trouble."

When Teddy Polito spoke again all of the playfulness was gone from his voice. "Talk to me, Michael. Tell me what you need."

ON THE DRIVE OUT TO Amesbury, Michael kept the radio off. It seemed a time for silence. His heartbeat provided a persistent rhythm, an ominous staccato that propelled him on too fast. The headlights of oncoming vehicles lit up the inside of the car with a golden shimmer that made it all the more surreal. He had no idea what he was going to say when he reached the Barnes house. Was he supposed to just barge in? The Michael he had always been cringed at the thought, yet that part of him was being slowly eroded. What remained was the core of him, where all that mattered was Jillian.

He would do whatever he had to do to protect her, no matter the cost. If that meant breaking down doors in the middle of the night, then that was the way it would have to be. He sensed that answers existed just at the edges of his mind, the same way the lost girl had lingered just out of view in his peripheral vision.

But he would have those answers. And soon.

Old Route 12 led right into the heart of Amesbury. Michael used the atlas to navigate along several long, winding streets and then through a small grid of roads that seemed to be one sprawling neighborhood development, two decades old. He slowed to study the house numbers. The Barnes place was set back slightly on a rise, a long ranch whose driveway had been cut into the hill so that a garage could be put underneath. A stone wall ran along the property beyond the house, and past that there was only woods. Michael felt a passing tremor looking at the trees. They reminded him of his search for Wildwood Road.

He pulled into the driveway, got out, and went up the front walk. The engine noise and the slam of the car door had drawn attention from inside, for the lights above the door went on, throwing a dome of illumination over the stoop. No sooner had he rung the bell than he heard the click of a deadbolt being thrown back, and the door swung open to reveal a thirty-something guy in a Red Sox T-shirt. His feet were bare and the cuffs of his jeans were ragged, but he was clean-cut, his dirty-blond hair neatly trimmed.

"You're him," the man said with a dreadful weariness. "The guy who called."

Michael had imagined having to introduce himself, even having to plead for the man to open the door. Now he was taken off guard.

"Yeah. Look, I can't apologize enough for just coming over here, intruding on your life like this. I swear to you I'm not a reporter or some kind of stalker. I just . . . I need to talk to your mother, Mr. Barnes."

With a sigh of resignation, Barnes leaned against the frame of the open door. "What's your name?"

"Sorry, yeah. I should've . . ." He thrust out his hand. "Michael Dansky."

Barnes did not bother to uncross his arms to shake. He only studied Michael.

"Well, you're here. I probably should call the cops but you've already made me think about things I don't want to think about. The harm's done. So take thirty seconds, tell me what you want to tell me, then go away."

His expectation of an argument defied, Michael faltered. "I'm not sure how to . . . all right, okay." He paused, then began again. "There's this house. I mentioned it on the phone. It's off of Old Route Twelve, on or near Wildwood Road."

Barnes flinched at that. Michael saw it, but didn't push. He knew there was something here, that the guy had gotten so upset on the phone because there was a connection that he did not want to share. Maybe that was why he was listening, now. Perhaps his mother's fate was its own mystery, and he thought Michael might be able to solve it.

"You were upset before. I don't want to upset you," he continued. "It's just that I have . . . an interest in that house. And I think your mother may know some things about it that no one's told me yet."

Barnes gave a little cynical sniff of a laugh. "Jesus, Dansky, that's pretty weak. You're harassing me at, what, quarter past eight at night and you can't be any less vague than that?" He gave Michael a dark look. "I'm closing the door now. I want you to leave my mother alone."

The man started to close the door. Michael's breath caught in his throat and he put out a hand to keep it open. Barnes was quick, and stronger than he looked. He grabbed Michael's wrist and forced him backward, moving out onto the stoop with him.

"You've got balls, buddy. Touch my door and I really will call the cops."

Michael ran his hands through his hair in frustration. He was at a loss. But Jillian couldn't afford for him to fuck this up, and neither could Susan Barnes. The problem was, how was he supposed to explain that to her son?

"It's about my wife."

Barnes scowled. "I don't know your wife. I don't know you. And clearly you don't know my mother, or you wouldn't be here asking about her. So for the last time—"

Michael's eyes burned with exhaustion and his patience ran out. "Listen to me. Just . . . just listen, all right? Something's wrong with my wife. I think it has something to do with that house. I'm getting the idea maybe something's wrong with your mother, too, from the way you're talking. If that's true, it may also have to do with this house."

They stood there in the light cast by the lanterns on either side of the door, only darkness beyond it. Barnes hesitated a moment, then peered even more closely at Michael.

"How did you know they called her Scooter?"

"I don't think you'd believe me if I answered that question."

Seconds ticked by as their words hung in the air. Michael thought Barnes had a sense that whatever had happened to his mother was out of the ordinary, but did not know how to deal with that.

"No," the man said at last. "No, I guess I probably wouldn't."

"Mr. Barnes—"

"Tom."

"Tom. I think some of this rings a bell with you. If it didn't, you wouldn't be talking to me. My wife . . . she needs help. Please."

The man could not meet Michael's gaze after that. He retreated over the threshold but paused inside the house to look back.

"You know she was a Realtor. The house on Wildwood Road was the last one she ever showed. It had been abandoned for years until the state took it over by eminent domain. She specialized in older homes, and she went up to take a look at the place. Showed it to a client that same day. After that—"

During the momentary pause in the man's words Michael felt

panic rising inside him. If Susan Barnes was dead . . . if the specter that had visited him over and over was truly her ghost . . . then all of his theories were wrong.

"What happened to her, Tom?"

Barnes shrugged, but he met Michael's gaze again. "I don't know. She was the kindest person you'd ever meet, but she was just never the same after that. You won't get much from her now but nastiness, but if you want to talk to her you'll find her over at Pentucket Hospital. She's a permanent resident in the psych ward there."

He began to close the door even as he spoke, disappearing from view. "You'd better hurry. Visiting hours are over at nine."

TEDDY FELT LIKE A BURGLAR in the Danskys' house. He sat on the sofa watching television, the volume on low, and surfed channels with the remote control. Nothing seemed to catch his attention. The strangeness of the situation was simply too distracting.

Her behavior is erratic, Michael had said. *She knows something is wrong with her, but . . . look, if she does anything stupid . . . she kind of scratched up her chest. If she tries to hurt herself again, just call the police.*

Well, what is *wrong with her?* Teddy had wanted to know.

Some kind of chemical imbalance, I think. It's hard to explain.

It sounded plausible enough. Put aside the phone call at dinner time and the urgency and there was no reason Teddy should have doubted him. There were all kinds of drugs these days for depression and bipolar disorder and all that kind of shit. He figured it was something like that. But where the hell was Michael off to, if what Jillian really needed was to see her doctor?

Teddy hadn't asked. If Michael had wanted him to know, he would have volunteered the information. In the scheme of things it was not a major inconvenience for him, and so Teddy had decided it was best to just be a friend, and help out, no questions asked. Not now, at least. Later, if it didn't

seem too sensitive a subject, he would want to know what was
going on.

Yet the longer he sat in Michael and Jillian's living room, the
more he felt that something was *off*. He did not feel welcome.
Though he was sort of hungry, he didn't get up and raid the
fridge or the cupboards. Teddy had been to the house dozens of
times and normally felt very much at home there. He ought to
have been able to grab some chips and a beer if he wanted them.
But the whole situation was just too odd for him, and so he
planted himself on the sofa with the remote and tried not to get
comfortable. Once, in the seventh grade, he had left for school
and purposefully missed the bus, hiding out until his parents had
left for work. But his day off had been completely spoiled by the
feeling that at any moment one of them might come home unex-
pectedly and catch him where he wasn't supposed to be.

That memory was strong tonight.

He surfed through the news channels, several movies, and finally left it alone when he found a comedy on BBC America.

"Comfortable?"

Teddy's pulse spiked and he nearly threw himself off the sofa,
twisting around to see Jillian watching him from the arched entrance to the room. Her hair was disheveled, and she had black
circles around her eyes that seemed a combination of exhaustion
and tear-streaked mascara. She wore only a cream-colored tank
top and pink panties, but there was nothing sexy about her
stance or her expression. The tank top was revealing enough that
he could see some of the scratches Michael had told him about.
Jillian's nostrils flared and her lip curled back in revulsion, as
though Teddy were the most distasteful creature she had ever
laid eyes upon.

"Jillian, hey. Are you okay? Can I get you anything?"

"Can *you* get *me* anything? It's my house, Ted."

The way she looked at him he felt like a fool, as though he
were the one standing there in his underpants.

"Wait, didn't Michael tell you I was here?"

"Yeah. Baby-sitting. You're a pal." She said this without

expression, voice desert dry, then turned and moved deeper into the house.

Teddy's face flushed and he stood awkwardly between sofa and television, listening to her open and close cabinet doors in the kitchen, probably rooting for a snack of some kind. The remote control was on the floor where it had fallen when she had startled him to his feet. He hesitated to sit down again. Teddy Polito had never felt more out of place in his life. But he sure as hell wasn't going to follow her into the kitchen to make conversation. For one thing, she was practically naked. And for another, she was behaving like an absolute bitch. If he had never met Jillian before he would have despised her. But Teddy knew her, and so instead he was worried.

Worried, and a little afraid.

It was possible that something had gone wrong between Michael and Jillian. An affair, maybe. Nothing else he could conceive of would have engendered so much spite. But if that was the case, why would Michael have asked him to come here? It confused the hell out of Teddy. Regardless of what was going on, whether it was something between them or some kind of personality disorder, he wanted them to work it out. Seeing Jillian like this gave him chills.

Whatever you're up to, Michael, I hope it helps.

When Jillian passed by again on her way back upstairs, Teddy was back on the sofa. His head was turned toward the television but he could not focus on it, all too aware of her. Only after he was sure she was back on the second floor did the tension begin to leave him, and even then, the awkwardness remained. He didn't belong here. He wanted to leave. But he had told Michael he would keep an eye on Jillian all night if he had to. Now Teddy regretted those words as he mentally hurried Michael along, hoping he would get home quickly.

It was going to be a long night.

THERE WERE PERHAPS TWO DOZEN cars in the main parking area behind Pentucket Hospital, all but one clustered near the front entrance. The other, a lone Cadillac, was three quarters of the way across the lot. Michael figured the people who'd parked up close were nighttime visitors, recently arrived, and whoever the poor bastard was who owned the Caddy, he had come much earlier in the day and had reason to stay until the hospital threw him out. It might have been for good reason, something happy like the arrival of a new baby . . . but odds were he had been there for a long time because something very unpleasant was going on in his life.

Out of an impulsive burst of solidarity, Michael parked beside the silver Cadillac and walked across the barren lot to the wide front entrance. As a boy he had loved revolving doors, but they were mostly electronic now and moved too slowly, so he hadn't stepped inside one in years.

The lobby was unlike most hospitals he had been inside. It reminded him far more of a hotel, with a sprawling oasis of greenery, comfortable chairs and carpets in the center, and all of the important counters, services, and stations ranged around the edges. Information. Gift shop. Au Bon Pain bakery. Florist. Patient services. There was a large clock on the wall that revealed the time as 8:36, and he worried that though visiting hours didn't end for more than twenty minutes, he might not be allowed in to see Susan Barnes. The prospect of this made his face flush and his pulse quicken as he approached the information counter.

"Can I help you?" The girl behind the counter had exotic features and caramel skin, with just the faintest accent. He thought she was Middle Eastern but wasn't certain. There was a tiny diamond piercing in her left nostril and it glinted in the light.

"I'm here to see a patient in the psychiatric ward. Where do I go from here?"

She was pleasant enough, giving him a small square map of the hospital and showing him which corridor to follow, even marking it with a pencil. But as she slid it across the counter she glanced at the clock.

"You should know that visiting hours are——"

"Almost over. I know. Thank you."

He hurried to the elevator and was lucky enough to catch one headed up almost instantly. On the third floor he stepped out and then strode quickly along the corridor, turned left, and walked through a long covered footbridge that separated the main hospital building from the psychiatric services center. Michael resolutely refused to look at his watch.

The double doors at the entrance to psych services swung open at his approach and he saw an abandoned waiting room beyond, with another door past that. There was a long desk by that door, and a formidable-looking black woman sat sentinel behind it. She glanced up at him as he entered, and her gaze flicked toward a clock before turning back to him.

"Can I help you, sir?" she asked, her tone and expression indicating that she thought he had lost his way.

"Yes. I've come to see a patient. What room is Susan Barnes in?"

She sighed and gave him a look to let him know he was a moron. "I'm sorry, sir, but you can't simply go to her room. That isn't the way it works in this part of the hospital. Also, are you aware that——"

"Visiting hours are almost over," he finished for her. "Yes, but I need to speak with Susan Barnes, please."

He hoped that his own urgency was enough to let her know that she was wasting his time asking questions. Whatever had to be done for him to talk to Susan Barnes, he had less than twenty minutes in which to get it done.

"Ms. Barnes is in a restricted wing. She cannot have visitors in her room. If you want to speak with her, I can have an orderly escort you to a public meeting room and have her brought to see you there."

"Please," he replied, now glancing at the clock himself.

If the nurse or receptionist or gatekeeper found his hurry odd, she did not remark upon it. Instead she picked up her phone and barked a couple of orders to have Susan brought from her room and for an orderly to fetch Michael from the entrance.

"It will just be a moment," she said, hanging up the phone. "Just fill this out."

"You knew just who she was," Michael noted with admiration as he put his name and address into the visitation form. "That she was in a restricted wing. You didn't even have to look up her file. That's pretty good. Do you remember all the patients?"

Her smile was thin and false. "Only the dangerous ones."

He blinked, taken slightly aback.

"Just don't turn your back on her," the woman said. Then a spark of amusement lit her eyes. "Anyway, her son called a little while ago, said someone would be coming to see his mother and that you had his permission. You think just anyone gets into this wing to see a patient when they want to?"

Michael stared at her a moment, amazed that Tom Barnes had made the call. "No, I . . . I guess I never thought about it."

Then the door beside the desk opened with a clank of a lock turning and an orderly emerged. He grabbed a clipboard upon which was the form Michael had just filled out. It included not only his own information, but the details on whom he was visiting. The man had not been young for twenty years, but his size and his bearing, the cut of his hair and the line of his jaw, all suggested military service in his past.

"All right, Mr. Dansky," he said. "Come on with me."

"Have a nice night," Michael told the receptionist out of reflex.

"Yeah," she said, apparently tickled by the concept. "You, too."

As they walked down hallways redolent with the smells of human sweat, ammonia, and disinfectant, Michael felt a shivery sort of dread creep up the back of his neck, as though dozens of sets of eyes were upon him. Most of the doors were closed, but he saw into some of the patients' rooms as he passed. A man sat in a rocking chair watching a television anchored to the wall and moved the chair in the tiniest jerks, this weird rhythm that could barely be called rocking. In another, an androgynous figure sat calmly knitting, softly singing an old Coca-Cola advertising jingle in a voice of ethereal beauty.

It struck him then that he actually missed the presence of the lost girl in his peripheral vision, or the passing sight of a figure in a shapeless coat on the side of the road. They were leaving him alone for the moment—perhaps because of whatever strange short circuit had happened when they had tried to control him earlier—and he should have been pleased. Instead he was unnerved. He did not want to be here, in this awful place. Some of these people had spiders crawling in their brains, at least metaphorically, and it made his skin go cold. It would have been better if his own madness was still with him. He might have felt more like he belonged here, but if not, at the very least it would have propelled him along. Terror and dread and helplessness were powerful motivators.

The orderly led him deeper into the ward. Michael knew that once upon a time the place would not have been so much like a hospital. Pentucket's psych services wing was all about patient treatment, observation, and in some cases, long-term care. But the latter was far less common in modern times than it had once been. In an earlier era, the place would have been filled with chronic patients, permanent residents. The laws had changed, and so had drug therapy. Depression, bipolar disorder, and so many other things that altered human behavior now had clinical cures. Miracle pills that could fix the problem, as long as the patient kept taking them.

But there were always some people who were simply crazy.

The orderly took him into a side corridor that opened up almost immediately into a large public room with an air hockey table, a large television set, and a number of sitting areas arranged with plush chairs, throw rugs, and card tables. On the far side of the room was a set of double doors with a red light above. Set into the wall beside it was a window into an office, where a tall, thin man sat behind a desk. Michael's escort waved to the man as they approached, and the tall man nodded and reached for something beneath the desk. The light above the heavy double doors turned green.

"Jesus, it's like a prison," Michael muttered, mostly to himself.

"Some of the patients can get violent," the orderly replied. "It usually isn't a problem, but that doesn't mean you don't take precautions. Particularly with the limitations of the facility. If it was built from scratch today, the layout of the place would be completely different. A lot more PC, at least on the outside. But we have to make do with what we have. With the way things are going, it's not like the state's going to pay for a shiny new upgrade."

"Yeah. Yeah, of course. No way to justify it in this economy," Michael agreed. But it still seemed like the place was a throwback to an earlier era. On the other hand, he had never been inside such a facility before.

They passed a glass wall on the right, beyond which was a long conference table with half a dozen chairs around it. There was a second identical room, but when they came adjacent to it, Michael saw that it was not empty.

A stocky female orderly stood in one corner. But she wasn't alone.

Susan Barnes sat at the table with her arms crossed like a sullen child. He had seen the resemblance in her Realtor photograph to the little lost girl who had been haunting him, but if it had ever been there, any similarity was gone now. She was too thin, her face gaunt, and her dirty-blond hair was fading to white. He'd never been able to establish her precise age, but he gauged it at just past fifty. Behind that glass wall, she looked sixty at least.

Then the woman noticed him and stared at him. Her face was

so thin that her eyes seemed huge and luminous, and in that moment, any hesitation about her identity left him. Physically she looked nothing like the lost girl . . . like Scooter. But those eyes were unmistakable.

"You've got about ten minutes, Mr. Dansky," the orderly noted, glancing at his clipboard again for Michael's name. Then a smirk twisted up the edges of his mouth. "If she gives you that long."

He stood aside. Michael pushed open the glass door. The female orderly appraised him silently but said nothing, not interfering with the visit. When Michael realized he did not have to deal with her, he focused on Susan Barnes. Her arms were still crossed, and one of her eyebrows was arched. Her upper lip was curled back in the threat of a sneer about to be born.

Come find me.

A shiver ran through him and he felt his breathing quicken. Emotions welled up inside him and nearly spilled over. Here she was, this ordinary madwoman, tangible proof of all that he had been living through since that terrible night after the masquerade.

"Well?"

He blinked. So strange to hear her speak. He recalled that tiny lost-girl voice, remembered the golden-haloed angel who had been silhouetted in his headlights in her peasant blouse and blue jeans. Her foot had crushed his D'Artagnan hat. Michael smiled as he thought of it. He had no idea how that detail could have been lost to him, in spite of all the chaos. Of course she had been real, if something like that . . . but, no. There were variations on the word "real," here, apparently. For this woman and that lost girl . . . they were the same and not the same at all.

"Hello? Who the fuck are you? Reporter? Lawyer? They said my son sent you. So talk to me, asshole. You dragged me away from my shows, so don't waste my time. The clock is fucking ticking."

Michael opened his mouth, his lips moved, but he could not seem to form words. How could it all be? Seeing her there like that and knowing, remembering that night on the side of the road . . . it was worse, in a way, than the sweet lost creature haunting his eyes, worse than those hollow, twisted women with their frigid touch and the memories they had infected him with. The filthy violation of his mind.

This is what that lost girl became, he thought. And he could not help but wonder if it was because he left her there at the house on Wildwood Road that night. If it was because he brought her home.

The female orderly was staring at him now. She had even taken a step away from the corner; he could see in her face that she was trying to figure out if he was going to be a problem.

"Scooter," Michael whispered.

Susan Barnes sneered. "What the fuck did you say?"

"Scooter," he rasped again. He shook himself, then slid into the chair across the table from her. "They used to call you Scooter. When you were growing up. Your . . . your sister couldn't say Susan and—"

A trace of fear breezed across her features before disappearing, buried once more beneath the sullenness and anger. "I don't remember much about growing up."

"No," Michael said, agreeing. "No, of course you don't."

He was still partially mesmerized by her presence. At any moment he expected those women to appear, or for the specter of the younger Susan Barnes to loom once more in his peripheral vision. But neither occurred. It was just the two of them and the orderly and the ticking clock.

His time was wasting.

"How long have you been here?" he asked.

"Two years? Three? What does it matter?" Some small doubt showed in her eyes, then. "Do I know you? I mean, did I?"

Michael understood what she meant. Did she know him from once upon a time, from her childhood, that black oil spill in her memory that blotted out everything good and innocent about growing up, that smeared and tainted her heart, ripping away all the kindness that she would otherwise have had? He did not bother to point out that he was young enough to be her son, that she could not have known him then.

"No. No, you don't know me. Not really. But I did speak to your son Tom earlier. He thought you might be able to help me."

She scowled. "That little fucker? Why would I want to help you? My son is an ungrateful shit, leaving me to rot in here. I'd like to rip his . . ." She smiled sweetly. "Did he tell you that I stabbed him?"

Michael shook his head.

Susan crossed her arms more tightly, smugly pleased. "You know those serrated spoons people used to use for grape-fruit? One of those. I stabbed him in the leg with one of those. Little bastard. Wish I'd hit the femoral artery. Living in my fucking house with my fucking things, sleeping in my fucking bed. His wife left him. Bet he didn't mention that, either. She was a goddamn bitch, but I still can't blame her. Kid's a dildo."

The stream of filth barely fazed him. Instead he felt his face flush warmly because of the freshness of his memories of Jillian. Once upon a time, Susan Barnes had been an ordinary, happy woman. Now she was this. Michael had been nurturing faith in the idea that he could help Jillian, that he could return her to who and what she had been. But seeing Susan Barnes like this . . .

He caught the orderly watching the clock.

Six minutes to nine.

Shit.

Panic raced through him. This was too important. Everything depended on it. His marriage. Jillian's life. And he was screwing it up.

"Look, Ms. Barnes, we only have a few minutes and I don't have time to dance around the questions I really want to ask."

Something troubled her. When he spoke, she narrowed her eyes as though trying to see him through the filter of her eyelashes.

"So what are you waiting for, then?"

No *fuck*. That seemed odd. Like she had been distracted from her stream of profanity by something else.

Michael took a deep breath and nodded. "Not long before you . . . before you ended up here, you took an interest in a house on Wildwood Road. I've been to that house once, very late at night. I wasn't entirely sober. Well, now I think it's really important that I get back there. I think maybe . . . a lot is riding on me going back."

Her gaze dropped and she seemed to want to look anywhere but at Michael. Her lips twisted bitterly and her nostrils flared. She wanted him gone. Her body language said as much.

"So? Go back."

"I . . ." His mind flashed on the woods, the hill, those misshapen women chasing him through the trees. He had been studiously avoiding thinking about the house itself, about being inside and what that had felt like. The voices. Singsong jumprope voices, of lost little girls. Now it all rushed into his head at once, and it was overwhelming. Michael sucked in a breath and sat back in his chair, pressing the heels of his palms against his eyes.

In the blackness inside his head, he saw a double image of Scooter as a girl, of the figure of that blond little angel going into that dilapidated old house and its door swallowing her whole.

"Shit," he said, opening his eyes and seeing that the female orderly, who now looked very imposing, had crossed half the distance between him and her corner. She paused and waited to see what he would do next.

Michael stared at Susan, seeing the ghost of her little-girl self in her face. "You've got to help me. Maybe I can help you, too. My wife . . . something's happened to her. There's something she lost, and I think maybe you've lost it, too. But I've been searching for that house . . . even for Wildwood Road . . . and I can't seem to find it."

In that moment he saw in Susan Barnes the same combination of pain and fury and hollowness he had seen in Jillian earlier that day. Her chest rose and fell and she played with her faded hair, wrapping a strand of it around one finger. But she was resolute in her unwillingness to look at him.

"I can't give you fucking directions. And you're not going to find it." She uttered a little sickening laugh. "I could find it, but . . ." Susan waved her hands to indicate the glass wall. "I'm unavailable. Indisposed. Otherwise fucking engaged."

Then, at length, she raised her eyes and met his gaze dead on. "But if I could find it . . . maybe if your wife lost something there, she could find it just as well."

Michael stared at her, slack-jawed, hardly daring to breathe.

Her eyes narrowed. "I do know you, don't I?"

And it occurred to him that maybe a part of her did know him. Maybe some part of that lost little girl, the stolen piece of her that was hiding in the ether somewhere, hiding from those twisted women . . . maybe it was still tethered to her, and she sensed a connection with him.

"Nine o'clock, Mr. Dansky," said his original escort from the hallway.

He glanced back at Susan.

"Does the name Moloch mean anything to you? Or a city, Kart-hadasht?"

Susan Barnes hugged herself and her gaze drifted, as though she had become lost inside her head. "They were so hungry, under the city. Moloch gave them scraps, but not enough. And there were so many of them. The Virgins of Carthage."

Her voice was a thin whisper, the voice of a little girl, weighted with sorrow.

"Mr. Dansky," the orderly snapped.

Susan's eyes cleared and focused. She frowned.

"What are they?" Michael asked her.

She seemed not to understand, as though she had not even been aware of what she had said. Susan scowled.

"Mr. Dansky, I'm going to have to insist," the orderly told him, the warning clear.

Susan met his gaze. "Don't come back," she said, as if the very sight of him was loathsome.

"No," he said. "I won't."

CHAPTER FIFTEEN

It is the middle of April, more than a year before the masquerade and the trip to Wildwood Road. The past four months at Krakow & Bester have been both the busiest and the most rewarding of Michael's career. All of the hope that his employers have had for him since they brought him on board has come to fruition with the campaign for Athena Sportswear, a national rollout that depended entirely on the client's confidence in him.

He should be flying high, cruising on the adrenaline and momentum of the kind of personal victory that just doesn't come very often. Hell, for some people, it doesn't happen at all. But as he makes his way home in the thick of the traffic on Route 125, his stomach is in knots. The day has been full of congratulations—both from grateful bosses and from envious coworkers—and thank-yous. The first of the Athena Sportswear ads is testing extremely well, and the president of the company called him at the office this morning and sent a fruit basket this afternoon. It sits on the passenger seat beside him. There is some cheese in with the fruit and he's tempted to nibble, though he isn't hungry. How could he be, after the dinner Paul Krakow took him out for tonight?

"What am I supposed to say, Jillian? He's the boss. When the boss says he's taking you to dinner, you go."

That little conversation from this morning has been festering in his gut all day. His skin has been tingling with a buzzing tension since breakfast. There is that old saw about not going to sleep angry . . . everyone has heard that one. But Michael thinks they ought to add that you should never go to work if you've had a fight with your wife and left it unresolved. All day he has been unable to really appreciate the current of good feeling coming his way because of his preoccupation with the argument.

Now, as he drives home far later than he had promised, streetlights strobing the windshield as he passes beneath them, Michael cannot help returning to the moments they'd shared that morning.

He had come downstairs in a hurry, rushing as usual. Jillian rose only a few minutes earlier than he did, but somehow she always seemed to be able to get herself ready without having to rush. Today had been no exception. He'd been putting on his belt with one hand, carrying his shoes with the other, and trying to figure out if his growling stomach would actually start to digest him from the inside out if he left the house without eating something.

"Hey, hey, sweetie, slow down," Jillian had said as she poured yogurt on top of a bowl of granola. "It takes me a lot longer to get to work than it takes you. What's the hurry?"

Michael had sighed and plopped down on the kitchen floor to get his shoes on. "The results from the test group for Athena should be in first thing this morning. I want to see them before anyone else. Then, supposedly, Paul wants to take me to dinner tonight to celebrate. It could be a long day."

Storm clouds had swept across her eyes. "When isn't it a long day? You've been working your ass off for them, Michael. The job is done now. Can't they cut you a little slack?"

He had been so tense for so long that his immediate reaction had been to go on the defensive. Michael had bristled and snapped at her. "They sign the checks, Jilly, or maybe you've forgotten that?"

"Oh, for fuck's sake!" she had muttered. "Look, I know you've been under pressure with this thing, but you're not the only one who brings money into this house. We don't compare the size of our paychecks around here, or how much work we're doing. Through all of this, you've been somewhere else, your mind on your work instead of at home. For the last couple of weeks I've been dealing with some really nasty crap at the firm. But have you even once *asked* me how things are?"

The memory of that question and the look on her face as she had asked it is haunting him now, as he passes the Dunkin' Donuts on the corner where he walks to get her coffee every Sunday morning. The radio is on, but he doesn't hear the music. He glances at the dashboard clock. It is nearly eleven P.M., and a small, guilty part of him hopes Jillian is asleep so they can finish their argument in the morning instead of tonight.

But he knows she isn't.

They don't fight very often. There might be the occasional argument over something her mother said, or where they're going to spend the holidays, but that doesn't really count. It isn't personal. But this . . .

He had stared at her, brows knitted. A nauseous little twist of guilt had begun to worm its way through his stomach. Jillian didn't curse a lot, so to hear her rattle off that language had made him flinch. "No. No, I guess I haven't. If I haven't been paying enough attention, I'm sorry about that. What's wrong? What's been going on?"

Then she had done it. Jillian had rolled her eyes and waved him away, dismissing the conversation. Dismissing him as though she could not be bothered. "It doesn't matter anymore. It's not important. It's been dealt with. Just forget it. Go to work."

"You know, maybe it's not Krakow & Bester that needs to cut me some slack. You've got the number two job in your field in the entire state, Jillian. In all of goddamned New England. I'm clawing my way up to number one or two in my agency. You don't have any competition, or maybe you'd have a clearer picture of what that's like."

They had fumed in silence as he finished getting ready, and though her commute took forty minutes longer than Michael's, Jillian had still been in the kitchen reading the newspaper when he had left, waves of antagonism radiating between them.

Now his headlights wash over the front of their house as he pulls into the driveway. The lights are out but there is the blue glow of the television in their bedroom windows. Michael shuts off the car but sits with his hand on the key in the ignition for a moment, dreading going inside. The engine ticks loudly as it cools. He feels like an ass. Jillian had been a little snippy, sure, but what she'd said was right, and he'd been too defensive to just apologize. He's going to tell her that now, of course, but she's had a whole day to get up a righteous head of steam and he isn't sure what to expect.

With a self-recriminating little chuckle he steps out of the car and pockets his keys. He goes up the walk and unlocks the door quietly, but not with any surreptitious intent. Now that he's here he doesn't want her to be sleeping. He just wants to talk it out, get it behind them, so he can slip into bed beside his best friend after a long day and just hold her. Michael Dansky has traveled around Europe and America; he's had blindingly good sex and some of the most exquisite food in the world. But for sheer bliss, there is nothing like the comfort he surrenders to every night as he climbs into bed with his wife.

Going to work angry had sucked. No way is he going to bed angry tonight.

Michael drapes his jacket over the banister at the bottom of the stairs and goes up. The bedroom door is open. He can hear the Channel Five news anchor running down the headlines as the eleven o'clock newscast begins. As he enters the room he takes in several things at once. There is a large suitcase on the floor, standing upright and zipped, but obviously full to bulging.

Another suitcase, this one smaller, is open on the bed and Jillian is folding a pair of khaki pants.

Packing.

"Jilly?" he ventures, just the beginning of a horrid conclusion tickling the back of his brain.

Then she looks up and she smiles mischievously.

"Help me finish packing. We have to get up really early in the morning and we're both going to be exhausted."

Her smile is infectious. Michael grins at her and shakes his head. "What are you doing? We're going somewhere in the morning?"

She finishes folding the pants and tucks them into the top of the suitcase neatly. "New Orleans."

Michael can only gape at her. He's always wanted to go to New Orleans and has never been. "What are you talking about? I can't . . . we're saving our vacation time for the summer. And I haven't cleared it. I can't just disappear."

Jillian picks up a hideous Hawaiian shirt that she had bought him once as a joke and begins to fold that into the suitcase as well. "Sure you can. I arranged it with Paul two weeks ago."

"Paul Krakow? You arranged it with my boss's boss?"

"Gotta go to the top, babe. He's good, I have to admit, keeping it a secret while you guys were at dinner tonight."

Michael laughs and goes to her, embracing her from behind as she tries to finish folding the shirt. She squirms, but not to get away from him. The way she moves she brushes against him suggestively.

"You're amazing, you know that?"

"Yes. I do."

"I'm sorry about this morning." His voice is softer.

"Me, too." Her back is still to him and she reaches for a small stack of her bras and panties to stuff them in the suitcase. "But we'll have all week to make it up to each other."

Pulling the bras and panties from her hands and letting them scatter on the bed, he spins her around to face him and their lips meet. He kisses her deeply, regretting every hour that has passed between this morning and tonight. His hands roam over her body and her fingernails run lightly down his back.

"Why wait until we reach New Orleans?" he asks.

Jillian's only response is a grin, and then she takes his hand and pulls him down to the floor. After all, there isn't room on the bed.

THE DANSKYS' LIVING ROOM WAS perfect in that way that only couples without children ever seemed to manage. Everything was dusted, and the knickknacks on the coffee table and the mantel were arranged just so. Even the paintings and prints on the walls hung straight. The irony was not lost on Teddy Polito. His friends led lives that, though filled with love and passion, were neat and orderly. And now something had happened to bring disorder into their house. It might not be visible in the meticulous arrangement of this room, but it was in the air. In the walls. And it was freaking him out.

Teddy sat in an overstuffed chair now and, despite its plushness, could not make himself comfortable. The television was on. After channel surfing until he was numb he had surrendered to the lure of celebrities behaving badly on the E! network. He fidgeted in the chair, his hands in constant motion as he tapped his fingers, then interlaced them, then slid them down beside him. He'd chosen this chair now because all he had to do was look to the left and he could see the bottom of the stairs. If Jillian came down again, he was sure to see her before she could startle him.

Bipolar, that's what he had figured. It had to be. Not that his guesswork made the baby-sitting job any easier. Teddy had known Jillian for years, but he still did not know her well. Michael was his friend and coworker. Jillian was funny and intelligent and had always been nice to him, but over the years she had remained *Michael's wife.* They shared no intimacy. Teddy knew how she felt about certain social and political issues, but not what was in her heart. Not the sort of thing you revealed to your closest friends.

But this, right here . . . this felt pretty goddamned intimate. And not in any way that was pleasant.

He had the volume on the television up just high enough to drown out some of the noise from upstairs, but not so high that it was likely to bring Jillian downstairs to snarl at him. No, he wanted her to stay right up in her room. Teddy hadn't a clue what he could say to her if she came down. From time to time he heard her up there, cussing at the top of her lungs. Shrieks of "fuck you!" and "bullshit!" drifted down to him and there was a great deal of her stomping around. He heard something shatter at one point—a lamp, a mirror, maybe a window?—and managed to convince himself that it was nothing to worry about. The fifteen or so minutes of silence that followed had frightened him horribly. He dreaded the idea of going up there and finding that she'd cut her wrists with broken glass and was bleeding to death and he'd just sat down there watching drunken celebrities make obscene gestures at the paparazzi on TV.

This went on and on. In a real sense, Michael had not been gone very long. Less than three hours. But the minutes seemed to tick by with a purgatorial slowness.

Teddy shifted in the plush chair now. His stomach rumbled. Something in the cookie family of snacks would have been welcome, but he wasn't about to go raid their kitchen. There was no way for him to know what might set Jillian off.

He glanced to the left, checking the stairs for any sign of her.

No Jillian, but there was something there on the carpeted steps that hadn't been there before. A square or rectangular white something. Teddy frowned and narrowed his eyes, trying to figure out what it was. He felt that actually getting up and walking over to the stairs was asking for trouble.

Then, as he watched, another rectangle sailed down the steps.

"I don't know you!" Jillian screamed. Her voice came from

upstairs but she had broken her silence so suddenly that he started in his chair. His focus had been on the photographs she had tossed down.

For that was what they were. The second one had made it further and landed with the picture side up rather than the white paper side. From what he could see at this distance it looked as though a portion of the photograph had been blacked out with heavy marker.

"And who the fuck are you? Who are *all* of you?"

There came a kind of roar from upstairs, a heartbreaking howl of grief and rage, and then a photo album came flying down the steps to crash to the ground, spilling photographs onto the floor, pages tearing out. A second album came tumbling down a moment later.

This was followed by the sound of Jillian's footsteps retreating along the upstairs hall and the slam of her bedroom door.

Teddy was tempted to get up and go over to have a look at those photo albums and at the pictures where she had blacked part of the image out. But his throat was dry and what he really wanted, he knew, was to get out of there and go home to a place where people were comparatively sane.

He gazed warily at the wreckage of the photo albums on the stairs but he did not get up. Instead, he raised the volume on the television just a bit and did his best to focus on the screen. There was a digital clock on the cable box.

Where are you, Michael? he wondered silently. Teddy Polito thought of himself as a good guy. A good friend. But the truth was, he was not at all certain how long he was going to be willing to wait for Jillian's husband to come home.

JILLIAN LAY ON THE FLOOR of her bedroom staring at the ceiling. She had thought she was far enough from the shattered mirror, but there was a small shard of glass digging into her right shoulder blade. It had punctured her shirt and the flesh beneath, and hot blood was soaking into the fabric and into the carpet under her, warm and sticky on her skin. The sensation was not entirely unpleasant. The pain . . . it meant she was feeling something. That was good.

Every time she heard the hum of an engine out on the street and saw the splash of illumination from headlights reach across the ceiling, she stiffened, clenching her fists so tightly that her fingernails cut little bloody crescents into her palms.

Where are you, Michael?

As though summoned by her anger and desperation, a new splash of headlights touched the ceiling, accompanied by the low snore of a car with a failing muffler. The lights turned into her driveway, illumination splashing the wall above her, a glimmer touching the shards of her mirror that still hung in its frame.

She sprang to her feet, a shard of glass cutting her heel. Jillian reached down and plucked it out, wincing only a little as she went out into the second-floor hall, still only in panties and the clean tank top she'd pulled on after cleaning up the gouges on her chest. But now she felt a trickle of fresh blood down her back as she reached the top of the stairs.

Quite a sight, Jillian. You're quite a sight.

The shattered mirror was testament to that. In her eyes, she'd seen a vacancy, an absence of something she knew ought to be there. It was related to her missing memories, but different, somehow. She felt it. And Michael knew, didn't he? Yes, he certainly did. That much had been obvious for a while now. Her husband had a pretty good idea of what had happened to her, why she didn't seem able to control herself.

At the moment, she didn't feel like controlling herself at all.

The front door opened as she was coming down the stairs, and she sped up her pace. Teddy was rising from his chair even as Michael stepped inside, pocketing his keys. The two men exchanged a look, likely would have exchanged a word as well, but that was when they noticed Jillian.

"Michael," Teddy began, a warning in his tone. She had spooked the shit out of him. Jillian liked that.

But Michael didn't need Teddy's warning. The moment he looked at her, she saw in his eyes that alarm bells were going off in his mind. And why not? She was a dead giveaway, wasn't she? Crazy-eyed woman with wild hair, practically naked. He should be nervous, motherfucker.

"Talk to me, Michael," she snarled. "No more running off. Tell me what you fucking know. Right now."

His brow furrowed. "What do you—"

Jillian slapped him hard enough that the sound echoed off the walls. Michael swore and recoiled, held up one hand to defend himself in case she tried it again.

"The next time has claws. Now talk to me or I kick your balls up into your throat."

"Jesus, Jillian!" Teddy said, horrified.

He started toward her and she rounded on him. "Not another step, you fat shit, or I'll cut your goddamn throat."

The astonishment on his features made her want to laugh. A flicker of that amusement went through her as she turned back to Michael . . . too late. He was already in motion. Her husband grabbed her hands and spun around behind her, hugging her tightly like that, pinning her arms to her sides.

She shrieked, an animal rage bubbling up in her, and she thrashed against him. Jillian threw her head back and felt a satisfying impact as her skull hit his. She only wished she had managed to break his nose.

"Let me go! Get your hands off of me!"

"Michael," Teddy ventured. "Come on, man. Let's dial it down, here, a little. I know she's—"

"Just shut up a second!" Michael snapped.

Teddy had a hurt-little-boy look on his face that made Jillian giggle. Michael held her tightly from behind, and there was no way she was going to break that embrace. He was much stronger than she was. Instead she started to grind her ass against his crotch, feeling the outline of his cock under his clothes.

"Is that how you like it now, honey?" Jillian asked, her voice going throaty. He loved that voice. "If that's the way you want it . . ."

"Enough! Cut that shit right now, Jilly."

She stomped her foot down on his, wishing she was still wearing her heels from work. But even barefoot it was enough to hurt him, enough to cause him to flinch. Then Jillian shot her heel up and back, aiming for his crotch. Michael had to twist away and she took advantage of the moment, getting herself just loose enough to slam an elbow back into his chest. The grunt of pain that issued from his lips was sublimely satisfying. Jillian tried to pull away.

But Michael wasn't letting go completely.

He grabbed for her, tried to get her into a bear hug again. Jillian tried to stomp his foot and ended up tripping him. Then they were both falling. The floor rushed up at her and the impact drove the air from her lungs. With Michael on top of her, she wheezed, struggling to draw air, even as Teddy Polito waddled over to fret like an old woman.

"Jesus, Michael, what the hell are you doing? Get off of her! I know she's got problems, but . . . Jesus!"

Michael forced her to be still and then straddled her back to keep her that way. She couldn't see his face, but that didn't stop her from wanting to smash it, to shatter his nose, to claw his cheeks, to tear at his eyes.

"Fucking bastard! You fucking bastard, you know what's wrong with me! Tell me!" she screamed, and kept on with a stream of invective and demands.

"Michael, Jesus!" Teddy said again, as if maybe Michael hadn't heard him the first time.

"Teddy, back off! Just give me a second," he roared.

Jillian snickered as Polito moved away from them. Her head was twisted to one side and she could see him rubbing the back of his chubby neck, his face red with anxiety and confusion.

"And you! Just be still. You want answers, fine! Just *stop*."

Anger seething, Jillian ceased struggling. Her chest hurt,

pressed against the floor, but she could breathe again. "Talk to me, then."

"You've lost something," Michael said. "You know that, don't you? That much you understand."

Jillian said nothing but she felt a kind of embarrassment to go along with the bitterness and resentment these words summoned.

"If you cooperate, I think we can get it back."

Fuck you, she wanted to say. *I don't want it back. Who needs it? Who needs you, Prince Charming riding in on your white horse?*

But the words did not come. Something *was* wrong with her. Though her bitterness and her frustration with just about everyone and everything did not really bother her, she could see what it was doing to her life. Her job was in jeopardy. Her political aspirations had been completely shot.

There was nothing pleasant in her. Nothing at all. She remembered pleasant. Remembered happy. Remembered laughter. Though it all seemed shallow now, she felt the void that had been left in her. She had lost something, no doubt of that. And she wanted it back.

"Just come for a ride with me," Michael said, emotion choking his voice.

"Listen to you," she sneered. "Are you going to cry now? Why should I go anywhere with you? How do I know you're even telling the truth?"

She turned to stare at Teddy. "And what are you doing, fat boy? Why haven't you called the cops yet? Shit, he's beating on me. And you're just going to stand there?"

"Michael?" Teddy said, sounding more lost than ever.

"She's sick, Ted. Really sick. I need to take her to see someone tonight, or she may never get better. You have to trust me on this."

"It's after ten o'clock, Mikey. Where are you going to take her?"

She heard Michael sigh, and then he bent to whisper in her

ear. "You're a miserable bitch. In more ways than one. You know there's something wrong with you. You're falling apart. I just came from seeing a woman who's in the psych ward at Pentucket Hospital and probably will be for the rest of her life. That's the path you're on. No matter what you can or can't feel, what you can remember, I know you don't want that. So those are your choices. Committed to some loony bin or coming with me tonight."

For nearly a full minute she just focused on the feeling of her body against the floor. At last she took a deep breath and let it come out, a ragged gasp from his weight on her.

"Fine. We'll go for a ride."

Michael got up off of her without another word. He took a step back but did not try to restrain her. Though he watched her carefully.

"Teddy, if you don't trust me, you can come along," Michael said. "But all you have to do is look at her and you can see she's a mess. Tonight may be my only chance to help her. So I *am* going. And I am taking her with me. What you want to do about it is your call."

The three of them stood there just inside the front door, staring at one another for a long time. Teddy looked undecided. He rubbed his hand on the back of his head and neck over and over, as though trying to jog loose some thoughts that had gotten stuck. At length he walked over to the bottom of the stairs and picked up some of the photographs she had defaced.

He held one of them in his hand for a few seconds and then looked at Michael and nodded. "I think I'd like to go home to Colleen and climb into bed and pull the covers over my head. But if I haven't gotten a phone call from you by eight-thirty tomorrow morning, I *will* call the cops."

Michael nodded. "Fair enough."

Jillian fought the urge to grab for Teddy's throat. That was half the reason she was going along with Michael. Whatever had been taken from her with those memories, she couldn't control her urges very well anymore. Hell, she could barely control herself. And it was getting worse.

The void in her was hungry for something to fill it, and that hunger was driving her mad.

If Michael could help her, it would be lunacy to hurt him now. But Jillian did not know how long she would be rational enough to remember that.

CHAPTER SIXTEEN

It was going on ten-thirty when Michael turned onto Old Route 12, and the world felt all too real to him. It seemed perverse in a way, but after everything he had been through it unnerved him that the night suddenly felt so . . . *ordinary*. In the passenger seat, dressed in the jeans and sweatshirt she had pulled from her closet, Jillian sat staring out her window in utter silence. Her arms were crossed petulantly and there was a sour twist to her mouth. He was pretty sure that some of that was just for show, that she was being torn up inside and trying to hide the turmoil. But he wasn't positive. Whoever his wife had become, he didn't know her anymore, except in those moments when he could look in her eyes and see the pain there, see how lost she was.

All along he had thought of Scooter as *the lost girl*. Jillian fit the bill just as well.

The steering wheel was solid in his hands. The weight of the car around him and its momentum were all as they should be. The window was down a few inches and he could smell the smoke from someone's fireplace as they rolled down Old Route 12. All familiar. Solid and reliable. What alarmed him was that it was so different from that night after the masquerade. They had both been drinking then, and Jilly had been passed out in the backseat. Though he hadn't put it into words yet, he figured he had been susceptible to . . . what? Outside influence? That was one way to put it.

But he hadn't been drinking today. He was tired, sure. But he was wired on the adrenaline of grief and hope and desperation. They were all he had to live on, lately.

His skin prickled with awareness of Jillian's nearness to him. The chill wind felt good, but normally she would have complained about it. Not tonight. She had every other thing in the world to bitch about, whoever she was now. The tires thrummed on the pavement. The headlights of oncoming cars flashed in his eyes and he raised a hand to shield them.

When the lights had passed and he lowered his hand, Scooter was there. She stood on the roadside just as she had that night, in the same peasant blouse and the same blue jeans. The illumination from his headlights splashed over her and he could see that she really was a specter tonight, the trees visible through her gossamer form. And he wondered what that meant. The lost girl watched the car pass by with an expression that might have been hope or sorrow, he was not at all sure.

Michael took a quick breath, full of emotion, and let it out.

Jillian turned toward him, dark suspicion in her eyes along with a flare of the anger that had become so much a part of her. "What the fuck was that?"

The words echoed.

"You saw her?"

"Yes, I saw her, goddammit. Don't play with me. That was the girl you told me about, but you just drove right by her."

Michael brought his focus back to the curving road. "I don't think I was supposed to pick her up this time."

Seconds ticked by with the hum of the engine the only company. Then Jillian whispered something.

"What?"

"I said I could see right through her!" she shrieked, pounding her hand on the dashboard and shooting him an accusatory stare that startled him so much he jerked the wheel, swerving into the oncoming lane, which, thankfully, was empty.

"So could I," he said quietly, maneuvering back onto his side of the road. *So much for the ordinary world.*

Part of him wanted to turn around. After all this time it seemed ridiculous, but the urge was strong. The only thing in the world he wanted was to go back to the way things had been before the masquerade, to have Jillian back. The lost girl had haunted him, and he hoped to help her if he could, but even his promise to her had lost much of its power. Where Jillian was concerned, everything else was secondary. Even his fear.

So he went on.

When he turned off of Old Route 12, following the path he had taken that night, Jillian slid down in her seat. Her arms were still crossed but there was something about it now that made him think not of anger or petulance but that she was hugging herself. She turned slightly sideways. Hiding.

Michael nearly missed the next turn. His head felt muzzy now and his hands moved too slowly on the steering wheel. He blinked several times, his eyes growing heavy. Sleepy. And as he followed the lead of his own headlights as they picked out the path before him, he glanced into the trees on the roadside and saw one of the hollow women there, watching him. The creature was stooped, cloaked in its shapeless coat, but its too-long face gleamed in the diminishing glow of the headlights as the car went by.

His head began to bob drunkenly, his eyes to close.

"Michael!" Jillian shouted.

It was shrill enough to send knives into his brain, not enough to dispel the disorientation entirely, but enough to make him stamp on the brake and throw the car into park. His face was so warm. His head heavy. With long, steady breaths he relaxed, slipping down again, down into a soft and welcoming darkness.

"For fuck's sake!" Jillian snarled.

He forced his eyes open and turned, groggily, toward her, and she slapped him hard across the face. The sting of it cleared his head. Michael's eyes went wide and he shook himself.

"Oh, you suck," he muttered, not knowing if he was talking

to himself for falling under their sway, or to those twisted women for their hideousness.

The one he had passed was still there, he saw. And up ahead, barely visible in the trees on the side of the road, he thought he could make out two others watching, waiting to see what would become of him. He hit his high beams and their distorted faces, those masks of inhumanity, gleamed.

"I'm afraid," Jillian said, and winced as though the confession hurt her. He supposed it did. "What are they?"

"You don't know?" he asked, almost afraid of the answer.

She shook her head. "They're lost. That's all I know. They're . . . victims. And they're hungry. Something terrible was done to them, a long time ago, and no one cared enough to help them."

"And now they're passing it along?" Michael asked. When Jillian nodded he cursed under his breath. "Misery loves company."

Michael threw the car into drive and hit the accelerator. As they tore up the road away from the hollow women, he waved his middle finger at one of them.

He wasn't stopping.

Jillian laughed softly in the passenger's seat. "Nice."

Awake now . . . wide awake . . . Michael drove on. He had this entire area of the valley mapped out in his head after searching for so long for that house that he no longer needed an atlas. He had never been able to find Wildwood Road again, but he knew where it was *supposed* to be. That curve in a narrow back road where it cut away up toward the peak of the hill. It had been hidden from him before. But Susan Barnes had said that Jillian would be able to find it, and he prayed that was true.

"I . . ." Jillian began, and there was something new in her voice. Something it took him a moment to recognize.

Intimacy.

For the first time in too long she sounded, just with that single syllable, as though she was talking to her husband instead of just some man she couldn't stand the sight of.

"What?" Michael asked. "What is it, Jilly?"

Her expression soured, disdain coming back into her eyes. But he thought perhaps this time it was directed inward as well as outward. "I remembered something."

A spark of hope ignited. "You . . . something from before? From when you were little?"

"Sort of." She dropped her gaze and shook her head slightly. "I don't know why, but I was thinking about our honeymoon. About Vienna . . . that night after the opera, waltzing in the square in front of the cathedral. I can remember being happy, but not why. And . . . thinking back, I remember how . . . magical it was."

Jillian sniffed and chuckled cynically. "I was fucking Princess Barbie." Then she softened, just slightly. "But I remember being so grateful to my father for teaching me how to waltz. And when that memory came . . . so did another, just a flash of me and my dad dancing in the living room at our house. I was so small that I stood on his feet and he taught me like that, moving me around the room."

Michael slowed the car. His eyes scanned the treeline in search of more of those stooped figures, but he saw none. The hill was on his left now, and soon enough, he knew, he would reach the curve where Wildwood Road should be. But he wanted to focus on this before they got there.

"How can that be?" he asked. "You didn't remember anything from back then."

"I don't know. It just . . . it felt like when I remembered Vienna, and thinking about the connection between then and my father, it just came back." Jillian raised her head and there was a faraway look in her eyes. "There's more. I was a flower girl in my cousin 'Stina's wedding when I was seven or eight. The church . . . it was like a smaller version of the cathedral in Vienna."

Michael let the car roll forward, barely accelerating. What the hell was going on? Was it their proximity to Wildwood Road?

To the hollow women? He assumed it must be. Maybe what they'd stolen wasn't completely in their control. Maybe there were stray memories drifting, like the trail of bread crumbs Hansel and Gretel left behind.

Or . . . and this was a far more intriguing prospect . . .

"Maybe you can steal them back," he whispered.

Jillian flinched as if stung. Her breathing quickened and her eyes searched the dark interior of the car. Then she nodded. "Maybe."

"Maybe one of them, out there, had those memories, and you took them back as you went by? Or . . . hell, I don't know, maybe they're just floating around."

"That doesn't sound right. Would they be that sloppy?"

Michael wondered. "I don't know. Scooter got away." An idea was forming in his head. "Listen," he said. "One of them . . . something happened when it touched me. It must have fed on some of the memories they stole from you, but I fought it, I wanted you back so much. The memories it stole . . . I got them."

Jillian stared sidelong at him. "What . . . what were they?"

He told her about her Communion, and the seventh-grade dance, and the bus trip to Chicago. About snowball fights with Hannah and her mother's brownies and her father singing silly songs to her to get her up for school in the morning.

"Try," he said as she gazed at him, empty and confused and yearning. "Try to take them back."

Jillian shook her head, but she reached for him anyway and touched his face. Michael felt nothing. Her fingers were solid. She was not one of them. . . . Whatever those hollow women had once been, they were no longer truly flesh and blood. Moloch, after all, had been a god . . . or what had passed for one in those ancient days.

"Moloch," he whispered, hands too tight on the wheel.

"Child-eater," Jillian rasped, turning to gaze out the window, looking away from him.

"What? How do you—" He did not continue the question. When they had stolen her past from her, she had obviously gotten some knowledge from them, just as he had. Yet he had seen it, had lived the memory of one of the Virgins of Carthage, or whatever they were.

"Moloch didn't eat children."

Her reply was a whisper, as though she were wishing on the first star of evening, staring out that window. "Yes. He did. The child inside."

They drove on. The curve was just ahead. Michael took it slowly, peering into the woods on the uphill side of the street, but the forest was as dense as ever there. When he had rounded the curve he picked up speed and drove well past the place where he had pulled over before, where the women—the childhood-eaters—had caught up to him in the woods. The memory of his feet slipping on wet leaves was still fresh in his mind . . . that was one recollection he would have been happy to do without.

"Why did you drive by it?" Jillian asked as he did a U-turn and started back.

"It wasn't there." He frowned and glanced at her. "You could see it?"

"The sign says Wildwood Road. How could you miss it?"

And this time as he approached the curve, Michael saw it for himself. He vaguely recalled there being no sign there before, but now there was a fresh green one whose white letters gleamed in his headlights. He put on his turn signal and slowed down, then took the right and started up Wildwood Road, as if it had always been there. As if it had never been hidden.

"Why do you think she had you bring her back?" Jillian asked in that same low whisper. "She was free. She'd escaped them. Why not just go and find . . . find herself?"

Michael drove slowly, letting the question echo in the darkened interior of the car a moment. "I don't know. I've been thinking about the whole thing, and I figure there have to be others there, not just her."

There must be a little Jilly Lopresti there right now, he thought, but those were words he would never speak.

"They're in the house," he said. "I heard them laughing. Singing. I think . . . Somehow she got free of their control for a little while and she's been doing it, a little bit here and there, ever since. Trying to get help but never able to really escape."

"That still doesn't explain why she had you take her back."

"No," he agreed. "It doesn't."

All but one of the homes they passed was completely dark inside, though it wasn't quite late enough for everyone to be in bed. And that one house that had a light on in an upstairs room . . . well, it might have been on a timer. The wind did not seem to blow as strongly up here. The bare autumn branches of the trees scratched the night sky but they looked frozen and helpless, and he thought that was best.

Throughout the impossible, terrible events of recent days he had felt anger and fear in equal measure, but his fear had mostly been for the lost girl, Scooter, and for Jillian. Now, as they began to crest the hill and the roof of that house came into sight, he felt a shiver that was far more personal. He remembered the revulsion he'd felt at their touch, the marionette clacking of his teeth as they forced words into his mouth.

Michael could not help imagining the same thing happening to him that had happened to Jillian, to Susan Barnes. He cherished his memories. They were the entire foundation of who he was. So many things he loved would be lost forever if his past was stolen from him. Images flashed through his mind of his first kiss, of building tree forts in the woods and body-surfing at Nauset Beach down the Cape with his parents, of discovering the way a pencil felt in his hands, finding that he could draw pictures that would make his friends' eyes go wide. He didn't want to lose any of that, not even the silly things, like when he discovered that downtown was just part of his own town, when all along he'd thought it was Boston, or wanting to name his dog

Charlie Brown, even though he was black. Christmas mornings. Hell, Christmas Eves.

Jillian had lost all of her childhood. Inside, Michael was terrified of having all of that stolen from him. But so far it seemed they wanted only the memories of women, and they had certainly had ample opportunity to steal from him. It was cold comfort. He wished he weren't so afraid. But fear wouldn't stop him. They'd been stupid, the hollow women. They wanted him to stop searching for the house on Wildwood Road, stop trying to find the lost girl. But they did not understand him, did not realize that he loved his wife enough that it could overwhelm his fear.

He did not hesitate when they came into the circle at the top of Wildwood Road and into the nighttime shadow of that house. It was just as he recalled through the haze of memory and the drunkenness of that night.

The same run-down façade with loose shutters and clapboards. The same cracked windows. The same rambling architecture, as though the builder had been unable to decide what style the house ought to be.

It isn't a house at all, really. Not anymore. Michael parked at the curb and killed the engine, tugged out the keys, and opened his door. *It's the remains of a house. The skeleton. And those hollow women have been feeding off of its corpse.*

"Let's go," he said, shutting the door.

Jillian hesitated only a moment before climbing out. She looked over the top of the car at him, afraid to see the house, to acknowledge it. Yet there was the trace of a smile on her features.

"Pilgrim Day Camp," she said, shivering. "I got a medal in archery, and one in swimming. They used to play music every morning when they raised the flag. We told ghost stories during sleepover nights. This older girl hit me in the stomach one time and made me throw up."

Despite it all, Michael could not help smiling at her. The little twist that his stomach did in that moment was not of nausea, but of excitement, like the butterflies he'd always felt during the school art show.

He went to the trunk and retrieved the tire iron that was set into a clamp beside the spare. Then he glanced up at the house again and for the first time saw the car, there in the darkness of the circular drive, right in front of the door.

Who the hell? he thought, but even as he did he saw them moving up the front steps.

Tom Barnes and his lunatic mother.

Scooter had come back to Wildwood Road after all.

JILLIAN STARED AT THE PEOPLE in front of the house. Ordinary people. Not the little ghostly girl or the freaks with the fucked-up Elephant Man faces. Just ordinary people. But what were they doing here? She would have been tempted to think that this was the wrong place, that Michael had screwed up, but she could feel the pull from the house. Like something inside had cast out invisible fishing line and she was hooked through the breast-bone . . . and now she was being reeled in. She was connected to this place.

That was her reason for being here. What was theirs?

"Who is that?" she asked Michael.

He tested his grip on the tire iron for a second or two, standing at the curb. Then he glanced at her and she could see that he was troubled. Jillian didn't like that. The fucker was supposed to know what was happening, was supposed to help her. Her fists clenched, nails cutting her palms again. Her upper lip curled back and her nostrils flared. Her breathing came faster and she was about to reach for his throat.

"It's her. Susan Barnes. The guy's her son. She's like you, but it happened to her a couple of years ago."

Years of this bitterness? she thought. *I'd have killed myself a dozen times over by then.*

Jillian stared at the two on the stairs, who by now had noticed the new arrivals. The son raised a hand to wave, then lowered it quickly as though he realized how absurd such a gesture was in the shadow of that house.

The hook in her breastbone tugged harder. Jillian started across the ragged lawn. Michael began to speak, then shut his mouth and followed, still clutching the tire iron. Her fury had abated a little. The two small memories that had returned to her in the car had been enough to give her a glimpse at what she had lost, and what was supposed to fill the emptiness inside her. It made her sick to think that such idiocy was what she was missing . . . and yet she hungered for it as well. Hungered to fill that void in any way possible. Because she could feel her mind fraying at the edges. Jillian couldn't tell Michael that, but she could feel herself falling apart, crumbling into some mental abyss. Without the center, the rest could not hold.

Her pace quickened and Michael hurried to keep up with her.

The two who had parked right in the circular drive in front of the main door—and why not, since the residents of that house already knew they were coming—waited for Michael and Jillian. When they reached the steps, Jillian caught the woman glaring at her. Her eyes held a challenge. *She's trying to fuck with me,* Jillian thought. *I'll rip her goddamned throat out.*

"Mr. Barnes," Michael whispered.

The guy on the steps nodded. "Dansky."

"I guess you believed me." Michael shot a wary look at Jillian, perhaps getting a taste of the tension between the two women. Then he turned to Barnes again. "Couldn't have been easy, getting her out after hours."

The man called Barnes, a square-jawed guy, late twenties, whose nose looked like it had been broken at least once, shrugged. "She's my mother," he whispered. He reached out for her, this older woman who looked like she was old enough to be his grandmother, withered and brittle. She twisted away from his touch.

"Fuck off."

Jillian smiled in admiration. The woman sneered, but there

was some strange communication between them. They understood each other.

Barnes took a breath and reached for the front door. His mother was behind him, Michael next and Jillian last. Barnes paused with his hand on the knob and glanced back. He dropped his gaze a second, then looked up at Michael.

"What is this place, really?"

Michael looked up at the face of the crumbling old manse and then back at Barnes. "It isn't the house you have to worry about."

The other man waited as if expecting more. When it didn't come, he grabbed the knob and tried to turn it, but it was locked. Jillian's heart pounded as though it would burst from her chest, and her breath came in short gasps. Of course it wouldn't open for him. She shoved roughly past them all, reached out for the knob, and twisted. It turned easily and the door swung open onto a shadowy foyer. The darkness within beckoned.

"Jilly, wait," Michael whispered.

She let him go past her. The others, too. Jillian was the last one there on the front steps; she spared one final glance out at the circle, at the ordinary, familiar world. But there was nothing ordinary about it, for just across the street that little blond girl, the lost girl, the ghost, stood beneath a willow tree, its branches whipping in the wind. She was just a phantom, a gossamer thing, but Jillian could see the fear and hope in her face, even from this distance.

Then she turned her back on the lost girl and stepped inside the house at the top of Wildwood Road, leaving the door open behind her, allowing what little starlight and moonlight there was to follow her in.

The place was a kind of ghost itself.

With a shiver, Jillian realized that she felt very much at home.

To MICHAEL IT WAS LIKE walking into a place he had previously only seen in his dreams. He knew he had been here before, but his memory was so veiled behind the fugue of ale and magic—

or whatever the hell they had done to him that night—that up until this point it had been only tatters of remembrance. Now, though . . .

The memory came back to him. The place was immaculately clean, but faded and yellowed with age, as though it had been sealed tight for a century and then opened, just for them. Michael clutched the crowbar tightly in his hand.

Jillian's breath came raggedly, and she glanced around the foyer in a series of flinches. Michael looked at Barnes and his mother. It was difficult for him to be around the woman. The lost girl who had haunted his heart and mind for almost two weeks had become so much a resident of his psyche that it was troubling to see what she was now.

He recalled his previous visit here. The memory echoed in him, along with a prickle of dread unlike anything he had felt before. The memory of that helplessness caught in his throat and for a moment he could not breathe. Tom and Susan were ahead of him, starting down the hall toward the kitchen, and now Michael hesitated, turning around to stare at the door. The way they'd come in. The way out.

He recalled that girlish laughter. Their names scrawled on the furniture upstairs. And those blackouts, when his body was not his to control.

"Shit," he whispered.

The front door beckoned and he felt himself pulled toward it. Michael squeezed his eyes shut and pinched the bridge of his nose, then looked up at Jillian, who had paused just a few feet ahead of him and was glaring at him with bitter disapproval.

"You're not going to wimp out on me now, are you?"

Michael shook his head. Once again he squeezed the crowbar, barely conscious of it. "No."

Tom and his mother had gone past the stairs down the hall, moving silently and cautiously investigating the open doorways on either side. Michael began to follow, sifting his memories of this place through his mind. The hall. The back dining room. The kitchen. The narrow servants' stairs at the rear of the house.

Upstairs. His little fugue moments, his blackouts, happened all through the house, but he had been upstairs when he had seen the scrawled names and heard the voices. He paused with one hand on the finial at the bottom of the grand staircase. Jillian made a curious little noise behind him.

"Tom," he whispered.

At the far end of the hall, almost to the kitchen, Tom Barnes turned quickly around, brows knitted in annoyance that the silence had been broken. Michael pointed up the stairs, not really caring if the others followed, and then he took the first step.

In the darkness at the top of the stairs, shadows stirred. His breath caught in his throat. A ripple of childish giggles moved through the darkness, low and distant, muffled . . . somewhere up there. Michael glanced along the hall and saw that Tom and Susan—Scooter—had started back toward the front of the house. Tom was watching him, but Susan's face was lost in the shadows as she passed between the splashes of moonlight that came through the doorways along the corridor.

Michael's nostrils flared. If this was the memory of a smell, it was an incredibly powerful memory. Not apple pie or popcorn. Not baking cookies. This was an earthier smell, something familiar and yet he could not quite . . .

"What is that smell?" he asked.

"It's New Year's Day," Jillian whispered.

He turned to find her weeping. A tiny smile played at the edges of her lips, but there was a bone-deep melancholy in that smile as well and in the way her eyes crinkled.

"Jilly?" Michael asked, hardly daring. She was remembering something. This scent was something of hers.

"It's needles from the Christmas tree, spread all over the floor because my dad just dragged it out the door and to the curb. We always took the tree down on New Year's Day. And when I'd vacuum up the needles they would heat up and the smell would just be everywhere, so strong, like a last little gift before Christmas went away completely."

He went to her, his free hand sliding behind her back as he gazed down at her. It was the first time in days he had touched her the way a husband touched his wife, with gentle love and comfort.

"Do you remember it? Really? You see it in your head?"

Jillian nodded slowly but her smile was turning bitter even as she did. The sour twist returned to her lips. "I do. But there's so many more. I can feel them." She glanced around the foyer, then glared up at the shadows at the top of the stairs. "They're here. But it's like they're just out of reach."

"Goddamn it, Dansky," Tom Barnes hissed. "Shut her up."

Michael shot him a hard look. If the man thought their presence here had gone unnoticed, he was an idiot. Even now he glanced upstairs once more at the shifting shadows and something silver flitted through the darkness up there. For the first time he noticed the singing. It was distant, and so low, but if he listened very carefully he could make it out. Another old jump-rope song, a local one, too. He recognized it.

"Halfway to Boston, halfway to Lynn . . ."

He didn't know how the rest went and could not make out the words, so low were the voices. The little-girl voices. Three or four of them at least, punctuated with laughter. Even nearer, perhaps just at the top of the stairs, there were whispers.

"Don't you hear that?" Tom Barnes muttered in a low voice.

Michael ignored him, glancing at Jillian. She had grown deathly pale, and she took the first step up toward the second floor, joining him there. Then she took another.

The ocean. Michael smelled the salt of the surf, could practically hear it crashing on the rocks, though they were twenty miles from the coast. Then that smell was washed away as though by some unfelt breeze and replaced by something else. *Ripe strawberries.* So delicious a smell that his stomach growled. *Maple syrup.*

Lilacs in bloom, the scent so strong it staggered him and he had to grasp the railing.

Then he got it at last. The scents belonged to the girls, part of those stolen memories. They might have coalesced and taken shape, but there must have been something about powerful sensory memory, olfactory and auditory, that lingered and drifted. Jillian had New Year's Day. And Scooter . . . the smells of popcorn and hot cocoa and the sound of the calliope music from the ice-cream truck, those must have been hers. They accompanied her.

And these other smells, and the jump-rope songs . . . he wondered how many girls were here, kept like the sweetest of delicacies and nibbled upon by the Virgins of Carthage. If that was truly what they were.

"Up," Jillian said. "We have to go up."

Her voice sounded as distant as the jump-rope girls and their giggling song, as though she was mesmerized. Jillian took another step up. Michael followed, crowbar at the ready. Though he had no idea what good it would do. He felt himself falling under whatever spell had touched his wife. The spell of perfect moments, of cherished bits of the past.

"Mom?"

Tom Barnes's voice broke the spell. There was fear in that voice, in that single syllable. Michael glanced over the railing at Barnes and his mother, where they had paused just at the threshold of the foyer. Susan had turned around, her back to Michael and Jillian. Tom put a hand on her arm, and only now did Michael hear the strange sounds coming from the older woman's throat. Not quite crying. It was a low moan, a whimper that spoke of pain with no hope of relief. Then it stopped.

"Mom, what is it?" Tom whispered.

From the shadows of the threshold, she turned at last to face her son, and the moonlight washing the foyer illuminated her features. Her misshapen, distended features, her skin now hard and smooth and gleaming in the moonlight that sifted through the windows.

No, Michael thought, flinching. *She's one of them? How can she be one of the Virgins of Carthage?*

The virgins . . . women sacrificed to their god thousands of years before, but still women. Ever since the memory he'd unwittingly tapped into, the recollection of the mythic thing that lived beneath the city of Carthage, he had assumed these hollow women were the same ones he had seen in those shadowed, subterranean tunnels. And perhaps some of them were. But others . . . this was what happened to the women whose memory, whose innocence, was stolen. *All of them, or just the ones who dare to come back, who come to this house, to the new Hall of Moloch? Oh, Jesus, Scooter. I promised I would—*

Then he couldn't think anymore. He could only watch as Tom Barnes cried out, reaching for his mother, frightened for her when he ought to have been frightened of her. Susan thrust her hands into her son's face, fingers ghosting right through his flesh.

"*Men*," Tom Barnes said, but the voice was not his own. It belonged to the thing that his mother had become. His mouth moved in an obscene parody of speech as that chilling voice issued forth. "*High priests and fathers and brothers. You called our fear shameful and told us to lift our chins, to smile for the god-king, to show him our beautiful faces . . . and then you fed us to him. And this is what we became.*"

Tears streamed down Tom's cheeks, his eyes wide. His mother plucked her fingers from his flesh and his eyes rolled back in his head. The man passed out, crumbling in a heap, his head striking the hardwood floor with a solid crack.

And he was still.

Michael stared at her, at the elongated face, and he knew he had failed her, failed the little lost girl who had only wanted to be found. Shaking his head in denial he moved away from her on the wide staircase, went up one more step, unable to tear his eyes away.

Then Jillian whispered his name.

He turned to her and felt his chest tighten. His lips parted but no words would come. His eyes burned but no tears would fall. Jillian was ugly, now, her features beginning to stretch hideously.

This wasn't Jillian, after all, but just a husk of her, left behind when the core of what she was had been taken away. Just a husk.

She wasn't one of them yet.

But she was changing.

CHAPTER SEVENTEEN

All of Michael's fear was overridden in a single moment. None of it mattered. There was no more hesitation in him, no awe, not even a hint of caution.

"Jilly!" he shouted, forgetting about Susan and her unconscious son, and about the things that shifted in the dark corners of this crumbling house. In his peripheral vision he saw silver-black figures begin to coalesce, several at the top of the stairs and others from the parlors on either side of the foyer. But he gave them no further notice.

Patches of Jillian's skin were hardening, soft flesh stretching. Her eyes were full of fear.

"No, Jilly. No, baby," he whispered. He dropped the crowbar and pulled her roughly to him and held her close, one hand cupped behind her head, fingers pushing up into her hair. "Don't let it happen. Remember that smell, the needles from the Christmas tree and the vacuum. Remember dancing with your father. Waltzing."

He bit his lower lip. How to get her to those memories? Her face was pressed against his cheek and he could feel it changing, stretching, becoming cold against his own flesh. She bucked against him and the fingernails of her right hand dug into the back of his neck.

"No," he rasped. Tears began to burn the corners of his eyes. But he would not give in to grief. That would be surrender. "Listen to me. Remember Vienna, waltzing in the cathedral square on the cobblestones, you and me on our honeymoon. And you laughed because it reminded you of your father teaching you to waltz. Remember? That's how you got that memory back, by thinking of a connection you still had. Those threads are still there. You said they were all around you in the air, just out of reach. The fuckers stole them, Jilly, and you've got to steal them back. You've got to. Grab those threads. Follow them back to your memories."

A flash of inspiration struck him, an image in his mind of the set of hardcover books between the bookends on her bureau, her favorite story of all time. She read the whole series every couple of years. "Close your eyes, Jilly. Go to Narnia. Peter and Susan and Lucy and—Jesus, what the fuck's the other one?"

She was so very still in his arms. "Edmund," she whispered.

Something broke inside him then. "Edmund. Yes, that's him. Just like waltzing with your father, Jilly. You're connected. It's a pipeline from now to then, to the first time you read them. You got the flu and had to stay home a few days, and you read them all in one go. The memory's here in this house somewhere, babe. You're here, the girl you were back then. You've got to grab hold of her."

Jillian's face was still against his. Suddenly it felt warm. Damp with tears. It *shifted* against his skin.

Her voice was tremulous. Innocent. "Michael?"

He pulled back from her, stared in broken wonder at her distended face as it returned to normal, at the eyes that seemed for the first time in too long to see him, to see her husband.

Which was when he felt the cold knives of phantom fingers plunge into the back of his head, thrusting through hair and skin and bone.

Michael went rigid, and then he tumbled down into a deep well of ancient memory.

Hunger is all she knows.

She and her sisters, there in the dark tunnels that wind beneath Kart-hadasht, away from the Hall of Moloch. They are hollow, the vast emptiness inside them a constant agony. Power radiates from the god-king, a black, chaotic force that has twisted them. They are leeches now, starving for a taste of what was stolen, yearning for a moment of happiness that will bring them no pleasure, that will be bitterly digested, but that they cannot survive without.

They have become both Brides and Daughters of Moloch, infused with his essence, even as he consumed theirs.

Each time a new virgin descends the stairs to her sacrifice, they are forced to watch as the god-king takes her, penetrates her, and drains her of her joy and purity. Childhood-eater, virgin-defiler, that is Moloch. And they watch in agonizing hunger, until at last he has used up the girl, and only then are they allowed to come to him, so that he may cradle each one and let them suckle from him. One memory each he gives them. One moment of youthful bliss to sustain them until the next time.

It only whets their appetite, maddening them with hunger, now that they have the taste of it in their hearts and on their lips.

And it is not enough.

So she waits in the darkness with her sisters, maddened by hunger. And now there comes a new girl, a slender, bronze-skinned thing, draped in thin linen, perfect skin and a perfect face. Beauty that is anathema to the Daughters of Moloch.

This time they do not wait.

The hunger is too much. One memory is not enough.

The moment the girl reaches the bottom of the stone stairs they rush from the shadowed tunnels into the flickering torchlight. The girl sees them and screams, alarming Moloch, who turns to face them. The Daughters of Moloch do not pause. There is sadness in the god-king's eyes, but no surprise, as they attack, tearing at him with long, clawed fingers. There are undigested stolen memories still within him, and they tear these delicacies from his breast.

Moloch begins to wither.

The light goes from his eyes.

The god-king is dead.

The virgin believes they are her saviors. She weeps with gratitude.

They fall upon her, and steal her essence, the innocent core of her. Surfeited, the Daughters of Moloch will not need this sustenance for some time, but they have been hungry too long, and so they shall let the dark power that forged them give shape to the girl's essence.

She will be their hoard, their store, to stave off hunger . . . until the city above sacrifices another virgin.

And another.

And another.

Michael blinked and the room swam back into focus. Pain seared his back where the husk's fingers plunged into his flesh. He cried out, twisting himself around, breaking its grip and the circuit that had been created between them. It had been trying to hurt him, somehow, perhaps to overwhelm him. Maybe Tom Barnes hadn't fainted from shock, but from some harm the thing his mother had been had done to him. But Michael was certain that this creature had not intended for him to draw those images from it. Beneath those memories all he had felt was a black void, an abyss, a howling vacuum of nothingness. All he felt was its hunger.

Whether they were its own recollections or some ancestral memory, passed down through generations of these things, did not matter at all.

What mattered was that it hurt them.

Just as before, on that wooded hillside, the thing that had touched his mind had withered. It truly was a husk, now, in form as well as function. It was a wrinkled, shriveled thing. Its long arms reached out for him, skeletal fingers questing.

"No!" he snarled, and he rammed his fist into its skull, shattering it with a single blow. The silver mist that was their blood plumed in the air as that twisted woman crumbled to the ground.

Jillian was still on the steps, near the bottom. Several of the hideous things in their shapeless coats had surrounded her, and others were above her on the stairs.

"Give them back, you fuckers! I want them back!" she screamed, sneering as she glared at them with savage fury.

They were hesitant to approach her.

Michael saw the crowbar on the ground where he had

dropped it and started for it. He saw the prone form of Tom Barnes, and too late he wondered where his mother had gotten to, where the creature she had become had gone. Then a shadow moved behind him, visible just out of the corner of his eye, and he felt himself tugged backward. He was thrown on his back and spikes of pain shot through him as he struck the hardwood floor.

Then she was above him. Susan Barnes. Or the thing that had been Susan and, once upon a kinder time, been Scooter. She wrapped her cold fingers around his throat and he tried to beat at her arms, but whatever dark magic had transformed her, she was too strong. His windpipe was cut off. He strained, neck muscles popping out, face burning with the rush of blood to his skin. Black dots speckled the edges of his vision as oxygen deprivation began to close in.

As his vision began to dim, Michael saw something bright move in his peripheral vision and let his eyes drift that way.

The little lost girl. Or what remained of her. She was little more than a suggestion now, a sketch of blond hair and a silhouette against the shadows. In her blue jeans and peasant blouse, the little phantom girl stood just inside the foyer staring down at unconscious Tom Barnes. Her head was tilted to one side as though she felt something, some sadness, but did not understand why she should feel such a thing. She was a wisp now, almost nothing. If they caught her, she would be consumed.

Only her husk would continue, eternally hungry for what she had lost.

Michael's legs twitched and his whole body spasmed. The back of his head hit the floor, hard. His vision began to fade.

JILLIAN SCREAMED AGAIN AT THE hideous women who now surrounded her. They hated her, but she gave them pause as well. With Michael's help, she had found scraps of her memory. The house was full of tattered bits of stolen innocence. These things consumed them. But the memories she had regained, though few, were enough to give her a tether to what she'd lost, to the girl she'd been. And she was not going to let go now. No matter what kind of terrible power there was in this place, in these creatures, she was not going to surrender to it now that she had regained even those precious few moments.

"Give them back!" she shouted again. Her hands trembled as she reached up to touch her own face, to feel her skin. All around her she could sense the memories. It seemed to her that if she squinted her eyes a little she might be able to see them, images flashing in a tornado just the way they had when Dorothy's house had been sucked up into the storm and dropped down in Oz. She could taste coconut ice cream on her tongue the way they had made it at Hanrahan's when she was a little girl, the way it tasted there and nowhere else. But Hanrahan's had been closed for twenty years.

They're here. They're all here. If she could only focus hard enough she could recall them, just the same way it felt when she'd misplaced her keys and was trying to remember where she'd put them.

Michael had fought off one of them, destroyed it. But now she heard him shout again and turned to see the thing that had been Susan Barnes grab him and drag him down. He was being choked. Strangled. Michael tried to tear the woman's arms away but could not. All around Jillian the others began to close in. Jillian felt a kinship with them. She shared their hunger.

But she remembered waltzing with her father.

Huddling under her blankets with the flu reading *The Lion, the Witch and the Wardrobe.*

You're not one of them, she thought. *They'll kill you to taste that coconut ice cream on your tongue.*

The hollow woman straddled Michael. He stared off to the left, toward the hall that led to the back of the house. There, above Tom Barnes's fallen form, was an apparition. A haunting trace in the air that might once have been a little girl. She was staring at the unconscious man, but now she looked up at Jillian.

So afraid.

She's afraid of me, Jillian thought. *Of all of these women, and of me.*

A flash of memory burst abruptly into her mind. *She is eight and it's Thanksgiving at her grandmother's house in Vermont. Everyone is there. Dozens of aunts, uncles, and distant cousins she has never even met. It is the most amazing Thanksgiving of her life. Her grandmother and her aunt Betty are in the kitchen cutting pasta for the last of the hundreds of ravioli they have made from scratch. Her cousin Jamie, who is in the fourth grade, has been wrapped completely in aluminum foil by his sisters, who are pretending he is a space alien. And they've invited Jillian to play. Space Alien Jamie chases the girls and they shriek with delight; the smell of meat sauce cooking in a pot, to be used for the ravioli later, fills the house along with the voices of her family and their families and their families, and she can smell her great-uncle's pipe.*

"Uncle Bull," she said to herself. "We called him Uncle Bull, even though his name was Bill."

He died of cancer the year after, but I didn't know it then. Didn't know it was coming. And it was perfect.

The mouths of all of the hollow women hung open like the beaks of baby birds, snapping at the nearness of a worm. She had gotten this memory back and they wanted it. Even the one on top of Michael stopped strangling him a moment and twisted her head around to stare at Jillian with hard, black eyes.

Jillian grabbed another memory out of the air. Sitting on a beach in Mexico drinking a piña colada with her mother—hers without the rum—while "Margaritaville" played on the radio.

She shook her head violently. More memories started to flicker across her mind, touching her, questing, as though they were moths and she had become an open flame.

The hollow women on the stairs hissed, openmouthed, and turned away from her, looking back up the way they had come. Jillian glanced around to be certain the others were still hesitant, then looked to see what had drawn their attention.

She could not breathe. Her eyes were wide. A smile of wonder touched her lips. For there, coming slowly down the stairs, she saw herself: Jillian Lopresti at nine years old, her hair tied back in a ponytail, in a purple tank top and beige capri pants with flowers embroidered on the legs.

The girl . . . the lost heart of her . . . hugged herself as she looked at the stooped, cruel forms of the hollow women. That shaped essence of Jillian, that little girl, took another step in spite of the terror in her eyes and the trembling of her lower lip.

The husks reached for her.

"No!" Jillian screamed.

With all the strength she had, she rammed her elbow into the head of the nearest one, then slammed into another, knocking it over the railing. She pushed past the third even as it scrabbled at her waist and legs, tried to stop her, fingers digging into her flesh.

The little girl smiled so sweetly, and opened her arms as though Jillian were going to lift her into an embrace. Jillian reached for her, and then touched . . .

And she knows. At last, she understands so much. She can feel the power in this house, in these monsters. She sees in her mind a room filled with little girls, with memories made manifest, kept like wheat harvested for a long winter. The women take only a few memories at a time; they can digest only so much at once, and gluttony is a waste. So they take their time and they search for girls whose memories of innocence shine like a beacon. There are blemishes, of course, but that is why they are careful in their choices.

They take only the choicest girls and slowly, over months, sometimes even years, they strip away the joyous memories, the pure moments, leaving only sadness behind. They relish each taste, even as the girls—these essences given form by the power in the house—are whittled to nothing. Some memories escape their grasp, precious smells, blissful sounds, and others that linger in the ether, separate from the manifestations of the girls. Some of them even drift beyond the walls of the house, dissipating somewhere out in the solid world.

This is how Scooter slipped away. Part of her began to drift and she followed it. After that, they searched for her, nearly caught her so many times, but she eluded them, just out of reach. And, after all, they had enough sustenance stored for many years to come. They could retrieve her at their leisure.

Sometimes she would appear to them. Whisper to them that she would not leave without them, that she would bring help to free them all. And sometimes she would cry because they were trapped there. If she strayed too far from the house she would begin to dissipate, the power that held her memories together giving way and her essence evaporating.

She would have to wait, she said. And be clever.

Little Jillian Lopresti knows all of this. Some she's learned firsthand, and some the other girls have told her.

Mostly she is scared. The hollow women frighten her, and so does Scooter, always begging them to try to slip away. Jillian doesn't dare. The hollow women are terrible, but to be nothing, to simply cease to exist, is worse. She's too frightened to try to leave.

And as her sweetest memories are torn from her, consumed by the twisted husks of her captors, she only cries harder.

Jillian fell on the stairs. The impact jarred her, but she understood it all immediately. The wraith, the essence of her, was within her again. Her face flushed with relief and gratitude and tears of happiness welled in her eyes.

"You're all right, sweetie," she whispered to the girl she'd once been, to the part of her she'd been missing. "I'm all right."

There came a hiss from behind her.

Jillian spun around, grabbing the railing and launching to her feet. There were seven of them now, coming up the stairs at her, hunger and hatred in their eyes.

"No *way*," she said. "Not again. I know what you are, now. I can feel what you took, inside me now, and this time, I'll fight you for every moment."

"*Michael?*" A tremulous voice came up from the foyer, a little-girl voice.

Jillian glanced down to see that Scooter had shaken off her fear. Her adult self, her husk, was throttling Michael, and now her essence rushed across the room toward them. Susan was much further gone than she had been, she had been completely altered, but Jillian wondered if they could be rejoined.

The hollow women on the stairs saw Scooter as well. The one that had escaped them. In that moment, Jillian was forgotten. As that phantom girl rushed toward Michael and the obscenity her body had become, the hideous things lunged down the stairs and across the foyer at her.

"No! Scooter, run away!" Jillian shouted.

Too late. They were upon her then. Hungry, ravenous mouths open wide, they reached long fingers toward her.

Jillian wanted to help her, but now that the creatures had been drawn away from her and she was free to move, Michael was her first concern. She rushed down the stairs. On the floor, hate filled the eyes of the thing that had been Susan Barnes. As Michael started to cough, his gaze clearing, it struck him hard in the face. Blood sprayed from his nose. Once more he tried to fend her off, his hands flailing but touching nothing but air.

Michael, Jillian's mind screamed.

Her memories of life with Michael had been the bridge for her, had given her the way to connect to the memories that had been stolen. Jillian loved him, and that was the key. Love was always naïve and innocent, in its way. They'd tried to steal that as well, but they couldn't take it. Only poison it for a time.

Jillian dropped into a crouch at the bottom of the stairs. Her fingers wrapped around the crowbar Michael had dropped. She lifted the crowbar, racing toward Michael and the thing that had been Susan Barnes. Curses and threats rose in the back of her mind, but she could not find the voice to speak them. Jillian grabbed the faded blond hair of the husk and yanked her head back. It tore out in patches, leaving only bloodless scalp behind.

The husk turned toward her and Jillian swung the crowbar. The metal cracked Susan Barnes's face as though it were made of porcelain, knocking her sideways off of Michael. The thing sprawled on the dusty wooden floor.

Jillian spun around, ready to fight as other husks rushed toward her and her husband. "Back off!" she screamed.

Six of them formed a loose circle around her and Michael. In the parlor and up the stairs, others shifted in the shadows as if holding their breath, waiting to see what would happen. They all hesitated now. The one on the floor, the one that had been Susan Barnes, twitched but did not rise. A kind of silver mist began to seep from the cracks in her face. The others shrank away from her.

A dozen feet away, across the huge foyer, the spectral apparition of the little girl, the core of the Barnes woman, began to scream. A trio of the husks had gathered around her. One of them had her by the hair and throat, holding her still while the other two thrust their hands into the wraith's chest, tearing bits and pieces out of her that looked to Jillian like nothing so much as cotton candy.

"Leave her alone!" Jillian shouted. She waved the crowbar at the husks nearer to her, and they flinched but did not back away. The three that were savaging the little girl's spirit reacted not at all.

On the ground, Michael moaned. Jillian looked down even as he sat up and grabbed hold of her leg. His eyes were wide with anguish.

"Jilly," he rasped. "We have to do something. I promised I'd find her. I can't let them . . ."

Frantic, she looked at Scooter and saw that the husks were eating what they stole from her, slipping long skeletal fingers into their misshapen mouths, bits of the girl's essence wriggling in their grasp.

Scooter was fading. Even her screams were diminishing. In the moonshine she seemed barely a trick of the light.

"Jillian, we've got to—"

Michael started toward the husks that were tearing Scooter apart. The other creatures opened those hideous mouths again and shifted to block their path. Her husband moved to attack them. Jillian grabbed his arm. She had an idea.

"Have I ever been to Mexico?" she asked him, desperate, that one confusing memory now seeming out of place in her mind.

"What?" He didn't tear his eyes away from Scooter and the husks. "No. What the hell—"

"No," Jillian repeated. "No, I haven't." *But I remember it.* Of all those stray memories in the air, she had snatched up one that wasn't hers. Not eaten it like the husks, but summoned it into her conscious mind to replace some of what they had stolen from her.

And there were others. She looked up and saw them flitting around the foyer, drifting toward the cracked windows and into the dusty corners. A little girl playing with toy horses on a grassy hill. Another kissing a second-grade boy in the schoolyard. Someone named Lizzie dancing on stage, her parents beaming up at her from the first row. Christina helping her dad at the grill during a cookout at the beach.

Jillian could smell sausages grilling. Could hear the music that made Lizzie's feet want to dance. Could smell the grass beneath those horses and feel the dream of one little girl to someday have a real horse to ride. All those memories . . . every one of them another moment's survival for the husks.

But not if Jillian got to them first.

"What the hell are you doing?" Michael asked.

She clutched the crowbar in her right hand and with her left she snatched memories out of the air. The husks had cried out before when she had done this, and now it happened again. With every memory she grasped, every image that came flooding into her mind, they twitched, opening their mouths in a wide, silent chorus of screams.

It enraged them. Maybe even hurt them.

Jillian liked that.

"The girl, Jilly! The girl!"

Michael was pulling away from her. The husks flinched with every memory she stole from their possession, but still they shuffled into his path, stooped over, their long fingers rising into claws. Jillian screamed at him to stop, to stay away from them, but even she could see that Scooter would not last much longer.

The husks latched on to Michael. One of them plunged its fingers into the back of his skull. Furiously he lashed out and his fist connected. A shout of satisfaction burst from his throat and he gripped a second husk by the throat and tossed her aside.

"Whatever you're doing, keep doing it!" he shouted to her.

"Wait!" Jillian called.

Michael tried to turn toward her but could not spare her a glance. Jillian plucked one more memory from the ether—nine-year-old Jennie crying while her brother packed for college—and ran to him. She grabbed Michael's wrist and thrust the crowbar into his hand.

He smiled.

And started for the tattered soul of a lost girl.

EVERY BREATH WAS LIKE SWALLOWING ground glass. Michael could still feel Susan's hands on his throat, strangling him. Could still hear the crack as Jilly shattered her face with the crowbar.

But Jilly was fighting. Doing something Michael didn't understand.

Mexico? What the hell was that about?

But it didn't matter.

All that mattered was that it seemed to force them to lose their focus, to distract them. Which meant Michael could fight them.

The moonlight lit the eerie tableau within the foyer, gleaming on the cracks in the windows. Dust swirled and eddied. The house seemed to shake with fury and grief in equal measure. And anticipation as well. The shadows rippled with the presence of other husks. Two of them stared at Jillian and snatched at the air like children, but they seemed bereft, lost.

The thing that had been Susan Barnes lay twitching on the floor, face splintered like a ceramic carnival mask. But the eyes were still alive, and they watched him. Her son Tom lay unconscious nearby. Between Michael and Scooter's remaining essence were seven ugly, twisted, hollow women.

Michael waded through them, ignoring their filthy, penetrating touch. One of the creatures pushed its fingers into Michael's face and he grabbed its wrist and swung the crowbar down, shattering its arm. Just before the impact, the thing recoiled, not from fear of his weapon but from the shock of contact with his mind. He had been tainted by them. Maybe whatever chaotic power was in them had poisoned him, but if they tried to violate his mind and memories now, they would begin to lose their own.

Hands clutched at him, fingers clawed at his clothing. Michael took one of the things and hurled it across the room to crash into the banister. He brought the crowbar down on the head of the next and when it crumbled to the ground he kicked it in the face. Like Susan's, the skin cracked. Shards of it fell away.

There was only blackness beneath. An endless void.

Michael tore his gaze away. He did not want to see, did not dare to look too deeply. Instead he drove through the other two in his way, thrashing at them to get to the three who still tore at Scooter, ripping ribbons of pink cotton from inside her. The ghost who was not a ghost turned her eyes to him, and in her gaze he saw that she was more lost than ever.

"No," he whispered.

Come find me, she had said. Michael had promised he would, and now he had, and this was where it had led. There was almost nothing left of her.

He clutched the crowbar like a spear in both hands and drove it through the back of the nearest woman's skull. It fell to the floorboards, gray mist spilling out of the hole in its head. The two others left off their attack on Scooter at last. The wisp of her drifted like a plume of cigarette smoke.

One of the hollow women pushed her entire hand into Michael's chest. He froze, throwing his head back in pain as the intrusion seemed to seize his heart.

"You're killing us," his voice said. His mouth. His lips. But not his words.

Michael snarled, fighting the pain. The husk had already started to wither from the contact, but he forced himself to raise the crowbar again. Before he could use it Jillian flew past him, driving the hollow woman down to the floor, her fist rising and falling. Michael heard small bones pop as Jillian struck the hard, twisted features again and again.

"We're doing our best," she said grimly. "We're doing our best." Her voice was distorted. Not really her voice at all, but the voices of half a dozen different women or more. And when she looked up at Michael her eyes were wild, shifting colors in a kaleidoscope, brown one moment and blue the next, hazel somewhere in between.

The two remaining creatures fled into the shadows, sifting themselves into the darkness so that in seconds it was as though they had never been there at all. But they were not alone. Michael had seen many more of the figures before, watching from the shadowy corners, shifting in the darkness, waiting for the outcome.

For a taste, perhaps.

"It's not over," he said, turning to Jillian.

Her wild eyes were full of hope and life, and she shook her head in agreement. "No. Not yet."

They were alone there in the foyer save for the twitching form of Susan Barnes. Her face had begun to revert now, something that had not happened to any of the others. It was less distorted; there were places where her skin seemed ordinary pale human skin. But he didn't know her. Not really.

He knew Scooter.

Michael turned to the lost girl, and his heart filled with sorrow. Once she had been an angel with a halo of blond hair, a pretty little girl with a precious smile, innocent in her peasant blouse and jeans. Now her presence was so faint that he had to focus to find any details, to see her eyes. This was all that was left of the girl Susan Barnes had once been.

In his mind he held an image of the way she had looked that night after the masquerade when he had nearly hit her. On the road, her face washed in red from his taillights. Wide-eyed and lost. How much of her remained he did not know.

"Scooter," he whispered. "I'm so sorry."

The wraith, little more than an outline in the moonlight, tilted her head and gazed at him with no recognition. *She doesn't remember,* Michael thought. He reached out to touch her, but his hand passed through her silhouette.

Jillian stood by him, and now she stretched out her own hand. Her fingers twined with the wisps that were Scooter's fingers, and Jillian led her across the moonlit foyer. With one hand touching the tattered essence of the woman's memories, Jillian pushed the fingers of her other hand into the still-flinching form of Susan Barnes, and the specter that had haunted his dreams and his waking life seemed to flow *into* Jillian and then on down her arm into the body on the floor.

Susan's face was even less distorted now, and one half of her face had returned to its natural flesh. The crack in that mask had now become a deep gash in flesh and, Michael was horrified to see, in bone as well.

The shattered woman drew a deep, shuddering breath.

Jillian's eyes had returned to normal. "They're together again now. And so am I, Michael."

Hope rose, quickening his pulse. "Really?"

She glanced at the floor. "Parts are missing. Things they've already . . . things that are gone forever. But I'm mostly me again. There were escaped memories in the house, bits of different girls. Echoes. I . . . I put them all in *her.* They took so much, I thought it might help."

A rasping breath came from Susan's lips.

"Upstairs, Michael," she rasped, her eyes unfocused. *"The others . . . I hid from them as long as I could, so they punished me, took without hunger. But you have to help the others."*

Michael tried to understand.

"But you and Jillian . . . you were here. The others . . . they've got nowhere to go."

"Better to be free . . . to become nothing . . . than to be torn apart, piece . . . piece by piece. You have to hurry. They'll try to take them all at once, now." Even shattered and aged, he could see Scooter in Susan's eyes, the fear there. *"They'll eat the girls all up."*

Michael shook his head, cursing again. He glanced at the stairs, gripping the crowbar, then at Jillian.

"Let's go."

Together they hurried up the stairs, images from his first visit flashing through Michael's mind. The shadows moved on the second floor. He pulled Jillian to the top of the stairs and was assaulted by the smells . . . cinnamon and apple pie, the salt spray of the ocean.

Michael stumbled once but caught himself. Jillian grabbed his hand and they ran side by side.

A corridor branched off to the right, and there was another staircase going up to the third floor, but the heart of the house was the main hall straight ahead. The same hallway he had found himself in after the masquerade. But his head was clear tonight. His throat was raw and he was desperate, but his mind was clear. There were nine doors leading off of the corridor, four on the left and five on the right.

Eight of them were open, letting moonlight spill in, flooding the place in a brassy gloom. The shadows had fallen still. It looked for all the world like an ordinary house. But the smells were still there, along with a ripple of distant laughter, the hushed, intimate, shared giggling of little girls.

With utter clarity he heard the voices. *One, two, buckle my shoe. Three, four* . . .

Jillian shuddered. Michael saw that she was crying. Crying for the lost girls.

He hurried her down the hall. Even if that one door—that one goddamned door—hadn't been closed, he would have guessed it. Would have known it. For of all the vague, disoriented bits of memory in his mind, that one was crystal.

A soft, lisping, baby-girl voice sings "I'm a Little Teapot." *He steps into a child's bedroom. Pale and bleached of life, washed in moonlight.* ". . . Here is my handle, here is my spout . . ." *Graffiti scrawled on the wall. Ruthie Loves Adam. Nikki and Danielle were here. Miss Friel Cuts the Cheese. Lizzie & Jason, TLA.*

True Love, Always.

He held Jillian up and she leaned into him the way she curled under his arm, conforming her body to his, every night in their bed.

With a roar he kicked the door in. It crashed open and they went together over the threshold into that pale, faded bedroom with its pretty white furniture. Some of the hollow women were there—eight all told. Five of them stood in a line across the room, herding the memory-wraiths of little girls against one wall. In the moonlight they were mere shapes, though some seemed more solid than others.

Then he was wading into the hollow women, the crowbar falling, cracks splitting in misshapen skulls, shards of faces crumbling to the floor. He had driven two of them to the ground and kicked a third, knocking it toward the same broken window he himself had crashed through once upon a time. Then he felt fingers twine in his hair and a powerful hand grip his wrist, and they had him.

Four of the husks. Hungry mouths wide open above him, they slammed him to the floor. His head banged the wood and blackness swam in his eyes. Michael tried to swing the crowbar again, but it was plucked from his hand. Cold knife fingers plunged into him—

You don't want this, he warned. *I'm not afraid of you, anymore. Not when I can look into* your *core, steal* your *past.*

The fingers left him. It was cold where they'd penetrated his flesh, but this time he did not feel dirty or tainted. The husks staggered back from him and Michael grinned. This time he was the one who had tainted them.

Against the wall, the lost girls—no, the *stolen* girls—huddled. One of the husks grabbed the nearest girl, barely a shadow now, and plunged its face into her chest, baring grotesque teeth from that distended jaw. It came back with pink ribbon squirming in its mouth like some animal at a trough.

He raised the crowbar.

"Die, damn you!"

It was Jillian's voice. He glanced over to see her struggling with one of the hollow women. Rage flushed his wife's face red. The husks on the floor began to stir, still alive, scratching at the wood, trying to drag themselves back up.

At the door to that faded bedroom, other broken husks appeared.

All of them hungry.

The lost girls who were herded into one end of the room began to scream. Some of the broken ones were reaching for them. Michael raised the crowbar again, ready to shatter the husks, to tear them apart . . .

"No," whispered one of the girls, a wraith so slight that he had not noticed her before, barely a glimmer of a memory. *"There are too many. You can't save us all that way."*

Michael hesitated. Then he turned and ran to Jillian. One of the husks was almost upon her and he crashed into it, driving it hard against the wall. He grabbed her by the arms and gazed into her eyes.

"You collected some of their memories before. Lost ones. Do it now! Share with them! Let them *all* in!"

Once more terrible fingers clawed at him, tried to burrow into his flesh and his soul. Michael shattered a malformed face.

"Yes," he heard Jillian say. "Come in. Come in, girls."

The spectral girls swept toward her, one of them shaking loose the grasp of a husk that tore one final bit of memory from her. One by one they struck Jillian like a gust of wind, blowing her back, disappearing into her chest. Jillian's eyes went wide with each entry, each impact. When it was over Michael shoved her into a corner and put himself between her and the rest of the room.

There was the window, that shattered window. But he was not going out that way again.

"Back off!" he shouted at the husks that shambled and crawled toward them. Only one was uninjured. The others were a nightmare vision, with their shapeless gray coats and their fingers curled into claws, their faces broken and impossible darkness beyond.

He grabbed the one that was nearest him. It clawed his arm, cutting deeply. Michael forced its hand against his chest; at first, nothing happened.

"Do it!" he screamed. "*Touch* me!"

It fell limp, its fingers slipping through his flesh.

Almost instantly, it began to wither. Michael shuddered with the contact, nearly slipping into the fugue state that had overcome him when they had touched him in the past. But he would not let himself succumb. Instead he only held the hollow woman as she shriveled, skin hanging on her cadaverous form.

"Out of the way, or I swear to God I'll do the same to every last one of you, even if it kills me."

They were unsure. Could he destroy them all? It seemed unlikely. There were more of them. How many more he did not know; others moved in the shadows outside that room. But they hesitated.

That was all he needed.

"Come on," he growled, grabbing Jillian's hand.

They knocked husks aside as they fled the room.

For the moment, the hollow women did not pursue them. The hall was suddenly empty, only silver blurs in the air to indicate that they were not alone. Downstairs they found Susan Barnes still alive, but only by a breath or two. Her body had reversed its own metamorphosis but her injuries were so severe it was miraculous that she was still breathing. Michael held Jillian's hand tightly as they walked over to her.

"Oh, no, Scooter," he whispered. "Oh, no."

Susan attempted a smile, and blood ran from the hatchet-split in her face. "Scooter," she said, her voice gurgling. "That's right. That's what they all called me." The woman laughed, a wet sound, filled with fluid that didn't belong in her lungs. "Hilly could never say Susan."

Her brow knitted into a frown. "I don't remember Hilly. What she looked like. I don't . . ." Her eyes were filled with despair.

Jillian crouched beside the dying woman. One by one the lost girls slipped out of her again. They made a circle around Susan, touched her, fingers slipping into her flesh, passing through her as though she was the ghost among them. Jillian could not perform this trick, but she brushed Susan's hair from her eyes.

Michael caught those familiar scents again. Cinnamon apple pie. The ocean. Others as well. Memories drifting off of these girls. He looked around, afraid it would bring the hollow women, but there was no sign of them yet. Just moonlight and dust in the crumbling foyer of the house on Wildwood Road. Moonlight and dust, and the ghosts of women who had never died.

"One from each of us," Jillian whispered to Susan, holding both of her hands. "The best memories. The happiest ones. Because if not for you—"

The thought went unfinished.

The smell of a Thanksgiving feast filled the house.

"Uncle Bull," Susan Barnes whispered, and a smile of love and wonder blossomed on her ruined face.

The wraiths began to leave, then. Passing out through the walls and windows like true ghosts. Lost girls searching for their future, memories set free. Some of them were dead now, the lost memories only ghosts that he supposed would slowly fade. But for the others, Michael wondered what would happen. Would the women they had been stolen from wake up different in the morning, completely changed? Would they think suddenly of something from their childhood, something that hadn't occurred to them in a very long time, and smile? He would not like to think that these others were now just lost girls as well, wandering in search of their shells, searching for completion. Or disappearing forever into nothing.

The thought would haunt him.

Alone at Susan's side now, Jillian beckoned to Michael. He went and knelt with her and took one of Susan's hands in his own. Her eyes were unfocused, lids fluttering, but for a moment they cleared and he could tell that she saw him. The flicker of recognition was impossible to mistake.

"Scooter—"

"It's you. D'Artagnan," Susan whispered, tears in her eyes. *"I'm sorry about your hat. I crushed it—"*

"Sssh. It's okay," he said, holding her hand tightly. "It's nothing."

She took a long, ragged breath. A tremor of pain crossed her face, but then she focused on him again and her smile returned. *"You came. You found me."*

"I made a promise," Michael told her.

A faint smile creased her lips. He could see cracked bone right through the torn flesh of her face. *"I . . . remember."*

And she was gone.

TOM BARNES HAD STRUCK HIS head hard on the wood floor. Hard enough to bring a trickle of blood across the boards. Even so, he stirred as Michael grabbed him beneath the arms and dragged him out of that house. His feet bounced on the steps going down to the front lawn.

When Michael emerged yet again from the house bearing the body of Susan Barnes, Tom was awake. Unsteady, he crawled over to her as Michael set her down, and he cradled his mother in his arms, weeping silently.

He was still holding her that way when the sound of an engine cut the night. Jillian had set off on an errand . . . a short drive to that elegantly antique gas station, so well preserved, an echo from another era.

A memory.

Michael took the gas can into the house and splashed curtains and mattresses and furniture, holding it upended until the last drop had fallen, and soaked into that house. When he came outside again, Tom Barnes had already gone, taking his mother's remains with him.

Jillian insisted that she be allowed to strike the match. Michael didn't argue.

The blaze lit the night, dispelling shadows. Some of those monsters, those hideous thieves, were still inside. He felt sure they would escape. But with the power that had gathered in that house for so long destroyed by cleansing fire, they would have to begin again. To find another place.

Another empty house to fill with stolen memories.

EPILOGUE

Springtime in Seville was all music and flowers and laughter. It was the kind of place anyone could fall in love with. The Old City was a labyrinth of cobblestoned streets, many barely wide enough for two cars to pass without scraping against one another. The architecture was breathtaking, so different from anything Michael and Jillian were used to. There were massive doors that seemed made for giants, with doors of a more ordinary size cut into them. Wrought-iron gates covered arched entrances that revealed interior courtyard gardens, where flowers blossomed in colors so bright they seemed impossible. Small religious icons were set into alcoves in the outer walls of buildings that might have been homes, hotels, or churches, though it was difficult to tell at times.

Michael led the way along a sidewalk that forced them into single file. He glanced back at Jillian; she offered him a bemused expression. A squat car that looked almost like a toy passed them, and they had to hug the wall to keep from being bumped by the side mirror. He heard Jillian laugh in amazement and a warm feeling flooded his chest. Michael stepped off the sidewalk and reached for her hand so they could walk together.

"You're going to get killed if you stay in the street."

"I'm pretty quick. I can jump out of the way."

"Ooh," Jilly said, squeezing his hand. "He's a rebel."

A loud whine erupted behind him and Michael started, heart galloping, adrenaline spiking through him as he leaped back to the sidewalk. He spun just in time to see a guy on a moped fly by at maniacal speed. *Probably a messenger*, he thought, seeing the packages strapped to the back.

"My hero," Jilly said, and laughed.

Michael whacked her lightly on the arm.

"Ow!" She shot him a withering glance.

Michael didn't wither. "You be nice or I'm not taking you to that flamenco show tonight."

The one thing she had made him promise when they had decided upon Seville as a destination was that he would take her to a flamenco show. The city had turned out to have an extraordinary charm all its own . . . or, rather, the Old City had. Seville proper was a sprawl of urban ugliness, depressing in its gray sameness and almost dystopic in its filth. But finding the Old City in the center was like peeling back the layers of a rotten onion and discovering a pearl.

"You promised," Jillian said, as the road opened up into a small plaza where the street forked. The main road continued to the right, but on the left was a narrow pedestrian path lined with restaurants and shops and what might have been apartments. In the middle of the fork was a bar with outdoor patio seats where waiters brought tapas to the tables of the tourists who needed a rest and a bite to eat.

Michael grinned and spun her around in a mad dance. Jilly laughed a moment, then nearly tripped and pulled him into a tight embrace. Her heart beat wildly in her chest from the fright.

"I'll take you anywhere you want to go," he whispered to her. Michael drew back just enough so that he could see her eyes. "Didn't I tell you that from the beginning?"

Jillian nodded. Michael pushed a stray lock of hair away from her face and bent to kiss her. They lingered there, breathing each other in. Several local boys drove by in a car and one of them hooted something out the window. Michael and Jillian only glanced over at the passing car and smiled. But then he squeezed her hand to draw her attention again.

"Whatever you want is fine with me."

She tilted her head to one side, a little-girl gesture that was a recent trait. "I want you to have a good time, too."

"I'm having a great time. The best. How could I not? God, the colors, the gardens . . . today was incredible."

And it had been. They had walked the Barrio de Santa Cruz, and then visited the royal Alcázar, taking their time as they wandered its rooms and gardens. Michael had taken dozens of pictures in a span of hours, his artist's eye taking in the Moorish influences and storing it all for another time. He knew he would not come away from Spain unchanged, that his creative imagination would be stoked by this place. And the Alcázar was only one of the city's wonders. The great cathedral at the heart of the Old City was perhaps the most breathtaking man-made structure Michael had ever seen. Its Gothic sprawl covered an entire block with intricate design, every surface—within and without—ornate in its way. And the Giralda, the tower, was equally impressive. What Jillian had loved best about it was that there were no stairs. The builders had constructed it so that there were only ramps going up and up and up inside that square structure. Legend had it that the king had wanted to be able to ride his horse all the way to the top.

Michael believed it.

In the shadow of the cathedral, in the square below it, he had been tempted to dance with his wife under the warm sun of the Spanish spring. But he did not. This was not the past, but the future. They were crafting new memories here, something Jillian desperately needed and Michael craved.

They had considered Vienna for this trip, but did not linger on it very long. Neither of them seemed inclined to travel old ground. Jillian had lost a lot of memories—she did not like to discuss it, so Michael had no way to know just how much of her past had been stolen from her, save the few memories of hers that still lingered in his own mind—and this trip was a fresh start. Here she would begin to weave a tapestry of bright thoughts and colorful moments that would help to give texture to her life.

They had both been fortunate in that they had employers who were understanding. Teddy had covered Michael's ass on the new ad campaign, and things had come out better than ever. Things were not quite as smooth for Jillian. She had been rude and insulting to several of the partners at her firm. And yet once she had gone back in to speak with them, to apologize and let them know that she hadn't been herself, that she'd been having personal problems, they were more than willing to let her show them that she had resolved those issues.

Her political aspirations had not been so fortunate. After her behavior toward Bob Ryan and the reporter from the *Tribune,* Jillian didn't have a chance in hell of making it onto the city council. Remarkably, she seemed to care very little. When he asked her about it, Jilly just shrugged it off, mystified that it had ever been important to her in the first place.

Jillian had reconciled with Hannah, however. Her bond with her sister was more important to her now than it ever had been before. When she had heard the news that the lump in Hannah's breast had turned out to be benign, she had wept openly. Not only for her sister, but for herself. She couldn't imagine losing Hannah, her one real connection to the memories she had lost.

As for Tom Barnes, they had seen reports on the news about the man being questioned by police in connection with his mother's death. The authorities seemed to think she had convinced him to take her out of the hospital, but that her mental illness and violent episodes had caused her to attack him, and that Barnes had killed his mother in self-defense. The investigation was ongoing. Michael thought it a shame that this was how Susan would be remembered, and that Tom had to go through all of this.

But, thus far, six months after that terrible night, there had been no mention of Wildwood Road. Tom had left the Danskys out of it, and Michael was grateful.

Now they were starting over with this trip to Spain, exploring the Old City of Seville. Jillian spoke Italian and so understood much of what was said to them in Spanish, but she could not speak the language. Michael could not understand a word of what was being said to them, but remembered enough college Spanish to reply after Jillian translated. They were a perfect team.

As they made their way down that alley—part of a maze of such passages that somehow always brought them back to one of the larger streets, or to a monument they could identify in the guidebook—they glanced in shop windows and instinctively began to slow down. To take their time. *Enough sightseeing*, Michael thought. Now they would just meander. They knew each other well enough that they were attuned to such rhythms.

Jillian gave a sudden mischievous laugh and darted away from him, up the alley. There was a tall door that hung open; a sign propped in front announced a flamenco show that night at half past nine. It wasn't until Michael had nearly caught up with her that he heard the music coming from that open door, the strumming of a guitar, a musician warming up for the evening. Jilly spun around snapping her fingers as though she wore castanets.

Michael watched her in amazement.

She must have seen something on his face, for she faltered and a wave of melancholy swept across her features.

"What, Jilly? What's wrong?" he asked.

Jillian glanced around but no one was nearby. Her eyes narrowed and there was something lost and plaintive in them, something that reminded him of Scooter Barnes.

"I'm different," she said, averting her eyes.

It was as though she had been reading his mind, but Michael knew that she had only been reading his face. And she felt it, deep down. It had come up before, but it still haunted her.

"A little," Michael told her. "Not so much that most people would notice."

"But you notice."

"I'm your husband."

He reached out for her and she took his hands.

Jillian gazed at him now, gnawing on her lower lip. "Different how?"

Michael smiled. "You're a little daffier. But that's not a bad thing, babe. It really isn't. You're . . . you seem happier."

Most of the time. That was the unspoken coda. And even during those times when she seemed happier than before, there was a kind of undercurrent in her voice, a gray cloud at the back of her eyes. Michael understood; he saw the same thing in his own eyes when he looked in the mirror. The two of them could still love, they could still laugh, but they had learned that the rules that had always defined the world were lies. And they were unsure how to go about learning the real ones . . . or even if they wanted to.

In light of things, Michael was prepared to be grateful for *Most of the time.* In a way, the hard knowledge they had found made him appreciate everything more. Ice cream tasted sweeter, jokes were funnier, Jilly's perfume was sexier.

But the fact that she was different, that she had changed in some small, fundamental way, troubled her, and Michael did not know how to fix that, to make that better.

"And you still love me?"

Michael pulled her nearer. "Still and always."

"Even though I'm . . . even though I've changed?"

They had both lost bits of themselves the previous autumn, Jillian quite literally and Michael more figuratively. Preconceptions. Expectations. Assumptions. Michael had come to the conclusion that life wasn't about avoiding sorrow—that was patently impossible. Instead, it was about recognizing it, and finding joy in spite of it.

"We all change," he shrugged, trying to find the words. "Life changes us. I have no idea how much we'll have changed by the time we're seventy. But I want to find out with you. The thing is, I don't think who we are, way down, ever changes. That's who I fell in love with, Jilly. And if you're different now, well, I get to fall in love all over again."

For a long moment she stared at him, searching his face. Then

she laughed, rolling her eyes heavenward. "Oh, that is so unbe-
lievably lame!"

Michael couldn't help laughing along with her. "It's true."

"It's still lame," Jilly said, shaking her head and tugging him
by the hand, pulling him deeper into the labyrinth of the Old
City.

Michael followed willingly. Evening shadows began to stretch
over the cobblestones now, even as he thought again about the
things they had learned, and the shadows that knowledge had
cast upon their lives. Moments later they emerged into a large
square where the late-day sun still shone brightly.

That was the thing about shadows. Stepping out of them always made the light seem so much brighter.

ABOUT THE AUTHOR

CHRISTOPHER GOLDEN is the award-winning, *Los Angeles Times* bestselling author of such novels as *Of Saints and Shadows, The Ferryman, Strangewood, The Gathering Dark,* and the Body of Evidence series of teen thrillers. Working with actress/writer/director Amber Benson, he cocreated and cowrote *Ghosts of Albion,* an animated supernatural drama for BBC online.

Golden has also written or cowritten several books and comic books related to the TV series *Buffy the Vampire Slayer* and *Angel,* as well as the scripts for two *Buffy the Vampire Slayer* video games. His recent comic book work includes the creator-owned *The Sisterhood* and DC Comics' *Doctor Fate: The Curse.*

As a pop-culture journalist, he was the editor of the Bram Stoker Award-winning book of criticism *CUT!: Horror Writers on Horror Film,* and coauthor of *The Stephen King Universe.*

Golden was born and raised in Massachusetts, where he still lives with his family. He graduated from Tufts University. There are more than eight million copies of his books in print. Please visit him at www.christophergolden.com.

Be sure not to miss

THE MYTH
HUNTERS

by Christopher Golden
On sale spring 2006

The first book in an arresting new trilogy entitled

THE VEIL

In a world where legends can come to life,
anything can happen.

Here's a special preview.

The Myth Hunters

On sale spring 2006

The promise of winter's first snowfall whispered across the low-slung evening sky. Oliver Bascombe shivered not from the December wind but with the same anticipation he had felt at his seventh birthday party, just before the magician performed his act. Oliver did not believe in magicians anymore, but he did still believe in magic. He was stubborn that way.

The green cable-knit sweater was insufficient to protect him from the cold, but Oliver did not mind. At the edge of a rocky cliff a hundred and twenty feet above the crashing surf, he hugged himself and closed his eyes, felt the north wind prodding him and smiled. His cheeks were numb but he cared not at all. There was a delicious taste to the air and the scent of it was wonderful, exhilarating.

Oliver loved being by the ocean, relished the air, but this scent was different. This was the storm coming on. Not the metallic tang of the imminent thunderstorm, but the pure, moist air of winter, when the sky was thick and each misting breath was almost crystalline.

It was bliss.

Oliver inhaled again and, eyes still closed, took a step closer to the edge of the bluff. All the magic in the world existed right here, right now. In the air, in the portentous gray sky, in the mischievous auguring of winter. A solemn oath from nature that soon it would bring beauty and stillness to the land, at least for a while.

A few more inches, a single step, and he would fly from the bluff down into the breakers and serenity would be his. One final enormous disappointment for his father to bear, and then he would not burden the old man any further.

One step.

A flutter against his cheek. A rustling in his hair. A gust swept off the water and struck him with enough force that he stumbled back a step. One step. Back instead of forward. The wind blew damp, icy stings against his cheeks.

Oliver opened his eyes.

Snow fell in a silent white cascade that stretched from the stone bluff and out across the ocean. For the longest of moments he stood and simply stared, his heart beating faster, his throat dry, holding his breath. Oliver Bascombe believed in magic. Whatever else life brought him, as long as he could hold on to such moments, he could endure.

He would endure.

Oliver chuckled softly to himself and shook his head in resignation. For another long moment he stared out at the ocean, his view obscured by this new veil of snow, then turned and strode across the frozen grounds of his father's estate. The rigid grass crunched beneath his shoes.

The enormous Victorian mansion was an antique red with trim the pink of birthday-cake frosting, though Oliver's mother had always insisted upon referring to it as rose so as not to impugn the masculinity of the household. Her husband wanted his home to be finely appointed, but drew the line at decoration that would be inarguably feminine.

Thus, *rose*.

The house was warmly lit from within. The broad bay windows of the formal living room on the south wing revealed the twinkling, multi-colored lights on the Bascombes' Christmas tree. Oliver strode up to the French doors, melting snow slipping down the back of his neck and into his shirt, and rattled the handles, sighing when he realized the doors were locked. He rapped softly on a glass pane, peering into the rear entryway of the house at dark wood and antique furniture, tapestries and sconces on the walls. When his mother was alive, his parents had done everything in their power to give the interior of their home a European flair, so that it looked more like a French bed-and-breakfast than a place in which people actually lived.

Oliver rapped again. The wind whipped up again and rattled the French doors in their frame. After another moment he raised his fist again, but then a figure appeared in the corridor. The house was lit so brightly that at first it was only a silhouette of a person, but from the hurried, precise gait of the figure he knew immediately that it must be Friedle. He was more than simply a caretaker, but that was how the man himself referred to his job, so the Bascombes did not argue the point.

The slim, bespectacled man smiled broadly and waved as he hurried in his peculiar way to unlock the doors.

"Oh, goodness, come in, come in!" Friedle urged in his curt Swiss accent, then he clucked his tongue. "I am sorry, Oliver. I locked the door without even considering that you might be out-side on such a chilly night."

A genuine smile blossomed on Oliver's face. "It's all right. All the preparations were becoming a bit overwhelming, so I thought I'd take a walk. And now it's snowing."

Friedle's eyebrows went up and he glanced out the door. "So it is," he noted appreciatively. But then his eyes narrowed and a mischievous sort of grin played at the edges of his lips. "We're not getting cold feet, are we?"

"I was out for a stroll in the first snow of winter. Of course my feet are cold."

"You know that isn't what I meant."

Oliver nodded amiably. "Yep."

Friedle handled all the day-to-day business of running the household, from the largest details to the smallest, leaving Max Bascombe to focus on his work. Friedle paid the bills, answered the mail, and attended to small repairs and general upkeep, while at the same time overseeing the employment of the twice-weekly cleaning service, the landscaping crew, and the snowplow man in winter.

When Oliver's mother had died, it was Friedle who realized that someone was going to have to be hired to cook for father and son, the two men living in that silent, old house. Mrs. Gray arrived promptly at seven o'clock every morning and remained until seven o'clock at night. Oliver hoped that she was paid well to spend so much time in someone else's home. Friedle was another story entirely. He lived in the carriage house on the south end of the property. This was his home.

Oliver smiled warmly at the man, wished him good night, then strode down the corridor. The paintings on the walls reflected his father's interest in the ocean—lighthouses and schooners and weathered lobstermen—and his mother's passion for odd antiques, in this case crude portraits most visitors mistook for Bascombe family ancestors.

His damp shoes had squeaked from the moment he entered the house and Oliver wiped them on the Oriental rug before striding through the formal living room and the vast dining room. Though it was still early in December, the entire house was decorated for the holidays, red ribbon bows and gold candles and wreaths all throughout the house. And from the other end of the house came the scent of a fire blazing in the hearth.

His path took him past the grand staircase and to a room his mother had always insisted upon referring to as the parlor, though nobody really had parlors anymore. Despite or perhaps because of the fact that it drove his father a bit crazy, Oliver had for years preferred to cozy up with a book or a movie in Mother's parlor than the so-called family room. Katherine Bascombe had always kept her parlor filled with sweet-smelling flowers and warm blankets. The furniture was delicate, like his mother; the one room in the house where Max Bascombe hadn't trampled upon his wife's decorative instincts.

Now he paused a moment at the door to the darkened room. The parlor was small by the standards of the Bascombe home, but it ran all the way to the rear of the house. The far end of the parlor was an array of tall windows that looked out upon the back of the property, at the gardens and the ocean beyond.

But tonight the view was obscured. Oliver could see nothing outside those windows but the snow that whipped icily against the glass. He looked at the small rolltop desk where his mother had liked to sit and write letters to old friends. Bookshelves revealed a combination of paperback Agatha Christie mysteries and antique leatherbound hardcovers. From time to time Oliver would take one of those older books down and read it, not minding the way the binding cracked and the yellowed paper crumbled. Books, he had always thought, were for reading. Writers put their heart and soul in between those covers and it seemed to Oliver that if the books were never opened, the ghosts of their passion might be trapped there forever.

He inhaled the lemon scent of wood polish in the room, noticeable even over the powerful smell of flowers, and he felt his mother's absence keenly. In the wake of her death, Oliver had done as his father asked. He had gone on to law school and become an attorney, passed the bar not only in Maine but in Massachusetts, New York, and California as well. You had to be versatile if you wanted to be a partner in the firm of Bascombe and Cox. The problem was, this particular junior partner had no interest in being a lawyer. He had spent all four years at Yale in the Drama Club doing Chekhov and Eugene O'Neill.

Oliver Bascombe was an actor. He wanted to live on the stage, to travel the world not in a private jet but by car and train. As an attorney it was his job to erase the trials and tribulations of others, yet he barely understood what his clients were experiencing.

He was a fly trapped in amber.

"What are you doing?"

Oliver started. He turned abruptly away from the parlor to find his sister, Collette, standing in the hall gazing at him. She had an odd smile on her face and he wondered how long she had been there, waiting for him to notice her arrival.

"Way to go," he said, a hand over his chest. "Give the groom a heart attack the night before his wedding."

"My, my, little brother. You're not *nervous*, are you?"

Collette laughed and a ripple of good feeling went through Oliver. So often he felt that the only warmth in this house came out of the heating ducts, but having Collette back in town, even if only for a few days, had been wonderful. Oliver, to his regret, was the image of his father, though somehow at once both thinner and more robust. But Collette was petite and her features fine and angular, so that she revealed in every glance the Irish heritage that had come down to them from their mother. A light of mischief gleamed in her eyes and though she was his elder by six years, Collette was often mistaken for a girl half her age.

"Why would I be nervous?" Oliver replied. "It's just my whole life changing forever tomorrow."

Collette smiled again, the skin around her eyes crinkling. "You make it sound like a death sentence."

A shudder went through Oliver and he caught his breath. His good humor faltered a moment and though he tried to summon it again, he saw in his sister's gaze that she had noticed this lapse.

"Oliver?" she ventured. "Oh, Oliver, don't."

Collette shook her head as though she could deny what she had seen in his face. He had no idea what *don't* meant, exactly. Don't say it? Don't feel this way? Don't get married? Don't fuck it up? But he could imagine some of what Collette was feeling just then. Her own marriage—to Bradley Kenton, a television news producer out of New York City—had failed spectacularly. They had no children, but Collette had friends in the city, a job she loved as an editor at *Billboard* magazine, and no desire to live with or even near her family again.

"I'm fine," he assured her. "Really," he lied.

His sister responded with a long sigh, then glanced around the hall before taking him by the elbow and ushering him into Mother's parlor. She turned on a tall floor lamp whose glass enclosure had been designed by Gaudi. It threw strange, almost grotesque arrays of colored light across the room and upon Collette's face. Oliver never used that lamp when he came here to hide away.

"Is it terror or dread?" Collette demanded, as though the question needed no more explanation than that.

Oliver was unnerved to discover that it didn't. He turned away from her searching gaze and went to sit upon a sofa rich with deep crimson and blue. The tasseled pillow he placed on his lap as though it might protect him. Collette sat on the edge of the coffee table, arms crossed, one hand over her mouth. *Speak no evil*, Oliver thought as he turned to look at her again.

"I'm not afraid to be married. I guess I ought to be. I'm not sure I know anyone whose marriage I can honestly say I admire. But the idea of it is pretty appealing. The way a marriage is supposed to be, who wouldn't want that?"

Collette frowned. "You don't think you can have that with Julianna?"

Oliver swallowed hard and found his throat dry. Slowly, he shook his head.

"I thought you loved her."

Images of Julianna crashed through Oliver's mind like the ocean against the rocks. She was laughing and dancing on the hardwood floor in nothing but white socks and Oliver's flannel pajama top, her raven black hair spilling around her face. She was playing the piano and singing so sweetly at her parents' fortieth anniversary party. What was that song? He could hear the melody in his head but was unable to put a name to it.

"I think I do," he replied at last. "But how can you ever be sure? Honestly. Still, the idea of being married is nice."

Collette leaned forward, her yellow hair draped across the left side of her face. She did not bother to push it away, but instead laid a comforting hand on his knee.

"So it's not terror. Where's the dread coming from?"

"I don't know."

His sister sat up straight, surveying him carefully.

"You lie."

A soft laugh escaped Oliver's lips. "Yes, I lie." The words were barely a whisper. "It isn't fair, is it? Not to me or to Julianna. It isn't fair that my cowardice has brought us to this."

Collette shook her head and threw up her hands. "You lost me, Ollie. Stop playing Riddler and elaborate already, if you please. How are you a coward? The only person in this world you won't stand up to is . . ."

Her words trailed off and Collette stared at him. She tilted her head slightly to one side as though seeing him from a new angle might shed further light upon their conversation.

"Daddy?" she ventured. "You're dreading getting married because of Dad? In what world does that make any sense at all?"

Oliver held the pillow more tightly and slid down into the sofa cushions. He turned to gaze across the long parlor at the darkness outside, the snow almost phosphorescent where it fell near enough to be illuminated by the lights of the house.

"It doesn't. Doesn't make a bit of sense. But it's been haunting me. Julianna's family are wealthy and they're local and they're very tightly knit. Her father is on the board of directors at the bank with Dad. They've golfed together at the club. If I marry Julianna, it's the final concession. It's not even defeat, but surrender. I'm giving up whatever chance still existed that I might someday do what I want instead of what he wants. Just like . . . just like Mom."

"Ollie, Mom never surrendered. She never stopped loving the things she had a passion for."

He laughed bitterly. "Maybe she never surrendered, but she was captured, sis. Think about it. Look at this house. One little room where she could do exactly what she wanted, where she could have it look like she pictured it, instead of how Mr. Imagination thought other people would expect it to look."

Collette put one comforting hand on his shoulder. "Oliver, I know he can be awful, but you're being unfair. All couples compromise. That's what marriage is. Yes, he can be bullying—"

Oliver cut off her words with a curt glance. "If she was forced to compromise her passions to mix with his, that I could understand. But he doesn't have any. His only passion is work. He had an image of how things should look that had nothing to do with what he liked or disliked, and everything to do with what he thought was the right image, what he thought was appropriate. And she was filled with passion, and . . . look, never mind." He brushed at the air. "I'm sorry I started. It's just . . . with her gone, I see it all around me, all through the house, and it's just so fucking tragic."

Collette hesitated a moment, gnawing her lower lip, then forged on. "And so, what? You think your life with Julianna's going to be the same thing, only in reverse? Is that it?"

Slowly, he nodded. "The really twisted part is, I'm going to end up resenting Julianna just as much as I already resent *him*. How is that fair?"

Collette shook her head. "It's not." For several seconds she only stared at him, then she ran her hands through her hair and laughed, not in amusement but in obvious disbelief. "Jesus, Oliver. Now what? It's two weeks before Christmas. You've got three hundred people coming to a wedding tomorrow. Flying in from LA and London and New York, some of them. The ones who made it in before this blizzard, anyway. I'm not telling you not to do it. I know as well as anyone what a mistake it is to get married if it just isn't right. But if you're going to call it off, you'd better be damned sure."

A chill ran through Oliver. He stroked his chin, taking some odd physical comfort in the rasp of the stubble he found there. Something burned in his gut but he had no idea if it was that dread he and Collette had discussed or simple guilt. His throat was still dry and his chest felt hollow, too quiet, as though his heart had paused to let him think. His lifted his eyes to gaze balefully at his sister.

"I guess running away isn't an option?"

Collette smiled tenderly. "I think you're a little too old for that."

"Pity."

He fell into contemplation once again and his sister rose and began to drift about the room as if she were seeing it for the first time. She caressed certain knickknacks that she recognized from their childhood, ran her fingers along the spines of several books, then slid one of the Agatha Christies off the shelf. Oliver took all this in very peripherally and only glanced over at her when she grunted softly in appreciation of the book and then continued to peruse the shelves, paperback clutched against her chest like some talisman.

Oliver lay back on the sofa, his head against the wall. It would not be a bad life with Julianna. She came from a similar background, but she still understood his dreams. Yet that was the worst of it, in a way, for though she understood what he dreamed of, she had never once considered it more than a dream.

He closed his eyes and imagined his future in this house or

one much like it; his future with this bright, funny, beautiful girl who wanted to marry him and raise a family with him. Perhaps it was the time of year, but images of Christmas mornings came into his head, of his children opening gifts beneath the boughs of a tree Oliver himself would decorate. If they were wealthy, so much the better. He would never have to fear for his children's well-being. That was a worthy pursuit, wasn't it?

"Shit," he whispered, one hand on his forehead.

Collette turned quickly to regard him once more. "What?"

Before Oliver could reply, a familiar voice boomed out in the hall, shouting his name. Brother and sister turned to stare at the open doorway of the parlor, then Collette glanced at him.

Oliver took a breath then shouted "In here!"

Heavy footfalls came nearer and a moment later the doorway was filled with the figure of their father, his face etched with the usual impatience. He was Maximilian Bascombe, after all, and it was not now nor had it ever been his place to go chasing about his own home for his children.

"I should have thought to look for you here first," the old man said.

Old man, Oliver thought. *What a quaint expression.* It seemed almost insultingly ironic when applied to Max, who at sixty-six was in better shape than Oliver had ever been, salt and pepper hair the only hint at his age. But the phrase had never been associated with age in Oliver's mind. Max had always been *the old man* in his mind. It was a crass term, reminiscent of bad sixties television. But as formal as they were in the Bascombe home, *father* seemed too generous an appellation.

"What's wrong?" Oliver asked.

"Nothing. I couldn't find Friedle," the old man replied dismissively. Then he held up a portable telephone Oliver had not noticed at first. "Julianna's on the phone."

For a moment Oliver froze. He stared at his father, his mouth slightly open, aware that he must look foolish, as though he had gone catatonic standing there in the parlor. His gaze ticked toward the phone and only when he reached out his hand to receive it did he understand what had happened within him.

"Thank you," he offered, more from practice than purpose.

"Ollie?" Collette ventured, her concern and wonder clear in her tone.

Oliver cast her a resigned glance, then took the phone from his father. The old man muttered something about wanting to talk to him later on a case that needed to be dealt with before he and Julianna left for their honeymoon in South America. Oliver barely heard him.

He put the phone to his ear. "Hello?"

"Hey," Julianna said, her voice soft and near, as though she spoke to him from a pillow beside his own. "What's shakin'?"

A melancholy smile spread across his face and Oliver turned his back to his father and his sister.

"Oh, just celebrating my last night as a bachelor with a bit of perverse revelry."

"As is to be expected," Julianna replied. "I'm just getting rid of the gigolos and the mule myself."

Oliver could not help himself. He laughed. Julianna was a wonderful person, kind and beautiful and intelligent. And he had made a promise to her. Wasn't it up to him to keep his own passions alive? His mother had surrendered. And where his father was concerned, Oliver had always done so as well. But that did not mean that his marriage had to be a cage. It was up to him.

"It's good to hear your voice," he said.

At his words, his father retreated into the hallway. Collette came over to kiss her brother on the cheek; she stroked his hair a moment and he saw the regret in her eyes and knew it was for him. He nodded to her. *It's going to be okay*, he thought, and hoped she would read his mind or at least his expression.

"So, what are you doing tomorrow?" he asked Julianna as Collette left the room, disappearing into the massive house after their father.

"Why?" Julianna asked. "Did you have something in mind?"

"As a matter of fact, I did."

HOURS LATER, OLIVER WAS STILL in the parlor. It was late enough that Mrs. Gray was long gone, so he had made a trip to the kitchen for some hot cocoa. Somehow, in the short time he was gone, Friedle had come into the parlor and laid a fire in the stone fireplace. When he returned with a large steaming mug, a dollop of whipped cream bobbing on top of the cocoa, the blaze was roaring. Oliver was more than happy to feed new logs into the flames from time to time. Friedle had put a large stack of wood aside for him, and now it was nearly gone. Across the room, one window was open several inches and there was something delicious about the combination of the heat of the fire and the chilly winter wind that swirled in. Snow had begun to build up on the windowpane and some landed on the wood floor, slowly melting there.

This was magic; right here in this room with his cocoa and a worn leatherbound copy of Jack London's *The Sea Wolf* in his hands. He had rescued the book from its lonely place amongst the other abandoned volumes on these shelves, but it was not the first time. *The Sea Wolf* was an adventure he had returned to many times over the years. Always in this room, in this chair, beneath this light.

With the snowstorm raging outside and the house gone quiet now, time slipped away. Oliver might have been twelve again. The fire crackled, casting ghostly orange flickers upon the walls.

He was lost in the book, adrift upon the sea aboard *The Ghost* with Wolf Larsen at the helm. All the world had been pushed aside so that Oliver existed now within the pages of *The Sea Wolf*, far from his concerns about the future and the delicate irony of his love for a woman destined to become, for better or worse, his anchor.

Oliver had shivered several times before he really noticed how cold it had grown in the parlor. The fire was down to one charred log licked by weak flames. Reluctantly he slipped a finger into his book, dry paper rasping against his skin, and went to kneel before the fireplace. He used a poker to push back the black iron mesh curtain in front of the burning log—the metal would long since have grown too hot to touch—and then carefully arranged two thin logs within.

The fire began to spread and Oliver picked up another log, this one fat with a thick layer of bark, and placed it diagonally atop the others. For a moment after he had closed the mesh curtain again he remained there, watching the blaze. Then, finger still holding his place in the book, he stood again and started back toward his chair.

Cold wind raced through the room, trailing chill fingers along the back of his neck. Again Oliver shivered, though this time he noticed it.

The open window rattled hard in its frame. He glanced over to see that the snow had built up much more than he had realized. One corner of the gap between window and sash was packed with pure white and enough of it had powdered the floor that it was no longer melting.

"Damn."

Oliver started toward the window. The edge of the Oriental rug was easily six feet from the wall but some of the snow had reached it. He paused to try to brush it away with his shoe but managed only to melt it into the carpet. The window rattled harder, buffeted by the storm. The sound was so loud and abrupt that Oliver jumped a bit and turned to squint in amazement at the snow outside his windows. The night seemed darker than before. The air whipped so hard against the panes of glass now that where it rushed through the opening it howled softly. More snow blew in with every gust.

"Wow," he whispered to himself as he stood peering out through the glass. Even in the dark, he could see that what had begun as a light snowfall had become nothing short of a full-fledged blizzard. The snow was thick and plentiful, the ground already completely blanketed with it, and the wind drove it in twisting swirls and waves.

Oliver held the book up against his chest with his left hand, keeping it away from the open window. For a moment he simply enjoyed the storm. Then the glass rattled again, the window seemed to bow inward as though the storm was trying to get in. He reached out to close the window, but enough snow had built up on the sill that it slid only a fraction of an inch before jamming. He brushed as much of it out as he could. Even then, it seemed frozen in place. Awkwardly, finger still holding his place in *The Sea Wolf*, he set both hands upon the top of the window and put his weight into it. The window began to slide down.

A powerful gust slammed against the house, shaking all of the parlor windows, as though in defiance. The open window seized again and he worked hard to force it closed. The storm raged outside, buffeting the walls of the house. The wind that passed through the narrow gap remaining between window and sash fairly shrieked now.

The wooden frame shook, banging loudly now, and a long crack appeared in the glass, stretching a tendril from one side of the window to the other. Oliver cursed under his breath and let the book fall from his hand. *The Sea Wolf* struck the damp floor on its spine and something in its binding tore. Oliver barely noticed that he had dropped it, never mind that he had lost his page.

Swearing again, he struggled to close the window, worried that at any moment the glass might splinter further, even shatter. It would not close that final inch, however, and his fingers were numb with the frigid air, the whipping snow. *So cold.* It seemed impossible that it could be so cold.

Oliver paused, suddenly certain that he was not alone in the room. Friedle or Collette, perhaps . . . someone had heard the banging and come to investigate. But no . . . the presence he felt was not within the room, but without.

He narrowed his gaze and for just that moment, twisting with the currents and eddies of the wind, he saw a figure dancing in the storm, eyes like diamonds staring in at him, a look of pure astonishment upon features carved of ice. All the air went out of Oliver then, as though he had died and his lungs expelled his final breath.

The wind drove in through that narrow opening with the force of a sliver hurricane. The crack in the glass spread no further, but the storm blew in so hard that it knocked Oliver backward. He stumbled, slipped upon the melting snow, and fell sprawling onto the Oriental rug.

Snow poured through the opening in the window and swirled and eddied about the parlor as though there were no difference between outside and inside. The storm had knocked, and now it had come in, uninvited. In a steady stream the blizzard slid through the inch-high gap between window and sash and raced around the room. Cold and damp, it slapped against his reading lamp and the bulb exploded, casting the room in darkness save for the light from the fire, which guttered weakly, only the iron mesh curtain keeping it from being doused completely.

Oliver gasped, sucked icy air into his lungs. His eyes were wide as he gazed about the room. He was too cold for this to be a dream, and his stomach hurt from the gust of solid air that had knocked him down. Splayed there on the carpet, he felt a sense of wonder but it was tainted by a primal fear that welled up now from somewhere deep within him.

The storm began to churn and then to spin more tightly at the center of the parlor. The fire surrendered and went out, smoke sifting from dead embers and being sucked into the white ice whirlwind that knocked knickknacks off the coffee table and twisted up the rug beneath its feet.

Oh, Oliver thought. *Oh, shit. What the fuck am I still doing here?*

It was as though the frozen wind had numbed his mind as well as his body. No longer. He scrambled to his feet and ran across the parlor, bent to one side to fight the wind. His cocoa mug slid off a side table and shattered on the floor.

As he ran for the door, a gust of wind rushed past him, nearly knocking him over again, and blew it shut.

Oliver stood unmoving in the middle of the parlor, staring at the door. There had been purpose behind that wind. He was not alone. The storm was here, but more than the storm.

He turned slowly. The vortex in front of the dark fireplace was changing, taking shape. Through the snow churning within that whirlwind, Oliver could see a figure, the same that he thought he had seen outside moments ago. A man, or so it seemed, made from ice, his body all perilously sharp edges, dagger fingers and hair that swung and tinkled musically like a crystal chandelier.

Its eyes gleamed pale blue and with every twist of the vortex, every swing of its arms, it stared directly at him. At first Oliver had thought it was dancing but now he saw that it was carried by the snow, by the storm.

"God, please, no," Oliver whispered, shaking his head. "What the hell *are* you?"

The vortex slowed and then stopped.

The snow fell to the floor, blanketing the wood and carpet and furniture.

The winter man stood, chin proudly lifted, and cast a cold, cruel eye upon Oliver. Then he staggered, icy tread heavy upon the floor, and his sharp features changed. Pale blue eyes narrowed with pain and exhaustion, and Oliver saw that there was a chink out of his left side, like someone had chipped away a large sliver of ice.

"Help me," the winter man whispered, voice like the gusting wind.

Then he fell hard, jagged features scoring the wooden floor. He lay half on the wood and half on the carpet. Where his wound was, water dripped onto the Oriental rug. Mind in a frantic tumult, Oliver stared at that spot and wondered if the winter man was melting.

Or bleeding.